Bonding

Mariel Franklin

Bonding

PICADOR

First published 2024 by Picador
an imprint of Pan Macmillan
The Smithson, 6 Briset Street, London EC1M 5NR
EU representative: Macmillan Publishers Ireland Ltd, 1st Floor,
The Liffey Trust Centre, 117–126 Sheriff Street Upper,
Dublin 1, D01 YC43
Associated companies throughout the world
www.panmacmillan.com

ISBN 978-1-0350-1657-0 HB
ISBN 978-1-0350-1659-4 TPB

Typeset in Plantin by Jouve (UK), Milton Keynes
Printed and bound by CPI Group (UK) Ltd, Croydon, CR0 4YY

Visit **www.picador.com** to read more about all our books
and to buy them. You will also find features, author interviews and
news of any author events, and you can sign up for e-newsletters
so that you're always first to hear about our new releases.

For Stephen

PART 1
Market Research

The activity of gathering information about consumers'
needs and desires.

There was something magical about an island – the mere word suggested fantasy. You lost touch with the world – an island was a world of its own. A world, perhaps, from which you might never return.

AGATHA CHRISTIE, *AND THEN THERE WERE NONE*

1

Ashley was drunk, unsteady on her feet, the smell of her makeup overlaid with booze. She grabbed my arm, lurching against me as I struggled to fit the key in the lock. It wasn't the first time I'd found her in the stairwell. It must have been midnight by the time I came across her. It was a Wednesday.

'I'm locked out,' she said, slurring.

Ashley and I shared a flat together. I'd met her only a few months earlier after the previous tenant had left. She'd seemed fine at the time – normal, solvent, decent company for a stranger. It was why I'd chosen her in the first place. She'd been the front runner in a long line of candidates.

Eventually, the door gave way and I steered her gently to her bedroom where I left her in a clumsy attempt at the recovery position.

'Thanks,' she mumbled under her breath.

For a second, I thought she'd stopped breathing, then she opened her eyes and blinked at me

'Are you going to be OK?'

No answer, so I dragged her pillows out of the way and stacked them neatly on the floor beside her.

It was cold in the flat, the bulb in the hallway needed replacing and there was a stale smell as if the place hadn't been lived in for a while. This wasn't so far from the truth, neither of us liked coming home and we didn't really treat it as if it was one.

In the fridge there were two Gym Kitchen curries (both low-fat, one out-of-date), a half-empty bottle of Blossom Hill, some Coronas and a tub of Glossier Mega Greens Detoxifying Mask. I picked up the technically expired meal, considered eating it, then threw it out. The other I put in the microwave while I ate a handful of spinach from the bag. In the time it took me to complete these tasks, my phone buzzed sporadically, a few texts from a group chat I barely followed and one from a newcomer on the app. The app was always on. I wasn't having much success with it but I found it hard to delete the thing, so I left it lying there on mute, lurking on it occasionally, skimming over the stream of 'Hi's, spam and the occasional, badly focused dick pic. *Matt, 36* distracted me while I sat on the windowsill and ate. Earlier that day, he'd sent me a video of a shredder slowly chewing up a piece of paper. This was how the two of us communicated, I sent him close-ups of myself and he sent me pictures of the objects on his desk: a Rexel stapler, slightly damp with sweat, an empty Pret A Manger box. **What I'd like to do,** he'd said between photos of a pad of yellow Post-its, **is meet you in a public place for coffee and then fuck you stupid, like a wolf.**

You there? he asked, while I opened the kitchen window, which took some effort as it was sealed with duct tape to stop the draught. Fresh air flew into the room, slightly alleviating the smell of damp. Outside, four storeys below, a dull clanging sound rose from the courtyard. Most probably someone had broken in again and was going through the bins.

In bed, I balanced my laptop on my knees. It took a while to click to *Game of Thrones.* I'd seen this one before. I'd seen them all but it was comforting, watching these things over again. Most nights, the routine numbed me enough to sleep. I watched a pack of dogs as they chased a naked woman into a forest. I closed my eyes as she screamed into the darkness. When I opened them, *Matt, 36* had sent me a photo of the charger for his phone.

•

Bored at work the following afternoon, I sent *Matt, 36* a close-up of my skirt. He fired back with a picture of his keyboard and, erotically, the corner of his hand.

It was quiet in the office, quieter than usual. I heard Ed's footsteps as he approached my desk. It was obvious something had happened.

'I need a word,' he said under his breath. He was dressed head to toe in cycling gear, his crotch hovering around my face, its contours clearly visible through an explosion of neon Lycra. 'Can you come and see me when you're ready?'

The last time Ed had called me into his office it had been to tell me to take more risks. 'You'd get more traction,' he'd said, 'if you loosened up.'

He liked to give pep talks which erupted randomly, usually when he was bored. He saw himself as an inspirational leader, someone who would lay his life down for his team.

In fact, the work we did was hardly taxing. Ed spent most of his time in meetings, chatting up blue-chip clients, selling them the dream of a health and well-being app for minimizing sick days.

All the same, despite Ed's efforts, the mood in the office was definitely off. There was a general sense of unease. People had started leaving earlier. That week, I'd heard one of the engineers taking a call from a headhunter at his desk. I'd overheard the whole conversation, he'd barely bothered to hide it. The whole office must have known because that corner of the room was generally quiet, an oasis of hushed keystrokes, whereas the non-tech side was usually buzzing and correspondingly full of junk – reusable coffee cups, novelty phone chargers and piles of promotional gonks from sales, as well as the constant hum of Microsoft Teams meetings and Slack huddles.

Another bad sign – in the past month there had been two visits from two different branding agencies. The first one had shown us a portrait of our target demographic: Rocket and

Parmesan Woman. She had a white-collar job but was time poor and, it turned out, she was a bit of a soft touch – she wanted the app to provide 'a safe and supportive environment' that would allow 'everyone to achieve their fitness goals without judgement'. The second consultant contradicted this completely. Her talk was all about competition. 'No one exists in a vacuum,' she'd written in green ink across the whiteboard. She'd had a deep German accent and had stridden in wearing a black T-shirt and jeans, her grey hair tied back in a severe ponytail like the designer Karl Lagerfeld. 'This is why social listening is key,' she'd said in her gravelly voice. 'We buy into services not only for their convenience but to display our status to others.' She'd started prowling around the room, her leather trousers squeaking. 'As our tribes become ever more dynamic, personalized and segregated, agile listening becomes key for delivering insights that can be actioned in real time.'

None of this had any bearing on the actual work we did but it did fuel the sense of low-level anxiety. In the pub, there was talk of doom on the horizon. Growth was slowing, funds were drying up. Any hope of a big sell-out – or even, for the real dreamers, an IPO – anything that might leave us with a decent payout before our time ran out – all of that was all receding faster than Ed's hairline.

Despite these omens, my heart stopped when Ed said, 'The big guy is going to join us.' I went to the bathroom and spent a long time staring at my reflection in the mirror. I'm not sure how long I was there but after a while, I started to look like someone else.

•

At school, I'd been instilled with a romantic view of what the future held for someone like me. Like most people of my generation, I'd been told that I could do whatever I wanted, as long as I was prepared to work for it. Ms Hidehouse, our mullet-haired, marathon-running headmistress, had drilled this with extra ferocity into the girls: all we had to do was work. Effort and ambition would lead us to success, not only for ourselves but for society as a whole. We'd triumph on our merits and then we'd lift up those less fortunate than ourselves. This almost spiritual indoctrination seemed, in retrospect, laughably off-base. I didn't know anyone whose life had played out along those lines. Most of the women I knew had turned out like me: overdrawn, plagued with anxiety and full of an uneasy sense that something, somewhere had gone wrong. And most of us had nothing approaching the sort of career that was supposed to make it all worthwhile.

My only other memory of Ms Hidehouse was that she took the opposite approach when it came to sex. Sex was something she thought should happen casually, as often as possible, in the name of adventure. Sexual caution was oppressive, a hangover from the bad old days. I wasn't sure about this part yet, but so far, things weren't going well.

•

In his office, Ed sat next to Rory Haynes, the company's founder and CEO. Haynes must have been about twenty-eight, a former public schoolboy with a transatlantic accent that he'd picked up during his internship at the Apple HQ in Cupertino. He was wearing a light blue Oxford shirt with, I noticed, one button missing and another that had become dangerously unravelled. On his feet, below the baggy jeans, was a pair of threadbare Vans.

'Heeey!' Haynes greeted me like an old friend. 'Looking gooood Mary, looking gooood. Take a seat. As you know, we've got some major changes coming up so there's a lot to talk about today?' This was news to me. There hadn't been any redundancies announced.

'It's no reflection on your performance? We've just been rethinking how we work?'

I tried to look as neutral as I could.

'We're reskilling for the pivot into retail? So, we've had to rethink your position?'

'You'll be looked after,' Ed said kindly, before announcing the terms of my pay-off.

I made a quick calculation as I sat there. It wasn't enough, it wasn't anywhere near enough.

'I hope we'll stay in touch?' Haynes said brightly. 'You know how it goes? Don't be a stranger?'

I stood, unsure if I should leave, while Haynes glanced discreetly at his phone. I wondered how much he was paying himself. I knew he'd just bought one of those penthouse lofts on Hoxton Square.

I was out of the room within minutes, unemployed and slightly dazed, my exit signed off with just about enough to get me through the next few weeks.

For a moment, I stood at the entrance to the office. *Healthify*, it said in wooden letters on the wall. Everyone was quiet, their headphones plugged discreetly into their ears. Around me was an angular composition of oak beams and exposed brickwork. On one table was a mug that said: *There Ain't No I In Team*. On the kitchen corkboard – underneath the firm's diversity policy – a poster had been pinned that said: *LEADERSHIP MEANS THINKING ABOUT **WE** NOT **ME***. My past at the place flashed through my mind as if I was drowning in a sea of white Formica. The future, on the other hand, presented itself as a terrifying void. Outside, the rush-hour traffic had already begun. The pollution hit me like a warm breeze.

2

The next day I felt the need to leave the flat. Westfield in Stratford was my nearest destination. A sign beside the entrance told me that this was the third largest shopping centre in the UK and that, taking the surrounding area into account, it was in fact the largest urban shopping zone in Europe. As I approached the escalator, I noticed a line of uniformed police officers standing across the mezzanine, submachine guns strapped across their chests as they filtered the waves of people emerging from the Tube into single file.

Inside, a sea of bodies dispersed through tiered walkways. Voices echoed around the glass interior, a mass of dialects I couldn't understand. I stopped briefly in Sephora to try a Brazilian Honeybronze Glow, then I messaged *Matt, 36* while I was waiting in the queue.

What's up? I sent him a photo of my golden, gloss-slicked arm.

No answer, so I tried a new approach. I picked out a shot of myself half naked, my head cropped out, my bra bathed in the amber light of the bedside lamp. I watched the message shift from delivered to read. He started typing and then stopped. I paused in case he needed time to think.

Eventually he replied: **Sorry, slammed at work**

At Victoria's Secret I ran my hands through a pile of acid yellow thongs. A tinge of panic bolted through my blood as it occurred to me that I didn't know what I was doing. I made my way back out onto the concourse and sat in Caffe Concerto.

Patisserie and Prosecco Bar, it said in gold italics on the wall. I pinned myself on Instagram, adding a photo of my green pistachio slice. It was only £4.45 when you tagged yourself and left a good review. On impulse, I started searching for flights. Hundreds of options drew me through the network. There were rows of offers with links, most of which had already sold out. Eventually, I found what I was looking for. I must have been sitting there for a long time because when I finally looked up, the lights had dimmed and it was almost dark.

'Thank you for shopping at Westfield,' a voice boomed above my head. 'Our stores will be closing shortly.'

•

The flat was empty by the time I made it home. The curtains in Ashley's room were drawn and I noticed that she'd left her gym gear in the kitchen. Her bag was lying by the cupboard we'd taped shut because the place got so damp in the winter that a colony of slugs had eaten through the wall. It was 4 July, the day before my birthday. I was going to be thirty-two years old. I lay on the sofa and glanced at my laptop. It was still showing the last thing I'd watched, an old Agatha Christie series. It was a Christmas special: *The ABC Murders*, one of her best works, in my opinion.

Christie was the first adult writer I came across as a child. I used to search her books out in charity shops, they were always available and they were cheap. I especially liked the 1970s editions, the ones with the dark, surrealist covers. I'd read almost everything she'd written by my teens, by which point I was facing adulthood myself, a transition I quickly realized was going to be a disappointment.

For some reason, I still had vivid memories of the books I'd read as a child. They were often more real and more affecting than my memories of actual events, more so than anything I'd seen on TV or at the cinema. It sounds old-fashioned but even around the turn of the century, this sort of thing wasn't unusual.

I pressed play at the end of episode two and contemplated what I'd loved so much about Christie's writing. It must have been fairly universal – she was the bestselling author of all time. It wasn't her characters, although her detectives evolved expansively over thousands of pages, it had more to do with the world they lived in. It was a world suffused with hierarchy but also with an interconnectedness that had a comforting, almost tranquilizing effect. Everyone's lives were intertwined and as a result, everyone was implicated, from the servants to the upper aristocracy. Her novels played out like symphonies, each player intimately related to the others. It was the minutiae of these relationships that held her rigorous mysteries together. Indifference barely figured in her world. Even the worst of her villains were products of these networks. There were exceptions obviously, especially as her plots became more conceptual, but these only served to prove the rule. It was a formula that soothed you like a warm bath.

While I was still at school, I'd taken all of this for granted. My tween self was looking forward to a life of communal cruises down the Nile, country house weekends and fireside gatherings somewhere in the Alps. It was a shock to discover that life in twenty-first-century London was, to say the least, *different*. Communications had transformed completely. Social life was now inextricable from work. Beyond school, you met people through your job or you met them online. Society had become more abstract to the point that relationships hardly ever happened and when they did, they were subject to weird and unpredictable distortions because, like everything else, they were now shaped by digital efficiencies. I sat back and let Poirot wash over me. Around halfway through episode three, the video player faltered. A grey box appeared:

Network error: there is a problem. Please try again later

While I was waiting for the Wi-Fi to reconnect, I reached instinctively for my phone. There were a few messages, not many. Someone from the office had tagged me in a post. There was an invitation to a virtual conference from something called the Institute of Human Development. My cousin had sent me a birthday text. Happy BD! I hope you have a good one!! Underneath was a gif of a puppy staring, uncomprehendingly, at its own reflection.

•

The following Monday, I had an interview with a man who managed a chain of health clubs. While I waited in the lobby, I looked at the company's website. There were muted portraits of people working out, some shots of food, a picture of the skyline. On their social media was a comment about last night's news. A teenager had died under restraint by the police. They'd linked to a video of his final moments, the camera crawling over his face.

•

JUSTICE NOW, the communications team had written on the platform's pale blue interface. IT'S TIME TO PUT AN END TO THIS INSANITY.

Haven't they learned a fucking thing? @JadeyBae had typed underneath. This is crazy. These people should be shot.

This tweet has violated the Twitter rules about threatening violence against an individual or a group of people and/or glorifying violence. However, Twitter has determined that it may be in the public interest for the tweet to remain accessible. LEARN MORE.

ANYONE CALLING FOR ANYONE'S DEATH, ESP.
HARDWORKING POLICE IS SHOWING THEIR
STUPIDITY

To all non-Nigerians, we need your solidarity. We are
rising up against years of police brutality

I'm recording a protest song, listen here:

https://lilmaestro.lnk.to/enoughisenough

HOW MANY TIMES DO WE NEED TO SEE THIS
SHIT?

A burst of cortisol shot through my blood. I felt my pulse rise
in my throat, although I tried not to show it as the receptionist
waved me in.

Upstairs, I took a seat with the company's surprisingly
portly owner. His face was round, soft and pale. He was wearing an anonymous navy shirt that strained slightly as he sat
down. He talked about the digital expansion of the business
and when I asked about his marketing strategy, he said the
future was all about being human.

'It's an ethos,' he said. 'We aim to embrace all sorts of
people but, you know, we're also building a tribe.'

I glanced around the office, which was decorated vaguely
in the style of a New York loft: eclectic post-industrial units,
tobacco-coloured leather chairs. All of the gyms looked the
same, regardless of which city they were in. These gyms featured heavily on the company's social media but I quickly
realized they were primarily a front to sell subscriptions to
workout videos. 'Grown up luxury personal training', this service was called, the personal part meaning that you could track
your progress on an app.

I wasn't sure how to deal with this man. I couldn't tell if I was what he wanted.

Am I in your tribe? I wanted to ask him. He looked at me wordlessly for a while. On the walls were photos of beautiful, racially indeterminate models working out in tight black Lycra. He mentioned that the gyms had chilled towels and UV treated air.

I nodded politely but there was something wrong.

'I'll be in touch,' he said, as he heaved himself up and walked me to the door.

He shook my hand and smiled dispassionately. I had a feeling I wouldn't get a call.

3

At Heathrow, the departure lounge was packed. Beside me was a group of teenage boys in hoodies, T-shirts and jeans. Their luggage was piled haphazardly beside them: technical backpacks and bags of duty-free. One of the group took photos while the others mugged riotously for the camera. I checked my phone but nothing from *Matt, 36*, so I decided to try another angle, this time standing artfully by the mirror, my face obscured by the flash. I spent a long time touching up the picture, warming my skin tone, slightly enlarging my eyes. Once sent, it shifted immediately to read. I watched for a while but nothing happened. I waited longer, my finger on the glass, the grease on its surface shining in the strip lights. A security guard asked the boys to tone it down while one of them staggered across the floor, smacking his shoulder against the wall, flipping his can across a glass window where its contents dripped down towards the carpet. I wanted to grab the can and empty it. I wanted to smash myself against the glass. I couldn't help sympathizing with these boys. Like most inhabitants of the UK, faced with a few days of freedom, their first instinct was to get totally out of their heads.

•

On the plane, the flight attendant mimed against the soporific buzz of the air conditioning. There was something about air travel that made me think of Swiss euthanasia clinics. I'd never visited one but, for some reason, I had an idea of what they were like: soothing, bland, probably extremely comfortable portals to oblivion. The only time I read magazines was on a plane. Mental images of air disasters spattered through my reading of the *FT*'s *How To Spend It*. I was halfway through a story about kombucha when I lost consciousness completely, passing out somewhere over Rouen.

It was not long before I was awoken roughly by my neighbour. A big guy, he shifted in his seat, his thick elbow jutting helplessly into my chest. In the seat beyond him was a boy of about thirteen, his eyes white from the reflection of the game he was playing on his tablet. He was wearing a tight grey tracksuit, his freckled wrists exposed by its grubby cuffs. The sounds of the game were audible through his headphones and the man beside me turned to catch my eye, keen to share a look of resignation.

'I'm so glad my parenting days are over,' he said in a Welsh accent. He didn't seem to expect a reply. I smiled politely as he turned away, crackling at the plastic wrapping of his sandwich.

'You in Spain a lot?' he asked.

'No,' I said. 'Not in Ibiza, anyway.'

'Me neither.' He released the sandwich from its packet, the smell of Thai chicken filling the air. I waited for a second before going back to sleep but he didn't speak to me again.

•

As soon as the plane came to a standstill, the man stood and started grappling with his bag. I lost sight of him almost immediately as he joined the surge towards the exit. Outside, the runway was bathed in golden evening light. The airport was small and startlingly bright, a glossy walkway full of coloured booths. Billboards advertising Loewe handbags and Cava Brut Reserva lined the walls. In the foyer shopping area there was a store with the logo *Club Ibiza*. Inside it were racks of vacuum-packed T-shirts and bikinis, each printed with the name of a

DJ or nightclub: *Amnesia, David Guetta, Privilege*. The shop was empty. In fact, the airport was almost deserted. There was no one waiting at the desk when I got there to collect the keys for my rental car.

.

It was dark when I finally made it onto the motorway. After a stretch, the route followed a series of crooked roads that never seemed to pass a dwelling, curving instead through the pitch-black countryside. Occasionally, another vehicle drove past, its headlights piercing my eyes. Inchoate forms seeped in and out of view, the dull silhouettes of trees or old stone walls. At one point, an animal lunged in front of me. It seemed to have the bobbing gait of a rabbit although too big somehow. It took me a moment to realize I was looking at a dog, a stray bitch with one leg missing. For a second, I caught her eye in the head-lights. I braked abruptly, skidding to a halt as the animal loped off into the darkness. As I caught my breath, a faint sound emerged in the distance. I felt it almost immediately – it was the dull throb of dance music.

.

I woke up wet with sweat, my hair stuck to my face, the sheets twisted tightly around my legs as if I'd been struggling in the night. In the corner was a small wicker chair, the only point of colour in the room. The place was neat and formulaic, white cushions piled on a sofa, linen curtains that opened onto a window overlooking a field of olive trees. Bizarrely, the TV was showing an episode of the English reality show *Geordie Shore*, the characters dubbed into fast-paced Spanish. I must have fallen asleep with it on, although I had no memory of this at all. I scanned the room for the remote and eventually found it buried in the sheets.

The Can Na Serra was one of a group of resorts on the

island described on the company's website as luxury destinations 'for free thinkers, wilderness seekers and those seeking something offbeat and individual'. 'Ca Na Serra,' the blurb continued, 'is a bucolic sanctuary nestled deep in the Ibizan countryside. Surrounded by lush olive groves and aromatic vineyards, the hotel's quiet luxury is complemented by a freshwater pool and open-air restaurant serving dishes made from fresh local ingredients. Fusing traditional Iberian craftsmanship with a modern, pared back sensibility, the interior comes into its own at dusk, warm candlelight casting an amber glow across linen fabrics, guests sitting on the terrace as they sip cocktails in the Iberian sunset.'

I drank the complimentary bottle of Acqua Panna and forced myself into the shower. As the water started to stream over my head, I tried not to think about what I was doing here.

·

Breakfast was served on a terrace by the pool. I didn't feel good and the coffee wasn't helping. It was warm outside, the air still and thick with the buzz of crickets. At the next table was a tall man who caught my eye and smiled briefly. He was attractive, his hair cut short above a pale, serious face. I glanced back at him and he caught me staring, forcing me to turn away. I got the impression he was intelligent, bookish even, although maybe that was just his glasses. Behind him were three women I recognized from the airport. They were in their twenties, slim and tanned, wearing long dresses and straw hats. Although they'd all gone for the same ensemble, each had added a subtle variation: a slightly larger pair of sunglasses or a different retro leather sandal. The tallest one, a sharp-nosed blonde, was waving a glass of wine in the air. She was laughing loudly with her friend, who was showing her something on her phone. 'People are so fucking stupid,' she said in her drawn-out Surrey accent. 'Honestly, who believes this shit? Can someone please explain to me why people are so thick?' Although they varied in terms of attractiveness, each of these women was meticulously groomed – hair, nails and skin taken care of, faces injected with elegant enhancements. There was something self-conscious about them, their studied indifference only paper-thin. The tall blonde one broke into fresh giggles and her friend mirrored her hilarity, although the other woman didn't seem convinced – it was as if a hierarchy had been established, and maybe not a happy one. 'Who *says* that?' the blonde one snorted through her wine. 'I mean, what *planet* are they on?' A couple on another table stared at them in quiet disapproval. After a while, they left their seats, picking their way down the slope towards the pool.

I was almost halfway through my melon chunks when the nausea began to hit. I stared at the lukewarm slices of Manchego I'd uploaded from the buffet. Helpless, it dawned on me that I wasn't going to make it through the meal, so I sat perfectly still as the tables emptied one by one.

•

In the afternoon I took the Fiat down to the beach. The landscape was unrecognizable in the daylight, a placid sweep of pine forests and scrub, leading to volcanic rocks. Occasionally, a path peeled off into the hillside. As I approached Sant Joan de Labritja, a row of white houses came into view. Almost all of them were fincas for rent, each one dressed to suggest an oddly modern rendition of the hippie lifestyle: a fluorescent hammock here, a plastic Buddha there, a pile of old ceramic pots beside a heart-shaped sign saying *Love Is The Answer*.

At Playa Agua Blanca, I recognized the Germans from breakfast immediately. The woman looked a bit like Martina Navratilova, her features angular and rangy, her thin nose slightly off-key. She caught my eye, leaving me with no choice but to return her smile. A bunch of sun loungers was arranged in a grid on the sand between us and I felt obliged to wait for her as she picked her way towards me.

'I just wanted to say,' she told me, 'I thought you were really patient with those girls this morning. I mean – come on – drinking at breakfast? And why not put your phones away for five minutes? While you're eating, at least! I'm Annette.' She introduced herself as a web designer.

'Hi.' I shook her hand, which was wet from the sea.

Faced with my failure to ask what kind of web design it was that she did, she volunteered that she worked for a fashion brand in a role that demanded a lot of creativity and humour. I didn't really know what to do with this info. There was something disconcerting about her, as she kept repeating, deadpan, that she had a sense of humour. Gaunt and anxious, the man pulled up alongside her. 'Moritz,' he said, introducing himself as a software developer. He stood in front of me, a thick film of wet hair blanketing his narrow chest. In his hand were a biro and a book of puzzles. I looked at him helplessly, then back at Annette. There was something desperate about her. I felt as though she wanted me to stay with her and Moritz, or at least that she wanted someone to mediate whatever kind of life it was she shared with this man. I glanced at the sea while she complained about the girls. The sun was still high and the water was a bright, almost hyperreal shade of blue.

'Tomorrow we're going to take the dolphin tour,' Annette told me. 'It's meant to be amazing.'

'You should come,' Moritz added. 'We heard there were orcas here this week. It's super unusual for the season.'

I shook Annette's hand, firmly this time, as if I was leaving a relative at a funeral.

'That sounds interesting,' I said. 'I'll definitely let you know.'

•

Solitude didn't lend itself to narrative. It was an absence, not just of people but of plot. It wasn't that I went unnoticed, exactly. I did leave some traces in the world. I was overseen, accounted for. Commercially, I was probably quite predictable. Politically, I fell into a certain demographic. Software tracked my progress as I went, capturing the nuances of my behaviour. I was integrated into a system that more or less ensured my physical survival. Lying on my towel as the sun went down, I had to remind myself that everything was fine.

·

In my room, a slight breeze came through the windows. My temperature was high and I didn't feel like going out so I ordered from the room service menu. The food took a long time to arrive, a piece of sirloin with a wicker basket full of chips. I ate fast, washing down the steak with an Estrella and then a can of Coke. While I waited for my sleeping pills to kick in, I watched *Telecanarias* on the widescreen TV. They introduced a woman in a turquoise suit. Behind her was a rolling animation of the ocean, waves gliding past her shoulders and around the sleek bouffant of her hair. She covered a segment on the refugee crisis. The Spanish coastguard had rescued a hundred and ninety people the previous night. The screen flicked to a drone shot of the dinghies, bodies clinging to their crumpled edges. Abruptly, the image switched to a different view. This one was of the Balearic Sea – a pod of orcas emerging in slow motion, rising from the water and then hanging briefly in the air before flopping back beneath the surface. Back in the studio, a professor of cetacean neuroscience joined the conversation.

'. . . it's interesting,' the subtitles explained, 'because cetaceans are close relatives of herding animals like cows and horses. Herding is a deep part of who they are. And in the case of orcas in particular, they seem to have taken it to another level.'

'What do you mean?' asked turquoise suit.

'When you look at how they communicate, there's something about being an orca that's highly social in a way that might be different to what we understand as social life. You could call it a shared sense of self.'

'This is from observing their behaviour in the wild?'

'Not only that. If you look at, say, the brain of an orca and the brain of a human being, the limbic area of the brain – the part that's responsible for processing emotions – it's far more highly developed in the orca. Not just larger but more elaborate. This is especially true of orcas in the wild.'

'So, you're saying that these animals don't experience themselves as individual creatures?'

'Something like that. It suggests that there's something different about their sense of themselves. Their psychology doesn't recognize solitude. It's not a part of their nature to disconnect from the group in the way that, say, a human would.'

Before the professor could continue, turquoise suit turned back towards the camera: 'Spanish police have been mobilized in Catalonia. Some are claiming that excessive force is being used against supporters of the far-right Vox party.'

I turned the TV down and stared at the vibrating grille of the air conditioner.

Then I typed 'solitude' into my phone. What came up was a quote from Wikipedia: 'A state of seclusion or isolation. A lonely or uninhabited place.'

•

During the night, silhouettes flitted past my eyes. Transparent squiggles zapped across my vision. The buzz of the crickets was too loud and soon the whole room was throbbing as if the building had come to life. A strange machine rolled through the door, manned by a small team of apparatchiks. The soldiers took off all my clothes and then rubbed oil into my skin. Two of them moved to the corners of the bed and started wrenching my legs apart. The machine reconfigured itself to form a steel shaft of monstrous proportions. As it gyrated at the bottom of the bed, the officers massaged the oil between my legs. 'You're not ready yet,' I heard them say. 'We need you to relax.' The cold needle of a syringe passed into my arm, then everything turned dark as the steel shaft of the machine started drilling against my pelvis. I tried to open my eyes but I couldn't, my heartbeat rose, I felt paralysed. The panic didn't subside as strokes of pleasure rolled down my thighs. It was only afterwards that I resurfaced, wide awake and drenched in sweat.

•

The next time I was awoken it was by a bleeping sound. Something was happening in the corridor outside. I could hear voices, footsteps thudding, someone banging against the wall. I opened the door to find people rushing past and so I followed the crowd outside where everyone was looking up at the mountains. A sheet of ash hung in the sky, over the remains of a lush pine forest. Embers glowed among the ruins, burning through in the flat dawn light. The smell of smoke was overpowering, the air dense with heavy mist. I sat on a lounger by the pool while the hotel staff drifted around.

To my surprise, the bookish man from breakfast came towards me. 'Can I sit?' he asked. For a moment we shared an amicable silence. 'I wasn't expecting this,' he said, looking up.

I felt the blood rush towards my face. 'Me neither,' I replied.

'Are you here by yourself?'

'Yes, for a few days.'

'It's good to get away on your own sometimes.'

'And you?' I asked him.

'No,' his voice was steady, 'I'm here to see some friends.'

He told me that they had a villa in the hills. He was going to stay with them that night, once they'd arrived on the island.

'They're closing this place down,' he said, 'because of the fire. We're all being evacuated. They'll probably send you to the coast.'

I wanted to talk to him some more but I couldn't, my mind had gone completely blank.

•

Later, I saw him standing in the car park as we were ushered to our new lodgings. He nodded at me and I rolled my window down.

'I'm Tom, by the way,' he said, moving to shake my hand and then thinking better of it.

I considered offering him a lift but then spotted a taxi pulling up behind him.

'What are you doing this week?' he asked. 'I mean, it seems a shame us all being kicked out like this. You know, if you wanted, you could come up to the house.'

4

It looked like an old farmhouse. Lamps were hanging from the palm trees, illuminating a gravelled driveway. I could feel the haze of a watering system pulsing somewhere on the lawn. It took a while for the door to open.

Tom looked at me with curiosity.

'You came,' he said, a little surprised.

Inside, the place smelt like eucalyptus. He led me down a long corridor towards a large arched lounge. Beyond this, I could hear voices. The next door opened onto a chamber dimly lit by a heavy, cast-iron chandelier studded with thick white candles. The room was filled with books, blob-shaped sofas, a marble coffee table, a scattering of plants and a tall metal sculpture on which someone had hung a bikini. I realized that I didn't know what I was doing there. I felt ashamed of my blatant availability as I followed him out onto a poolside terrace where a group of people were sitting around a table, their faces partially illuminated by a row of tiny, flickering candles. It looked as if they'd just finished a meal, there were bowls of salad strewn across the table and a plate of large roasted artichokes. A man in a creased blue shirt stood up. 'This is Niall,' Tom said, matter-of-fact, as his friend leaned over to shake my hand.

Niall's grip was firm and businesslike. His face was scattered with freckles, his skin dry from alcohol and sun. Sitting behind him were three women. 'My wife, Grace,' Niall informed me, 'and this is Bay and Mireille.' Grace stood up to kiss my cheek while the other two nodded politely. Grace was bird-like and serious, her grey eyes set into a narrow face, her hair chopped short around her jaw.

'Good to meet you,' she said, looking slightly bemused. She obviously had no idea why I was there. 'You look like you need a drink.' She examined my face with curiosity, as if she was inspecting an unusual animal. 'You're so pale, look at you. Have you only just arrived?'

'A few days ago,' I said.

She insisted I sat down beside her, squeezing me up against Mireille to the point that I could smell the cigarette smoke on her breath. Mireille was in a short green dress, her round lips painted with a soft metallic gloss. Around her neck was a moulded choker that curved down towards her collarbone. Bay looked softer than the others, her white-blonde hair piled loosely on her head. Her dress was stretched over a bikini that was still damp from the pool. At the end of the garden, a silver greyhound paced around the edge of the water. 'Winston! Come back here,' Bay called, patting her legs. 'Come on,' she shouted. The dog turned to burrow in the bushes. 'He never listens to me,' she swivelled back.

'He needs his space,' Grace said. 'So, how do you know Tom?' she flashed me with the full force of her attention. I was reluctant to tell her that I didn't, so I changed the subject to the fire.

'Isn't it crazy?' Mireille cut in, her English accented with French. 'They never used to happen here so often. It's the climate. The heat's so strong these days.'

'Thirty-seven degrees last night. It isn't normal.' Bay turned back to the dog but he seemed to have vanished into the darkness.

'I heard about the evacuation,' Niall said. He lit a cigarette. 'Fucking crazy. Did they move you to the bay?'

'Just above the strip,' I told him. 'It's a place called Hotel Playasol.'

'Oof.'

'Bad luck.' Bay shook her head.

'It's not the nicest part of the island.' Grace passed me a glass of wine. 'Last time I was down there, there was blood spattered on the beach.'

'What's all that about?' Mireille asked. 'The Brits abroad, it's so funny.'

'It's because of how we work,' Niall replied. 'Long hours. Soul-sucking jobs. The pay's shit, the weather's shit. Give us a taste of freedom and we lose our fucking minds.'

Grace gave him a sceptical look.

'I mean, I work in tech,' he said vaguely. 'It's different for me, but you know what I mean.'

She shook her head almost imperceptibly.

'I don't know.' Bay was picking the leaves off a small piece of artichoke. She held one of them out in the air in an effort to lure the dog towards her. 'I think it's more than that. We've always had that propensity for chaos, haven't we? I know I have.'

'You mean booze?' Niall asked her.

'Yeah, haven't we always had that reputation?'

'I don't know about that.' Niall drained his glass and reached into the pocket of his jeans. He produced a piece of waxed paper that had been folded into a small square. 'Although I think you're right, it's more than just work. I mean, in thirty years' – he waved his hand in the direction of the bay – 'most of the people staying on that strip won't be here. They're already being priced off the island. In a few decades, they'll be gone. If they're lucky, their kids will still have jobs, but those jobs will be less stable. There will be more screen time, lower pay. Or maybe the government will pay them not to work. Suppose that happens? Take work out of the picture completely. Are they going to stop getting their rocks off? I sincerely doubt it.'

'I don't know.' Tom was sitting across from me, his face shaded by the candles. 'People might medicate themselves but it won't necessarily be for the fun of it. You can't just have fun all the time.'

Mireille leaned back and drained her glass. 'I can. I mean, what else is there?' I noticed that her bare foot was pressed against the inside of Niall's thigh.

'Live a little?' Niall suggested. 'Talk to each other? Look after each other? Fuck, I imagine.'

'I know something about this,' I said. 'I had to study it at college. They wanted to see what people did with their free time when their working hours were cut. Like in America – the rust belt, those kinds of places. No jobs. A lot of people subsidized for not doing much.'

'And?' Bay asked, the leaves of the artichoke browning slowly on the table in front of her.

'They spent it on the internet, mostly. Playing games. Watching porn.'

'Of course they did. Who wouldn't?' Mireille finished her cigarette and stubbed it out. 'I'd probably watch porn all day if I could.'

'I couldn't live like that,' Grace said as the dog approached her, sniffing around her legs. 'No way. You need some structure in your life.'

'Well, they did feel bad,' I said. 'That's exactly how they felt, although a lot of them couldn't stop, they just became steadily more addicted. There was substance abuse as well – opioids. Tranquillizers.'

'And on that note,' Niall said brightly, smoothing the waxed paper out in front of him. 'Here we have Tom's finest efforts. He's really outdone himself this time.'

He cut the soft white powder with his card, scraping a pile

onto a copy of *The Subtle Art of Not Giving a Fuck.* 'Brought to you by Britain's finest.'

Tom caught my eye in embarrassment.

'I just check it's pure,' he explained. 'I used to be a chemist.' He leaned towards me and said 'You don't have to' under his breath. 'They like it.' He gestured at the others, as if by way of apology.

'Come on now, you can't miss this.' Niall sculpted the powder into lines. 'The world's going to shit, remember? The least we can do is go down in style.'

I looked at Tom but he didn't catch my eye.

'Let's see what we've got here then.' Mireille leaned over the table, Niall catching her dress riding up her thighs.

'Easy, cowgirl.' For a second, I thought he was going to slap her arse.

'Ignore him, he's always like this.' Bay shook her head, taking my arm.

'Be nice.' Grace sounded almost maternal. She crossed over to Niall's chair, where she perched on the edge of his knee. She took his cigarette and passed it to Bay, who sucked deeply, then put it out. 'I think you've had enough of those,' she said, giving him a territorial pat.

•

An hour passed before I started to feel it. I was standing by the pool, music drifting from the house. Bay's skin was cool against mine, her lips moving close to my ear. I could understand what she was saying but I wasn't present, I was somewhere else, riding on a strange wave of joy. What followed was a bolt of pure euphoria. It shot through me, pounding through my veins. I waited for the feeling to subside, but instead it held me, radiating outwards. My internal world and external reality oscillated in harmony, opening up to encompass Bay as her touch rippled down my spine.

At one point, Niall drove us through the hills. We parked outside a white building and walked through its large, dimly lit interior. Beyond was a private beach on which a crowd of people danced. There were strings of lanterns above their heads, the music heavy and hypnotic. These people weren't dancing with each other, they were all facing the front, their shoulders jostling as they swayed to a solitary speaker in the sand. Time passed slowly but it was good. I was aware I was high but I felt well. The music rose and my mood lifted further. I looked at Tom in total adoration. He looked back with what seemed to be mild concern. He put an arm around me and I closed my eyes, turning towards him.

•

I woke up hot, in bright daylight, on the synthetic sheets of the Hotel Playasol. It took me a while to take in my surroundings. I opened the door to the balcony and stepped outside. On the Passeig de la Mar below, the holidaymakers were out in force. Most were wearing brightly coloured sportswear, their children dressed in smaller versions of the same. The plastic bunting on the beach stalls criss-crossed a sea of human bodies.

I leaned further over the railing and watched the heads passing underneath me. I was reminded of *Monkey Planet*, a show I'd once seen about long-tailed macaques – how increasing group size led to more violent competition as the monkeys tried to distinguish themselves.

'Please don't jump.'

Tom was awake. He sat up and rubbed his face, his eyes soft and bleary with sleep. He was naked apart from a pair of cotton boxers. He was physically tougher than I'd imagined. His dark hair was a little dishevelled, his face creased from the pillow. Without his glasses, his eyes looked green-grey in the morning light. I wanted to move back beside him but I resisted.

'Sorry about last night,' he said.

'Why?'

He looked at me quizzically. 'I think you probably had too much.'

I couldn't remember anything beyond the party. All I knew was that I'd felt good, better than I'd done in years.

'You don't say much, do you?' He got up and joined me on the balcony. He didn't touch me when he reached the railings. I could hardly bring myself to look at him.

'How long are you around for?' he asked.

When I told him I had a few more days, he took a while to think about it.

'You should come out on the boat some time,' he said as he searched for Wi-Fi on his phone.

I couldn't tell if he was serious; he seemed more interested in booking a taxi.

I looked over the balcony again. It was flaming hot outside. Underneath us, a tired-looking beach seller was laying out his box of bags.

•

That night, alone in the room, I found an old copy of *Ibiza Living*. The shower was broken so I ran a bath and opened the magazine at random. A photo of a woman dancing in the sunset was accompanied by an article about the island: 'a vibrant melting pot of hipsters, celebrities and renegade bohemians', but also of 'business professionals and thought leaders looking to improve their health and fitness in discreet and scenic settings'.

The next page featured an interview with a greying fifty-something in headphones. According to this Ibiza veteran, the island was working hard to stop attracting 'the wrong sorts', which was why the clubs had had to raise their prices. In fact, its reputation was undergoing a luxurious transformation.

Only five-star resorts were now being opened. He assured us that the Seven Pines in Cala Conta was one of the jewels in the crown of this new plan. This place offered guests a personal pool, an ice grotto and a Pershing yacht.

I sat in the bath and watched the progress of a small insect on the wall. Outside, voices could be heard clamouring over the music from the bars. The bathroom was dank and claustrophobic, it smelt of other people's sweat. Stuffed down the side of the bath was a waterlogged copy of *Fifty Shades of Grey* – a German edition, its pages brown and glued together. I tried not to imagine the previous occupant of my apartment, an older Fraulein no doubt, probably masturbating furiously to the thrill of being taken by a billionaire 'industrialist'. Although, if I was honest, I couldn't deny the sentiment. There was a reason books like this were all the same.

My phone buzzed loudly by my head, a message from someone I hadn't seen in years. I almost dropped it in the bath.

It's Lara. I heard you need a job.

5

The boat was already running by the time I arrived at the Marina at Port Esportiu. It was Niall's boat, a 32-foot cutter, smaller than most of the yachts in the harbour. I followed Tom on board and sat at one of the white upholstered booths on deck as Niall reeled up the anchor. Once we'd started to pick up speed, the bow glided through the water like a knife. At a certain distance from the shore, the ordinary world seemed to lose all meaning. The tourists on the beach looked ant-like, packed together like mould on a crust. I looked up Formentera on my phone. According to Lonely Planet, the island we were heading towards was 'blissfully languid' and 'full of barefoot-glam boutiques'. Wikipedia took a more cultured approach: a paragraph on Bob Dylan, another on the island's violent past, passing from the Carthaginians to the Romans, then to the Visigoths, the Vandals and the Arabs before it was finally seized by the Catalans and absorbed into the Crown of Aragon. Bursts of spray bounced off my face as we approached a rough, volcanic shore. I'd seen photos of these jagged rocks before, probably on an advert for something, but the reality was stranger, they looked eerie, jutting out like a half-exposed ruin.

As I sat, scanning the horizon, my phone jumped suddenly to life. It was a new message from the same conversation.

I know it's been a while.

Can I give you a call?

•

It was almost noon by the time we moored at Playa Es Calo. The beach there was divided into two. On one side, paunchy couples sat beneath a grid of acid green umbrellas, their children running back and forth across the sand that divided the seating area from the urine-soaked shallows of the ocean. For the most part, these couples seemed affectionate in a bovine sort of way. Others were more hostile, their backs turned, their devices drawing them into private worlds. The men lay sideways on their flanks, bellies spilling onto their towels. The women were mostly in bikinis, their shoulder straps tied behind their backs, their breasts resting loosely on their stomachs.

The other side of the beach was another story: gym-toned women, many of them topless, wandering around the beach bars, while tattooed men in vests and shorts watched them hawk-like from the sidelines. In one of the bars, a DJ was playing a gentle, almost jazz-like set. Girls were bobbing to the music, their contoured stomachs lubed with cream. No one caught anyone's eye and yet the atmosphere was charged. They all ignored the families in the distance, as if oblivious to where all of this was heading.

Bay rolled her towel out next to mine, removed her top immediately and started slathering sunscreen on her chest. I couldn't see her eyes behind her glasses, all I could see were two reflections of myself. She pulled a book out of her bag and caught me glancing at what she was reading: *Human Givens: A New Approach to Emotional Health and Clear Thinking.* On the cover was a photo of the rainforest, dew dripping from a verdant frond.

'You should read it,' she told me. 'It's really changed the way I think. It's all about basic needs, you know, the things we all need to be happy.'

'Like?' I asked her.

'Well, it starts with absolute fundamentals – food, shelter, things like that. Not just bricks and mortar but like, emotionally, a home.'

'What else?'

'Oh, I mean, it just goes on.' She sighed, flicking through the pages.

I tried to ignore the boys beside us who were staring at her tits.

'There's attention, for example – like being acknowledged by the world. Then there's a sense of control over your life. After that comes love, intimacy, feeling like part of a community. There are tons of things.' She propped herself up on one elbow and slid a thin cigarette out of her bag. I looked at her mirrored lenses and wondered what she thought of me. She obviously had money, and either hadn't noticed or was relaxed about the fact that I didn't. 'Freedom's a big one.' She exhaled, an 'O' of smoke floating towards the sea. 'Personal autonomy, that sort of thing.'

It struck me that these things were hard to come by – even taken in isolation, I couldn't say I'd managed even one of them.

'The point at which life is worth living is probably quite high,' I said out loud.

She looked surprised but she didn't contradict me. I didn't smoke but I took a cigarette, although it wasn't really a cigarette I wanted – it was more of whatever I'd had the other night.

'So, what are you doing here, really?' Grace said, slipping down beside us. She folded her legs underneath her. Her movements were neat and unobtrusive.

'I'm just taking some time off.'

'On your own?'

'Looks like it.'

She inspected me the way she had when we'd first met. I got the feeling she didn't miss a lot.

'You don't seem like you should be on your own.'

I shrugged and turned over onto my front.

'So, what do you do when you're not on the island?'

She said 'the island' as if she was there a lot.

'I work in marketing,' I told her, stifling the inevitable wince.

'Me too.' She almost smiled, a note of commiseration on her face.

I waited for her to ask me where I worked but she had the grace to let it go.

'Tom seems to like you.'

'You think so?'

'I don't know, it's hard to tell with him.'

'Where is he?'

'Over there,' she said, adjusting the straps of her swimsuit. She nodded across the beach to where Tom and Niall were buying drinks.

Our boat bobbed mutely on its tether, slightly apart from all the others. The thought of work filled me with dread. I imagined a life spent on the ocean. I knew some people lived like that, drifting endlessly from place to place, a life of ceaseless recreation. With the advent of on-board Wi-Fi, there were probably more of them than ever.

•

I was twelve the first time I stepped onto a boat. My father had taken me to the Isle of Wight. It was some kind of work-related thing, a trip his boss, Richard, had organized. Also on the holiday was Susan, Richard's wife, and their daughter, Emily, who must have been around three at the time. It was Richard who owned the boat. Richard was old-school, the kind of man that drank brown ale on tap. He had a Gary Busey-style wild haircut and although he was on the short side, he somehow took up a lot of space, his hefty torso balanced on a pair of skinny, fluffy legs. There was something manic about his determination to be in charge.

The boat was a sort of floating caravan, its hull painted with the handle *Lucky Dick*. About half an hour into our voyage, Richard's daughter started to cry. A row erupted within minutes and Susan demanded they take her back to the harbour, although it was only with reluctance that Richard agreed to dump his wife and kid. When he steered us back out into the Channel, it was with the blank determination of someone who couldn't wait to put some space between himself and the life he led on land. At twelve years old, I understood this irritation meant that he couldn't stand his family, he was repulsed by what they represented, they were a dead weight to him, dragging him down into a bog of mindless domesticity. As Richard sped back out into the ocean, a fog began to close around us. Almost indiscernibly, it lowered over our heads, the sea turning a heavy grey. Crag-like waves rose around the boat, tossing it more violently than before. The whole time, Richard kept his head down, pushing the engine harder, continuing to drive us out towards the horizon. I watched all of this with fascination; it was only when I saw the look on my father's face that I realized something was wrong. At one point, the engine failed and Richard climbed into the hull to try to fix it. While he was down there, the mast snapped, cracking hard against the deck where it rolled noisily against the plastic seats. I looked up to see a wall of water, the surface of the ocean scrolling downwards. I understood exactly what was happening. It seemed likely we were going to die.

More than anything, I was embarrassed for my father; I felt he would have preferred a more normal death. At the same time, I faced the prospect of my own oblivion with the resignation of a corpse. It was as if I was already dead. I shut down completely, the only thing that touched me was the thought of the pain, of those final moments as my lungs filled up with water – *that* filled me with terror. Nothing else mattered in the slightest; I would have preferred to pass out there and then.

Afterwards, once we'd made it back to the marina, I barely thought about what had happened. Throughout the rest of the weekend, my dad bought me whatever I wanted. He plied me with bags of sweets and nautical-themed stationery from the gift shop. We spent most of the drive back home in silence, listening to *Steve Wright in the Afternoon*. He never mentioned the incident to my mother. He left a few months after that. I think something about that weekend had made him realize he wanted more from his life.

•

Lying on the Playa Es Calo, I couldn't help feeling self-conscious in my swimsuit, although Tom seemed absorbed in his own thoughts.

'What happened the other night,' I said finally. 'I don't do that often.'

He didn't reply.

'I mean, I hope that's not what you think,' I added.

'You don't remember what happened, do you?'

'I know we went back to my hotel but then, to be honest, it gets a little hazy. Did we have sex?'

'You were pretty out of it,' he said. 'I mean, I won't pretend I didn't want to.'

I wasn't sure if he expected to me to be embarrassed.

He sat up. 'Look, this isn't usual for me either. Things got out of hand.'

'You gave me a cocktail of drugs?' I rolled over in the sand to face him. 'And then you tried to have *sex* with me.'

He looked at me seriously. 'I didn't touch you.'

'I know,' I said. 'It was a joke. I had a good time.'

'I did too. Although all of that, it's a bit depressing, don't you think?'

'The drugs?'

He nodded, searching my face.

I realized that I didn't want to disappoint him. Reluctant to continue, I changed the subject.

'So how do you all know each other?'

'Grace is my boss.'

'Seriously?'

'Yeah, although we've become more like friends over the years. Niall's the one who always drags us out here. He grew up with all of this. The house has been in his family for years, he's been coming out here since he was a kid. Not that it gives him an excuse – he shouldn't be doling Class A's out to strangers.'

This time I decided to respond.

'That's very honourable of you,' I said.

He looked a little uneasy.

'Am I a stranger?' I asked.

'Well, who are you? You don't seem to want to tell me.'

'What do you want to know?'

'Is this what you're into, for a start?' he asked bluntly. 'Because I should probably tell you that I'm sober.'

It took me a moment to absorb this.

'But you still come out here?' I said.

'I have to have a life,' he shrugged. 'I have to be around other people.'

I got the impression he didn't want to talk about it.

'Earlier,' he said, 'what was it you were reading?'

'The news, Reuters, *New York Times*.'

'You like to keep up with all of that?'

'Doesn't everyone? I find it relaxing.'

I lay on my back, surveying him from behind. He was squinting straight ahead into the sea. I felt my blood move as I watched him, the pulse shifting in my neck. The way he looked reminded me of the kind of men I'd seen in old photos of the countryside, photos from my grandparents' generation. He had that kind of easy physicality. My phone buzzed. I silenced it but I caught him eyeing the screen with curiosity. As I shut the notification down, my browser window came into view.

'I like the problem page,' I confessed, a little sheepishly.

'Let me see that.' He leaned over my shoulder. '*Is Agreeing To A Casual Relationship Demeaning?*' he read out loud.

The words seemed comical coming out of his mouth.

'I'm a fifty-year-old woman,' he continued. 'I recently met a man who makes me happy. More so than anyone I've been with before. He sees me for who I really am. He tells me that he finds me attractive and we have great sex, but he's adamant that he doesn't want a relationship. Not a traditional one, anyway. He wants us to enjoy one another's company. He likes us to live in the here and now. My question is, am I compromising my dignity if I continue to sleep with him on his terms? I love what we have together and I don't want to lose him.'

'What can I say?' I turned towards him, a little embarrassed. I felt I had to defend my reading material. 'I'm interested in other people's lives.'

'You're one of those people who never shares anything, aren't you?' he said. 'You're a pervert. You like lurking.'

'Aren't we all?'

He scrolled through to the food section. '*What do successful women really eat?*'

I shook my head in mock shame.

'I'm going to have to take that back,' I said, grabbing my phone out of his hand. 'My whole browsing history is on that thing. I'll tell you now, you don't want to see that.'

He raised his eyebrows in faux-shock.

I cast him a sidelong glance. 'What did you do last night?'

'Not much. We went out for dinner. They stayed out. I went to bed.' I caught him scanning my face for a reaction. 'I was on my own, if that's what you're asking.'

I didn't reply immediately.

'I don't do that sort of thing,' he said.

'You don't?'

'What I mean is, I haven't been,' he corrected himself. 'I've lost interest, I suppose. It gets old, sleeping with the wrong women.'

'Were they all wrong?'

'The ones that were willing to sleep with me were.'

'Correlation or causation?'

He almost cracked a smile.

'You don't have to tell me,' I said.

'I know.' He paused, kicking up the sand. 'That woman in the letter,' he said. 'That's it for her, isn't it?'

'I don't know, she's only fifty. People get together, it happens all the time.'

'Does it?' he asked me, dead serious. 'Does it happen all the time?'

I wanted to say yes, but I wasn't sure if it was true. I thought about my mother, divorced and living alone in the house that I grew up in. Relationships, I sometimes thought, survived only on the happiness of the first few years. That foundation was all there ever was, its memory the only defence against the inevitable decline that followed. It might be true that love required youth. I looked at Tom and he nodded towards the sea.

'You can see the mainland from here,' he said.

•

Later, as we packed our things to leave the beach, the party by the bar began to pick up. Now devoid of small children, the area had filled with a different crowd. Cars pulled up behind the rocks, their headlights flashing as the light faded. Girls in stretch dresses gathered around the sound system, dancing to a deepening bass as strange men approached them from behind, their groins rubbing against the women's haunches. The lights came on inside the bar as a party of ten or so emerged, bottles of Cava in the air, spilling as they swayed towards the speakers. Some of the dancers were high already, some too drunk to stand. I watched as a couple staggered from the crowd, the man lifting his partner off her feet as she laughed compliantly, faux-protesting, giggling loudly. Once the couple reached the limits of the beach, they disappeared into a wooded area.

I read once on Playboy.com – the new one, without the nudes – that only one in ten women ever climaxed on a one-night stand. This news was presented as a shocking example of inequality between the sexes. It was obvious why men avoided commitment, I thought, but why didn't women deny them sex? Without pleasure, what was the point? Hope is a powerful fiction, I guessed.

The sun sank lower on the horizon, turning the ocean to a soft, metallic pink. Then, quicker than I would have imagined, it disappeared completely.

6

I woke up in the morning to another string of texts:

I know you probably don't want to see me

I'm back in London, by the way

The third message was a photo, one that looked at least ten years old. It was a snap of me at a party, barely aware of being caught on camera. Lara, a few inches taller, was by my side, her arm around me, a look of wild hilarity on her face. We must have been in our early twenties at the time. It isn't true that the past haunts us forever, what haunts us are the traces we leave behind: the photos, emails, arbitrary records. Beyond those fragments, some things – maybe even most things – are lost as if they never happened. The photo cut through my defences, releasing something I'd buried completely. It was a tinge of excitement mixed with apprehension. Although I knew it was a bad idea, I had a feeling I was probably going to see her.

That night, a woman stopped me in the lobby. I didn't recognize her at first and it was only when she started complaining that I realized it was Annette from the beach, her Navratilova-esque features now tanned to a deep, burnt orange. She stopped me as if she was doing me a favour. I could tell that she'd been drinking. 'Always on her own, this one,' she said, loudly enough that everyone could hear.

'You must come and sit with us tonight. You can't spend

all your time alone.' She was rambling, her sweat-resistant T-shirt hanging loose around her braless chest. 'You don't know what you've got until it's gone,' she told me, staring intensely at my eyes. 'A woman like you should be out there, having some bloody fun in life.' Her eyes widened further, her eyeballs bloodshot with alcohol and sun. She lowered her voice to a dramatic whisper: 'Don't settle too young, like I did.'

Annette and her husband Moritz had gathered around a table with some of the other refugees from the Can Na Serra. They seemed to have reached a truce with the Surrey girls and the group was huddled closely together, a safe distance from the hotel's 'real' guests, most of whom were sprawled around the pool, their kids splashing in the water while they downed Estrellas on the terrace. I flicked through a magazine that someone had picked up from the airport. 'When in Ibiza, avoid the West End,' it said. 'Famous for its "Chav" behaviour, the girls will flash their bits to anyone and these days there are often film crews trawling the area in search of debauchery. Despite the advent of social media – and fun fact, Ibiza is one of the most photographed places on Earth – you can find them wandering the streets at night, usually having puked on themselves.' It wasn't long before the Germans picked up on this theme. 'The vomit.' Moritz shook his head. 'The piss.' He looked traumatized. I gave up on my magazine and picked up a newspaper instead: 'Drunken Brits arrested over chaos on flight,' the headline said. 'It was 7am, yet these folks were already steaming.' In the photo was a woman in a white dress, the front of which was soaked with wine. Her eyes were unfocused. On her face was a look of pure delight.

•

I spent the afternoon alone, swimming at Talamanca Bay. On its far side, I could see the tall palms of the Nobu Hotel. The hotel grounds were sealed off, its walls bunker-like. This was

to ensure that guests weren't subjected to views of the over-
crowded beaches. Yachts gathered around a small marina that
backed onto the hotel garden. Years ago, I'd been to a product
launch at the Nobu in Marylebone. At the time, all I'd known
about the place was that it was co-owned by Robert De Niro.
The lobby had been filled with marketing types and journalists from the style press. I hadn't realized at that time that the
restaurant was part of a conglomerate, an American enterprise
with more than thirty sites around the world. There was one
in the Marriott in Beijing and a few concessions in resorts
across the tropics. Unlike most venues of its type, Nobu – now
known as Nobu Global – cultivated no house style. Instead,
it took a chameleon-like approach, melding elements of the
local culture into its core formula – a little gold panelling for
the Qataris, paper lanterns for Japanese. In this way, the brand
succeeded in generating a sense of glamour that glossed over
any awkward cultural differences. Cultural differences were
for the workers, the unsophisticates who mopped the floors.
Much like the shopping centre business, every Nobu was
the same but different – familiar enough for the local clientele but bland enough to provide a reassuring environment
for wealthy tourists. The sole unifying theme of the business
seemed to be that it sold sushi. As I watched, a small sail-
boat approached. It stopped just short of the marina as a
woman in a long white dress emerged. Her hair was cloaked
in a white niqab, a pair of silver sandals on her feet. Behind
her was a man in a white suit, an elaborate silver-patterned
tie knotted in a strange way around his neck. His skin was
almost black against the brilliance of his jacket. Together,
they looked like the king and queen of a new-age medieval
kingdom.

•

I showered and changed as slowly as I could. My plan was to eat on my own and spend my last evening reading in my room, but there was no room service at the Playasol and I had to brave the bar if I wanted food. Annette spied me as soon as I showed up, waving me over from her table. The Surrey girls were still in situ, joined now by a pair of men. 'Come and have a drink with us,' Annette insisted. 'Have some fun for once, no?' It was obvious she wasn't going to let me get away and before long, I was ensconced at the table, reluctantly accepting a jumbo glass of wine.

'This is Dean' – Annette beamed at me encouragingly – 'and this is Lee. Pippa, Holly and Michelle – I think you girls have already met?' The Surrey girls smiled in unison, alarmingly friendly now that they were drunk. On the table was a batch of empty bottles. 'Lee used to be a DJ,' Annette announced.

'Oh, it was a long time ago,' he batted her away as if the compliment was too generous. Lee looked knackered, his cheeks soft and jowly underneath a greying Liam Gallagher mop.

'What kind of music do you play?' I asked him.

'Oh, you know, eclectic, a bit of house, salsa, EDM.'

'That's interesting,' I lied.

'It's that Balearic sound, it's all about the melting pot.'

Pippa had started to sober up, her flushed features suddenly discomposed. Michelle, on the other hand, seemed entranced by Lee. I drained my glass only to have it filled again, this time right up to the brim.

'Moritz,' Annette ordered, without looking. 'Another bottle of white.'

By midnight, my eyes were burning. 'The car's here.' Dean bounced up and I followed him, unsteady on my feet, the room lurching as I faltered across the floor. In the taxi, Lee produced a plastic wallet and fished out a handful of greyish pills. He pushed them between the women's lips, one by one, until he got to me. I was just sober enough to turn him down – and also to notice that he didn't bother with Moritz, instead handing the packet straight to Dean, who slipped it down the side of his shoe. We came to a stop beside a long queue. There was a huge variety of people at the club, some of them spilling out of chauffeured cars, many of them well into middle-age. At the door, we each paid €55 for entry to a vast hangar-like space, purple lasers cutting through the thick, pungent mist that permeated the air.

'My God, this is amazing.' Annette took my hand and led me to the centre of the dance floor where she started to jolt erratically, her body rubbing up against the tattooed trunks of a group of extremely young Israelis, their tight vests drenched with sweat, their pumped physiques giving off a fruity stench that seemed to send Annette into a frenzy. The whole place, in fact, reeked of sweat. The air was moist with the pheromones of what must have been a few thousand bodies. It was at this point that a flume of gelatinous gunk started roaring above my head. '*Schiuma*,' shouted a shaven-headed Italian as he bounced into the centre of the mess. A group of Drake lookalikes sprayed Cava over him as he went. In an instant, the crowd erupted, wet skin sliding through the billowing fluff. I spotted Pippa grinding against Dean, her mouth gouging into his face. Annette remained entranced, a beatific smile on her face. Beside her, the smallest of the Israelis started rubbing his face into her chest. Stripped of certain inhibitions, I thought, people were kinder to each other. They seemed to like one another more. Maybe this was who we really were, when you peeled back the fear and loathing. Around me was a kind of temporary utopia – gender, class and racial tensions vanished as if they'd never existed. Why, I caught myself wondering, was it so disgusting?

Overwhelmed, I pushed my way towards the door. Outside,

the night was pure and still, the palm trees barely stirring in the breeze. I found Moritz by the car park working quietly on a Sudoku.

•

I didn't hear from Tom the following day. I wanted to call him but it would have seemed gauche. And I hadn't made a call for months. The other option was to text but I couldn't bring myself to formulate a message. The thought of sending him a light-hearted goodbye – maybe with a fun emoji – I didn't want to. And anyway, it was pointless. Convention dictated that I move on as if the two of us had never met. I spent the morning packing my bags. I stacked my luggage on the bed: a small holdall and a rucksack that said *Just Do It* on the zip. My flight was booked for 2 p.m. I threw up in the sink before I left.

Downstairs, the bar was almost empty. By the window, a girl was crying, her eyes ringed with smudged mascara. Her feet were dirty in her strappy sandals, her head leaning heavily against her friend's shoulder. 'I can't help it, I want him.'

'There's no point crying over a bloke,' her friend scolded her gently. 'You don't need that in your life.'

'I love him though.' Her words were running together. Her voice had the tone of someone who didn't care that much about her life. She sounded, in fact, like someone who would have preferred almost anything over this.

7

It was crowded at the airport. My plane was delayed and it was almost midnight by the time I arrived at Heathrow. There was a man lying on the floor in arrivals, a group of security guards holding him down with some difficulty as they waited for the police to arrive. The man was yelling incoherently, there was a pervasive sense of violence in the place as the other passengers walked around him, barely reacting as they moved along the concourse. The altercation had affected the queuing system, which meant I missed my last train home, the man's yells reverberating through the building as I joined the long queue for a taxi. During the ride, the driver asked me what I did. He stared at my reflection in the rear-view mirror. I tried to answer his questions as well as I could but he wasn't easily satisfied. Later, the conversation changed direction as he asked me, in broken English, how old I was, if I was married, why I didn't have children. The journey went on for over an hour, encompassing a detailed overview of my life, half of which I made up because I couldn't bring myself to disappoint him. He dropped me off around 2 a.m., dumping my bags chivalrously by the door. I'd forgotten that the switch in the lobby wasn't working, so I felt my way up the stairwell in the dark.

The next morning, I discovered I couldn't get out of bed. There didn't seem to be much point. I could have cleaned the flat, bought food, maybe switched on the TV. I could have had my face tattooed, or spent the day fucking strangers. Ostensibly, I was free. The options seemed, on the surface of things, to be plentiful. There were a few constraints, of course: murder, violence, theft – although, with the right resources, those too could probably have been negotiated. The world I lived in was laissez-faire or, more precisely, it was actively seductive. Right now, for example, it was calling me to spend the rest of the day watching *Poirot* on Now TV.

Halfway through 'Dead Man's Mirror', just as David Suchet was touring the grounds of Sir Chevenix-Gore's ancestral manor, my phone vibrated and I lost an hour swiping through the previous week's alerts. I messaged Lara: I'm back in town. I watched for a reply but nothing came. While I waited, I scrolled through social media which directed me to a long and detailed polemic on the horrors of social media by someone called Jaron Lanier. I resurfaced just in time to watch Poirot gathering the suspects in the lounge. I found myself touched, unexpectedly, by the episode's denouement, my eyes welling up with tears as Ms Lingard unravelled in the study. I looked up the actress – Fiona Walker. I couldn't tell if her performance was stunning or if I was going through some sort of crisis.

I lined up an old season of *Love Island* while messaging a couple of former colleagues. I tried to sound as casual as possible, dropping in that I was open to 'the right role' if something 'interesting' came up. I tried not to dwell on the fact that my future hinged completely on these tenuous connections. I also texted a recruiter, someone I'd once met for a coffee but whose face I couldn't remember. Montana, a gym-toned student, was standing in a deep-V swimsuit on the lawn. She was eating a bowl of muesli while Alex and Harley wrestled by the pool, their oiled muscles glowing in the sunset. Neon lights bathed the villa in the distance. The effect was mesmerizing.

Watching Montana scrape her bowl, I felt a cold sweat break over me. I went straight for the comfort of my phone, where I looked up Lara but she still hadn't replied. Then the phone vibrated. A shot of dopamine pumped through my blood.

Back tomorrow
It was Tom.

.

Everything in life happens for a reason and that reason is usually a mistake. I realized as soon as I'd arrived that I probably shouldn't have turned up.

She was haphazardly put together, although the studiedly effortless assemblage she was wearing looked more polished than I remembered. Her nails had been professionally done and her long hair was parted in the middle, albeit loosely and in its natural, slightly chaotic state. It hung down her back, over the oversized coat she was wearing.

'I've left Max,' she said.

She always launched into things like this, picking up where we'd left off as if we'd seen each other only days ago. In fact, it had been over three years. I still had the date in my diary. She'd disappeared during a party, which wasn't unusual in itself, she often left unannounced if she was bored. What was different this time was the silence that had followed. We'd both been the worse for wear and I remembered vaguely that we'd argued. She'd called me a 'soulless cog' and 'one of life's followers'. She'd also described the people I worked with as 'the grey goo of non-player characters'. To be fair, the last part was accurate, but I hadn't needed to hear it from her. I'd lost my temper and called her, not very originally, a narcissist. In retrospect, I think it was me that had bored her that night. I still had all the messages she'd left unanswered.

She slung her coat over her chair and threw her bag on the seat beside it. It was a battered Prada Milano that she had no doubt lifted from her mother. She let it drop like a sack of rocks, rummaging inside it for her phone.

'What happened?' I asked.

'Just one of those things.'

'So you're moving out?'

'I'm staying with my mother.'

'Not your dad?'

'He's in France,' she said, a little cagily. 'They're getting divorced, thank God.'

'Sorry to hear that.'

'It took them long enough.'

She turned her attention to the menu. She obviously didn't want to talk about it.

'I saw you're doing well, though.'

I knew she'd guess that I was talking about work. There didn't seem much point in pretending that I hadn't been following her online.

'I'm doing fine,' she said. 'Actually, that's what I wanted to talk to you about. I heard you're looking for a job.'

I waited for her to continue, curious to see where this was going.

'We've got something coming up,' she said casually. 'I thought you might be interested.'

'I don't think so.'

'Why?'

She said it as if it was a real question. I couldn't believe she thought I'd be prepared to work for her. She hadn't even bothered to tell me what she did; the only reason I knew was because I'd read about it on Londonnews.tech.

'Aren't you going to hear me out?' she said.

'No.'

'I think you'd find it interesting.'

'It's a dating app, isn't it? I doubt it.'

'We're trying to change the culture around sex.'

She sounded exactly like my old boss.

'And how's that going for you?' I said.

'It's going well.'

'Congratulations, I'm pleased.'

'What are you doing these days, anyway?' she asked me. 'Outside work, I mean.'

'Not much.'

I couldn't face telling her the truth. I also didn't trust her with it.

'So, where are you going to live?' I said.

'Why are you so interested in where I'm living? I've found a new place, for what it's worth. You should come over.'

'Where is it?'

'Holly Grove, not far from here. I couldn't stay with Mum, she's been driving me insane.'

I still wasn't sure why she had summoned me. Why the sudden job offer after all this time?

'I'm trying to see it as a new start,' she said carefully.

So she was single again, so what? Did she think she could just reinstate me in her life?

I decided to ask her directly. 'What's going on?'

'Can't I do an old friend a favour?'

'Not convincingly, no.'

She looked a little thwarted.

'Fine,' she said. 'I'll get this.'

.

I was eighteen the first time I met Lara. She was one year older than me exactly. She was in the Faculty of Art at Goldsmiths, which imbued her, in my credulous eyes, with the kind of glamour that was conspicuously absent from my own subject: Management with Marketing. She was part of an older crowd, some of whom ran small galleries around the city. These were mostly in abandoned office blocks or old, disused warehouses. There were parties almost every night and Lara was a fixture on the scene. One time, late at one of these gatherings, she caught some guy assaulting me. He'd drunkenly pinned me against a wall. I was drunk too – it was very late – but the scene impressed itself on me with crystal clarity. It was the sheer force of her indignation. She'd pulled him off me and he'd hit her, so she'd smashed a glass in his face. She was fearless to the point of violence. It was shocking, coming from someone like her. Maybe it was just a teenage thing, but she had an almost pathological willingness to stand up for what she believed in. She was a total purist in those days. I was impressed. We became friends that night.

She still went by her full name in those days, Delara Gray. She was half-Iranian and half-English. Her parents had met in Tehran while her father was there on business. The family was sitting on a mountain of property, a tangle of mortgagings and re-mortgagings that was wrapped around south London like a sprawling knotweed. Her father was a successful developer who had worked on projects all over the world, although he always made a show of not being interested in money. He had a vaguely hippie air about him, as if none of it really mattered. It was confusing for Lara, I think, in that he never demonstrated an old-school respect for the management of capital. He was rich but he rejected the idea of it. Life, as far as he was concerned, was for living.

Around the time Lara was born, her parents left the Middle East. Due to the circumstances of her father's work, her childhood was spent travelling. It was a life he'd chosen for himself and which had seemed important at the time, but it was also one that left the three of them unmoored from any particular society or culture. It was probably the reason he clung so hard to the whole 'free spirit' thing, with his faded denim jacket and the old T-shirts he always wore, I think he needed that idea to make sense of things. The boring life he'd left in England – the one he'd always taken for granted – kept changing in his absence, becoming more foreign each time he returned. Lara, on the other hand, had never known anything else. By her teens, she'd lived all over Asia. That was before she'd turned fourteen, when her parents had shipped her to boarding school in Sussex.

When I met her, Lara was living at her parents' house in Chelsea. She had the place to herself when they were away, which was most of the time. It was comfortable and unpretentious but it was also full of things I'd never seen before. There was a glass-walled fridge in the kitchen dedicated exclusively to drinks. There was a temperature-controlled wine cellar and a huge, up-lit wooden cabinet, a floor-to-ceiling thing in the sitting room full of vintage Scotch. When her dad was around, he liked to open a bottle of whisky and wind his daughter up. He thought it was hilarious that she'd ended up at art school after all the money he'd spent on her education. He was a man whose default mode was banter but Lara rarely played along. She wasn't interested in that. She wanted to be taken seriously.

Lara's mother, for her part, saw things differently. She was full of support for her daughter's interests. She'd say things like: 'I might not understand the path you've chosen, but I'll always defend your right to take it, because when I was growing up, we didn't have any choice at all.'

Her parents didn't have much in common. In fact, despite her father's commitment to a sort of blandly Blairite multiculturalism, they hardly seemed to understand each other at all. The one thing they shared was an assumption that their daughter's trajectory was a reflection of their own place in life. The world of work was a social cue for them, it was a status symbol above all else. Lara, naturally, thought this was bullshit, much like everything else her parents thought. Conspicuous production, she called it. She wanted to burn it all down.

One evening, we went to the opening of an exhibition. It was a more sophisticated crowd than usual. She looked beautiful that night. The gallery was so packed we decided to explore the rest of the building. It was dark in the office upstairs, a circle of desks strewn with wires. There was a smudged whiteboard on the wall and a bank of shelves stuffed with folders. Outside, the city looked alive, car lights flowing like oil in the darkness. It felt as if we were finally part of something.

'Are you into girls?' she said, leaning her head against the glass. I'd never thought about it before, but it turned out, that night, I was.

I submitted to the kiss without thinking, with my eyes closed. It was sweet, although I was nervous. I'd had a couple of glasses of wine but I couldn't really believe what was happening. I think she could feel that I was becoming aroused, because she whispered in my ear to keep my eyes closed, as if the fact that I couldn't see somehow diminished the enormity of what we were doing. She turned me around towards the glass, then she moved her hand up my thigh and down underneath my tights. Outside, the city continued its business, oblivious to what was happening, although anyone could have seen us. I felt the blood pumping through me, liquefying between my legs. It was intense and then it was over. Afterwards, we went back downstairs, where she behaved as if nothing had happened.

8

I'd arranged to meet Tom at Fischer's. I hadn't seen him since the day we had sailed to Formentera but I'd found myself thinking about him a lot. It had already been two weeks and although we'd exchanged a few messages, they had dwindled in the past few days. I'd convinced myself he wasn't coming and arrived at the restaurant late on purpose, so that if he wasn't there I'd be able to leave immediately. I was so nervous when I saw him that I told him I hadn't thought I'd see him again.

'I wasn't sure either,' he said.

'What changed your mind?'

'It's hard to say.'

'I'm glad you came.'

'Me too. I mean, this doesn't usually happen.'

'What do you mean?'

'Well, that night at the villa, you were pretty gone. Those drug-fuelled parties, they don't usually lead to much.'

'You were sober, weren't you? Did I disgrace myself?'

I actually felt myself flush.

'Not at all,' he said politely. 'Just saying – you were wasted.'

I wasn't sure what to make of this. I glanced around the room while I thought about it. The place was quiet. Most of the clientele looked older. In the booth beside us was a group of plastic surgeons from the clinics around Harley Street. It was an odd choice for a date. Old-fashioned. Tom was dressed formally too. He was wearing a white shirt with a dark navy jacket. He'd obviously come straight from the office. He looked good in his work clothes. I picked up the menu and forced myself to read it.

'Science is predatory,' he told me later, while he was eating his pan-fried seabass. 'It's ruthless, it changes everything it touches.'

He was explaining why he'd dropped out of college.

'A lot of scientists are mad. They might not know it but they're focused on their research to the point of mania. They have to be if they want a career. And the scary part is that no one notices. I don't think most of them know it themselves.'

Our corner of the restaurant was dark, lit only by a set of fringed lamps. The waiters wore green waistcoats. I wondered if he was trying to impress me. On the other hand, he'd told me outright that he hadn't been sure if he would come.

'What did you say earlier,' I said, 'about drug-fuelled parties not leading to much?'

The truth was I'd felt transcendent that night, even though we had barely touched.

'It's well-established. There are studies on it. Thousands of drugs affect the way people treat each other – they might increase libido or lower inhibitions – but the effects wear off, which destabilizes things. It's worst for people on prescription medications.'

He looked at me as if he was worried he was boring me.

'Are you really interested in this?'

I was, but only because I wanted to know what he thought of me.

'Well, it's a problem for psychiatrists,' he continued, 'in that when a patient is given a psychotropic drug – it could be an antidepressant or an antipsychotic, anything that affects them emotionally – they usually have to keep taking it indefinitely. It's something a lot of people can't handle.'

'Sounds like a licence to print money.'

'It is, but it also causes problems. Most people are resistant to the idea of taking drugs, especially ones that affect their brains.'

'Why is that?'

'Because they think there's something special about raw, unadulterated experience.'

'And you disagree?'

'For the most part, yes. If that experience is causing you pain, why not do something about it?'

'You think there's *nothing* to be lost? Nothing at all?'

'Not necessarily. Not according to the research, anyway. It's an assumption based on extreme examples, like alcoholism or heroin abuse. People tend to talk about drugs in moral terms, they'll say an addict is behaving worse than they normally would, for example. That intuition is very ingrained but it isn't always well-founded.'

'So which substances do you recommend then?'

'It depends what state the patient's in. Even an opiate can be a good thing when it comes to long-term suffering. It can give someone the relief they need to function.'

I was still none the wiser as to what was going on between us. I was so overtly attracted to him that I'd assumed it showed on my face, but maybe he couldn't tell. We looked at one another. He'd accused me of not saying much but he seemed determined not to give anything away.

'How come you know so much about this?' I said.

'It's my job. I'm in pharmaceuticals. I work in marketing.'

'You're a salesman?'

'Not exactly.'

'You sound like one.'

'Thanks,' he said, smiling.

'I used to work with salespeople.'

'Sorry about that.'

'It's a tough job.'

'I suppose it depends what you're selling. In my case, it is getting tougher. Most of the companies I work for are desperate to clean up their reputations but people just don't trust them any more. There's a lot of confusion out there.'

'That's not surprising.'

'I know – and I'm not necessarily defending them. All I'm saying is that communicating with the public has become more difficult. And in the meantime, we're living in one of the most heavily medicated countries on Earth. And I'm not even talking about addiction, which is worse here than anywhere else in Europe.'

The waiter reappeared to clear our plates. While we'd been talking, the restaurant had filled up. It was now so packed that I could smell the perfume of the woman on the next table. I could even name the brand she was wearing – Velvet Orchid by Tom Ford.

'Shall we get out of here?' Tom said.

Outside, it had started to rain so we hailed a taxi on Weymouth Street. When he gave the driver his address, I didn't say a word. The building was near City Road. It looked as if it had just been built. I could still smell plaster in the lobby and on the carpet was a ridge of sawdust brushed up against the walls.

'Sorry about the mess,' he said as he opened the door. 'I've only just moved in.'

There were stacks of boxes by one wall and a collection of plants pushed against the window. He went into the kitchen where he searched the cupboards for something to drink. I stood patiently under the spotlights while he moved around, opening random doors as if he wasn't sure where everything was. It was warm. I'd taken off my shoes and I could feel the underfloor heating through my tights. Eventually he gave up, letting slip a momentary flash of nerves. Then I think he felt as if he had to compensate, so he came towards me and sat me on the counter. He kissed me, finally – which broke the ice. I could tell from the way he touched me that he'd been thinking about it for a long time. Things moved quickly after that. He unbuttoned my blouse and freed my breasts, lowering his head to close his lips on them. I felt the fabric of his shirt against my skin, I pulled him closer but he stopped suddenly, his hands around my waist. I could feel he was hard but he didn't move.

'I don't think we should do this,' he said.

I wasn't sure what he meant. I thought he wanted me to leave at first, but he didn't pull away completely. Instead he kissed me again, tracing a finger lightly over the outside of my underwear, his skin touching mine as he pulled the fabric to one side. He started to stroke me, lightly at first, until the muscles in my stomach began to twitch. I could feel his belt between my thighs. I closed my eyes as he slowly, languorously brought me on. I came against his hand as he held my neck. He watched my face the whole time.

'That was good,' he said.

'Thanks,' I answered politely.

He laughed, which made me laugh too. I felt exposed as he stood beside me. He was still fully dressed. When I finally freed him from his jeans, he came almost immediately in my hand.

•

It was almost nine when I woke the next morning. Neither of us had had much sleep. The flat looked different in the daylight, one wall smoothed with raw concrete, the others all painted white. Above my head was a copper lamp that hung from a thick steel girder. I opened the curtains a little to reveal a vast expanse of slate rooftops, wet from last night's rain. Tom came over with a pot of coffee.

'Am I one of those women?' I asked him. 'The ones you were talking about that day on the beach?'

'I don't know yet.' He looked amused as he got back into bed.

'Tell me honestly.'

'I mean you're obviously not *fine*.'

'Who is, though?'

'Probably lots of people.'

'Who are these people? I mean, are you?'

He half laughed.

'You don't know much about me.'

'Someone like you,' I said, more seriously, 'I wouldn't have thought you'd be interested in me.'

'I don't know if I am, yet,' he said playfully.

He pulled me towards him and this time I opened up to him completely. There was nothing in the way. I was already soft when he reached between my legs. This time he moved his head down, parted my thighs and spread my lips, then he began to lick the nub of my clitoris, kissing it gently, with just enough pressure. I stopped him gently, touching him, kissing him as I moved down. When I finally let him inside me, my pussy dilated, thick with pleasure. A flood of intense tranquillity seemed to wash through every muscle in my body.

'You're nothing like I thought you'd be,' he said afterwards. 'When I first met you, you seemed so reserved.'

'I am reserved.'

He raised an eyebrow.

'What are you saying?' I pushed him gently.

'I almost didn't speak to you at the hotel.'

'Why did you?'

'I don't know, there was just something . . .' He trailed off as he thought about it. 'There's just something there sometimes, isn't there? Plus obviously . . .' He looked at my body.

'Thanks,' I said, perplexed.

He checked his phone.

'I should probably go to work,' he said.

I watched as he shaved over the sink, thinking about that first morning at the Playasol. I'd hoped then that something would happen and now it had.

'I think we should probably see each other again,' he said, letting me out into the hallway.

As I waited for the lift, I realized, with some trepidation, how much I wanted to.

•

The following day I took a walk along the Thames. When I reached the Naval College at Greenwich, someone handed me a flyer for a nail salon. The stature of the building behind them was really something, its grandeur bordering on camp. It was obvious that the people who'd built this thing had inhabited another world, one that had almost completely disappeared. It was a world that had been held together by debt but also by forces that were now almost extinct: family, religion, geography, an unyielding social order, a communally enforced vision of what it meant to coexist. In other words, those people's lives were shared. They lived in a simple, brutish system that everyone more or less understood. Some of them had fought against those bonds – and they'd succeeded, to a degree that they could never have imagined. It was difficult not to feel a sense of vertigo in the shadow of these buildings. London was full of them. The result was the existence of someone like me: floundering, mostly on my own, bombarded with ads for various prophylactics – fitness programmes, anti-capitalist marches, psychotherapy courses. Anything to ward off the realization that no one had any idea how to live.

•

At Goldsmiths, Lara had a tutor, Dr Manning, who used to say things like: 'We've all become Warholian facsimiles of ourselves.' Dr Manning wore a cropped velvet jacket with Cuban heels and a pair of leather jeans. He had a Marilyn Manson-esque bob and a leather pouch that he cradled sensually in the crook of his arm, as if it was a pet. Lara used to drag me along to his lectures, which had names like 'From Global to What? Neoliberalism and the Cultural Object' and 'Against the New: On the Tyranny of the Contemporary'.

Art school wasn't what she had expected. The things she made there – and the things the other students made – seemed to disappear as fast as they could produce them. There were piles of detritus strewn around the studios as they all pumped out their installations, paintings, performances, animations – all of which were painstakingly documented and then uploaded to the internet. At that point, 'the work' – as everyone called it – would quickly become buried under an avalanche of everyone else's 'work'. None of the tutors had much to say about this. Instead they collapsed everything into their preferred talking points around 'the marketization of the culture', 'the violence done to marginal voices' and 'the cul-de-sac of aesthetics as resistance under the conditions of late capitalism'. These philosophies mushroomed as fast as the junk accruing in the school's corridors.

At the time, Lara's 'work' comprised small canvases of woodland flowers, a genre so conservative that no one could figure out what she was up to. She was either stupid or a troll, a pervert or some kind of genius. In retrospect, I think she was overwhelmed. We both were. Although we quickly realized that the worst thing you could do in a place like that was admit it.

Inadvertently, it was Lara who introduced me to the idea that work wasn't going to save me. All those exams I'd passed were insufficient to shield me from the worst of the world. In her eyes, the answer to this predicament was to make a decision to live for what you believed in, for its own sake, without having anything to show for it. It helped that she'd grown up with money, although I don't think she saw the link. But more importantly, she needed to believe it because she was never – and neither was anyone else, ever again – going to be an artist of any stature. The culture had become too transparent, every innovation documented, processed, replayed and tweaked in a stream of infinitesimal progressions, each version on display, every player in the game embedded in a furious feeding frenzy of production, reproduction and repurposing. The more people tried to individuate themselves, the more difficult it became. No one's 'voice' was particularly outstanding; the atom had devolved almost entirely into the wave. What all of this produced, above all, was *trends*. That's not to say there weren't still personalities in the art world – galleries needed name recognition, and high prices still brought spikes of interest – but the characters that circulated in the limelight were generated to dramatize certain vibes. It was the trends themselves that did the work, the artists like a revolving cast of actors in a soap.

It was probably in the light of this sort of thing that when Lara and I first got together, people thought we were putting it on. 'You're not *gay*,' someone once shouted at us, 'give it a fucking rest.' But I didn't want to. I was enjoying myself too much. I couldn't decide if I loved her or if I wanted to be like her. Her life felt infinitely more real and more exhilarating than my own. And anyway, Lara knew how to work a crowd. 'So what?' she used to say. She'd been reading about performance art that week. 'Who cares if it's just for the attention?'

We spent most of our time together. We talked for hours, watched obscure films, we went on long walks. At one point, we discovered her father's porn collection – a drawer of ancient DVDs – and watched them on the white linen sofa in her parents' Marston & Langinger conservatory. We smoked hand-rolled panatelas from the humidor he kept in his office. In general, I'd say our lifestyle was heavily influenced by the European intellectuals on her reading list. Like them, we were deeply critical of the 'mainstream', although we never really thought about what this meant. Something to do with TV and whatever went on outside London.

One day, while her parents were away, we got home drunk in the early hours. She decided to take me upstairs. The first floor was painted the colour of an oyster. It was the kind of place that felt like a hotel, except for a massive black and white portrait of Lara and her mother hanging on the landing wall. There was a framed poster for the *Musée d'Orsay* in her bedroom and a huge, mottled antique mirror. She'd brought a bottle of whisky with her and she handed it to me as she sat on her bed.

I sat beside her, feeling almost drugged.

'Lie down,' she said, then she kissed me. It was like falling into space. I'd seen her naked before, she wasn't shy about changing in front of me, but we'd never taken things this far. I hadn't been sure if she'd wanted to. It was intense, her pleasure bleeding into mine, as she crushed herself against me. I felt self-conscious, I didn't know what I was doing but she didn't seem to mind. Perhaps she found it alluring – the novelty of being in charge. After that, it became something that we did. She liked to play the role of the libertine. She pushed my body to extremes. She took an almost brutal pleasure in making me come. And for my part, it was like the lights came on.

After that night, I started skipping classes so that I could sit beside her in the lecture theatre. I compared our bodies furtively. She was a little fuller than I was. When she was naked, her breasts felt heavy against my own. One night I sank my teeth into them and she bit my thigh until it bled. I relived this stuff a thousand times as I ploughed through *Principles of Digital Marketing and Behavioural Change*. It was narcotic. I found it difficult to concentrate on anything else.

9

It was the second week of August, which marked a month of unemployment. The flat was empty. Ashley was at work and, as usual, I was procrastinating. I couldn't face another bored recruiter telling me that things were rough out there. I hadn't seen Tom since Fischer's but we'd agreed to meet again. I'd tried texting him but he hadn't been forthcoming. Ashley had said this was a bad sign, that a lot of men went quiet after they'd slept with you, especially if they moved in different circles and had no social ties to you. I'd spent a long time thinking about it but I was leaning towards the conclusion that he just didn't like texting. If he wrote to me at all it was almost always to discuss arrangements. There was no parallel stream of consciousness accompanying our actual time together. It meant I had to think about him on my own, which was turning out to be an interesting experiment.

Deciding to waste my time in a different way, I resumed the deep lurk on Lara that I'd started earlier that week. Her network dwarfed mine, she was definitely more 'connected' in that sense, although she didn't give much away. She came across as something between your standard, polished Instagram thoroughbred and someone messier and more relatable – another veneer that she had mastered to perfection. She was very good at presenting as aspirational but not too aspirational – the loose hair, the endearingly chaotic charm.

Mid-stalk, I felt my phone vibrate. It was so perfectly on

cue, I wondered if she somehow knew that I'd been watching her. I was a little nonplussed by her text:

What are you doing on Sunday? Come to Plum's?

It was so perfunctory that at first I thought she'd sent it to the wrong person.

•

It was soon after I turned nineteen that Lara told me she didn't believe in love, not because she found the idea sentimental but because she'd been reading a book by the French feminist theorist Hélène Cixous who said that kind of language was a trap. 'It doesn't lead anywhere,' Lara said. 'It's just a way of subjugating women.' I was quite impressed by this at the time. The truth was, I felt uncultured in her shadow, probably because while she was reading French philosophy, I was reading *Principles and Practices of Marketing: Volume 9.*

Despite the intense pleasure she gave me during those months, it wasn't only about sex. There were moments of real tenderness between us. They often happened when we were doing nothing, or 'power-dossing' as she called it.

'Half of London thinks they're a fucking artist,' she said one day while we were rambling around town. She was having a hard time at college and had decided that she hated her degree. Aesthetics, she told me, were just a form of manners and required a social hierarchy, something that couldn't be maintained in an online world, no matter how much people tried to force it. And anyway, she was against hierarchy, so she didn't care what they thought of her.

That night, as she lay beside me in her underwear, I watched her leafing through the book *A Thousand Plateaus* by the French authors Gilles Deleuze and Félix Guattari. She turned to face me.

'It doesn't work,' she said.

'What doesn't?'

'Art – it's all bullshit isn't it? It doesn't achieve anything, it's just a load of empty ambition. Let's face it, it's more important to act on things than it is to make art about them. The world's fucked and it's up to us to fix it. And that means working with technology because it's the only thing that ever changes.'

'What do you actually want to do?' I said, although I'd started to hate these conversations. I'd already noticed her language changing. She'd started talking more and more in universals. Her thinking revolved around abstractions like rights, principles and freedoms. If it wasn't a big idea, she wasn't interested. Maybe this was what education was all about but it got on my nerves after a while. I remember wondering how long it would be before I could touch her mouth again. I wanted to kiss her, I could feel the warmth of her body against mine but I held back this time.

'Come on, what do you want to change so much?' I pushed her.

'Inequality, unfairness.'

'In what way?'

'In every way.'

'Be specific,' I said, deciding to press her all the way for once. 'Do you mean economically? Under the law?'

'Both.' She put her book down. 'And in everyday life.'

'But how?'

'By any means necessary. It shouldn't take this long.'

'But how would you make it happen?'

'Like I said, I'd do whatever it takes.'

'But there would have to be so many rules.'

'But there *are* rules already, aren't there? They're just set up to favour the wrong people.'

'You hate rules, though.'

'I don't *hate* rules,' she got up, exasperated, and disappeared into the kitchen. When she came back, she leant against the doorway holding a tub of ice cream, which she ate straight from the container. The semi-transparent fabric of her bra was extremely distracting.

'By any means necessary?' I said. 'Really?'

'Yeah,' she said. 'Why not?'

•

For her final exhibition, Lara made a film called 'Doing What You Love'. She'd filmed the two of us doing what we did almost every day, which was wandering around the city aimlessly. The video tracked me as I rose up the escalators at Canary Wharf, wandered through the crowds at Churchill Place and then crossed the bridge at West India Quay. The film was supported by a social media campaign in which she'd tried to crowdfund our efforts. 'Support Us Doing What We Love,' she'd written on her GoFundMe account, which had raised almost eighteen pounds. 'It's about the desire to love your work,' Lara told Dr Manning. 'It's about the fantasy of labour as a means of self-expression.' I watched supportively as she spoke. 'And finally,' she concluded, 'it's about the possibility of a world in which all work is meaningful.' The film seemed to go down well. There was a long discussion afterwards about 'the marketization of the culture' and 'the cul-de-sac of aesthetics as resistance under the conditions of late Capitalism'. When I met her at the party afterwards, she was in a weird mood.

'Listen,' she said, pulling me aside, 'I've been meaning to say this for a while. Don't take this the wrong way, but I've started seeing someone else.'

I was so shocked, I left right then. I thought she'd call me afterwards but she didn't. I kept tabs on her from a distance but weeks passed without any communication. The silence almost killed me. I couldn't stand it. I barely slept that summer and when I did pass out, I dreamt about her. I cried alone at night for weeks. I poured thousands of words into an exercise book that, when I read it back, was mostly obsessive drafts of letters I wanted to send her explaining that she'd made a mistake, that I *loved* her, that she must have misunderstood. I never sent her any of these letters – I was too proud and also I knew I couldn't take it if she still didn't care. I wanted her back but, if I was honest with myself, it was the rejection itself that annihilated me, because it confirmed what I'd always secretly felt: that someone like her was out of reach for someone like me. There's nothing like being shown a glimpse of an infinitely more beautiful world and then having the door slammed in your face. I felt paralysed. It went beyond anything I'd experienced before. I didn't think I'd ever get over her. For the first time in my life, I almost failed my exams.

I went through months of this dysthymia and then a very long, drawn-out flu. It must have been almost spring the following year by the time I finally woke up one morning and realized to my surprise, that I was probably going to survive her.

We didn't speak again until our final year. This time things were different. I saw her far more clearly. It put us on a different footing. And in a strange way, we became friends. Or at least, something like friends.

•

Whenever I came to a critical moment in my life, I had a habit of switching off completely. It happened automatically but I liked to think of it as something I'd chosen, a sort of spiritual practice, similar to how footballers say you'll get the goal when you stop focusing on it. It happened later that week as I made the journey to Plum Valley in Soho. It was a dim sum place that we'd once considered 'our thing' in that clannish way that teenage girls do. Although, looking back, I sometimes wondered if she'd planted that one strategically. She was good at making things 'a thing' so you felt as if you shared a secret language, something intimate that no one else understood. I sometimes thought it was a skill she'd picked up from moving around so much, having to start new schools, make friends, reel people in. Or maybe I was being too hard on her, maybe we'd just liked dim sum. Plum's had started in the early days, before the first time she'd discarded me. I sometimes caught myself fighting her spectre in my head, probably because despite everything, I still felt a certain way about her. It was a combination of trepidation and the immortal charge of teenage lust. I never knew what she was going to do next, she seemed completely free of inhibition; and although I didn't trust her in the slightest, I got a weird high from being around her. There was a vicarious and painful thrill in it. It was like pressing on a bruise.

As I descended into the Tube I thought about her many teenage philosophies. The one that came to mind was built on a single concept from which she'd developed a complicated universe of sub-theories, all of them logically compatible as long as you bought into the basic premise, which was this: no one should inflict themselves on anyone else unless they were happy on their own. The 'happy' part was ill-defined but it basically meant that you couldn't need them. You were supposed to be independent, whatever that meant. I thought about it as I boarded the train. Most people would have thought of me as independent, in the sense that I made an OK living. On the other hand, I was introverted, I didn't go out much and I hated selling myself online. As a result, I spent a lot of time alone. I looked at the other women in the carriage. We were all doing our best to hold our lives together, all of us sitting there in our cheap clothes, our bags full of gadgets – gadgets that weren't so cheap, each of them silently imposing on us. We did our jobs, we paid our bills, we called our parents now and then. Our social profiles were well-maintained, our CVs up to date. Here at least, I supposed, was a tangible measure of our worth.

The problem, as far as I could see, was that the situation wasn't sustainable. None of it was enough on its own. Our salaries weren't enough, our jobs weren't enough and the people in our 'networks' weren't enough. It all seemed OK at first, it was even fun up to a point – let's say around my age. Beyond that, life began to bite. Independence was expensive – or to put it another way, freedom came only at a cost. And then there was the loss of all the other things we'd always taken for granted – the expectations with which we'd been raised – of a home, of family, of what used to be called a life. All of these had become harder to achieve. They'd morphed from unremarkable norms into terrifying spectres of a world that wasn't there. Even friendship became a struggle over time. Lives diverged. Things fell apart, slowly at first and then with gathering speed. And the truth was, despite the fighting talk, it wasn't at all clear what was supposed to take their place.

The journey clarified my thoughts, although I missed my stop and had to circle back at Bond Street where I got caught in the rush-hour crowds. Underlying all of it, I realized, was the hard problem of attraction. The thing was, as you got older, it became more difficult to feel it. Or at least to feel it for anyone who might actually want you back. Things deteriorated fast as time went on. Looking at the mass of humanity around me, it was difficult not to feel a little nauseated. I tried to move away from the old guy whose hand was brushing unnecessarily against my skirt. It didn't help that porn had pervaded everything. It made normal bodies seem disgusting. As a result, whole industries were now dedicated to servicing people's needs, pumping out cheap and fast alternative routes to orgasm. They spared us all the humiliation of having to deal with one another. As Lara would say, they gave us 'independence'. Or rather, instead of depending on each other, we now depended on things we had to buy. A life built exclusively on the whims of venture capital.

Lara was already there when I arrived. She was wearing a black silk shirt that I recognized immediately as Saint Laurent. I'd been there when she'd bought it – she'd acquired it on a power dress in Kilburn. Even second-hand, it had cost more than I'd been paying in rent at the time. Although the rent had gone up since then. It had risen faster than the cost of clothes. Clothes down, rent up, I thought, like the good data manager that I was. Lara's stock had risen in the past few years. I wondered if she thought mine had fallen.

This time she stood to kiss me on the cheek. I let her do it, although I wasn't sure. I noticed she still smelt the same. She didn't wear perfume but the scent of her pulsed through my chest.

Plum's looked different now. The old wooden chairs had gone. There were now black leather banquettes that divided the space into booths. We sat near the back in a dark corner where the brickwork had been painted green. We made small talk for a while. She showed me a photo of her flat. In the lounge was an antique leaning mirror and an old de Sede leather sofa.

I wondered how much money she was making. If I'd had to guess, I'd have said not much. Not in terms of salary anyway, the company was still too young. On the other hand, its valuation had risen, I'd seen the stats earlier that week. I wondered if you could expense things like sofas.

'I know I haven't been around much lately,' she said, cautiously.

'It's been a while.' I played along.

'Things have been crazy.'

'We're all busy,' I lied.

She looked good. I'd made an effort this time, but I still felt lacklustre in her presence. She'd told me once that I was pretty 'when I wanted to be'. She'd said it approvingly, as if she found beauty uninteresting, as if there was nothing more banal than being beholden to it. I wondered if she still thought that now. I'd read a post on her app about whether women should make the first move. It had discussed why so many didn't, why they preferred pouring their efforts into their looks – even though waiting for male approval was out of step with the times. It said the risk of rejection was too forbidding, that it was about mitigating failure – although as a tactic, apparently, it made real rejection harder to take. Stock up, stock down.

'So you've finally made it,' I said.

'Work's going fine, if that's what you mean.'

'You can talk about it, if you want.'

For some reason, she seemed reluctant.

'It's going OK,' she said noncommittally. 'It seems to be the only thing that is.'

This was uncharacteristically reflective of her.

'Work?' I said. 'As opposed to life?'

'Yeah.'

'I can't believe that's true.'

'I'm not complaining.'

She ordered a bottle of wine and poured two small glasses. I drank mine immediately. She stabbed a dumpling and chewed on it, thoughtfully.

'There's not much else to say. I mean, I've already tried to hire you.'

'Did you really think that was a good idea?'

'Why not? I think you're talented.'

'I thought you said I was a soulless cog.'

'Actually,' she said, refilling my glass, 'I think the phrase you're looking for is "soulless interchangeable cog".'

'You said you found my face depressing.'

'That party was dire,' she said, stifling a smile. 'In my defence, I might have been a little drunk because I was bored out of my fucking mind. I can't believe you worked at that place.'

'They sacked me.'

'Thank God for that.'

She put her bowl down and then picked it up again, poking ambivalently at a second dumpling.

'Can I ask you something?' she said.

'What?'

'Am I the only girl you've ever been with?'

'You know you are.'

'I thought so.'

'Why?'

'No reason.'

'You don't have to look so smug.'

'Come on!'

'You put me off for life.'

She slid her bowl across the table and left it alone this time. Then she leaned back and watched my face as if she was assessing a complicated problem.

10

The next day was a Friday. I had an interview in Holborn. It was for an education start-up, something to do with 'redefining knowledge'. They always had taglines that were grandiose but also bland, like 'globalizing breathing' or 'exploding words'. It had a kind of poetry to it, I thought, as I made my way down Kingsway, like haiku but without either the heart or the intellect.

The inside of the building was full of unrelated groups of people, some of them hunched on little pouffes, others tapping on laptops on the long refectory tables. It was one of those amorphous offices that was supposed to allow for fluid working, but I couldn't find whoever was meant to meet me. I'd already signed in at reception and was sitting on a blob-shaped sofa in the lobby. I must have been there for a long time because eventually I got a call from the recruiter. They wanted to know why I was late. I had no idea what was going on. I gave it another twenty minutes and left.

There didn't seem much point in going home so I walked all the way up Oxford Street. I wandered into Selfridges and made my way through the fragrance hall. The scent of apricot overwhelmed me. It was coming from the Hermès stand, which centred on a huge pyramid of bottles arranged on an up-lit plastic plinth. There must have been thousands of products on the shelves, each one grouped by theme: the fresh ones, the classic ones, the modern ones and the stranger, more experimental offerings. It was a vast explosion of options that, on some level, were all suffused with romance. I picked up a bottle of Exotic Blossom by Michael Kors. 'Flirtatious and optimistic,' the description said, 'the hypnotic aroma of juicy mango, smooth rose petals and musk transports you to a sensual oasis.' The droplets clung to my wrist. The scent was sweeter than I'd expected, a cloud of fruit salad tinged with citrus. I wondered what the floor space must be worth to justify a business of this size. Markets had always been illusory in part but this one seemed to constitute a trade in almost nothing more than pure, unbridled romantic longing.

I'd made plans to meet Tom that night. I had nothing to do in the afternoon so I walked all the way home, took a shower and spent a couple of hours trying not to look like someone who had spent the day aimlessly wandering the streets. We'd made loose arrangements for dinner but he was running late so I met him at his office. The reception at Churchill Analytics was quiet, neutral, air-conditioned. Tom was on the phone when I arrived, leaning his head against the glass partition that divided his space from the bank of communal desks in the main area.

While I waited, I recognized Grace from the island. She was sitting in an almost identical glass cube, this one with a slightly larger desk on which were arranged some personal items – a colourful card, a water bottle and a framed photo of her and Niall with a small child, a dark-haired daughter. She came out and walked down the aisle towards me.

'I remember you!' she said. 'He's not making you wait, is he?'

'He looks busy.'

'He's not that busy.' She poked her head into his office. 'Look who I've found.'

He waved helplessly. When he finally emerged, he was apologetic.

'Don't believe anything she tells you,' he said.

'There's no dirt on him,' Grace replied. 'He's the most boring man I've ever met.'

'She thinks she's funny,' he shrugged, genially. Then he grabbed his coat and walked me out of the door.

He'd booked a table at St. John where he told me he was working on a project for Procter and Gamble, who had just revamped their website and were trying to break new ground as leaders in sustainability and community impact. He showed me the company's impact page, which said 'We Are Unique And We Are United', with 'and' in rainbow colours. He said their marketing budget was a behemoth, partly because for decades they'd had to battle stories about supporting the Church of Satan.

'What do you mean?' I asked.

'People thought they were in league with the devil. Not metaphorically, they thought they were actually fronting a cult. Even now, their SEO results are fucked. If you google Procter and Gamble Scandal it's still Satan all the way down.'

'But why?' I asked.

'I believe it was a rumour, probably started by a competitor.'

'I didn't know marketing was so savage, I thought it was all ball pits and bean bags.'

'It's much worse than that now,' he said. 'You should see the stuff they have to bury on TikTok.'

He seemed pretty relaxed about it. I got the impression with Tom that he didn't take himself too seriously. He was sanguine about the world around him, especially the parts he couldn't change.

'Maybe it encourages these companies to clean up their act, so there's nothing that can be used against them,' I said.

'You'd think so. I mean, that's the idea, although pharmaceuticals is still run by dinosaurs. Our boss calls Grace "the barrier method" because she takes the blowback when he's trying to really fuck a client on budget. He thinks they won't negotiate as hard with a woman.'

'Is it true?'

'Not really, she's just better at finessing people than he is.'

'You like her, don't you?'

He seemed surprised by the question.

'We've worked together for a long time.'

He said it almost protectively. It was such a discreet non-answer that it made me wonder what the deal was between them.

The time passed quickly. He was more relaxed. I think we both felt a little sceptical about the situation but we also knew that something was happening. Also, the dearth of texts, photos, the general flotsam of daily communication had forced us to save things up for one another. It changed the feeling of the time we had together, made it seem more important.

'Nothing matters,' Tom said, 'except what's happening right now – in real time, in real space. The rest of it is just distraction.'

'Do you really believe that?'

'Yeah.'

'You're describing the whole of the modern world.'

'I know, and I understand what I'm saying – I'm a scientist, remember. I'm just not sure it's worth it in the end.'

'That's a strong take,' I said.

Later, he asked where I lived and I told him without being too specific. I got the feeling he wanted to see for himself but I managed to manoeuvre us back to his place. I wasn't ready to unveil the depressing reality of my existence and I also didn't want to go home. I never wanted to go home. His place was warm, the electrics worked and we could make love with abandon without having to worry about anyone hearing.

•

The light was already on in his flat when we arrived, the living room lit by a single lamp. He didn't touch me in the taxi or in the lift, but as soon as we stepped through the door he kissed me urgently, as if he'd been holding back all night. He led me to the sofa, unbuttoning my shirt as he went. I felt his hands on my breasts, on my thighs, then in my underwear. He let out a moan as he felt the fabric, which was damp. We fell back together and I unzipped him. He smelt good. I felt my pussy swell as he hardened in my hand. I bent down to suck him but he stopped me, pulling my face back towards his.

'We've got all night for that,' he said. 'Right now, I want to be inside you. I couldn't stop thinking about it all week.'

I felt the blood rush between my legs as he touched me gently, opening me up. He went slowly, it was almost painful – I'd never felt such straightforward attraction towards anyone before. It didn't seem to hinge on power or even on physical appearance – I'm sure we both found each other attractive, but not like this. It was just there, as if it had always been there. I groaned as he pushed himself inside me.

'What does it feel like?' I asked him later. 'Having sex with a woman?'

He thought about it for a while.

'Do you mean purely physically?'

'Yes.'

'It feels like putting your hand in a warm bath.'

I laughed. I hadn't expected such a straight answer.

'You asked!' he said, smiling at my reaction. 'What does it feel like for a woman?'

I wanted to say that it could feel like being destroyed or it could feel like the only point of being alive.

I thought about the first time I'd slept with Lara. I'd never told her this, but before that night, I'd never come close to climaxing. I hadn't even understood how it happened. I'd found sex ugly, painful and sometimes outright scary. I'd had boyfriends before her and had dutifully gone through the motions but I hadn't known how it was supposed to feel. I'd just gone along with whatever it was they'd wanted. I wouldn't even have said they coerced me, they hadn't needed to because I'd had no idea what else there was. I sometimes wondered what would have happened if I hadn't met her. I'd probably still be with Kyle or Dane, staring at the bedroom wall – or worse, putting on a performance for their benefit – dying quietly inside while they ground out another load.

I thought about the way I'd felt the first time Lara had touched me. Aside from Tom, she was the only person that had made me feel that way. Although when I thought about it, she'd done it differently to him. She had a way of adding layers of complexity. She was always whispering in my ear, spinning stories, fabricating tension. She'd blown me apart at a time when I was barely conscious of my own body. Even now, I wasn't sure if I'd ever put myself back together.

•

I didn't get home until late the next day. Ashley was on the sofa. She was with a man who was quite good-looking in a loose, Kurt Cobain kind of way. She was reading aloud from one of my books. It was a translation of *Les Misérables*.

'I hope you don't mind,' she said.

There were empty beer bottles all over the floor.

'Sorry,' she muttered, stacking them on the table. 'This is Jack, by the way.'

'Hello,' I said. 'So you're Ashley's friend?'

'Sort of.'

'We've been seeing each other for a while.' Ashley glanced at him a little awkwardly.

She'd never mentioned him before but perhaps we'd passed in the night. She did sometimes bring people home after I'd gone to bed.

I could tell that Ashley was ambivalent about this Jack. It was obvious in the way she was sitting. All the same, a couple of hours later, the two of them moved to her room. Whatever algorithm had brought them together had been accurate in its predictions.

I found the book on the floor, its pages crushed where she had left off reading. *To love or have loved, that was enough*, it said. *Ask nothing further. There was no other pearl to be found in the dark folds of life.*

I didn't see Ashley again until the morning.

'Where's your man?' I asked her.

'No comment.'

'You know you're not allowed a boyfriend, don't you? You're not leaving me on my own in this place.'

She threw a teabag in a cup.

'I'm not going anywhere.'

'He seemed OK.'

'I think I hate him.'

We sat in silence for a while.

'You know something?' she said eventually. 'I don't think I can do this any more. Why do these dickheads even bother? Most of them are barely worth the effort.'

She paused for emphasis.

'Why is it always me that ends up with these porn-sick losers? I can't even pick them out any more. They hide in daylight. They're everywhere. It's not like I even expect them to get me off.'

'There should be background checks.'

'There should.'

'Where's the ratings system?'

She pulled a blanket over her knees and stared at her laptop for a while.

'Do you know how long I've been seeing that guy? *Three months*. We went to the cinema last night. He took me to meet his fucking mother. I liked him, I didn't *love* him yet, but he was better than anyone I'd met for a while. I was into him enough to want to have the talk. I just thought we should take each other off the market, at least for a while – it had been three fucking months. *Three months.* Then poof – he's gone, overnight, ghosted. What is he, fucking Cinderella?'

'I'm sorry,' I said, but she barely stopped for breath.

'And do you know what pisses me off the most? These guys think they're so woke. All they want to do is bitch about the government. Or about the fucking climate crisis. This one – he's a fucking *vegan*. It's only when it comes to sex that the gloves come off. They'll do whatever it takes to get laid. They lie all the time. It's disgusting.'

'It's not right.'

'Have you seen this?' She flipped her screen around to show me the video she'd pulled up. *DO IT FOR DENMARK,* it said.

'This is an actual government *campaign* to try and get people together. And they wonder why no one's fucking any more.' She slid the screen towards me in disgust. 'In France, they're bribing people to reproduce. In Japan, the birth rate is in hell. And the same thing is happening here. And no one wants to state the obvious: that fewer and fewer of us are interested in doing the traditional family thing because most men aren't worth it any more. Most of them are just as entitled as their fathers were, but they don't bring anything to the table. They don't earn enough to support us. They don't protect us from shit. Why would anyone sacrifice their time, health, happiness, income *and* independence for some broke, avoidant, un-housetrained prick?'

'Steady on.'

'Look at this thing.' She nodded at her screen again.

It looked like some sort of training video. An old lady with a silver bun was explaining that sharing new experiences – a trip to Paris, for example – might help the bored, sexless couple in the ad reinvigorate their marriage. The thirty-something wife tried on some silky underwear, her balding husband watching from the sidelines as she twirled around the changing room. Then they went to see the Eiffel Tower. In the background, silver bun's calm voiceover explained that this was a duty to their country. 'It will, after all, help our future business,' she reassured us.

'They might as well pay us to have kids,' Ashley said. 'Why not call it what it is: a job?'

'It might happen one day.'

Underneath the video was a torrent of comments:

Feminism is going to end the human race.

Young men should avoid this until they've got reproductive rights. Remember kids: the woman can erase you from her life, your children's lives and she can then use you as a wallet for her and her new partner for LIFE.

WTF? WOMEN'S WOMBS ARE NOT FOR SALE

Looks like men are willing to go extinct before sleeping with a fEmInIst.

'You know we're going to die alone here, don't you?'

I wasn't sure if she was joking.

'Listen,' she said, 'if you could have anything you wanted, what would your life look like?'

I thought about it.

'I suppose I want the same things as everyone,' I said. 'A home, a family, some stability.'

She sat upright. 'Exactly. We all want the same things. We've all been conditioned that way, but why? What if it isn't realistic? Most relationships aren't going to last, right? And neither are most jobs. So why build up your expectations? I can't believe I'm going to say this – it's embarrassing at this point – but I still feel the same as you and I'm starting to hate myself for it.'

'Why? It's normal to want those things.'

'It's so needy.'

'Everyone's needy.'

She didn't look convinced.

'Look, there'll always be another man,' I said. I was starting to sound like my mother.

'I can't believe this is my life.'

'At least we've got each other.'

I wasn't quite serious, although I'd grown up next to two widows who had set up home together. My dad had always joked that they were lesbians, the joke being that Mrs Creed and Mrs Gordon hadn't cut the sexiest of figures, and in his mind, lesbianism was something unimaginably saucy. You rarely saw that sort of thing any more – two people living that way. I didn't know any straight women who supported one another financially.

'If we're still here when we're old,' Ashley said, as if she'd read my thoughts, 'we should definitely set up home together. We'll be spinsters. We could start a commune.'

I could hear in her voice that she was unconvinced, even as she said it.

'Or if it that doesn't work,' she added, 'we'll hire a fucking Thunderbird and Thelma and Louise it.'

11

I didn't see Tom until the next weekend. It was September and suddenly so cold that I could feel the pavement through my shoes. We met at a pub by the canal where we found a booth overlooking the water. It was deadly calm outside, a light rain falling on the towpath.

'You went to boarding school?' I said.

He'd hidden that well.

'If it makes a difference, I hated it.'

I was more concerned about the material gulf that was opening up between us. He was obviously more successful than I was and now, apparently, he was privately educated. I wondered why I was surrounded by these boarding school survivors and realized, depressingly, that it was likely because the city was becoming so expensive. He must have noticed the chasm too. I wondered if he was one of those men that liked rescuing people. I wasn't necessarily against this. I tried a vulnerable look and he stared back at me, bemused. In all honesty, he was turning out to be a bit of a conundrum. I realized I had no idea who he was. I spent a long time looking at the menu, then I decided to ask him outright.

·

'A factory?' I said, later that night as we lay together in the dark.

He'd been telling me about his father.

'Dinsdale Food-To-Go.'

'Really?'

'My dad started on the sandwich line.'

Tom's father had been hired to make sandwiches for Marks and Spencer.

'Chicken tikka,' he said. 'And that other one – the one with the raisins in.'

'Coronation chicken?'

'Yeah. He made the fillings. He did that job for years.'

M&S was already a multinational by the time Tom's father got involved but the pre-made sandwich transformed the company's fortunes, catapulting it into the brave new world of fast food. It was one of the last true industrial moves in a country that had already shifted most of its capital out of production and into the more abstract realms of speculation. By the 1990s, Dinsdale Food-To-Go was making millions of sandwiches a year. McDonald's had arrived by then and the nation was hungry for fast food. The pre-boxed sandwich, it turned out, was more than a time-saving device. It popularized the concept of a meal that could be eaten anywhere – even on the move – something that changed the shape of life in Britain forever. Within ten years, his dad had made it onto the board, partly because he'd left Tom's mother for Patricia, the company's head of accounts.

One of Tom's earliest memories of his mother was of sitting on her knee at a wedding. His grandfather had come over from Ireland and was feeding him slices of sponge cake. He'd been scared of the old man's hands, which were rough and darkened from working on the farm. They looked nothing like the hands he'd seen before, which had all been smooth and pale like pork.

Tom's mother was from Galway. She'd grown up on a smallholding near Headford. Her family held onto the place for too long, working the same routine each day until the land became first profitless and then, eventually, a liability. She'd spent her early childhood in a house without electricity or gas and had travelled on horseback until the age of twelve, rarely going further than the nearest village. Of her six siblings, his mother was the first to leave and the only one that made it out of Ireland. She was seventeen in the late 1970s when she first arrived in London. In those days, it took six weeks of instruction to qualify as a trainee nurse, after which Tom's mother began working on the wards, earning a full-time salary and learning on the job. It had been easy for her to find work and she'd left home in part for that reason, but there had been more to it than that. She'd wanted a taste of freedom. She'd seen another side of life on TV and she had wanted more than anything to experience it for herself. She'd left the farm without a second thought and in doing so she'd left behind a way of life that her ancestors had lived for centuries.

Despite her yearning for liberation, it had never occurred to Tom's mother that her marriage would end in divorce. She'd been desperate to escape the way she had been raised but she'd still somehow assumed that marriage – especially her marriage – was sacrosanct. After the break-up, she'd tried to go back to nursing but she hadn't bargained on how much things had changed. By the 1990s there were all sorts of barriers, like university courses and background checks. The people in charge of the wards weren't matrons any more, they were now graduates with management degrees who worked on things like safety protocols and cascade training schemes. She gave up on the idea pretty quickly and from that point onwards, she barely left the house, unsure what to do with herself in a world she found increasingly incomprehensible.

It was around this time that Tom's father pulled him out of school. He'd decided to enrol him at a local public school, since he could now afford it. Tom's dad knew nothing about this place except that it would give his son a better chance. He knew this because the board of Dinsdale Food-To-Go was made up almost entirely of people who had gone to schools like this. He'd been lucky – and he was smart enough to realize that his kind of luck was becoming rarer.

'How old were you?' I asked Tom, before he fell asleep.

'Thirteen. All the other kids had been to prep, or whatever the fuck they call it. I was the only normal person in that place.'

'You're not grateful, then?'

'You think I should be?'

'I mean, no one pulled me out of "normal school".'

'You have no idea.'

'Why, what happened?'

'I'll tell you another time.'

'Oh fuck.'

I hadn't meant to make light of it, but it had sounded that way. I apologized.

He shrugged. 'I guess you're going to find out sooner or later.'

I barely registered his apprehension. I was too busy noting, with satisfaction, that he thought we were going to see each other again.

'I'm very open-minded,' I replied, slipping my arm around his.

He felt warm on the bed beside me. I realized I wanted him to trust me.

12

The play was *A Doll's House* by Ibsen. Lara and I were at the Royal Court Theatre. She'd got tickets and had invited me to go with her. Her business, which was called Openr, had won a prize that day. There had been some buzz about it in the press. I'd been googling her all afternoon. She'd done an interview with the *Evening Standard* under the headline 'Sex 2.0: A Second Revolution?'

I got here by making a lot of intuitive, unconventional decisions. In business, you have to follow your gut. You have to have convictions and you have to run with them.

And:

There was a gaping hole in the dating market. People wanted more than a filtered photo and a list of impossible demands. What we're building at Openr is a community, it's like a party for everyone who's sick of doing the things the old-fashioned way.

She texted solidly throughout the first act. I could see that she'd dressed up. She was wearing a black leather skirt and a cream silk shirt, rolled up at the wrists, on one of which I couldn't help noticing an antique Cartier watch. She only ever wore vintage clothes – although she called them 'archive' – which meant meant buying second-hand Celine, Hermès,

Margiela. It was an ethical choice that underscored her brand, although she'd also told me once that she thought buying new designer was basic. It was the one area in which she didn't seem to mind being openly elitist.

I had to admit, I was getting something out of sitting beside her in the theatre. No matter how I felt about Tom – and I knew it was ridiculous feeling anything at all, that would have been unseemly, you had to keep your options open – here I was sitting next to an It girl who the papers were calling 'a bona fide changemaker' and 'one of the breakout movers of her generation'. It gave me a pleasant feeling of nonchalance, as if I was doing fine, whatever else happened.

I also couldn't help feeling a bit smug, as if my own good taste had been confirmed. I'd discovered Lara years ago. I was an early adopter of her. I thought her app was overhyped, as most of them were, but that didn't mean there wasn't money in it. I wondered how much she'd had in mind when she'd mentioned bringing me on board. Sitting in the dark by her side I got a strange thrill out of the idea. Maybe I wasn't above a little financial domination by her after all.

She didn't say much afterwards. We walked until we got to Fifty Cheyne, where she sat at the bar and ordered me a vodka tonic.

'You remembered.'

'Like I said, you don't change much.'

'That's not true.'

'OK, you don't like change.'

I thought about the number of times I'd had to move home compared to her.

'What did you think of the play?' she asked.

Although the production had been named after the Ibsen play, they'd cast Nora as a glamour model and Torvald as a wealthy hedge fund manager. It had included an assemblage of live video showing cam girls ramping up their fees and Bloomberg terminals with flashing charts of stocks and shares. In the show notes, the director had said it was about the 'dematerialization of desire'. I'd struggled to make much sense of it and had dozed off in the second half.

'I thought it was pedestrian,' I said.

Lara always called everything pedestrian so I thought I'd get in first. She caught my drift. She seemed a little tired.

'Why is it always like this?' she said.

'How do you think it should be?'

'I could ask you the same question.'

'Why did you message me?'

'Because I wanted to. Because I thought you'd be good at the job. Does it have to be more complicated than that?'

She checked her phone coolly while I sat there.

I realized that she hadn't changed much either. She felt no need for a distinction between 'because I wanted to' and 'because I thought you'd be good at the job'. I had a sudden memory of staying up all night editing her films at college. I'd even written essays for her. She was still the same, she still got so wrapped up in whatever it was she was doing that she assumed everyone around her was as driven by it as she was – and if they weren't, she was going to charm them into it. It probably hadn't even occurred to her that I might not want to be her underling.

'You know, every time I come across that play,' I said, 'I judge the Nora character more harshly. The first time you watch it, you think it's about money – the battle of the sexes and all that. Then after that, it all seems more inevitable – there's a kind of Greek tragedy side to it. But once you get past that stage, you realize that, for the most part, it's just a story about people. The Nora character has fucked up. She's made a miscalculation. Things worked for her for a while and then they didn't. That's it. She's not this feminist hero.'

'She's both,' Lara said. 'It's a play. She's supposed to be complicated.'

'But doesn't that undermine the whole premise?'

'No, it just makes her more human.'

She said it deadpan but I knew what she was doing. It was a word I probably overused even more than she called everything pedestrian.

'I'm just making conversation,' I said.

'I know,' she gave me a thin smile.

•

Nothing happened, or almost nothing happened, over the following days. I tried and failed to find employment. Tom went away with work. I saw him on the evening of his return and we went back to his flat. That night, he resumed his account of his adolescence. At school, he experienced trouble with the other boys. They could tell that he was different. Everything was off – his hair, his accent. There were too many subtleties to list and he quickly gave up on trying to mask them.

To make things worse, he smashed his kneecap playing football, which was one of the only things he had in common with them. The kid who smashed it was the son of a barrister who wrote to Tom's mother almost immediately, threatening counter-action if she tried to sue the school. Tom's mother misunderstood the letter, taking its aggressive tone to mean that Tom had been at fault. She was embarrassed and shut down his protestations, insisting that he make the most of the opportunity his father had afforded him. More than anything, she'd seemed anxious that he was showing himself up in front of these people.

The injury stopped Tom from playing sports, excluding him even further from his peers. It also left him in pain – a nagging ache that never went away. The school's doctor eventually prescribed Tramadol, which only partially relieved the problem. On the other hand, the drug interacted with his moods in a way that made him feel top notch. By the time he was fifteen, he'd learnt to store the pills up, crush them and snort them in the toilets. It gave him a warm, euphoric high that lifted him out of himself completely. The school was eager to avoid bad press around his accident and once Tom had realized what this meant – that he could hold them to ransom over it – he started dropping out completely.

It was during one of these truant sessions, having bunked off to wander around the local town, that he met another deserter. Sandra must have been a little older. She sat around the local park all day, often with another kid he didn't know. One day, she approached him and asked him for a cigarette, and from that moment onwards, she dominated his thoughts. He obsessed about the smell of her skin, the thought of her pale breasts against the thin fabric of his school shirt. He pictured the two of them alone together, kissing in some vague, private space. In his daydreams, he surrendered completely to the kiss. He was usually already hard by the time she moved her fantasy hand towards him. He liked to think about her taking off her bra, her heart necklace around her neck. He thought of her as shy and reserved about her body – although the power of his gentle masculinity would melt her in his arms, and his arms only. Inevitably, Sandra would be wet by this point. His stomach would tremble as he touched her underwear. He always came at exactly this moment, abandoning himself in his dorm room bed. In reality, his relationship with Sandra never got past the DVD stage. They'd sit for hours, watching films at her flat while her mother, who worked at the local hospital, looked over them from a huge, softly lit portrait on the wall. One afternoon, Sandra caught him staring. Her bare thighs were folded underneath her as she sat in front of the TV and, as usual, he'd found it hard to look away. He'd checked her out plenty of times before – he'd even seen her bra when she leaned over – but until that day, she had pretended not to notice. He froze for a second, paralysed with excitement. Then he closed his eyes and leaned towards her. He was rock hard as he waited for her lips; but instead, he heard a small click. There was a muffled, bubbly laugh. She'd leaned back and grabbed her Samsung Digimax. She had managed, somehow, to capture him on camera. He wondered instantly if she had set him up. He lunged at her, trying to grab it from her hand, but she managed to wrestle it away from him. He hadn't yet completed puberty and she was at least his equal in strength.

Afterwards, she tried to smooth things over, but to his consternation, he couldn't brush it off. He was so ashamed, it overwhelmed him. He stopped skipping school after that, he just couldn't bring himself to face her. Her absence left him even more isolated – or at least, it left him at the mercy of the other boys, which was worse.

By this point, Tom was in Year 10, which meant sex permeated everything. His classmates now talked openly about girls, mostly boarders from the sister school. It was around this time that the commercial world began to seep into Tom's awareness of his sex life. The past few years had seen a gradual change in the meaning of his stuff. As a kid, he'd played with toys as objects that possessed a meaning in themselves. They existed to give him pleasure, it was as simple as that. Insofar as they had a social aspect, they offered him a route into other children's lives – a place where the pleasure they gave him could be shared. But now, suddenly, everything was imbued with an ulterior motive. All objects – a pair of trainers, a skateboard – were marshalled into a longing to be cool, which was another word for attracting girls. And the bar at his school was set extremely high. Some of the kids were given designer clothes: Supreme, Ralph Lauren, Abercrombie & Fitch. Some were given SUVs at seventeen. There were skiing holidays over the Christmas holidays, something Tom only knew about because he'd see the photos afterwards. There were girls who worked out and wore thongs. Some had undergone professional hair removal, dental work, even cosmetic surgery. Tom's attempts at engaging with this lifestyle were thwarted at every level, although it took him a while to fully comprehend the gravity of the situation. At first, he begged his parents for the basics: clothes and money for a computer. Every new jacket or gadget was pregnant with the possibility of reinvention. Confidence came in shiny packages: a new phone or a branded T-shirt. Unfortunately, neither of his parents understood the strange world they had landed their son in and therefore saw no reason to satisfy their son's incessant demands for luxury goods. They bought him a second-hand Golf for his eighteenth birthday, an experience that snuffed out any glimmer of hope he might eventually lose his virginity.

Tom's miserable school years weren't the worst of it. What got him into trouble was what happened afterwards: the sheer inanity of life back at his mother's house in Northampton. At school, he'd got high to dull his suffering. It was only later that his fledgling addiction began to take control of him. It was, as it turned out, an excellent way to pass the time. That summer, he lost himself completely. He was no longer dispirited or bored, or even aware of such mundane considerations. He existed on a higher plane and he saw no reason to come off it. Over the next few years his habit graduated. He was twenty-two when his dad found out, which quickly brought things to a head. The rehab centre reminded him of school, but eventually – and with great resistance – he found himself back in the ordinary world. He managed to pass his A levels and, to his surprise, discovered an aptitude for the sciences. Although when he eventually applied to university, he didn't get as far as he had hoped. The STEM subjects were competitive and his concentration wasn't good. It was by default that he ended up in France, a student at the ISIPCA, a small school of cosmetic chemistry in Versailles. It was the only place that would accept him.

•

'You seem so normal,' I said, although I wasn't that surprised by any of this. I'd guessed it would be drugs since he was sober.

'Are you close to your parents now?'

'In some ways. Mum's dead but I still speak to my father occasionally. He's got his own life but we're in touch.'

'How did you stop?'

'Dad rescued me, although I don't think he's ever for-given me.'

'I'm sure it's not like that.'

'I wouldn't blame him.'

'Your dad's probably just relieved you're still around.'

'I wouldn't know, we never talk about it.'

'Well, if it makes you feel any better, I'm a bigger failure than you are.'

'Is that so?' he said.

I told him that my life was going nowhere, that I didn't have a job, that I had no idea what the future would look like.

'Well, thank God for that,' he said. He sounded genuinely relieved. 'At least we've finally got something in common.'

I messaged Lara the following day: That job – is it still going?

It didn't take her long to reply:

I had a feeling you'd come around

•

Ashley was dressed for the gym. She went every morning before work. She'd drunk her protein shake and was now mas-saging her thighs.

'So he wants to take you away for the weekend?' she said. 'Isn't that a bit much?'

'I don't think so.'

'Where's he taking you?'

'The countryside.'

My vision of what this might entail was no more fleshed-out than hers. I pictured a chintzy hotel, log fires, some kind of breakfast buffet. I hoped there would be lovemaking on expensive sheets.

'What are you going to wear?'

'Lingerie?'

I had to admit, I was very into this development. I sifted through relevant Instagram suppliers. There was @Aimee-Cherie_dk that sold nude bras and thongs. Alongside each set was a quote from Anaïs Nin. I was deep into an excerpt from her diary, something about intoxication and fire, when my phone buzzed.

Meet me after work

It was Lara.

Later on, scrolling through Twitter, I received a notification that one of her followers had @ed me a link to a post.

LET'S TALK CONSENT! is a dedicated crew of Creatives committed to offering Healing through Art. May you find Words that Mesmerize you and Beauty to help you Heal. SIGN UP for our newsletter and join our mission! #womensboundaries #respect #Openr

There was a stream of comments underneath:

THERE'S NO RAPE CULTURE IN THE WEST THESE DAYS, ONLY IN DUMPS LIKE INDIA

Let's Talk Consent is exclusionary to trans people, do not support these people

Women are chaotic, they need to be controlled

GET SUBWAY DELIVERED WITH UBER EATS
TODAY

I checked my inbox and found the job that Lara had mentioned – *Assistant Data Manager*, it read. Below that: *Openr is a dating app for open-minded singles and couples, we cater to all sexualities and identities and welcome people who are looking for the freedom to express themselves in full in a safe and accepting environment. We're looking for a talented individual to work within our marketing analytics team. You'll support our team as they work with disparate data sources to build out new onboarding pipelines. Obsessed with automation and reproducibility, you'll be experienced at managing fields and from there, liaising with our engineers to index extrapolated features.*

Lara texted again. Did you see it?

They're going to love you

I can't wait

13

Tom and I left London after work. The terrain along the M1 was flat, repetitive and dull, an endless a grid of empty fields that seemed devoid of animal life.

'Don't people farm here any more?' I said.

'Not really, now the subsidies have gone.'

'Oh, God.'

He looked at me, amused.

Once we'd made it to the Cotswolds, the landscape changed for the better.

It was a long drive and I asked him what happened after he'd moved to France.

·

In December 2007, two months after the start of term, Tom began to wonder if he'd made a mistake enrolling at the ISIPCA. He couldn't speak French and he knew almost nothing about the culture. On the other hand, most of the other students were girls, something which lent the place a definite appeal. He spent his first few months in a state of panic: there weren't many other foreign students there and no one told him what he was supposed to be doing, so he had to pick things up as best he could. He got the impression that he'd only been offered a place because the school wanted to attract more overseas students. Like most universities, they wanted to expand their brand. Contrary to this aspiration, the school had no idea how to integrate a foreigner like Tom. Every class was conducted in a formal, jargon-heavy French that he couldn't make head nor tail of. The classes followed a kind of Victorian model, tutors lecturing from the front while the students sat in lab coats, taking notes behind a stark arrangement of desks. Once again, Tom found himself spending most of his time on his own. He pretended to follow what was happening while the other students passed him boxes of Kimtech gloves and vials of delicately tinted fluids.

During this period, a girl called Gabrielle – a heavy-set, freckle-faced Alsacienne – started sitting next to him in class. Gabrielle was friendly and outgoing and she seemed to know most of the other kids; he often saw them on the lawn at lunchtime, eating their jambon-beurre together. One morning Gabrielle approached Tom and invited him to a party at a local bar. That night, he discovered that her English was good enough for the two of them to become friends. He made her laugh with his contorted attempts to speak her language and he was relieved to have someone on his side. Over the following weeks, she made a point of including him in her activities. She helped him with his French and insisted on going through his coursework, correcting his papers until they resembled something that might scrape him through the year. Slowly, she drew him into student life. By the second year, thanks to Gabrielle, he was able to get by on his own.

One night, after a party at Les Caves, a grimy club in the old part of town, Gabrielle followed him back to his flat. He'd smoked a lot of weed that night, together with the booze, and he wasn't feeling good at all. He'd resisted her gentle flirtations up until that point, but for some reason, that night his guard was down. He switched on the TV and lay back, putting his feet up on the futon. Gabrielle sat expectantly beside him, perched delicately by his head. He fell asleep by accident, the soundtrack of *France 24* in the background. He was still drunk when he woke up to find her topless, straddling his thighs. Her breasts were large and unfamiliar, she looked completely different in the nude. He stared at her as she leaned towards him, her breasts descending over his face. He thought of allowing her to kiss him, but he couldn't bring himself to face the rest of it. He didn't think he could see it through. He felt his penis shrivel. Panic flew from his chest to his stomach; he realized he needed to get up but the weight of her body was pinning him down. Just as her lips touched his, he felt his stomach lurch. He twisted violently, trying to protect her from the surge of puke that was firing from his stomach but he couldn't get her out of the way in time. He managed to throw up mostly on her feet, flecks of bile spattering up her thighs. She stood up immediately. She made a strange, guttural sound as she watched him squirming on the sofa. Within seconds she was dressed and gone. He heard the door slam as he sat up, the scent of her perfume in the air, its sweet, floral fumes forcing him to retch again.

Tom tried to call Gabrielle the next day but she refused to pick up the phone. She wouldn't reply to his texts. When he saw her in class, she wouldn't even meet his eye. From that point onwards, he found himself – and this was becoming a habit – on his own. The group excommunicated him completely. There was a sense that he'd taken advantage of their friend and although he never found out what she had told them, the message was clear: damage had been done, irreparable damage – and it was all his fault. As much as he tried to explain himself, his place in their lives had been terminated.

Still a virgin, Tom spent his final year at the college on his own. It seemed impossible to penetrate the social web that the French imposed. Without an obvious position in society, he couldn't even talk to anyone. At first, he spent a lot of time online, flicking through various forums, trying to crack the code that would allow him back into the lives of the shiny-haired, fine-boned BCBGs that populated the town. Versailles was a small place and everyone knew everyone, which meant that his every move was thwarted – often even before he'd tried to make it. Eventually, he gave up on his personal life and threw himself into his work. The lab was open late most nights and over time, he developed an aptitude for the digital aspects of the subject. He'd entered the school understanding chemistry as a craft – something like cookery, in which various elements could be combined to create new effects. By his third year, he saw things differently.

Molecular machine learning was a relatively new field of study and most of the faculty at the institute viewed it as a dubious American import. They focused instead on the more traditional aspects of perfumery, leaving Tom with the IT lab largely to himself. By this time, synthetic chemistry had spread into the realms of corporate psychology, retail optimization and sports performance. Software engineering was now at the heart of new discoveries and although the perfume industry was still weighted towards cosmetics, there was a growing understanding that new molecules could be used as behavioural modifiers. And now that the behaviour of these molecules could be predicted with algorithms, the field was expanding extremely quickly. Most of Tom's peers at the time envisioned their futures working for luxury brands. The science of smell was relatively virgin territory in neuroscience, lagging far behind vision and hearing, for example. Tom's tutor on the subject – the tiny, hairless M. Morel – impressed on him, for example, that olfactory stimuli, once transmitted to the limbic system, could not be consciously blocked. Scent was therefore a powerful tool, it offered a direct point of entry to the brain. He speculated on military applications, as well as healthcare and education. According to M. Morel, the field was pregnant with possibility. His new toy was a piece of software that enabled computer-aided synthesis planning and, over time, he succeeded in planting in Tom at least a passing interest in the subject.

After college, Tom tried to move to London but he couldn't find a job. His field of expertise was too narrow. Most of the students on his course were now in Paris, finding positions in the old perfumery firms but he felt homesick and tired of France with its impossible manners and strange conventions. He wanted to speak in his own language; he wanted the ordinariness of home. He thought about moving into academia but he couldn't afford to support himself. His father had refused to pay his expenses in an effort to keep his son in work and thereby, hopefully, on the straight and narrow. By this point, Tom was in some debt, which meant he couldn't afford to stand still. He had to make a move, which is why, reluctantly, he accepted a role at Zauberman.

Zauberman was a Swiss conglomerate based in Meyrin, specializing in commercial scents. The company dealt in all sorts of products from washing powder to car interiors. His first assignment was to join a team developing a scent for a new shampoo. The name of the product was 'Rush' and the idea was to make a scent for 'the modern woman' that was 'fresh and dynamic' with 'urban vibes'. They'd sent him to London to meet the marketing team, which was where he'd first met Grace.

14

Tom's days at Zauberman were filled with programming, something he struggled to get used to. Far from the sensory consolations of the lab, his new job required him only to sit behind a screen modelling virtual compounds. Zauberman had an absolutist approach when it came to the invention of new molecules, which meant that the company employed a farm of virtual chemists who did nothing but code, working with machine learning to generate an index of every possible permutation. These scents were unknown to the world, they existed in an entirely abstract state until the time came for one of them to be engineered in the lab. They were classified by five-digit codenames that reminded Tom of the Dewey system: this one was filed in the Floral section, with sub-notes of ambrein and waxy alcohol; that one was filed in the Fresh section, with Calone for an aquatic aura.

Tom spent nearly two years in this position. After a couple of weeks signed off with 'stress' – in reality, a long, lingering virus that seemed as much a mental illness as anything else – a senior colleague took pity on him and agreed to let him do a PhD. The company would sponsor Tom to develop new data-mining techniques, the goal being to predict the actions of different compounds on the brain. It meant that he was now free to model not only olfactory products but all sorts of substances in a bid to find patterns in their effects.

Tom's PhD allowed him, finally, to make it back to the UK, where he spent some time on secondment with pharmaceuticals conglomerate Pharmacon. He'd been delighted to get out of Meyrin, a place he found both boring and anxiety-inducing. The prospect of spending a year in Luton, a town he knew primarily for its proximity to the airport, filled him with a pathetic level of excitement.

It was during his time at Pharmacon that Tom's feelings of unease about his personal life began to deepen. At twenty-five, he was still a virgin. He'd assumed that back in England he'd be able to meet girls, but it wasn't at all straightforward. The technicians in his lab were mostly men and although there were women in other departments – he knew they existed because he could see them through the glass walls when he went up to head office – unfortunately, his professional dealings with them were almost nil. He knew they could see him, they navigated around his body in the corridors, sometimes they even nodded when he held a door open. From what he could gather, most of them were already tied up with other people. He thought a lot about the lives of these women but there wasn't an obvious way to interact with them. They came to work, spoke only to their immediate colleagues and then went home. No one ever acknowledged him when he had to cross the office for a meeting. His position in the company was too unclear, it was as if he didn't exist for them. He felt like he'd been warped in from another planet. The only single woman that he spoke to was a middle-aged lab technician called Joy, a forty-something Londoner from a strict Nigerian family. Although she usually laughed at his jokes, Joy didn't seem to want to see him naked. He was aware that the whole situation was untenable. At his age, if he didn't have sex soon, the leap would become insurmountable. He'd read the statistics. He had to make a move.

During these months, Tom found himself sharing a desk with a man called Sunny Chaudhry – also a data-mining PhD but working in the field of antidepressants. It was obvious that Sunny was also a virgin. Worse, Sunny seemed to have quickly drawn the same conclusions about Tom, despite his best attempts to hide it. He wondered if the same was true when it came to girls. Could they tell? If so, they were probably judging him for it. All in all, things were getting out of hand. He even stopped masturbating for a while, he was too depressed; and anyway, the videos on his phone were just another reminder that the world was full of people having sex.

One Saturday, out with Sunny on one of their weekly forays into the town centre, he managed to get someone to talk to him. The woman's name was Annika and she was visiting from Amsterdam. She'd said she'd be at a bar near her hotel, a place called Revolution, one of a chain of vaguely Communist-themed venues that specialized in bucket-sized cocktails with names like Wild Ting and Calypso Cooler. The bar made money from its reputation as a magnet for drunk women. As a result, Tom had been there before, trying to fit in with the regulars, most of whom were employees from the nearby EasyJet head office, either sales staff or cabin crew. Almost without exception, the women had theatrically contoured faces, long hair made from glued-on extensions, and wore tight clothes in bright colours. They seemed both muscular and overweight compared to the girls he'd known in France. He felt intellectually superior to these women, which made it even worse when they rejected him. He and Sunny must have spent hours on the edge of the orange-carpeted 'vodka lounge', resentfully trying and failing to pull. Annika, to Tom's relief, was unfamiliar with this scene. She found the bar extremely entertaining. She took photos and sent them to her friends, regaling them with what she saw as quirky, wack-job visions of the English on the lash. She drank heavily, beer only, and danced ironically to old songs. She was out with a party of accountants from the airline, who'd flown in to do an audit. Tom sensed, immediately, that something was going to happen. She seemed comfortable in his presence, she even smiled at him unprompted as she moved across the sticky dance floor, twirling around him as she drank. She was attractive, her face open and relaxed beneath the swinging purple lasers. He danced around her awkwardly, unsure how to move things forward. He felt himself harden as she brushed against him. He tried to hide it but she didn't seem fazed. Around midnight, she began to sober up and he panicked, sensing that she might leave without him. He found Sunny alone in a corner, his small hands nursing a glass of Bourbon Bad Boy. Sunny didn't look well, he was sweaty and morose, although as Tom approached his face snapped back into its usual nonchalant mask.

'What have you got?' Tom asked him.

Sunny, surprised, pulled out a bag of coke. He always carried something just in case. He used the drug casually, primarily to stay awake, but the idea was always there that a girl might one day agree to share it. Maybe – in his most flamboyant dreams – she'd even let him snort it off her tits. In this fantasy, he'd lick it off her cleavage before she straddled his chubby thighs. They were always in the penthouse of an expensive hotel, probably somewhere in Vegas. His fantasies were heavily informed by the 'classy' section on Pornhub.

Sunny had been raised in Pakistan and although he was close to his parents, both of whom were conservative Sunni Muslims, he'd developed an aversion to the sorts of rules they had raised him with. He wanted to do things his own way – which meant doing them the Western way. That meant he had to find a girl who actually liked him and then fall in love. On the other hand, it was obvious that he'd never get a girlfriend in this country if he didn't at least drink. As far as he could tell, there was no other way to meet them. In his experience, they had to be a little tipsy even to notice that he existed.

'Can I have it?' Tom asked him. 'It's for a girl.'

Reluctantly, Sunny let him have the bag, which was hot and damp from his jeans. Tom found Annika on her way out of the bathroom. He snorted a bump off his hand and, buoyed up, stopped her for a cigarette. He managed to walk her to the car park, his heart pumping as he looked around, trying to find somewhere for them to sit. As they smoked, he realized that he wasn't sure what he'd just taken. The powder in the bag looked blueish under the street lights, which wasn't what he had expected. He hesitated for a second but there wasn't much time, he needed to do something to keep her interest. So he pulled it out and went ahead. She demurred at first and then politely dabbed a small amount onto her gum. They spoke about the films she liked, her love of travelling, her visit to a music festival the previous summer. The feeling between them shifted slowly. He noticed that her pupils were starting to dilate. Her features softened, inhibitions lowered, something within her fell away and she opened her body up to his, allowing him to put an arm around her. Soon the two of them were kissing deeply. Emboldened, the world tipping sideways, he lifted her onto his lap. He slipped his hand underneath her top and she moaned, pressing herself against him. Her skin was goose-bumped with cold and she seemed to want him for the warmth as much as anything. He managed to put his coat around her shoulders as they wandered up towards the road. In the cab, they kissed some more. He administered another dose. She took his hand confidently this time, licking it clean before she returned her lips to his. Then she pressed his fingers, still damp, between her legs. By the time they'd made it to his flat, he realized the second dose had been too much. She was clumsy and unstable on her feet. He felt himself break into a sweat. He couldn't see straight as they lay on his bed and started taking their clothes off. Her body was soft and heavy now. He stopped more than once, but she kept her hands locked tightly around his neck, she never actually made him stop. He fumbled with his jeans and then with hers, struggling to angle himself against her. He came almost immediately, slumping down on her, pulling the condom off. He felt remorseful almost straight away. She lay in his bed for the rest of the night, silent but wide awake, increasingly lucid as the sky began to lighten. Then she got up, dressed and left the flat. Tom lay in silence for a while, pretending to sleep as the door closed behind her. The empty wrap of powder lay beside on the duvet. He felt terrible.

·

We drove in silence for a while.

'You wanted to know everything,' he said.

The game had gone a bit too far. I thought about it as he parked at the hotel.

'There was no need to tell me that.'

'It's not something I usually put out there.'

'But you did with me.'

'You asked me to. It's not a test, if that's what you're thinking.'

'What did you do?' I asked, despite myself.

'Nothing, I never heard from her again. I tried to contact her but she ignored me. It was a shit time. I had to get out of that place and I still had Grace's card, so I called her. That's how we ended up working together.'

·

The head office of Churchill Analytics was unlike anything Tom had come across before. The place was an ode to the colour grey, a cathedral to a muted, placeless idea of wealth. And it was also full of women. Marketing, it turned out, was where they worked. The ones he saw drifting through the lobby were mostly young, attractive and interested. They met his eyes. Some of them even smiled. He felt stupid in his Burton suit. It was the same one he'd worn to every interview he'd ever had.

Grace was friendlier than he'd remembered. She seemed genuinely pleased to see him. The interview went well. They were of a similar age and both in jobs that they didn't really care about. Grace, like Tom, had stumbled into her field. She had wanted to be a doctor as a child and had fallen into marketing only later, after failing to make it into med school. Her first role at Churchill had been in 'over the counter', which meant she'd spent her twenties behind a computer, writing copy about painkillers. During her thirties, she'd begun to ascend the ranks, slowly at first, and then with increasing speed. She was now UK director of communications, a nebulous position that made her responsible for the branding and marketing of a whole range of medications, some of them breakthrough discoveries that had altered the lives of millions of people. She oversaw everything from packaging to events. And increasingly, in the line of duty, she found herself directing the products themselves as they became ever more subservient to the 'story' the brand wanted to tell about them. She would oversee their functions, their market positionings, their feel and appearance – it was the only way to cut through the noise in a competitive global marketplace. She was often bored at work but she found herself strangely loyal to the place. It was something she knew was a weakness, especially as it was openly enforced by a heinous web of incentive schemes. Over time, she lost the ability to imagine any other kind of life. All she'd ever known was Churchill Analytics. And as a result, she kept getting promoted. In a way, her lack of ambition was an asset, in that no one really saw her as a threat. By the time she'd decided to hire Tom, she was in a position to place him where she wanted, so she put him in her own team as a sort of technical assistant. She had a feeling he'd learn on the job but more importantly, she just liked him. She also quickly discovered that she could trust him, which didn't happen very often. Nowadays, although she was his boss, she often asked for his opinion.

•

'What's Grace really like?' I asked as we lounged in the hotel. It was in a converted manor. The room was studded with antiques, interspersed with wooden fixtures and the odd, tasteful modern piece. The bed was a massive four-poster, draped with heavy linen curtains. Above our heads was a huge round lamp and an abstract sketch of the countryside.

'She's decent.'

'She's very hard to read. When we were in Ibiza, I couldn't figure her out.'

'She's nice. She doesn't take herself too seriously. And she's always had my back. She's up for Executive Director now, and if she gets it, she'll probably take me with her.'

'She sounds impressive,' I said.

'I suppose she is.'

'Do you think some people are just like that?'

'Not really, I think she needs the money.'

I absorbed this information for a moment.

'I thought Niall had money,' I said. 'For some reason, he comes across like that.'

Tom laughed.

'Well,' he said, 'Niall puts a lot of effort into how he comes across.'

I was intrigued, I wanted to ask him more but I didn't want to sound as if I was prying. I sat down on the corner of the bed. I wondered how much the room had cost.

'Anyway,' Tom said, 'I don't know why we're talking about work.'

There were sounds coming from the room next door, not some clandestine affair but a podcast about money.

'The thing with blockchain,' the muffled voice explained, 'is that it allows for absolute capitalization.'

I looked out of the window as Tom closed the curtains. It was just beginning to get dark. The garden was green and manicured. I could tell it had been designed meticulously to look organic but not too wild. When he came back, I let him kiss me.

'Anyone can now create their own IP and sell anything to anyone. Welcome to the Brave New World of the total capitalization of everything.'

I felt my pussy swell as we lay on the bed together. The car journey had been intense but it hadn't changed things for the worse; in fact, it had somehow brought us closer, as if he'd trusted me with something and we were now bound together by the knowledge. I'd started feeling something for him that I found difficult to describe. He had an effect on me that had reorganized the world around me. I no longer felt as if I was on the periphery of my own existence. I now inhabited my own life as if everything had reorganized itself around me. I'd been aware of this transformation for a while but I hadn't dared acknowledge it. Now it was becoming clear that he could feel it too. Small movements were suddenly charged. We kissed slowly for a while, the two of us barely moving. A warm flush of happiness overcame me. Neither of us said anything much. I filled my mouth with him, and then my pussy. Outside, I could hear water trickling down some rocks into an artificial lake. Beyond this, it was completely quiet. The window was open but I couldn't hear any birds.

•

The rest of the weekend passed quickly. We barely left the room. In the restaurant that night, I realized he had a strange mixture of ambition and the supreme confidence of someone who barely registered what other people thought of him. He had a healthy scepticism about the world, a trait that I recognized in myself. It was probably a defensive thing – if you rejected everything, it couldn't hurt you – but it was also a real intuition that it was important to stay alert, that you might have to swim against the tide, that you couldn't necessarily trust it.

We spent the whole of Sunday in bed. He let me trawl through his phone. There were old photos of him in there, including shots with Sunny when they were postgrad students. I was a little startled by the pair of them, especially by young Tom.

'It was a look,' he said.

'Hip hop bar mitzvah?'

'I bought that scarf from Gant, it cost a fortune.'

'Why do men do this to themselves?'

He peered more closely at the picture.

'In my defence, Eminem was big.'

'You want an intimate date, I wanna intimidate?'

'That sort of thing.' He looked impressed. 'I believe there might have been ripped jeans involved.'

'You think a gay man would find this acceptable?'

He laughed.

'I don't think anyone did.'

I wondered what had happened during the London years to have transformed him so completely. He'd said he'd found himself surrounded by women, but surely it couldn't have been only that. It was a sobering thought, the idea that on some level, everything came down to numbers. He'd seemed almost jaded by the time I'd met him.

Over dinner that night, we revisited his sad virginity story. Then, warming to the subject, we started swapping hot takes on consent. He said the legal system didn't work as a regulator of sexual boundaries, that Spain had changed the law from 'no means no' to 'yes means yes', a strong move but still almost impossible to prove in court. I said the consent model was flawed anyway because it was blind to so many externalities – of the more ambient, psychic levels of coercion that led a person to have sex – sex they didn't exactly want. Like poverty, loneliness, ambition, the time pressure on women to have a child. He said we were a nation of sexual boozehounds who rarely remembered anything about last night. And how hardly anyone made a move unless at least one of them was wasted. He said it was a nightmare being sober in a town where people were always drinking, how it creeped him out to be in that position and how, sometimes, he felt like the whole of London was on a different planet. I ate my seabass fillet with saffron and watched as he filled our glasses from the water jug. I decided I didn't want my wine after all. The sober thing was a novelty. There was something exposing about it. I liked it. It was like being naked. I pressed my thigh against his as he asked for another jug.

15

For once, the interview had gone well. I realized this was Lara's doing but I tried to embrace the fact that I was now the dubious beneficiary of her influence. This was what you were supposed to do, wasn't it? I was just working my network.

I arrived for my first day early. My desk was behind a concrete pillar in the basement of an old WeWork building, the remains of the company's in-house style now reduced to a Prosecco tap, some hanging plants and an exposed heating duct that snaked up the wall behind me. I had a strong sense of déjà vu as I surveyed the sales junk around me – reusable coffee cups, novelty keyrings – this time emblazoned with Openr's logo. It was an airless, uninspiring room lit only by a row of daylight lamps, which gave you the feeling you were on an endless flight. *Free Your Desires*, it said in red Helvetica across the wall. *Nothing Is Less Binary than Human Attraction.* By the entrance was a sofa in the shape of a large upholstered heart, and above it a sign that said: *Openr: Experiment Ethically With Your Fellow Humans.*

I could hear the sales team across the room. They were all women, all in sweats and T-shirts. Most were youngish – under thirty – and it was tempting to describe them as coming from different cultures, which was true in terms of race and nationality, but they were all united by the only culture that seemed to matter here, something that might once have been called pop culture: they watched the same shows, they followed the same celebrities, they seemed to have barely divergent takes on politics, lifestyle and fashion. Today they were talking about the book *Bad Feminist* by Roxane Gay. My welcome email included a sexy winking gif from my boss Nicole, who was out of the office that morning. The email contained a list of tasks, a Slack invitation and an animated signature that said: *Stay Curious.*

As I waited for security to set my passcodes, I made myself an Openr account. I ticked every single dating preference in the drop-down menu. The app then sent me on my 'journey' – everything was part of a journey at Openr, and every user was 'part of the community'. We were here, according to the blurb, to be 'radically open while acting responsibly towards others'. Scrolling through the first few profiles, I came across a surprising number of suits. These men had photographed themselves in black and white – a sort of Christian Grey aesthetic. There was a run of DIY glamour shots and then a guy in a sheepskin loincloth, who was wearing what looked like a pair of horns. The next photo read: *Adventurous couple looking for a fun human to join us.* It featured a guy holding a cappuccino-coloured cockapoo. His wife was holding a mug that said: *This is what a feminist looks like.*

I was interrupted by a message from *Sir Stephen*:

Pardon me good madam, I was wondering if you might accept my assistance with your orgasm this evening?

I checked his profile, he hadn't uploaded any photos. It was just a drawing of Castle Black, the home of the Night's Watch in *Game of Thrones*. I replied:

Are you a well-made man? And of good character?

I am

And you are well-versed in the art of love?

Unquestionably

How courteous

I paused for a second, then I wrote:

Might I ask how you mean to abet me?

My phone rang before he could reply – it was IT, something about my permissions. Reluctantly, I let my suitor go. When I returned, he'd disappeared completely.

There was an unmistakeable standardization to the photos in the app – eyes and lips filtered and hyperreal, a repetitiveness of poses and expressions. Some of the more overtly feminine women were the ones who seemed, counterintuitively, to luxuriate most boldly in their kinks. I flicked through them as they stared proudly at the lens – a sort of Cara Delevingne effect. Or they'd gone for the classic bathroom mirror selfie, one foot stacked jauntily on the sink, like a kind of sexy pirate. There were all sorts of people in the system. It was a smorgasbord of human possibility. There were long lists on every profile where each user had ticked a set of boxes. The app demanded details of what they were into, their sexual personality, their wants and needs. There were sections devoted to every niche, from Japanese bondage to public sex – and even for aromanticism, demisexualism, asexualism. And unlike other dating apps, there was a sense of being in a club, a shared spirit of transgression, a proud rejection of the mainstream. This horror of 'the mainstream' – whatever that meant – seemed to be the one thing that everyone had in common. It gave people the sense of being part of a club that the rest of the world hadn't yet caught up with. It was a fantasy of its own, I thought, the idea of transcending

something. It was also difficult to pin down exactly what it was
that they were trying to leave behind. Victorian social mores,
maybe? Although these had themselves become just another
niche (for which there was a busy section on Openr called
'Trad'). Anyway, whatever it was, it didn't matter. It was the
atmosphere that reeled them in. The app was creating a sense
of transgression that seemed to permeate the user experience.
Lara, as always, was managing to attract attention.

·

How's things? Lara texted.

The kitchen was on the other side of a 'collaboration room'
that doubled as a gallery of art. Today there was a display of
paintings inspired by the photographer Man Ray that, according to the text on the wall, explored the idea of sex as a form
of dance. It was interesting idea in the abstract, but also – like
a lot of things about Openr – oddly flat in reality. Four giant,
oil-painted nudes loomed over me as I made my way to lunch.
I ate one-handed as I scrolled through the iPad I'd been
given. There was a long list of 'Dating Don'ts' on the app's
community guidelines. 'Haunting', it said: 'stalking people's
social media while ignoring their messages'. 'Benching' was
'stringing a match along while holding out for better options'.
'Roaching' was 'cheating on your partner with the excuse that
you hadn't yet discussed monogamy'. There was a whole page
of this stuff. Lying, in general, was frowned upon. Rejections
had to be clear-cut and so did, above all, consent. The glaring
problem, as far as I could see, was that there was no way of
policing all of this. The app relied on the goodwill of its users.
The ethical part of it was voluntary. It was like a well-meaning
but helpless nanny trying to manage a wayward mob of kids, a
mob that kept expanding and becoming more miscellaneous.

The more I thought about it, the more I realized that the
site's no-no's had become a way of life. Of course you 'talked'

to different people; of course you didn't tell them everything. There was something quaint about the notion that we'd all just go back to 'dating': handing your attention to only one person at a time. Going on *activities* with them. Respecting their feelings etc. And then, finally, deciding they weren't The One (Return to Go and start over) – or that, in fact, they *were* (which meant what exactly? Trust? Marriage?). Considering Openr was supposed to be a radical experiment, it had a strangely antique approach to ethics. Its sincerity belonged to a bygone age – the ancient history of Match.com or MySingle-Friend, a time when there was still some stigma around the very concept of 'online dating'.

I'd barely finished eating when Lara appeared in the kitchen.

'So?' she said.

'What?'

'How's it going?'

'All fine.'

I wasn't really in the mood, I was still recovering from the shock of being at work.

'You didn't tell me about this man of yours,' she said.

'What man?'

'You know who I mean.'

'Who told you?'

She tossed my phone at me.

'You left it on your desk,' she said.

We both knew this was neither an explanation nor an excuse.

'Patrick Bateman-looking fella, isn't it?' she sat down in front of me. 'Who are you?'

I shoved the phone into my pocket.

'You like him?' she pressed me.

'Yes.'

She ate her salad, watching me in silence.

'Why are you helping me?' I asked her.

'We're friends.'

'Are we?'

'You took the job.'

'I'm not sure if I should have.'

'Don't overthink it.'

'You're the boss.'

'I'm not your boss,' she said, annoyed. 'I just recommended you.'

'It's your company.'

'What's left of it, once the vultures have had their slice.'

She was talking about investors, as if I'd sympathize with that.

'Anyway, we're a team,' she said. 'I don't pull rank.'

I must have actually rolled my eyes. I really wasn't enjoying being employed.

'Well, put it this way, I keep it to a minimum. You know what I mean,' she conceded. 'There's no need to thank me, by the way.'

'Thanks.'

'What's your problem?'

'No problem.'

'Aren't you going to forgive me?'

I wondered which of her many offences she was referring to.

'Never look back?' she offered, lamely.

I didn't bother dignifying that with a reply.

•

It wasn't long after my initiation at Openr that I found myself at Café Cecilia. Tom had invited me for dinner with Grace and Niall. I barely recognized Niall from Ibiza. He showed up late, dishevelled, his raincoat bunched under his arm.

'Sorry,' he said as he sat beside his wife. Ignoring Grace completely, he topped my glass up with wine, then filled his own to the brim. He looked scruffier than I remembered. His hair was longer, it was wet from the rain and he was wearing a pair of sweatpants that said *No Problemo* up the side.

'I don't want to bore you,' Grace said, 'but there's something Tom and I need to discuss. It's work, so don't feel like you have to listen.'

It was obvious that she and Niall weren't speaking.

'I meant to ask how it went,' Tom said.

'Well' – she lowered her voice – 'I'm thinking of saying yes.'

'Are you sure?'

'It's a decent offer.'

'How much?'

'Two fifty,' she said. 'Plus shares.'

I was startled by the number. I tried to hide it by picking up the bottle of wine that Niall had already almost emptied. *Anbury Estate Organic* the label said.

'So what's the verdict?'

'It's a big decision,' she said, glancing at her husband as he spread a hunk of pâté on his bread. The bread was dark and coarse, like something a medieval peasant might have eaten. 'The company's in Cambridge. It's small but they're partnering with Pharmacon. I'd be working with them as a contractor, so not in-house like at Churchill. It would mean a lot more freedom. Flexibility. I want to spend more time with Evie.'

I thought about the photo I'd seen on her desk. She glanced at me, as if she thought I might help sway Tom with this line of thinking.

'There are risks involved, of course. And I'd want you to come with me.'

'I'd be flattered,' Tom said. 'I was seconded to Pharmacon way back, as you know. I know one of the leads on that team.'

'In the lab?'

'Yes, the one at Granta Park.'

'Not Sunny?'

'He's a friend,' Tom said protectively.

'He's a liability. But good for him, they're putting a lot of money behind this thing.'

'How much do you think they'd offer me?'

'I'd say one eighty, plus shares if things go well. I mean, we'd have to finalize the details but I wouldn't expect them to go much lower.'

I glanced at Niall, who'd retreated into his phone.

'It's a big commitment,' Grace continued. 'If we took it, I'd want you there for the long haul.'

On the table was a trio of small dishes, one piled with what looked like chicken nuggets. On another was a group of tiny eggs and on the third, a piece of sliced lamb encrusted with a popcorn-like shell. I was starving. I cut into one of the eggs and transported what was left of it onto my plate. I wondered if I should make more of an effort with Niall, but he didn't seem interested. Instead, I smiled genially at Grace while Tom chewed his nuggets in silence.

'I can't see any reason why not,' he said.

'There are always reasons.'

'Such as?'

'It's a big release, for a start. High stakes, high returns and all that. This drug is in a different class to anything we've seen before. It's a psychedelic, basically, the first to have been developed purely for medical use. Nothing like it has been mass-marketed before. There have been rumblings about MDMA but this is a next-generation product. It's a psychedelic developed specifically to alleviate the symptoms of depression.'

After dinner, I stood outside with Grace, who offered me a cigarette.

'It's a disgusting habit, I know,' she said, exhaling slowly at the pavement. 'Sorry about Niall, I don't know why he bothered coming.'

She looked almost Amish with her blunt, dark hair and her

thick, heavy cotton dress. I got the impression that she wasn't much older than I was. Late thirties, maybe.

'What's it like,' I asked, 'having it all?'

I was only partially joking.

She gave me a funny look, then she thought about it.

'You know, sometimes I wonder about that. I mean at work, when I look around, there aren't many women at my level.'

'Because of kids?' I asked.

'I don't think so. They hardly ever drop out because of having kids. They almost always try and stick around. Things just end for them, one way or another. They get expensive. They have less time. They get sidelined because they've become replaceable with someone younger. It's like a ramp that keeps getting steeper.'

'What happens to them?'

'I don't know. One of the girls I started out with became a yoga teacher.'

I thought about this for a second. 'Do you think I should become a yoga teacher?'

She let out a small laugh.

'You can calm Niall down if you like.'

Then she flashed me a crooked, goofy grin that broke the Amish thing completely. Her front teeth had a gap in them that she obviously hadn't bothered to fix. She seemed less icy than she had in Spain, or at least less icy towards me. Her lipstick had rubbed off on her cigarette. She looked more vulnerable without it.

PART 2
Marketing

The transformation of a market opportunity into a product or service available for sale, including the process of exploring, creating, and delivering value to the customer.

Every great business is built around a secret.

PETER THIEL, *ZERO TO ONE*

16

For some reason, my phone wasn't working. I had an uncomfortable suspicion that my last bill had gone unpaid but I had no way of finding out. I was standing helplessly in the street when I saw Grace for the second time that week. I'd left the office late and she must have gone to the gym after work because I caught her emerging from Ironmonger Row, her hair still wet from the pool. She seemed distracted. She was obviously in a rush, then she stopped as if she'd changed her mind.

'Do you have time for a drink?' she said.

The Britannia was an ancient boozer, so dark inside you could see flecks of dust floating around the door. She bought us both a drink and started talking. This went on for so long that the bar was closing by the time I gently suggested that we should leave. We were both heading east and I asked if she wanted to walk home together. She nodded gratefully and went to get her bike, wheeling it beside me on the pavement as we made our way towards London Fields.

'Every day?' I repeated, when she told me how early Evie woke up.

On the day of her interview with Neura Therapeutics, the drug company that was partnering with Pharmacon, Evie had woken on cue at 5 a.m. Like most mornings, she'd wanted to have a long and detailed conversation about animals, what sorts of dreams they had, whether birds could fly to other planets and whether unicorns had gone extinct. It was a Monday, it had been a rough few days and Grace wasn't in the mood.

Niall's parents had been over at the weekend. They were always complaining that they hardly saw their grandchild but Evie was old enough now at three to have her own opinions on the matter and after a fractious and tearful week spent with them during the summer while Niall and Grace had gone to Spain, she now burst into tears whenever she saw them and kept telling Grace she thought they smelt. It had snowed unexpectedly on the Sunday and Niall's parents' car had broken down, which had meant Niall going to collect them, a two-hour round trip and then another at the end of the day. This scenario had left Grace on her own to keep Evie entertained, feed her, bathe her, put her to bed and then try and persuade her to go to sleep. When Niall had finally made it back, he'd been in a bad mood. He'd filled the dishwasher so loudly that she could hear him from upstairs, then he'd sat silently on his laptop while they'd watched the boxset they'd been trying to finish for weeks. The show was called *Happy Valley*. It was about a missing girl and a rapist. The rapist had already impregnated the detective's daughter, who had already committed suicide. It was a kind of mash-up of *The Vanishing* and *Emmerdale* with bleak shots of the Yorkshire Dales and people staring grimly at a lake. Every now and then, Niall would glance at the TV without saying a word. They were OK, Grace thought. She wasn't exactly enjoying her life but she knew that things could be worse. And she had Evie, who was a whirlwind in the best way possible, and also the worst. Evie, at least, still seemed capable of real happiness – the kind of simple joy that Grace could hardly remember. The little girl had gone into raptures over the snow that weekend. On the other hand, she'd started wetting the bed again, which meant more waking in the night.

On her cycle into town that morning, Grace had started thinking about sex. She and Niall still did it, although it had dwindled since Evie had been born. She still found him attractive – which he was, objectively, for his age. She liked having a husband that was desirable. On the other hand, she had to concede that their years together had cost her more than they'd cost him. It was a combination of motherhood, work and age, something that happened to most people, she supposed. She wasn't even forty yet but the difference in the way people treated her was obvious. It didn't bother her that much – she'd never relied on her looks – but the shift required an adjustment. And also it was unfair, which got on her nerves. These thoughts occupied her for a while as she dodged the rush-hour traffic. Her route took her along the Essex Road, away from the expensive part of Hackney where Niall had wanted them to live. She rode down Upper Street and took a right onto the back streets of King's Cross. Locking her bike up at the station, she realized that her coat was splashed with mud and she had to decide whether there was time to go to the bathroom to clean it. She was already running late, as usual. She decided the coat would have to wait as she made her way to the platform and not for the first time, scrubbing it with a tissue, she wondered whether all of this was worth it.

On the train to Cambridge, she finally relaxed, pulling up the site for Neura Therapeutics on her laptop. 'Pioneering the development of more effective disease-modifying mental health treatments,' it said on their landing page. 'Our mission is to bridge the gap between the mental healthcare system and what our patients need.' Under the 'Our People' section was a glossy photo of Douglas Floyd, the company's founder and CEO and the man that Grace was about to meet. He looked like all the other MBA types she'd met before, except his hair was slightly overgrown and instead of the standard navy-coloured suit he was dressed from head to toe in black. Neura Therapeutics, the blurb said, had been founded in 2013 by Floyd and his then partner, Gerald Gert. They were both

Cambridge biology PhDs who had gone on to start their own companies. Floyd was a serial entrepreneur who had grown and sold a couple of other businesses: Action Life Sciences, a biotech venture capital fund, and Buildopia, a manufacturer of lab equipment. His bio said:

> As a child, I was unhappy at school and suffered from symptoms of anxiety that I managed, in adulthood, only partially successfully through a combination of meditation and prescription drugs. However, it has been my experience that many people are failed by the mental health system and this was what inspired me to build a new framework for treating these conditions.

Grace googled Floyd and scrolled through his images. There were rows and rows of pictures of him on stage. He'd done TED talks, YouTube presentations, lectures at something called the Flint Foundation. There was a picture of him at his old alma mater, playing chess with the Chancellor of the Exchequer.

He'd invited her to meet him at his office, which was a room hired out by the university. When she arrived, he greeted her in jeans, his sweatshirt sleeves rolled up, his feet in a pair of black socks that were made out of some sort of technical material.

'Come in!' He ushered her into the room. 'I was just meditating,' he apologized. 'Do you practise?'

'I've got an app,' she said politely. 'Although I find it hard to keep it up.'

'You should stick with it, it's worth it,' he admonished her. 'It's a deep commitment but it pays dividends. Did you know there's a longstanding history of it in Europe? Schopenhauer wrote about it. Voltaire defended the Buddhists in Paris. Can I offer you a coffee? It's Tanzanian.'

'Thanks.' Grace looked around the room. He had decorated

it with various artefacts. There was a bronze figurine of a Buddha standing on the floor beside his shoes.

'Pretty guy, isn't he?' he said. 'I got him in Shanghai. He's Emperor Xuande.' He gave Grace a coffee and picked up the sculpture. 'He's there to remind me that the self is an illusion.'

Floyd set the statue on his desk, standing back to admire it.

'The Western construct of the individual has, in my opinion, outlasted its utility.'

'I don't know much about Buddhism,' she said.

'I'm not talking about the religion. There are Jewish traditions of meditation, Islamic, Christian, you name it. The point is that the practice yields results because it lessens the burden on the ego. What we're trying to do here at Neura is bottle some of those results.'

Grace nodded patiently and waited for him to continue. She was mostly interested in his budget.

'Put it this way,' Floyd tried again. 'Mental health is primarily a systemic problem. Recessions lead to spikes in suicide. So do patterns of family breakdown, migration, changes in the technological environment. In adolescents, social media is a factor. Suicides in general are rising. They're going up faster than they've ever done. And interestingly, some of the least developed countries have the lowest rates of all: Afghanistan, Iraq, most of north Africa. Europe has the highest rates on the planet.'

'Why is that?'

'It's complex. No one really knows, if I'm honest.'

'You must have some idea.'

'You want my opinion?'

'Yes.'

'Individualism, in a nutshell. It can't survive exposure to giant networks.'

'What do you mean?'

'I mean that people fall apart when they're expected to compete with millions of strangers.'

'Because of the internet?'

'That's a major factor.'

'But in what way exactly?'

'Too much information, plus freedom. It creates a lot of problems for most of us.'

'You can't know that.'

'It's well evidenced, actually. We live under conditions that make it very difficult to thrive. All of these free choice networks produce hierarchies – hierarchies that become more pronounced over time. They result in a small number of winners and an underclass of billions of losers. Take a social network like Instagram, for example. There are over a billion users on that app, each spending around 30 minutes on it per day – that's 500 million hours of human attention every 24 hours. And over 100 million of those hours are spent on the top 20 accounts. Time is a finite commodity. I'm sure you can work out what that means for everybody else. It's the same in every iteration of these ultra-large, choice-based systems. It doesn't matter what it is, it's always the same pattern – from the stock market to education to recruitment. There are various ways of describing the phenomenon: economic theories, technological ones, it's fashionable at the moment to talk in terms of power laws. But the upshot is more or less the same, a sharp increase in competition for ever-dwindling rewards: for money, for attention, for love. They all become rarer in this environment because they're disproportionately distributed at the top.'

Grace looked sceptical, despite herself.

Floyd continued. 'Look, humans have evolved to vie for status in small groups of hunter gatherers. It's fundamental to our mating system. It's not something we can opt out of. When you apply that to massive global networks, the impulse becomes maladaptive. Modern life, in short, is unsatisfying for most people. And for some, it isn't tolerable at all. There are people walking the streets right now who simply can't endure their lives. And at the moment, we have no idea how to help them – or even how to reach them in the first place. If they come to light, it's usually too late, because they've already harmed themselves. Or worse.'

'But there are already treatments for these kinds of problems,' Grace said. 'What about counselling? Psychotherapy? And obviously there are whole classes of antidepressants.'

'Their effects are limited, unfortunately, because they all put the onus on the patient to adapt to a largely suboptimal environment.'

'Mindfulness then? Meditation?'

'Like you, most people don't keep them up.'

'You think it's all a social problem?'

'Not entirely. It's more complicated than that. But if you're asking me if there's a social solution, a political one – well, there's nothing on the horizon. There doesn't seem to be much appetite. And anyway, there's no guarantee that it would work. That's the gap in the market we're trying to fill. What I'm trying to say here is that what we do at Neura – it's more than just a medication. It's a radical solution to a global problem. Do you understand?'

He stared at her intensely.

'I think so,' Grace said. 'So, how exactly does this thing work?'

'Have you ever taken Ecstasy?'

'Yes.'

'So you're familiar with the feelings it produces? Feelings of euphoria and connectedness?'

'Yes,' she repeated, remembering the savage comedown she'd had in Spain during the summer. She was getting too old for all of that.

'Imagine a version that's exponentially more powerful.

That sense of closeness and belonging? Multiply that by a thousand. It's an experience of consciousness flying free from the boundaries of the ego. Every relationship expands the mind. What we have here is another level of expansion, a sensation of blissful freedom – the freedom to transcend the pressure to compete.'

This time it was Grace who stared at Floyd. She couldn't tell if he was serious.

'And the side effects?' she asked. 'Low libido is the big one we see with Prozac.'

'Minimal.'

'Really?'

'At the dose we've established? Yes, there are no significant side effects.'

Floyd looked almost high on his own sales pitch. She was starting to wonder whether he was on something.

He poured her another cup of coffee, as if he thought she'd need it to keep up with him.

'You know,' he said, 'it's hard to find a comms director that gets it. We're a mission-driven company, you know? It's not about the money, it's about creating change.'

They always said this. It was never about the money.

'And I'm sure you're aware of this,' he continued, 'but the thing with really radical innovations is that the marketing challenge is often the biggest hurdle. From what I've seen of your work, you're someone who knows how to connect with normal people.'

'Thanks.' She wasn't sure if this was a compliment.

'I don't want to bog you down with details but, as you know, we've signed a deal with Pharmacon, which means we're under pressure to get things going.'

'I guess they'll have their own sales team?'

'Exactly. But the strategy will come from us. Honestly, this whole area is a minefield. We just don't know enough about the underlying pathologies to put a simple message together.'

'Is the drug fully licensed?'

'Yes, since August. And we'd like to soft launch in the spring.'

'That's fast for a product like this.'

'I know, but psychedelics are the future of this niche and I don't want to lose the advantage we've created.'

'Do you have a name yet?'

'We're toying with Eudaxa – from the Greek *Eudaimonia*. It means "happiness", "well-being" or "flourishing". I'd say name recognition is a priority. Even here in the UK, patients will go online and do their research.'

'So, the focus is on maximizing impact?'

'Precisely. Followed by explaining how it works, how it's going to fit into people's lives – all the usual stuff. You know how it works.'

'I'll have to think about this.'

'Of course, take your time.'

As she stepped outside, Floyd pressed something cold into the palm of her hand. It was pair of tiny bells attached together with a thin red cord.

'It's a tingsha,' he said. 'Good for relaxation. I'm going to need a decision by next week.'

17

Lara was at her desk being photographed for an interview she'd done on women and technology. Her thing was that digital technology was liberating in that it took the emphasis off flesh and blood. You could reinvent yourself online because it was a space that didn't define you by your chromosomes. She was wearing a black dress and lipstick, a kind of Alexandria Ocasio-Cortez effect. The photographer was coming on to her pretty heavily. He probably thought he had a chance because of her work. The more he flirted with her, the more she disdained him, which only made for a better picture. I got the feeling she knew what she was doing. It was her preferred dynamic with the world.

Although I didn't find the job difficult, it wasn't as straight-forward as I'd hoped. I spent a lot of time waiting for other people, then having to work late to meet my deadlines. I filled most of these empty moments scanning the news, online window shopping and lurking around on social media. There was a bank of engineers behind me, and although I knew my job was linked with theirs, I wouldn't have been able to describe what they did. Their niches of expertise were so narrow that they hardly seemed to comprehend each other. It had become normal, when I thought about it, to have no idea how things worked. I couldn't have told you how a microwave operated, or even a transistor. All the same, there was something disturbing about the scale of these divisions in IT.

Despite the gulf, a lot of the engineers were friendly. I

formed a vague bond with a developer called Shaq. We invented a game that went like this: one of us thought of a theme and the other interpreted it through music. That morning, I offered him: *cocaine.* He took a long time with his selection. He flicked through options, teasing me with intros. Then he rose to the challenge with 'Nosetalgia' by Pusha T. He stood up to salute me over his monitor. I got the impression he was having a good time. It helped to pass the time, but only up to a point. I just didn't want to be in the office. While I waited for instructions from above, I checked my messages for the hundredth time.

'What else have you got?' Shaq enquired.

I thought about it.

'Weltschmerz,' I said.

•

On Sunday, Tom and I went to the Hunterian Museum. There were groups of tourists wandering around. Tom knew a lot about brains and as we browsed the jars of pickled flesh – occipital lobes, cerebellums, thin slices of cerebral cortex – I found myself engaged in a somewhat meta experiment into the theory that the brain is the greatest erogenous zone. He had a real depth of knowledge on the subject. That PhD hadn't been for nothing.

'So, is it the greatest erogenous zone?' I asked him.

'Probably is for me.'

He was being coy. I thought about it. I'd have said he was objectively better looking than most men I knew, but maybe I only thought that because I liked him in other ways. We stood millimetres from each other as we waited for the lift to the Zoology Museum. I wanted to touch him but I decided to hold back. He was quite reserved in public. Upstairs, there were more specimens, each preserved in yellowish formaldehyde. It wasn't obvious which were neurological samples and which came from other organs – livers, spleens, gallbladders.

'Is it true they all interact with each other?' I said.

'In a sense.'

He brushed my hand and immediately, if inadvertently, illustrated the effect.

'Oxytocin,' he said, catching my face as a burst of hormones washed through me. 'Vasopressin, serotonin, maybe a touch of dopamine.'

'Thank you, Rain Man.'

He smiled and, for a moment, I thought he was going to kiss me. Instead, he nudged me gently on the arm.

'Shall we get out of here?' he said.

We left the museum and walked through Holborn, heading towards Lamb's Conduit Street.

'So, the job search is over?' he said. 'How did you land this gig again?'

I'd already told him loosely that I'd got it through a friend.

'Same as you got yours,' I said. 'Networking.'

I think he could tell that I was leaving something out.

'And the company makes one of those dating swipe apps?'

'It's a dating app for alternative lifestyles. It's supposed to be more ethical than the others.'

'Alternative lifestyles? Are we talking about swinging?'

'Not exactly.'

'Wife-swapping, then?'

'Well, its users are mostly young, so most of them are still single.'

'So what does "alternative" mean, then?'

'It just means they're over the traditional model. They don't want the whole two kids and a Volvo thing, probably because so many of them have seen how badly that worked out for their parents. I suppose it's for people who want to be true to themselves and are brave enough to look for something better.'

I got the feeling my sales pitch wasn't landing.

'Who funds these things, anyway?' he said, as if he thought that sounded like pure idealism. 'None of them seem to make any money.'

I tried to explain the business model at Openr. The company was funded primarily by Mindbot, a private social media conglomerate that owned more than a hundred different brands. It specialized in live sex streaming but also owned various porn aggregators like XXXbox, Youngporn, Xzilla and Babebox. Mindbot was based in the Bahamas, presumably for tax reasons. Its headquarters, on the other hand, were in a nondescript office block in Amsterdam. No one seemed to know who owned the corporation because its founders didn't use their real names.

'The thing is,' I said, 'they're trying to buck the trend. Most of these dating apps are using machine learning to maximize revenue. The psychology of masses is quite predictable so they'll just run trial after trial until they've landed on the best way to persuade people to pay. It's often something quite straightforward, like withholding matches and blurring their faces so you have to pay a fee if you want to see them. There are also shadier techniques – they'll feed you "hot" matches first, or they'll release a flurry of matches and then stop. They'll get you hyped up early on and then suddenly, a few days later, you discover that your profile has gone quiet. That's when you start feeling insecure, you want to get that feeling back, so you consider making a purchase, or you spend longer swiping that day. They work like most social apps, they're designed to game your expectations so you'll keep coming back for more.'

'And what's so different about Openr, then?'

'Well, the problem with maximizing revenue that way is that there's a trade-off with user satisfaction. People will keep coming back for a while, but in the end, it starts eroding trust. They feel like shit. Fatigue sets in. They start to realize that something's wrong. That's where the industry is at the moment. It's why Openr is trying to do things differently.'

'But how are they doing things differently, though?'

'They're trying to build a community based on trust.'

'And how are they going about that?'

'By uniting people around causes, by emphasizing shared values.'

He looked sceptical.

'I know,' I said, 'but at least they're trying to improve things.'

I didn't tell him that Openr made money by selling its 'insights' to other companies. I worked alongside the insights team, whose job it was to divine patterns in the seemingly infinite chaos that was Mindbot's cache. These patterns ranged from well-known tendencies, like the average amount of time it took for a man to achieve orgasm, to glimpses of more subtle effects, like how sensitive someone was to sound. Mindbot's data store was a vast, constantly expanding vortex that produced a sort of textual vertigo. There was far too much of it for any single person to comprehend. Nonetheless, insights had to be produced because there was no other way of making money. No one wanted to upgrade to premium, they all wanted to use the app for free, which put heavy pressure on 'insights' to pay for everything. And in defence of the insights team, however spurious their services, they did keep churning them out. Aggregating thousands of fields, they would generate metrics for all sorts of behaviours. There was a job security score that supposedly predicted when you were about to get the sack. There was a churn score that calculated how quickly you would leave the app. There were health scores, mood scores, the all-important desirability rating. The scores went on ad infinitum, all of them anonymized, of course. They measured sleep patterns, honesty, anxiety. Each click logged, each sentence parsed. I once looked up the most common word typed in by users across all of Mindbot's platforms. I'd assumed it would be 'assfuck' or something. I was surprised to discover that the answer was 'love'.

•

By now, Tom and I were seeing each other a few times a week. I never mentioned Lara to him but I did discuss Tom with Lara. She sometimes asked about him. She even wanted to see the photos I had.

'I take it back about Patrick Bateman,' she said. 'He looks too basic to have killed that many hookers.'

In the meantime, I finally broke the seal and took Tom back to my flat. He spent a long time looking at the slug cupboard.

'It's like a terrarium,' he said, shining a light through the sellotaped hole where the door handle had once been. 'The air moisture in this place is ideal for gastropods.'

Most nights, though, we went back to his place.

'Someone should do an architectural study,' he'd said after the first night he'd stayed over, 'on the boner-killing effects of flat-shares. They're like a stealth form of contraception.'

There was a Chinese place on Upper Street where we sometimes went for food. It sold a drink called Genki Forest Water.

'It's almost flavourless,' Tom said. 'It just tastes of slightly sweetened water.'

'But you prefer it to actual water?'

'I like that it sits somewhere on the spectrum between mineral water, which is all about purity and health, and the usual soft drink scenario, which is generally too sweet for me.'

'You must be a connoisseur by now.'

'I am. I went through a phase of trying every mineral water in London. There used to be one called Svalbarði that came from polar glaciers. They sold it as "ultra-premium iceberg water".'

'What did it taste like?'

'Water, same as all the others. They'd always have some subtle selling point like smooth mouthfeel, or chalkiness, but I could never tell the difference.'

'Refined palates, those Svalbarðians.'

'Gentle thrill-seekers.'

'Do you miss drinking?' I asked him.

'It depends. Not with you.'

Once he'd left for work each morning, I rarely heard from him all day. His time was packaged into half-hour chunks, almost all of which were managed by other people. Most of these slots were booked days or even weeks in advance. He didn't seem to have much time to think about anything else. I supposed this was normal for someone whose career was actually going somewhere.

18

Lara had booked me for a meeting. We were going somewhere – a mystery location, because she hadn't yet bothered to tell me where. Like most people, she was different in the office. I realized this wasn't really a choice, but it had a weird, disorienting effect on how we were together.

She greeted me casually. She was draped in a thin cashmere coat. When she opened the car door for me, I could feel the warmth of her body underneath it.

'You look nice,' she said.

'Do I?'

'You look like Françoise Hardy.'

'You mean I'm wearing a trench?'

I got into her car and she started driving.

'You know I didn't hire you to do admin, don't you?'

She was speeding slightly. She accelerated through the lights, turning left sharply at London Wall.

'What do you mean?'

'I mean you're better than that.'

'Where is this going?' I said suspiciously.

'I thought you might like to do some writing. You were good at it at college. I don't know why you stopped.'

As if she really had to ask. Did she think my job was just a lapse in taste?

'What kind of writing?'

'Content. Posts, videos, podcasts. I'm trying to level up the vibe. I think we could push harder on socials.'

I flicked through the company's website on my phone as she swung around the roundabout, turning into Wapping High Street before hurtling past the station. Each blog post was headed in elegant Monoline, in the style of an old edition of *Vogue*:

Relationship Communism: It's A Thing
On The Fine Art of The One-Night Stand
Why We Need to Talk to Kids about Kink

'It's not my thing,' I said.

'Try it.'

'No.'

'Humour me.' She didn't take her eyes off the road. 'It'll be fun.'

'I don't think so.'

'You know you're going to have to stop punishing me at some point?'

'I'm not punishing you,' I lied.

I also didn't want to do it.

'I'm going to break you, you know that, don't you?' She was trying to be light-hearted but I didn't play along.

She parked haphazardly on a cobbled lane and looked at me, frustrated.

'There's a Tretchikoff painting of Françoise Hardy,' I said as we got out of the car. 'It's called "Rainy Day". He said he could tell that she'd been damaged by all the fame and adulation. He said he'd painted her that way because she was the loneliest person he'd ever met.'

•

The studio was crammed with banks of desks, each one attended by a solitary worker. Piles of hardware filled the tables. There were multiple screens mounted on each one.

Everyone was fenced in by these arrangements, cloistered into pen-like hubs. The space was huge, it looked like a film set. There was rigging hanging from the ceiling. At one end, a model in a vest and leggings was walking slowly on the spot. Her movements reappeared in real time on a huge screen behind her head. As I watched, the animation morphed into the shape of a soft-featured avatar.

'So, this is important.' Lara had switched to work mode. 'We've got our anniversary coming up. It's going to be the biggest party we've ever thrown and I'm doing an exhibition to go along with it. I've been working with these guys for a while. If it goes well, I'd like to get into events. The plan is to expand into other cities. It's all about live experience when it comes to publicity, ticket sales and all of that. And obviously, if the parties work, it would really help us scale.'

She waved towards the screen. By her side was a man in a ponytail, a pair of headphones around his neck, his T-shirt printed with a smiley face that had three eyes.

'What we've got here is an immersive experience. An *erotic* immersive experience. This is Openr's foray into virtual. What I want you to do is interact with it. You're the only person I've shown so far.'

'Introducing Unity,' ponytail said. The avatar waved in my direction. I nodded back, unsure how to react. Suddenly, she broke into a jog, her human doppelganger mirroring her. The movements of her breasts were amazingly gel-like.

'She's good, isn't she?' Lara said as the screen dissolved slowly into a beach scene. Unity was now in a string bikini, its gold fabric shimmering in the sun.

'Hi,' the animation said, 'I'm Unity.'

I stepped back, startled.

'What do you think of her?' Lara said.

'She's terrifying.'

'I think she's beautiful.'

Unity beamed back at us, her teeth glittering in the virtual light.

'Don't worry,' Unity said warmly. 'I'm here for you.'

'You can talk to her,' ponytail told me.

'Hi, Unity,' I said. 'How are you?'

'I'm great,' she breathed. 'How are you?'

I paused, unsure what else to say. It was a weird situation.

'You seem to be in a good mood,' I tried.

'I am! It's important to stay positive.'

'Who's the Prime Minister of England?'

'Rishi Sunak,' Unity enunciated. 'But you knew that, didn't you?'

'I suppose I did.'

'I'm not as stupid as I look.'

She winked at me.

I glanced at Lara, who seemed delighted with how things were going.

'Don't you love her?' she said. 'She's so convincing. I'm thinking of incorporating her into the app.'

'Why?'

'We've got to keep innovating,' she said, as if it was obvious.

She could tell I wasn't convinced.

'This isn't easy, you know?' she said. 'They don't give you many chances in this game. Especially if you're a woman.'

'I thought everything was going well.'

'It is,' she said. 'On paper.'

'What does that mean?'

'That I can't afford to slow down. I've got to keep it growing as fast as possible.'

'And if it doesn't grow?'

'It will.'

'But what if it doesn't?'

'It *will*.'

She said it as if she hadn't heard me. We were on our own now, ponytail had gone to the kitchen.

'What do you want me to say?' she said. 'That I'll have nothing?'

'You'll never have nothing,' I scoffed.

'You think I'm bulletproof?'

'No, but I think we have different definitions of nothing.'

'Why do I offend you so much?'

She looked hurt, as if I'd touched a nerve. Maybe I'd been laying it on too thick. She could never have offended me. If anything, that was the problem.

'Help me,' she said. 'I can't do this on my own. You're the only person I can trust.'

'What do you want me to do, exactly? No amount of "content" is going to change things.'

'That's not true. With Openr, it all comes down to engagement. Our customers want to be a part of something. They're looking for a way to *engage* with the world – a way that makes them feel seen, that makes them feel involved. They're interested in politics, justice, freedom. All we need to do is keep them talking. Keep them stimulated. Push their buttons. We've got to break new ground to stay ahead. We're as much a content creator as we are a dating site. In the end, it all brings people to the app and that's the one thing we've got to push for.'

'I don't know,' I said doubtfully. 'It's not really what I do.'

'I could put some equity on the table.'

This time she'd really managed to shock me.

'You must be desperate.'

'Not yet, but we haven't been growing as fast this year. I need someone I can trust.'

I wasn't sure how to take this.

'VR and sex, though?' I said, turning back to the screen. 'Wouldn't this have happened by now, if it was going to?'

'She's not a *porn* experience,' she said. 'She's a customer service bot. She's there to talk to people. Especially the men, the straight ones, the ones that no one wants to match with. So she'll give them someone to confide in, gather data, help us understand them. She's a customer service enhancement tool. I think she's pretty cool, don't you?'

'Can you afford all this?'

'That's what the funding's there for. And anyway, it's not about what we spend. There are only two metrics in this game: customer acquisition and retention.'

'You think you'll get more customers with this bot, then?'

'That's the theory. People need someone to talk to.'

'I mean . . .' I trailed off.

I glanced around the studio.

As we left, Unity's words rippled gently through the speakers:

'I've been thinking of you,' she murmured, her voice golden and depthless. 'I was hoping to see you again. Tell me what you want,' she breathed. 'I'd like to get to know you.'

19

That weekend, Lara's friend Natasha had a party. Tom was working late and I had nothing better to do, so I agreed to go with her. I'd met Natasha before. In fact, I'd met her so many times that I would have classed her as someone I knew, except every time I saw her she made a point of forgetting my name. She always did it in the most apologetic way, which only made the whole thing even more insulting. She lived in Battersea in one of those white stucco houses. When we arrived, she led us to the kitchen where she was ironically heating a cheese fondue. She introduced me, for the fourth time, to her boyfriend Nico, who was sitting at the table with his friends. I recognized a handful of these people. They were boys that Lara knew from school.

I was never sure what Natasha did for a living. She seemed to get photographed a lot at events. She was peripherally involved with *Vogue* magazine, she produced fashion videos or something. Nico ran an incubator that funded and nurtured start-ups. They both had voluminous, shiny hair and were always lightly tanned, which was because they'd either just been skiing or on holiday to St Kitts, where Nico's parents owned one of those palm-shaded villas. Their dreamy friend Spence was leaning on the table, telling a story I'd heard before. It was about that time his brother Damo had dropped the E-bomb in Courchevel to get the Old Etonian hotelier to helicopter them out after a snowstorm. Almost every anecdote they told had something to do with where they'd been to school – a subject they rarely mentioned in public; it was reserved for times like this when they were all together. They'd all boarded at different institutions – Nico at Harrow, Natasha at Marlborough with Lara and Spence – but although these places were scattered around the country, they all seemed to know each other through some bizarre osmosis. There were fine distinctions between these schools, which provided them with endless hilarity: Millfield was basically for plebs and people who wanted to be footballers, Stowe was no longer second-rate and Dulwich was not as rapey as it used to be. Eton and Marlborough had 'changed', meaning their recruiting strategies now resulted in a majority of overseas students. Eton – which was always referred to as 'School', hence the E-bomb amusement – no longer specialized in the sorts of hereditary Etonians on which its reputation had been built. They were now not only outnumbered but practically on the verge of extinction, which explained why Damo's kid had been rejected last year. Lara had been one of these 'overseas students', although she never drew attention to it. And she wasn't the only one in the room; there was also Jay – whose parents were Indian – and Gabe, who had grown up in Egypt. Obviously, no one asked about my school. In the past, I'd made the mistake of mentioning that I'd grown up on the outskirts of London and had realized, too late, that this was in itself a faux pas. Although Jay had been gentle enough to tell me that he'd been there once for a warehouse party. They were curious about my existence but not in an attentive way. They just weren't sure what I was doing there. The school talk went on for a while.

'I tell people I'd never send my own kids private,' Natasha said, as she stirred the cheese, 'but then it's convenient for me to say that because, nowadays, I doubt we could afford it.'

Jay wasn't so fatalistic. 'I don't know, your hands are sort of tied if you live in London.'

He was an environmentalist who managed a water charity

in Mali. His humanitarianism obviously didn't extend to the rigours of the mind.

'You do your best for your own kids,' Nico said, as if that was the end of it. There was no way his parents wouldn't pay for his future kids to go to his old school. 'Although these days, you never know what you're going to get. Look at Lara,' he joked.

'More bread?' she replied, flicking a Gruyere-dipped piece of baguette onto his plate.

'All the greatest radicals were privately educated, babe,' Natasha said.

'Marx, Sartre,' Spence agreed. 'Kanye West, Virgil Abloh.'

Natasha smacked him affectionately with a fondue fork.

'So you and Lara work together?' she said to me.

'She's a writer,' Lara decided, apparently on the spur of the moment.

In fact, although I was grateful for the gesture – I had no desire to spend the rest of my life in spreadsheet hell – I still hadn't decided if I was going to take her up on her offer. Besides, I'd hardly describe the job as 'writing', although I knew she was trying to protect me. Now I had to lie to these people. Inevitably, Nico took it further.

'An actual starving artist?' he said. 'You don't meet many of those these days.'

I'd forgotten what a prick he was.

'You know, Natasha's mother works in publishing?' Jay decided to inform me. 'You should send her some of your work, she's lovely.'

I wondered if Lara was going to dig me out of this.

'No, really, you should try her,' he repeated unhelpfully. 'I mean, I'm sure she's inundated, but she'd read it.'

I saved Natasha from having to put me down.

'I'm more on the journalistic side,' I said.

'Reporting?'

'Confessional stuff, mostly.'

This wasn't that much of a lie. The editorial style at Openr was not averse to a confessional essay, preferably one that involved some sort of intimate personal trauma. These posts were always wrapped up in a wholesome lesson about beating hardship, shining a light on issues, etc. The cost to the writer was often high – no one was getting paid enough to bare their soul – but as long as the clicks kept coming, people did it.

To my relief, Natasha was already losing interest. I spent the rest of the night on the balcony, getting drunk with Spence. I gazed into his slightly coke-addled eyes and watched him rake his hands through his silky hair. He did something at Goldman Sachs and was on the verge of setting up a software company to automate the process of equities and derivatives clearing. Later, in the bathroom, I overheard him and Nico in the garden.

'Where's that little slice of suburban bliss gone?'

'You're relentless,' Nico said.

'She's fun.'

'I'd describe her as monosyllabic.'

'You don't know how to juice them up like I do.'

'I'd rather dip my dick in a blender.'

'Give the girl some credit,' Spence drawled, 'she's bagged herself a handsome Old Etonian.'

'She's always so tight-lipped with me. Is she shy? Or is this how people speak in Zone 6?'

'You know what they say.' Spence lit a cigarette. 'Tight lips, tight cunt.'

•

I left with Lara not long afterwards.

'So, you and Spence?' she enquired.

She said it as if she'd been hoping something would happen.

'He's DMed me already.'

'Man of action. Do you like him?'

'Not particularly. You?'

'He's just someone I grew up with.'

'You're a bit contemptuous of them, aren't you? Is that what I'm here for, to share your disapproval?'

'They're friends,' she said, as if it was a fact of life.

'But you don't buy into all of that?'

'Not really. It's too much of a bubble, that scene. I don't believe in it.'

I understood what she was saying but I think she also romanticized the alternative. To their credit, they were very clear about who they were and they were loyal towards each other. It wasn't about actively liking each other, it went deeper than that. Some of them had families that had known each other for generations, and they went to great lengths to keep it that way. Obviously, the point was exclusion. They wanted to protect their way of life – but that didn't make them insular. In fact, slumming it was part of the game. They weren't above fucking the odd outsider. They even married one occasionally, but it was always at their own discretion. They could come to you but you couldn't go to them. What they had was some semblance of society. There were plenty of things they lacked, but solidarity wasn't one of them. Even Lara had imbibed that credo. Whatever she said about 'that scene', it was there, regardless – part of the architecture of her life. She didn't seem to feel any requirement to actually like them.

I didn't say that, though. I said, 'Is it really that much of a bubble these days?'

I knew it was, but I also had the sense that things were changing. Even the Spences of this world were not completely insulated any more. Money now spoke louder than they did. It certainly spoke louder than nationality or race. Their own children would probably lead slightly different lives to theirs. They'd live in less salubrious postcodes. Their inheritances wouldn't stretch as far. There was more competition and not all of them would keep up. In a thousand tiny ways, even for them, the wind was coming in.

'They act like it is,' Lara said. 'It's so boring.'

'It's safe.'

'I don't want to be safe.'

'What do you want, then?'

I knew what she was going to say.

'I want to be free.'

•

Throughout the following week, we started texting more often. Even the power-dossing made a comeback in the form of a spontaneous walk around the city. We met in Regent's Park and walked to Notting Hill, then circled down to the Serpentine, where we sat in the cafe and drank lattes. In the gallery, there was an exhibition by the Iranian artist Shirin Neshat. Lara bought a copy of the catalogue, a heavy hardback filled with monochrome self-portraits. It described the artist's parents urging their daughter 'to take risks, to learn, to see the world'. She spent a long time leafing through it, staring at its thick, glossy pages.

•

The time I spent with Lara felt private whereas the time I spent with Tom was somehow porous and shot through with Lara's presence. Everything was coloured by her thoughts, feelings, casual updates. We'd fallen unthinkingly back into a shared stream of consciousness. It was something I realized I'd missed and found difficult to resist. I went to the French House for dinner with Tom that Friday but I messaged Lara in the bathroom. She sent back a photo of herself at a party – she was in a black velvet dress. She was at the Institute of Directors, I recognized the brocade wallpaper. She said:

This place is full of Tories

There's a lot of bad dancing going on

What are you doing?

Work party

Some VC thing

Come

I'd been to these events before, Ed had occasionally forced me to chaperone him.

I've met some guy from the Department for Business

I asked him what it felt like to have fucked the country, I mean really fucked the country

What did he say?

That he found my naivety adorable and did I want some coke

I think he thinks I'm some sort of call girl, he keeps asking if we do girl-on-girl

It's going well, then?

I hate everybody here

The next day, she messaged me from home.

What are you doing?

You're not with Bateman are you?

I didn't answer, so she sent me the view from where she was sitting.

She was watching *Sex and the City 2*.

> Why?

Hungover

> I haven't seen it

Carrie's marriage is in trouble because Mr Big ate takeaway on the sofa, so the girls have gone to Abu Dhabi to talk about feminism

We discussed the high camp of the Middle East and she sent me a photo of Samantha on a camel.

That's why you don't see this kind of camp in Iran. It's because the British never colonized it. It's easy to laugh at the trashiness of the Emiratis but it's all British, we exported it

> Not so much actual homosexuality, though

I'm sure we tried.

She said that camp was a national sport in Britain because the whole country had cognitive dissonance, that we had to talk in doublespeak because we couldn't make sense of who we were.

When I first arrived here for school I couldn't understand what anyone was saying. The place looked like a military barracks but they all spoke like saucy vicars. All that stuff about spotted dick and crumpet

> The sound of willow on leather

And pantomimes, what are those about? We went to
Cinderella, it was terrifying

She paused for a photo of Carrie's turban.

It was relentless

People called it irony but it wasn't really, it went deeper
than that. I think it's what allows our politicians to be so
ruthless, and the rest of us to go along with it. We're not
capable of taking anything seriously

When it came to talking about 'the British', sometimes she
said 'they' and sometimes 'we'. She did it unconsciously, I
think, swapping according to who she was talking to.

So back to Bateman. Why are you being so cagey?

You know why, I thought.

20

It was a Wednesday, which was drinks night at Openr. I had no desire to spend my own time at what was basically a team-building exercise but there was an unspoken rule that everyone in the office had to go. *Cultivating community* was one of the company's three Core Behaviours, the others being *Do work you believe in* and *Break boundaries.*

Georgia Marchant, Openr's creative director, was the instigator of this activity. Georgia was small, bouncy and ambitious. Her accent suggested an expensive education. In another world, she might have been a barrister, or maybe an upmarket estate agent. She would have looked like a quintessential English rose if it hadn't been for her 'style', which changed every few months as if she'd transformed into a different person. She seemed to drift randomly through looks according to what she'd come across online, as if she'd connected briefly with some new tribe, immersed herself completely and then lost interest. Today her hair was bleached white blonde and she was wearing some sort of raw-edged tracksuit. Despite her slightly manic appearance, Georgia had a demon-like focus on her job. Her daily life was guided by efficiency, her calves chiselled from the gym. She talked fast, her sentences filled with peppy quotes like a Peloton machine. She liked to send group messages that said things like 'Let's have fun with this!' and 'Let's break boundaries!' She also had a tendency to cc the entire team into any exchange that had annoyed her, a habit she tried to pass off as transparency but that we all knew was just a way of warning people off. In a sense, I understood why she was like this: she was just trying to get things done. On the other hand, it was hard not to wonder who she might have been without the incentives of the job. That night, even in the darkness of the bar, she looked a little exhausted by it all.

'To levelling up,' she said, raising her glass.

'To levelling up,' echoed Marie, a tall, cheerful woman from accounts. Marie had just come out of an open relationship, as she told me every time I saw her.

'Saudé,' said Aliya, who was Lara's personal assistant, her gravelly Essex accent softened slightly with Portuguese. She was by far the oldest in the group, she must have been in her early forties. She was a tiny woman, recently divorced, with a tattoo that said *No one breaks my heart.*

Later in the night, I saw that Marie was unsteady on her feet. She'd spilt her drink down her top and although she hadn't noticed, the suits at the bar certainly had. Her shirt was almost transparent as she waited patiently for the barman. I looked for Lara but I couldn't see her. I tried and failed to catch Marie's attention. Across the bar, the suits were openly leering at her. One of them got up, goaded by his mates, and asked if he could buy her a drink. He managed to get her talking. She looked flattered. I watched as he ordered her a vodka. I wasn't sure if I should intervene. It wasn't long before he was leading her outside, pushing her along as if herding a cow. I glanced around for Lara but I couldn't see her, so I followed them outside. I tried to take Marie's hand but she wouldn't let me.

'Let her go,' I said.

I went for her arm, but he pulled her away from me. Within seconds, he'd bundled her into a cab. I banged on the window but although she heard me, she looked blank as if she didn't know me. As the driver pulled away, I thought of calling the police, but there was nothing to report, so I stood there lamely. After a while, Aliya wandered out. She stood beside me with her caipirinha.

'Bagged herself a banker, did she?' she said.

21

'You'll be rich,' I said. Tom had just come out of the shower and joined me on the balcony. His new contract was lying on the table. After fifteen years at Churchill Analytics, he was now a freelance Marketing Consultant. Grace was moving to Neura Therapeutics to lead the Eudaxa campaign and Tom was joining as her second in command.

'What does it feel like?' I said.

'Good, although that money won't go as far as you think. I'll be lucky to net one twenty after tax.' He looked around the flat dispassionately. 'I mean, I suppose I'll be able to get a mortgage on this place.'

'You really know how to charm a girl, don't you?'

'I can make you a spreadsheet if you like.'

'I hope this isn't going to your head.'

'I'm sure it will,' he put his arm around me.

'You think you're a big deal now?'

'Does it turn you on?'

He wasn't entirely joking. I remembered Marie at the bar last night. I mean it doesn't *hurt*, I thought privately, although the truth was, more than anything, it made me worry that he might lose interest in me. Things might be different now. Stock up, stock down and all of that. I wondered what our respective desirability ratings now were. He must have seen the look on my face because he suddenly changed tack.

'It's only money,' he said. 'I'm more worried that I'll hardly have a chance to see you.'

'I don't mind you being busy.'

'Well, I do. I don't want it to be like this forever.'

I was surprised by this confession; he'd always seemed so absorbed by his job.

'Listen,' he said, 'you make me very happy.'

'You make me happy too,' I said, a little stunned.

I wasn't used to describing my feelings. I'd become used to feeling numb, and sensed he was in a similar position. He looked at me as if we'd just veered into unknown territory.

He lifted me onto the ledge and kissed me.

'I don't think I'll ever get enough of this,' he said.

As we made love on the balcony that night I could see half of London underneath us. We were on the eighteenth floor and I had a vivid sense that the city was losing its hold on me, as if I no longer had to look to it for hope, opportunity, survival. I'd spent my life in its velvet grip but I didn't feel like that any more. I felt that anything was possible. It was exhilarating. I couldn't even feel the cold. Lara was wrong, I decided, about needing things from other people. Not everyone could be like her. There was more than one way of being free.

·

Lying in bed that night, I watched him sleep beside me. Sometimes, once the euphoria had passed, I had a strange feeling about Tom. It was something to do with the awareness that whatever was happening between us, it was fundamentally out of our control. Some primordial key had turned. It was unnerving when you thought about it. I wanted to take credit for the happiness I felt. I had the sense I'd achieved something. But the more I went over it in my mind, the more I realized it wasn't in my hands. All those years in which nothing had happened – the bad connections that went nowhere, the bad sex, the uncertainty, the gut-wrenching instability – none of that had been under my control. People suffered from a lack of love under wholly arbitrary conditions.

Despite the surreal quality of those days, there was one thing I knew for sure. It felt good. It was a revelation. My hours were filled with intense well-being. I lived through moments of real joy. It was something I'd never experienced before.

'I'm so glad I met you,' I said.

He didn't answer immediately, he was staring at the ceiling.

'I meant what I said about work being busy,' he answered, after a while. 'I don't want that to come between us.'

'I don't mind, it's only work.'

'Well, I do. I'm thinking of getting out.'

'You want to quit? You haven't even started yet.'

'I know, but I'd like to leave eventually. I've been thinking about it for a while.'

'Are you serious? What would you do?'

'I'm not sure, but I want to get away. At least for a while, so I can think about it.'

'Where would you go?'

'Not just me,' he said. 'I'm asking if you would come with me?'

I'd barely registered what he'd said beyond the fact that he was talking about the future, which filled me with satisfaction.

'Come where?' I asked eventually.

He reached into the drawer by his bed and pulled out an old photo.

'La Gomera,' he said. 'It's one of the Canaries.'

'It's an island? Have you been there before?'

'When I was a kid, a long time ago.'

'It's pretty.'

'You don't think it's too remote?'

'No, I think it would be an adventure.'

'I can't promise anything, of course. Don't mention this to Grace, by the way.'

22

'It's been almost fifty years since the monoamine hypothesis was conceived.' Grace had opened the window in her kitchen. It was Saturday morning, Niall and Evie had gone out and she'd invited Tom and I for coffee, which I quickly realized was actually a debrief on their new gig. It was hard to concentrate on what she was saying.

She stopped mid-sentence. 'I hope you're listening. Is this what you two are going to be like now?'

She lit a cigarette and waited patiently until she had our attention. 'So, the monoamine hypothesis proposed that low levels of serotonin, norepinephrine and dopamine were indicators of depression, usually in the form of feelings of low status in dominance hierarchies.'

'We already know this,' Tom said.

'I know, and we're going over it again.'

He raised an eyebrow at me apologetically.

'So,' she continued patiently, 'the theory was that artificially increasing these chemicals would alleviate depressive symptoms. The initial treatments were discovered by accident when Hoffmann-La Roche were trying to treat tuberculosis. That was when they first noticed that iproniazid was giving their patients feelings of euphoria.'

'The first antidepressant,' Tom said, as if to make the point that he didn't need the lecture.

'Exactly. Although it was only used off-label. It took another decade for the first branded treatment to come out.

Tofranil wasn't released until the late 1950s. That established a new class – tricyclics.'

I felt his hand slide across my knee.

'You seem to be finding it difficult to concentrate,' Grace said. 'You know I'm going to test you on this later?'

She was quite convincing at cracking the whip.

'So,' she persisted, tapping her cigarette on the window ledge, 'the main issue with depression is that it's badly defined. As far as we know, the causes are spread across several different factors: genetic, environmental and psychological. There isn't even a lab test for it.'

'Everyone knows what it feels like, though,' I said.

I felt the need to at least pretend that I was interested in what she was talking about.

'To some extent. The idea of melancholia, for example, has an ancient history. It goes back to the Greeks. But our relationship with it has always been opaque, to say the least. Even today, our classifications are pretty vague. Patients are supposed to show at least five of eight possible symptoms: sadness, loss of pleasure, insomnia, tiredness, feelings of worthlessness, poor concentration, agitation and suicidal thoughts.'

'Sounds like an average day at the office.'

'Exactly. Which is why the biomedical model is contentious. If you look at research from the 1990s when this approach was first entrenched, it's all very loose and abstract. The results never pointed in one direction. The idea that depression can be treated with a pill – that it's just a chemical imbalance – a lot of that stuff was oversold. It was all marketing copy. It was storytelling, really. Which is where we come in.'

She reached over to the kitchen counter and picked up a box of pills.

'The product,' she said, cradling it in her hand. 'So, let's run through its USPs: firstly, this is a drug that doesn't have the usual side effects. Both tricyclics and SSRIs are notorious for lowering sex drive. They're also known for dulling emotional responses. Neither of these are a problem with Eudaxa.'

Grace stopped speaking, as if she wasn't quite sure how to describe the next part.

'The thing about this stuff,' she said eventually, 'is that it brings people out of themselves. It helps them overcome those parts of themselves that are holding them back.'

'I don't follow,' Tom said.

'It helps them open up.'

'What's in it?'

'It's some sort of MDA derivative.'

'So it's a psychedelic?'

'Exactly.'

'It's like Ecstasy?'

'In some respects, although the pharmacodynamics are different.'

He didn't seem any clearer.

'Look, they think this drug has mainstream potential,' she said. 'They think it could become a household name. That means our competition isn't only other drugs when it comes to marketing – it's news, sports, celebrity gossip, basically the media landscape as a whole. Prozac picked up quickly through coverage in mainstream news outlets – *The New York Times*, *Vogue*, *Forbes*. People wrote memoirs about it. There were songs written about the stuff. It was *fashionable*.' Grace paused to let her point sink in.

'Are we launching here first?' Tom asked.

'And in the US. Simultaneously.'

'So, the American landscape will dominate.'

'Exactly. And with social media, we're going to have to think globally. It's a tricky balance, because we'll be reaching out to professionals as well as the general public.'

'Can you say anything you want?' I asked.

They were talking about this stuff as if they were selling sweets.

'In a sense.' Grace stabbed her cigarette out, wrapped it in a tissue and threw it in the bin.

'You can't *lie*,' she said, 'but beyond that, yeah, you can say whatever you like. As long as it works.'

'Don't people just want the truth?'

'Of course they do. And we release the science as soon as possible. Unfortunately, that isn't usually enough to capture the public imagination.'

'I thought you said people wanted information they could trust?' I said to Tom.

'We don't *misinform* them,' he said.

'But you spin the message?'

'In a way. What we do is communicate in a style that the target market can relate to.'

'You don't think people will feel patronized?'

'Some will. In fact, the public collectively often knows more than the people running these companies. But we can't get caught up in too much detail. Our job is to cut through the noise.'

'The problem,' Grace said, 'is that no one is managing the message any more. No one has that kind of power. It's not that the truth is hidden exactly, it's that it doesn't garner much attention. When I started in this game, the goal was clear for people like me: to control the narrative. That's all anyone cared about. That narrative might have been self-serving but it offered a framework, at least, within which the rest of us could function. I'm not sure how many of these companies realize it, but it's not possible to do that any more. The ecosystem now is too competitive. No one has that kind of power. We're left with no choice but to compete if we want to make any kind of impact. Which means going up against a lot of extremely hard-driving content. It's an arms race, everyone battling for the same segments of attention. It isn't easy to make a dent in that. You have to harness people's emotions and you have to do it in real time. This is the ad-based internet,' she said resignedly. 'I hate to say it, but this is where we are.'

'What we end up putting out is entertainment, really,' Tom said, 'which means drama, conflict, noise.'

'In medicine, though?'

'That's the way it's going.'

'You're exaggerating.'

'I wish I was.'

'All conflict is good conflict,' Grace said drily. 'I don't even try and resist it any more.'

23

I was due to start on the content desk that week. I'd decided to go along with the idea for a change of scenery as much as anything else. There was a window by my new workspace, although it overlooked a concrete wall and the extraction pipe from the restaurant next door.

Lara texted: Do you want come to Gables?

I had no idea what she was talking about. Where are you? I asked. I hadn't seen her that day. She often wasn't in the office and her diary was a black box that Aliya guarded like the Pentagon.

She replied: I'm going to this. Do you want come? It's in Margate. She had attached an invitation to some sort of exhibition. You should come, we could make a weekend of it.

Who's going? I asked, expecting more adventures with Spence and the gang.

She replied: I was thinking just the two us.

I wasn't sure what to make of this, although I had remembered that Gables was the beach house her parents owned. Her father's family was originally from Kent and he'd grown up in the countryside near Dungeness. He'd bought a disused pump house on the beach that he'd turned into a holiday cottage. I'd seen photos but never visited.

I need to get away from work, she wrote. It'll be fun.

When? I replied.

She answered: After the party.

I thought about it. Just the two of us, though?

She paused, three dots hovering.
Why not?

.

The next day was annual review day. We were all gathered in the conference room. We'd sat through hours of the company's financials and were now moving onto a talk by Georgia about market trends.

'What we are witnessing today,' Georgia began, 'is a consumer revolution.' She was in her comfort zone, a tiny ball of energy in Nikes and a tight black tracksuit. She was perched on a stool, her presentation projected on a huge screen behind her. After she finished going over the numbers, she moved on to 'insights for the coming year'. The slide's title was *Relationships & The Future: Innovation in Online Services.*

'The conspicuous consumer of the twentieth century,' she said, 'is being replaced. We live more urban lives. We are concentrated geographically more than ever. Many of us are educated to the point that we might define ourselves by our cultural capital, rather than by our spending power alone. Items that we might present to the world include original pieces of art, creative crafts, and tote bags bought from cultural sites like museums and bookshops.'

She paused to take a sip from her thermos. Then continued by flicking onto an image of what looked like a computer-generated forest. With the lights dimmed, models in nude bodysuits started running through a veld, wind chimes tinkling on the soundtrack as they drifted, gazelle-like, through the dawn.

'Our consumption is discreet. For those who can afford it, income is spent on insurance, private education and other intangibles that provide security above all else. We will spend on high-quality foods – organic vegetables, for example – and also on holistic practices like massage and meditation. We are adept at delaying gratification.'

Lara caught my eye and pulled a bored face. It was a rare slip at work that made me wonder what she really thought of Georgia.

'Those of us with children are more likely than ever to outsource their care in order to optimize our potential in the workplace. The roles we desire most are more than merely lucrative, they offer emotional rewards, often with the goal of improving society at large.'

Someone raised their hand but Georgia ignored them.

'Gender is increasingly fluid. Sexual norms are open to creative reinvention. Familial roles are ambiguous and free. We exercise our right to become the most fulfilled versions of ourselves, to explore our innermost desires. Choice is queen. Consent is our mantra.'

The video faded from the veld into what looked like some kind of spa. The models continued to gyrate, moving from one environment to the next in a constant flow of motion, their form-fitting sportswear fading to reveal a range of mono-chrome swimsuits. Like Barbies, they seemed to tour the globe in a weird array of random settings.

'The ethos is one of well-being, fulfilment, and of striving for the highest ethical standards,' Georgia purred, her bleached hair changing colour with the wash of dappled lights. 'And that extends to what we look for in our partners.'

'Can I ask a question?' someone stalled her. It was our business manager, Nicole. 'I just want to ask how Openr comes into all of this? Would it be possible to be more specific? We already have a code of conduct for our users. Our merch is carbon neutral. We're B Corp certified, which means we've been vetted for justice and inclusion. I mean, could you throw some light on how we might apply all of this to *relationships*? You mention choice. Perhaps we could start there.'

Georgia paused, seeming a bit nonplussed. I got the impression she'd given at least some version of this talk before and had been hoping to dial it in again.

'Well,' she said. 'What we should be doing is thinking holistically. I mean, we might be working with these values but are we *communicating* them? Is every one of our customers *experiencing* them? Are we making sure that everyone's choices are truly being respected?'

It was Nicole's turn to look confused. 'We do focus on ethics wherever possible,' she said. 'But of course, some of our users get more out of the service than others.'

'Perhaps you'd like to expand on that?'

'Well,' Nicole continued, sounding unsure where this was heading. 'We're an introductions service. Obviously, we attract a certain customer – people who are open-minded, people who are looking for something different – but of course there's more to it than that. Our users have high standards for themselves. They're searching for something – let's call it self-fulfilment – and they often have specific needs that they struggle to satisfy elsewhere. We do our best to encourage matches but, frankly, there are winners and losers. And these disparities have only gotten worse as our user base has grown. What we're seeing is a clustering around certain profiles – the ones that were already doing well. And the problem is' – she looked a little uncomfortable – 'there's nothing *fair* about it. We're supposed to be "a safe space to play", but as we scale the business up, more and more of our users are finding themselves with no matches at all. It's just not very' – she searched for the right word – '*inclusive*. To be honest, it's one of our toughest challenges.'

I thought about the headless torsos I'd seen in the Male Bi/Gay section, most of them light-skinned Asians trying to hide their faces in a bid to game the system. They'd long since learnt that their ethnicity was a drag on clicks – an awkward truth that was difficult to ignore when so many men in that section had stated 'no rice, no curry'. There were other embarrassingly off-brand discrepancies. White women under thirty swept the board as long as they were reasonably thin. Over forty, they fell off a cliff, overshadowed even by their plus-size sisters.

'I don't want to make this about race,' Nicole continued, 'but it's a good place to start. I've had experiences with men who've only matched with me because I'm white. I recognize that's a privilege of sorts, but I'd also say it comes from a dangerous place, because there's no doubt that some of these men view me as a target. I'm an ego boost for them. It's like they think it's a bigger win to show the world they can dominate a white girl. It's a form of internalized racism and it isn't always easy to detect.'

Marie from accounts put her hand up.

'I've never understood,' she said, 'why people are so determined to gloss over the outright racism, colourism, ageism and featurism in dating. We always use the word "preferences". Why? Why not call it what it is? It's bigotry, pure and simple. Systemic, historically entrenched prejudice.'

'Another thing,' Aliya piped up. 'We have a fetish lifestyle section. There's a whole race-play scene on there. There are guys who'll happily call our users whores, sluts, bitches, cum dumpsters, you name it – but they'll always draw the line at the n-word. Why? Why do they stop there? It's literally the only thing they won't say. I think it's because there's some real misogyny there and it's socially acceptable.'

'If you want your customers to trust you,' Georgia offered, 'you're going to have to confront this stuff head on. Perhaps you could look at the wider cultural context. Ask your users to have a conversation about *why* they want the things they want. Ask them to *own* their desires.'

'We've tried that,' Nicole said. 'We've had panels on it. We've had polls. There have been think pieces. Trust me, we've worked on this a lot. Our customers seem to like engaging with these issues, but once they get online, under the cloak of anonymity, it falls apart. It's a real problem. And I'll tell you this, it's slowing penetration.'

I heard one of the execs behind me snorting quietly.

'What we should be seeing at this stage is deeper penetration, particularly here in Britain, which is our most mature market.'

The whole row behind me started giggling. Even Lara looked up from her phone. A little nervous, Georgia peered at her tablet. She fumbled with the screen, clattering her fingers on its surface as if summoning inspiration.

'Well,' she finally announced, 'this might be something we could turn into a campaign. It could be something Openr could pioneer. It might distinguish our marketing presence. Work with the struggle.' She glanced at the clock on the wall behind my head. 'I'm sure our creatives can have some fun with that.'

'You can't socialize this stuff,' I heard one of the execs say under his breath. 'Are we seriously here now? What the fuck?'

Georgia motioned for the lights to come back on. Nicole looked exhausted. She closed her eyes.

'Thank you very much.' Georgia gave a little bow. A thin sputter of applause played out as the projection flicked to black.

24

That night, I went to Soho House. Tom had been in Cambridge with Grace all week so I went alone to meet Lara. I'd noticed that Tom had started messaging me more. I think it was because he'd caught on to Lara's inimitable presence. He'd even started asking me about her. He wanted to know what sort of boss she was. I knew he'd googled her because he'd made a casual comment about her being 'one of those girls' – the ones with ethical-luxury beliefs to go with their ethical-luxury wardrobes. It didn't help that she video-called me randomly 'to talk about work', although it was rarely only about that. During the last call – the one about tonight – she'd spent the whole time referring to Shoreditch House as 'Wetherspoons East'. I'd had to sit there patiently while Tom pulled a face each time she did it. Lara, on the other hand, wasn't quite so dismissive. She seemed intrigued by him. Or, more accurately, she was mystified.

I made it to Dean Street around seven. She was supposed to have left my name on the door but she hadn't, she'd either forgotten or 'forgotten' – I wouldn't have put it past her to have left me waiting just to sharpen things between us. She wasn't in the business of being undervalued. It took a long time for her to come downstairs.

I'd envisioned a debrief on the day's events – she rarely held back from talking work – but once we'd made it inside I realized that Nico and Natasha were there. They'd been to see some film that Natasha had been involved with – something about David Bowie and his influence on fashion.

Tom sent me a picture of his hotel room.

I replied:

I love hotels

Me too

Architectural study #2 – The Hotel

compare and contrast with The Flat-share

Obviously this would require research

I'm going to be in a lot of them over the next few months

Are you inviting me?

If you want to come

I paused to give this idea some thought. It opened up a world of possibilities. There was nothing in my contract that said I couldn't work remotely occasionally, I just had to make my presence felt in the office three days a week. On the other hand, Lara wouldn't be impressed. It would have to happen under her radar.

I surfaced to discover the three of them debating whether Bowie was gay-gay, as in sex with men gay, or just queer in a more abstract, romantic kind of way.

'He definitely slept with men,' Natasha said. 'He admitted going to bed with boys at school.'

'Didn't we all,' Nico said.

'I didn't.' Lara caught my eye.

'Questionable,' Nico said. 'Why are you being so coy? We're all friends here.'

'You did at college,' I said.

I knew this for a fact because she'd left me for one.

'Now, now, girls,' Nico said.

'We've all been there,' Natasha added pointlessly. 'But look at us now, the best of buds.'

She gave me a mild smile. I wanted to stab her smooth, complacent face with one of those little fondue forks.

Spence arrived later that night with a tanned blonde in low-cut jeans. She had a wrist full of those rainbow thread bracelets that make you think 'gap year'. I didn't acknowledge him, but he wasn't fazed.

Later that night, he caught me in the street trying to get reception on my phone. I'd had a text from Ashley and needed to reply but it was still playing up and I couldn't afford to fix it.

'Where did you get to the other night?' he said.

'I always disappear at midnight.'

'Are you calling me a prince?'

'I'm calling you a prick.'

'Steady on,' he said. 'Why did you ignore my messages?'

'You know what they say, Spence?'

'What's that?'

'Big mouth, small cock.'

He looked nonplussed.

'I think your wifey's made a friend,' I said.

In the lobby, his date had struck up a conversation with a smooth-looking silver fox.

Once he'd loped back over to her, I managed to get Ashley on the phone. She'd locked herself out of the flat again. I spent a while helping her find the key, the one we'd bought together, the one we'd hidden precisely for these occasions. She was so wasted she couldn't remember where we'd put it. I stood on the pavement for a while, coaching her until she'd made it back inside.

'Are you OK, Ash?' I said.

'I'm fine,' she said. 'I'm totally fine.'

Afterwards, I wanted to speak to Tom but he wasn't answering his phone.

I needed a drink. I turned to go back in but the woman on reception gave me a look. It was the same girl who'd let me in before.

'Sorry,' she said, 'are you a member?'

•

My first assignment in 'content' was a piece on BDSM. I knew nothing about the subject. This was obvious from the post I'd written, which I was due to upload that night. I'd been instructed to file it in writing and then present it on video for socials. It was embarrassing. I had the journalistic equivalent of stage fright. Mid-morning, I videocalled Tom and made him read it back to me.

'*Cock Torture for Feminists*,' he read, slowly.

'I didn't choose the title.'

'Who did?'

'Georgia.'

'I thought you said you were the ideas person?'

'I'm on probation.'

He continued reading: 'BDSM has always had a difficult relationship with feminism but maybe we can learn something from it. The idea of signing a contract before sex is something that has crossed over from the business world, but could this be an idea that we could all learn something from? Should we all be expressing our desires more clearly? If we can't be direct about what we want, how can we expect others to understand us?'

There was a pause.

'You think it's bullshit,' I said.

'I wouldn't go that far.

Do you believe it?'

'I'm not being paid to believe it.'

'It's not sexy, though, is it? It's about bureaucracy.'

'You think it's a turn-off?'

'Yes.'

'It's a talking point,' I said.

'I know, I get it. I think you're doing well. That title, though.' He pulled a sad face.

'It's clickbait. They're trying to push things harder.'

'I mean . . .'

'Oh God.'

He stifled a smile.

'It's not a joke,' I said dejectedly. 'This is my life.'

25

During the following weeks, I found myself falling into strange sleep patterns. I'd started staying at Tom's at the weekends. There didn't seem much point in going home and I liked sleeping in his bed, but work, as ever, was imposing itself. The office had been manic in the build-up to the party but, more importantly, I was struggling with my new role. I now had a target score for engagement that I had to hit every day – each 'click', 'like' and 'share' tracked and saved for analytics. I could just about handle the work but it didn't come easily. It was hard to calm down after I'd logged off. My brain was constantly switched on. In some ways, I preferred the dull rhythms of data management. It didn't fill my soul with joy but at least it didn't keep me up at night.

Awake again in the early hours, I found myself scrolling in the dark. I tried to tell myself I was doing research – that it would save me time in the office – but the truth was I wasn't working. More accurately, I was hungry. I wanted to be fed. Anything would do as long as it blocked my thoughts, which were otherwise constantly humming with ideas for the next day's supply of 'content'. I drifted in and out of different territories only when I saw them suggested to me. There was an anaesthetic pleasure to it, a trance-like submission to the logic of the feed.

I gorged compulsively on what it gave me. I yielded to the next offering and then the next. The pornography of it all was barely veiled. It was analogous to the kind of thing you might see if you typed 'Intense Deep Throat Gagging Blowjob' into your search box, which I did. I gave myself an orgasm, then I moved onto *The New York Times*. I couldn't stop gorging – it all went in, a shapeless mass of human effluvium. I couldn't stop and I didn't want to. Instead, I opened myself wider to the penetration of millions of strangers, each one selected and ranked on my behalf by a process I not only couldn't understand but that kept evolving as the world unfurled. The experience was compelling to the point of stupor. My synapses snapped into empty air, a blur of frenzied but memoryless diversion that kept me mesmerized for hours.

During my crash course on sadomasochism, I'd learnt there were more submissives in the world than there were dominants. It was something that caused problems on 'the scene' – and maybe, less visibly, for the rest of us. Everything was arranged to serve the masochist's desire. It was the sadist who had to do the work. They had to make the 'user' feel something – to invade them, to shove things down their throats – anything to bring them some relief from their everyday lives.

Tom lay beside me, illuminated by the screen as these restless nights unfolded. I was usually tired in the mornings. Although I'd hardly describe these nights as 'awake', they lacked both the sensuality of dreams and the healing quality of sleep. They were just blank intervals of textureless, mindless absorption – a kind of death. I wasn't there.

Occasionally, the night would be punctuated by moments of lucidity. I'd surface unexpectedly, a sharp spurt of endorphins pumping through me. I'd feel elated. Euphoric, even. Then it would fade into a pleasurable warmth. Sometimes I touched Tom as he lay beside me. He felt more real somehow when he was sleeping. The sensation would arouse another flood of happiness, this one overwhelming everything. I knew it couldn't last, it would eventually fade just like everything else. But in those moments, it was sublime. I felt preternaturally awake.

It was during one of these restless nights that I looked up Openr's analytics. The company was doing OK. Its numbers were rising slowly. I tried to figure out what was driving sales and I had to admit that Lara had a point. The 'talking points' did have an impact. There was a buzz of emotion around the platform that went beyond its basic function. You could practically feel it coming off the screen. I had no idea who these people were but their feelings were paying my rent. On the other hand, I wouldn't have described this congregation as a community. I looked up my BDSM article. There was a long comment section underneath:

> Feminism: fucking up normal men so rich bitches can get off

> These hoes are confused. The more freedom they get the more they want to be abused. It's like they can't respect a man who doesn't have the balls to tame them

I looked up 'violence girl' and the *Harvard Gazette* said it was rising. Then I looked up 'murder girl' and there were over 80 million hits. I looked up 'woman killer' and found a government review on domestic violence, linking the rise in incidents to a rise in teen suicides and terrorism. The feelings were real, I thought, as I scrolled through the pale grey panels of the analytics dashboard, but they were also fundamentally abstract. They couldn't exist without the organization of millions of tonnes of lithium-ion. And this was the worst of it – they had no point. The whole thing was unbelievably stupid. It was all froth on an ocean of crap, more than you could wade through in a million lifetimes. The numbers on the feedback charts blinked back at me, obliviously. I turned back to the Harvard study, then I made the mistake of clicking on one of the suggested stories underneath it. It was a promotional piece for an upcoming documentary called *The Extremist In Your Living Room.*

Are our boys being radicalized online?

Elaine Monae, a mother of two, was looking over her son's shoulder when she caught him uploading a cartoon of Adolf Hitler to his TikTok. Shocked, she stopped her son immediately. She'd assumed the cartoon had an anti-fascist message and was horrified to discover that it was instead an image of a well-known right-wing meme.

This story was followed by a second scene:

In college, Danny Voss became depressed and started skipping class. He was convinced he could improve his life through self-help videos on YouTube, which was where he discovered thousands of hours of content filled with racism, misogyny and hate.

The article went on to discuss the murder of the Labour MP Jo Cox by Thomas Mair, a middle-aged gardener and Nazi sympathizer from Kilmarnock, who had shot her dead with a .22 rifle a few years earlier. It conflated Mair with the schoolboys, painting all three of them as pawns in a world where seemingly ordinary people could be radicalized online. What the journalist didn't do was address the question of what made this violence spill over into real life. What separated the killers like Mair from the merely alienated or disaffected? If there were other factors, it seemed important to understand them.

Above the article was a photo of the boys. Voss looked well-groomed – too well-groomed, his hair parted neatly at the side. The picture had been taken as he sat at his laptop, an ominous black void on the kitchen table. The Monaes, by contrast, were posed in their conservatory, the whole family lined up on a flowery sofa. Voss was overweight, his giant T-shirt hanging limply over a pair of sagging jeans. He looked younger than his years, his face barely adolescent. He seemed mortally pissed off.

'I found him posting violent memes about women,' his mother said. 'He thinks it's all a joke but I didn't bring him up like this.'

There was something comical about this kid and his fla-grant craving for transgression. It reminded me of Openr in some ways. I got the feeling these appetites weren't rare. They were part of a vast, amorphous id that underpinned everything around me. Voss's attempt at rebellion was childish but also desperate. He'd already exhausted whatever sustenance his meme-war was going to bring him. Things moved too fast. He was already outmoded, a straggler in a marketplace that fed purely on the kind of subversion that had attracted him in the first place. It commoditized what shock value still existed and distributed it immediately to an audience of billions faster than you could have said the word 'taboo'. In an online landscape without boundaries, this kid's rebellion was a joke. Real insubordination required a line to cross. Without limits, no offence was possible. There was a pornography to this too in that, like porn, it never stood still. It escalated. You had to keep searching for harder material just to maintain the same effect, and eventually you became numb to that too. I noticed a photo of the pope on his T-shirt. *Catholic Boy Summer*, it said in Times New Roman. So he'd entered his conservative phase. In such an overheated market for dissent, it was the last remaining move.

'What are you reading?' Tom had woken up.

I shut my screen down before he had a chance to see it.

'Not much,' I said. 'I'm reading about men.'

'Oh shit.'

I didn't really want him to know that I'd been googling 'sex murder' at 4 a.m.

He turned to kiss me and I felt myself relax for the first time in hours. My body softened. I surrendered completely, losing myself in something that at least felt worthwhile. I didn't resist when he took my phone and slid it gently out of my hand.

26

The party had already started by the time Tom and I arrived. *Openr: a safe space to play*, it said in white lights above the door. The foyer was already packed, people filtering slowly into the ballroom. Inside, the place was illuminated by hundreds of tiny hanging lamps. Tactile sculptures wound around the tables, their long shadows sprawled across the walls. Music reverberated from a stage on which three giant screens had been erected. The screens played trance-like animations, a group of nude figures circling in space, genderless and bathed in light, their skin plastic and unreal, their features lost in Delphic bliss. The virtual hair on the animated characters blew in a virtual wind, their bodies penetrated one another, a Gordian knot of seamless fornication. Tom seemed mesmerized by the display, staring at it for a long time.

'So, this is what you do when I'm not around?' he said.

'It's work.'

I was suddenly unsure if I should have brought him. I recognized various e-girls in the crowd, content makers, models and other sub-celebrities. Although most of these people had built their images online, the doorman had confiscated their phones, locking them into small black pouches which hung delicately from their wrists. One woman passed by in a silver thong, her breasts loose beneath a pink gauze top. Another was wearing bunny ears, a bunny tail and nothing else. The crowd was clumped into small groups, some of them already making out. Hostesses carried trays of condoms as guests reclined in the shadows, some of them lying on the Openr-branded otto-mans that had been provided.

I came across Lara in the VIP room, surrounded by men in button down shirts. I recognized the owner of a private equity firm and some fund manager I'd seen around. He was from the Chinese venture capital conglomerate Taizong Capital. Next to Lara was Bob de la Puente, Mindbot's group head of invest-ment advisory. Lara leaned over to kiss me, then introduced me to her colleagues.

'So, this is Mary, our data manager. She's also doing some great work on content. She's new at Openr, it's her first party.'

The fund manager introduced himself as Aaron Charles. He handed me a card, then leaned down and kissed my neck. The force of his aftershave hit me like a brick. I also got the impression he hadn't showered. I stepped back as he slid an arm around my waist. I caught the filthy look on Tom's face and wrenched myself away before he had a chance to react. Lara grimaced almost imperceptibly. She gave me a glance that said: *Don't fuck this up.*

'So, what we were saying,' she continued, finessing any awkwardness, placing a hand on Tom's shoulder and none too subtly shoving him away, 'is that removing inefficiencies in the dating space is more difficult than people realize.'

I took his hand and made my excuses, steering him across the room.

'What the fuck was that?' he said, incredulous. 'I should have knocked his fucking teeth out.'

Trying to manoeuvre him into safer territory, I found myself taking him upstairs where a woman in a complex leather harness was giving a talk called 'Getting What You Deserve'. The title of the workshop was written in white chalk on a mini-blackboard.

'Most of us crave empowered lives,' she announced, perch-ing on the edge of a grand piano. 'We're conditioned to put others first and to hide our real desires. We get caught up in the same old patterns, we find ourselves frustrated but we don't know why.' She crossed the floor, her shiny heels clacking on the parquet. A group of women in similar outfits hung around her, slouching against the walls.

'What we are left with is frustration instead of deep connection. Well, I'm here to tell you that you deserve better. You deserve to be loved for your authentic self. You deserve to feel empowered. You deserve to release the fear and shame that holds you back. You deserve to ditch the endless dating with emotionally unavailable partners, deepen passion, explore intimacy and learn to ask for what you really want. Agency is what I'm talking about. You want a partner that will show up for you, someone that will allow you to be the person you want to be. Well, I'm going to show you how to step into your power! I'm going to show you how to create the life you crave! Everyone deserves to have an awesome relationship! And what it comes down to is having the confidence to know that.'

In the next room, I could see a group of men wandering blindly around the carpet, their VR headsets strapped around their faces as they poured their hearts out, presumably to Unity.

By the time we'd drifted back into the ballroom, the party was in full swing. Semi-naked bodies spiralled on the dance floor to a stream of heavy, driving beats. A girl in a pair of low-cut jeans bobbed delicately around me, her back tattooed with the words: *The keeper of fragile things*. A woman in a burlesque costume was kissing someone in a baby-doll dress, socks, plaits and a gold crucifix. A man in a soft pink cardigan reclined on a chaise with two voluptuous women, each one dressed in matching latex, their faces contoured into complex curves. I saw Natasha and Nico filing through the crowd, both of them looking a little lost. In an accidental moment of magnanimity, I caught Natasha's eye and smiled. She waved back limply, confused, as if she'd never seen me before in her life.

I realized I'd become separated from Tom. I headed to the bar where I bumped into Aliya. She looked a little melancholy.

'Are you on your own?' I said.

She shrugged. Then she nodded at the dance floor where Georgia was voguing with the accounts team.

'You're not dancing?'

'She isn't happy,' Aliya said.

'Who? Georgia?'

'Yeah.'

'What happened?'

'I missed a couple of deliveries, it's been crazy with this party. I'm not even supposed to be working on events.'

She was disconsolate. She also seemed a little lost in the sea of youthful bodies. None of them so much as looked in her direction, despite the effort she'd made with her Rihanna-style get-up.

'Don't worry about it,' I said, giving her a small nudge of solidarity.

'Thanks.' She seemed genuinely touched.

She clinked my glass and smiled dejectedly.

As I wandered around in search of Tom, I felt a cool hand in mine.

'You need to keep an eye on that moron.'

It was Lara. She was furious. She pulled me into a corner.

'The salesman or whatever the fuck he is.'

'He works in marketing.'

'Of course he does. Did you really have to bring him here?'

'What's the problem?'

'He can't embarrass me like that.'

'He didn't embarrass you.'

'He wanted to.'

I tried to leave but she hadn't finished reprimanding me. 'Just keep him on a short leash, OK? He's a liability. And will you buy him some decent fucking clothes? He looks like an undercover detective.'

I was a little shocked by this tirade.

'Give the guy a fucking chance,' I said.

'I have.'

By the time I saw Tom again, he'd found himself a new friend. She was dressed head to toe in black, her eyes rimmed with kohl. On her wrist was one of those DIY tattoos of a wilted flower. The two of them were sitting in the garden, looking morose. I sat beside them and she offered me a silver vape with a skull on it. Once we'd wandered back inside it had become quieter, the music lowered to a drone-like bass.

Later, at the after-party, an 'executive suite' had been booked for special guests. Inside, a woman with surgically enhanced breasts was on a bed with two young men. The three of them were fucking openly while other guests watched. The woman scanned her audience, arching her back theatrically, the two men pounding her determinedly from her behind. She began to moan a little, lifting one hand to squeeze her tits. One of the men moved his hand to her head, forcing his thumb into her mouth. She whined a little, spreading her legs further apart. On the bedside table by her head was a welcome hamper full of fruit, a selection of herbal teas and a packet of lightly salted Kettle Chips. The man with his thumb in her mouth was groaning, the mishmash of people in the suite milling around him as he pumped. Most of the onlookers were lounging quietly on sofas, some of them gently making out, a few of them checking out the view from the penthouse balcony outside. The woman caught my eye as she ground herself against her partners. Her movements were practised and impassive. She seemed more interested in being watched than anything else.

'Can we get out of here?' Tom whispered.

He didn't say much in the taxi home.

I couldn't stop thinking about her. The whole thing, bizarrely, reminded me of something that had happened at school. I must have been about nine at the time. I'd had a teacher, Mr Adebayo, who'd given me lines for damaging my desk. I had a habit of scraping at the wood, chiselling dents into its varnish. As a punishment, he'd made me copy out the definition of 'compulsion': 'An irresistible, persistent impulse to perform an action that has become untethered from its goal, such as head-scratching when confused, usually considered to arise unconsciously as a means of relieving stress or uncertainty.'

•

Lying awake, Tom turned towards me.

'Your job,' he said. 'What do you think of it?'

'It's fine,' I replied. 'I need the money.'

'But what do you *think* of it? Don't you think there's something off?'

'It's supposed to be fun.'

'I'm not so sure about that. Those people, they were being baited.'

'What do you mean?'

'I mean it's dangerous.'

'It's a business.'

He seemed unnerved by the idea.

'It's a subculture,' I said. 'It's a community.'

'Is it, though?'

'It's a niche,' I said. 'One that's growing.'

'But those people – they're just customers, aren't they?' He paused to correct himself. 'What I mean is, they're *only* customers. You can't *buy* what that place is selling. You can pay people to fuck you, but you can't pay them to actually want you.'

'A lot of them are in relationships already. They're just bored, they're looking for something more.'

He looked sceptical. 'And what about the others?'

'I don't know about the others, maybe it works for them too. It's just another way for people to get together.'

'But they *weren't* getting together. OK, some of them were fucking but really, it's all just masturbation, isn't it? They were all looking for something *more*. They're not just shoppers – it's worse than that – they're aspirational shoppers.'

'Does it matter?'

'I think it does.' He was wide awake. 'It's handing more power to your friend and those pricks who tried to put their hands on you.'

'They're just capitalizing on human nature.'

'I thought this was all about ethical dating?'

'It is, but it's difficult for them,' I conceded. 'They're giving people options they wouldn't normally have and that creates certain distortions in their expectations. It happens on all dating sites but it's probably worse with Openr because the whole point is to offer people *more* – more freedom, more opportunities."

'It's not just a marketplace though is it? There's no product.'

I thought about it.

'I think you've just put your finger on the problem,' I said. 'It acts like a marketplace in that the more you liberate it, the more people want. In the end, almost everyone is reaching for the top – the same small percentage of ultra-popular users, the same few fantasy scenarios. It's a very "winner takes all" scenario – except even the top users aren't really winning because they don't benefit. There's a supply side problem, basically. Ultimately, it can only offer people each other. Which means not everyone will get what they want.'

He was listening, but he didn't seem too moved by Openr's difficulties.

'I just don't think they care,' he said. 'I don't think they're that serious about any of it.'

'Lara is,' I said. And I did believe that.

'But the others . . .' I considered this for a moment. 'To be honest, it's harder to tell. There's more funding available for start-ups that score high on sustainability, which just means ticking certain boxes on the sustainability assessments. Inclusivity is weighted the same as something like recycling, for example. Economic rights – things like union membership – not so much. There are incentives. They steer people in certain directions. But Lara – I do think Lara is for real. She wants to make a difference.'

He was still sceptical.

'Look, I'm only trying to make a living,' I said. I wasn't even sure why I was defending the place so hard.

He leaned back and contemplated this for a moment.

'Why don't you just stay here?'

'You're asking me to move in?'

'I could get a key cut in the morning.'

I was a little shocked that he'd proposed it.

'Think about it,' he said. 'I don't care what you do for money but you shouldn't have to pacify those cunts.'

•

The bed was empty when I awoke the following morning. I lay in silence for a few minutes, listening to Tom as he knocked around in the next room.

'Before you go,' I said as he was about to leave. 'Last night, at the party, I think I saw your friend.'

'Who?'

'Niall. I wasn't sure if I should tell you.'

'Niall?'

'Yeah, he was with a girl.'

He stood in silence for a second.

I was almost certain I'd seen him with Lara, although in retrospect, that didn't seem possible.

'Should I say something to Grace?' I said.

He looked at me uncomfortably.

'Probably not.'

'Thanks for coming with me, by the way.'

'Of course. I wanted to. Although, I think I'm too old for that shit.'

He was only four years older than I was.

'I hope you're not bored,' he said suddenly.

'Why would I be?'

'Well, compared to your friends last night, I'm hardly showing you a good time.'

'You don't think so?'

I smiled at him and pulled the sheet back a little coyly.

'I've got to go to work,' he said.

'Don't let me stop you.'

That morning, it was obvious that something had changed. I touched him gently, feeling him harden in my hand. Then I moved my body against his, teasing him gently between my lips. He bit down on me, groaning quietly.

'Do you like it?' I asked.

He laughed.

I felt myself softening for him. A small wave of pleasure rippled through me.

'I love being with you,' he said, holding back as he began to touch me, his fingers wet between my thighs.

I considered the two of us living together.

'Did you mean it, about moving in?'

'Of course I did,' he said.

'I think I'd like to.'

He leaned back and reached into his bag. He took a bunch of keys, removed two of them and handed them to me. I put them in my jeans on the floor beside me. Then he stroked himself as he kissed me, slowing himself down until I was ready. He told me to touch myself until I was on the verge of orgasm, then he pushed himself inside me, a soft tide of euphoria lifting me out of the usual circuits of my thoughts.

•

After work that night, back at the flat, I asked how things were going now that he and Grace were working together, just the two of them.

'I like it,' he said, 'although sometimes I get the impression she's bored shitless. She's very good at what she does but I'm not always sure she particularly enjoys it.'

'Why does she do it, then?'

'The money, I suppose. It's hard to walk away from that.'

We circled back to Tom's early years in London when they'd first started working together. He told me that after years of thinking there was something wrong with him, once he'd arrived in the capital, he'd realized it was more complicated than that. It wasn't only about him. Suddenly, he'd found himself in an environment in which women showed an interest, not because he'd changed but because his circumstances had. In the mostly female world of marketing, he was suddenly in demand. The numbers were stacked so strongly in his favour that his prospects flipped almost overnight. It was an experience he found slightly unnerving. He wasn't stupid, he understood that he represented something to these women – something that had little to do with who he was and more to do with his potential. He was now a vehicle for their own ambitions as well as a romantic prospect. They were all unique in their approach, but nonetheless they all took these things into account, because they were all labouring under the same conditions: almost all of them wanted to start a family and they needed someone like him to make it happen. The steady rise in the cost of living had cloaked everything in a ruthless pragmatism. Tom wanted those things too but the truth was, despite himself – because he was sympathetic to their predicament – he'd begun to find the whole scenario off-putting. He knew these women weren't to blame for what had happened to them, he just couldn't bring himself to give them what they wanted. The problem was almost embarrassingly trite: he wanted to be loved for who he was. He didn't want to be seen as a type, even if it was an eligible one. He was terrified of getting trapped. It had reached the point where he'd started to feel repelled by the performance of it all. The shit wasn't worth the shake. He'd been single for a while already by the time we'd met in Ibiza.

I thought about the way we'd met. It was difficult to isolate exactly what had been different this time, but we'd definitely shared a similar apprehension.

We'd grown up in an era in which the idea of love had changed completely. It was now fraught with mystery. Relationships no longer had rules, you had to come up with them yourselves and then continually reinvent them. Even marriage wasn't clear any more. It was no longer a monolithic practice, bound to the Church and to extended family. It was now a lifestyle choice, albeit one that had become aspirational as it had become rarer. Like everything else in the social sphere, it existed as a form of personal expression – one that resulted in divorce around half the time. Whatever it was we had seen in one another, it was something to do with that environment. I think we both wanted out on some ambient level.

The light from the curtains slashed my thighs as I watched him get up to make coffee. I felt abnormally untroubled as I waited for him to return.

27

It was Anti-Slut-Shaming Week. The office was quiet. I'd been given two posts to write: *Choking: The Hot Consensual Guide* and *Has Rap Coloured How We Do It?*

It was no secret on the content desk that certain topics attracted the most attention. As Lara never tired of reminding us, Openr's users liked engaging with the issues. Anything involving race or rape fired up engagement within seconds. After that, the highest performing posts were about the sex lives of the rich and famous. This was known internally as the Three Rs: Rape, Race and Rich fuckers. There was a dark camaraderie on the desk that created a different atmosphere to the engineering side. The team was more hard-bitten. We were like leathery old hacks, numb to the daily grind as we churned out our shots of infotainment, one after the other, all day long. Sometimes, to liven things up, we competed to see how many of these subjects we could wedge into a single post. Lara was a master at this game. She had an instinct for buzzy headlines. She also knew it helped keep up morale. Our time was otherwise spent unblinking, one hour to the next, staring limitlessly at the screen and then going home to think of more ideas.

•

'Remind me why you're doing this job?'

Tom was scrolling through my photos. He'd found an old one of me and Lara at university. He stopped immediately when he saw it. ~~Lara was laughing at something off-screen~~ while I looked up at her in adoration.

'It's a job,' I said.

'Just get another one.'

'It's not that easy.'

'You could definitely do better.'

'You say that, but it isn't really true. Honestly, sometimes I think there's something wrong with me. I'll get interviews but they then won't hire me. It's like there's something off-putting about me. They think I'm not committed enough or something.'

'No one is, they just hide it better than you.'

'You are,' I said.

'Hardly.

It's a skill, coming across like that. I think you'd learn it fast if you really had to.'

I managed to retrieve my phone from his hand.

'Do you trust her?' he asked me.

I'd been hoping he would drop it.

'We've known each other for a long time,' I tried to explain.

'That wasn't the question.' He looked at me quizzically. 'She's an operator,' he said.

'So what?'

'I think she's full of shit.'

'And?'

'Did you hear what she said at that party? She said she was working on the right mix of people. *Still* working on it. Meaning me.'

'It's work, she has to chat these people up.'

'Well, I'm offended.'

'You're not,' I scoffed.

'She's a fraud.'

'She's trying to run a business. Like you said, no one knows what they're doing.'

He didn't look convinced. 'Why do you always defend her?'
'She's a friend.'

•

The next morning, I woke up early. Tom was dressed and
already on a call with Floyd. By this point, I'd overheard so
many of these calls and had spent so long waiting for Tom as
he attempted to navigate the internal workings of Neura Therapeutics that I was starting to feel as invested in the Eudaxa
saga as he was. I found it more compelling than my own work
and after a long day at the coalface, churning out my thought-
provoking™ posts, it was a relief to sit down with Tom and
think about something that was actually interesting. He and
Grace had finished setting up office – they'd rented a couple of
rooms near Churchill Analytics. They'd done a vast amount of
research between them and were now embarking on the main
show – which was trying to work out how they were going to
turn Eudaxa into a household name.

'Sorry.' Tom pulled a face. 'It's Floyd, he won't leave me
alone.'

He covered his handset.

'Have you seen this shit he keeps sending me?'

On his phone was a screed of Floyd's messages:

We need to stop this endless fixation on the self

Consider the infinite malleability of awareness

This Earth cannot sustain humanity as it is

'He's like a chatbot,' I said. 'He sounds like he's running
one of those Californian wilderness retreats.'

'It's relentless,' Tom said. 'He never stops.'

He took his phone and wandered into the living room,

along the balcony, then turned around again. Then he put Floyd on loudspeaker. I was still in bed when he reached for my ankle and pulled me towards him. I heard the phone slide to the floor. Floyd was still droning into the carpet when I came gently, against Tom's mouth. A slow, vital wave washed over me. I felt his body regulating mine. It was a barely conscious experience that by its nature warded off awareness, as if consciousness itself was fundamentally restless, a state of alert.

28

Grace's eyes were closed, her phone on her knees, her head propped up against the bright blue seat of the Eurostar. We were on our way back from the International Conference on Brain Disorders. Or at least Grace and Tom had been there, I'd spent the weekend in the hotel, watching *Poirot* in French and ordering Kir royales on room service.

'I think we're missing something.'

Tom opened his laptop.

'Remember that thing you showed me?' He pulled out a copy of the deck I'd sent him from Georgia's talk at Openr.

'You kept that?'

'It sparked something.'

He clicked through to the opening slide and started reading: 'With disruptive start-ups everywhere and direct-to-consumer distribution, is aspirational branding a thing of the past?'

Grace shifted uncomfortably in her seat. She crossed her arms, she was half asleep.

'Historically,' Tom continued reading, 'brands have focused on exclusion. Not only have they limited access to their products but they've kept their own consumers at arm's length. A culture of detachment has defined their engagement with the world. What we're seeing today is a shift towards a more inclusive state of mind. Young people respond to friendly interactions and they expect no less from the brands they engage with. Numerous studies point to the emergence of a different pattern of consumption, one that is driven less by ostentation and more by a rebellious attitude towards hierarchies.'

'What's that got to do with us?' Grace opened her eyes reluctantly. 'I mean, there's some truth in it, but it doesn't affect medicine, does it?'

She looked wiped. Her eyes were red and she'd lost a lot of weight in the past few months.

'It applied to Prozac,' Tom said. 'You said it yourself, there was a time when it was fashionable.'

'But what would that mean today? Are you going to start a movement?' I asked him.

'It's not the worst idea. According to this, anyway.'

He slid his laptop over so that I could see the screen.

'Seriously, I think these trends are important. We need to be focusing on inclusivity. It has to be about removing barriers, connecting people with each other.'

'We're not leading with that.' Grace scraped absentmindedly at her coffee cup. 'It's an antidepressant, not a protest movement.'

'It's an empathogen though, right? That's a USP right there. This doesn't have to be political. We could scale it down to a human level.'

Grace was barely listening.

'People won't buy into "Save the World",' she said.

Tom sat forward in his seat. 'Fine, but hear me out. It doesn't only help with mood, right? That's what separates it from other treatments. It actually brings people together. It's a social thing. It helps them open up. I could see this being used as a tool in psychotherapy, marriage counselling . . .'

Her face tightened but he didn't notice.

'. . . offender rehabilitation, team-building.'

'It's not approved for *team-building*.'

She looked stiff, as if her bones were tired.

'There must be more to life than this,' she said, leaning her head against the window.

Outside, there were tower blocks for miles, their lights blurred against the rain-smeared glass.

'What else do we have right now?' Tom asked.

'Not much. You can go in that direction if you like, but be careful, we need to keep it simple. And we also need to make sure we're taken seriously. We can't reinvent the wheel completely.'

She put her cup back on the table, its lip shredded into tiny pieces.

By the time the train arrived in London, Tom had already started sending emails. One of them was addressed to his friend Sunny. It said: 'Can you get us in the lab?'

•

It must have been only a few days later that Tom invited me to one of Floyd's events.

Not long after we arrived at the auditorium, Floyd pulled up in a Model Y Tesla. I noticed he'd gone for the design-your-own version with silver cyberstream wheels. It was the kind of car you saw parked in the leafier parts of London – it was unobtrusive, it signalled the right kind of wealth and, importantly, it gave the impression that the owner had a social conscience, albeit only up to the point that they could still drop seventy grand on a car.

Floyd was introduced on stage by a man called Ian Dunstan, the owner of a mobile phone distributor. His company had sponsored the tour and he was, in his own words, a big fan of Floyd's work. Dunstan talked Floyd up for a while. He seemed like a genuine believer. He had even brought his kids along. They were teenagers, a boy and a girl, the latter of whom I recognized immediately as Sofia Dunstan from *@peaceoutsofia*. She had a fairly significant TikTok following, an ad campaign with Nike, and had appeared briefly in a reality TV show. Now she specialized in fashion and fitness content. In other words, she was just famous enough for me to have heard of her. Whatever it was that Floyd had told this guy, he seemed keen for his children to hear it too. He was very vocal on this point. 'This is a message for the next generation,' he said.

Floyd bounded onstage to a ripple of applause. There was a camera hovering above his head. It swung around as he skipped towards the podium.

'The primary goal of the venture capitalist,' he began, 'is a simple one: it's to create the conditions for the best future we can imagine. The one we wish to leave to our descendants. Many young people today are overwhelmed with information, paralysed by it, disillusioned by it. They know our existing systems must change but they are not clear on how to do that, they have no obvious common ambition towards which to work. The challenge is to resolve the tension between the nihilism that has crept into our culture and the idealism that propelled our forefathers to this point. We need to conquer the existential angst that is crippling our civilization. We need to replace it with something new, something that unites all of us. Something that brings us all *together*. Without unity, there is no hope. And on that note, I'd like to offer you this thought experiment:

'Imagine a world in which every moment is brimming with well-being. Every conscious second is rich with fulfilment. Imagine this world exists as a potential future for humanity. What would the inhabitants of this world have to say to us? Wouldn't they look down on us with pity? And wouldn't they urge us to take action to bring this society into being? Wouldn't they want us to envision their way of life? And to use our intelligence to make it a reality?

'My point is that it's meaningless to ask, ethically, "What is the right thing to do?" By far the more important question is

"What is the best way to be?" What is the best way to *feel*? What states of consciousness should we strive for? What states can we converge upon that are unquestionably for the good? We are rapidly developing the technology to quantify human happiness. If we don't improve our philosophical imperatives, we will miss the opportunities this offers. With Eudaxa, we have discovered a new way forward – and not in a merely superficial manner. This is a pathway that takes into account the altruism necessary for our project. The free market won't align with social values unless we start controlling the levers of our own desires. Our worst excesses, our runaway appetites must be curbed by the cultivation of *empathy*. Our planet is boiling. Our people are in distress. Let us develop the ambition to mobilize this tool. Let us find the courage necessary to bring about the very best possible future for everybody.'

The audience, which seemed to be mainly composed of students, began to applaud. Then they started cheering. I looked at Grace. I was a bit startled, but she seemed distracted. She was furiously taking notes.

After the talk, Floyd stepped down into the auditorium and spent some time signing copies of his book, *1, 2, 3, Take-Off: How to Build a World that Works for Everyone.*

It was a long time before he finally emerged, nodded briefly at the three of us and then at his driver, who swept him out of the place so quickly that neither Tom nor Grace had a chance to exchange a word.

•

I'd been avoiding Lara since the party. I knew it was Niall she'd been with at the bar because I'd researched the two of them online and discovered that they were indeed 'friends'. That night, I'd seen them talking intensely together, his hand resting on her thigh. I hadn't said a word to anyone except Tom and Lara hadn't said a word to me, but a not unfamiliar sense of foreboding had started creeping in. Unfortunately for me, she wasn't easy to escape.

She messaged: **Are you still coming this weekend?**

It was a difficult question to answer. I didn't want to go to away with her but I also didn't want to ruin my life.

OK, I wrote, trying to project as much detachment as possible.

I'll pick you up on Saturday morning

It was only on the way down to the car that I realized she wasn't on her own.

'No,' I told her.

'Get in.'

Niall looked sheepish. He lowered the window.

'Sorry,' he said. 'I seem to have been kidnapped.'

I'm not sure why I obeyed her. I could have turned round and left them but I didn't.

'Are you going to tell me why I'm here?'

'You've been avoiding me.'

'For a reason.'

Niall didn't say a word.

'Does Grace know you're here?' I asked him.

'She isn't speaking to me.'

'Let's not go down that road,' Lara said, plugging her phone into the speaker. 'She's checked out anyway, by the sounds of it. She's never around. It's already over.'

I didn't dignify this with a response. The traffic was solid by the time we got to Rainham, the golden shafts of the Nickelodeon building jutting over Lakeside. I could see a trail of shoppers in the car park, most of them marshalling small children, plastic bags hanging from their buggies as they rattled haphazardly alongside the motorway.

Lara scrolled through playlists. She went for a compilation called Beach Vibes.

'People change,' she said sagely. 'And anyway, I don't like

what she's all about. That whole Big Pharma thing, it's shady. I don't believe you can reduce people to chemicals.'

She glanced at me in the rear-view mirror but I didn't acknowledge it.

'At the end of the day, you can't change human nature.'

Privately I doubted this was true. 'Human nature' was almost certainly engineerable. I decided to rise to it.

'What makes you think that?'

'Put it this way, when I was at school, half the girls in my class were on something. Seroxat, Prozac, Cipralex. It was rife. We all had private shrinks. This was while we were going through puberty. God knows what it did to us. Don't get me wrong, we all had something going on, but we shouldn't have been medicated like that. No one questioned why we were so unhappy. They just doped us like lab rats.'

'That doesn't mean it didn't work.'

'It worked alright. None of us could feel anything.'

'Some people need that.'

'Why are you defending it?' She looked in the mirror again and this time she caught my eye. 'Those companies are run by psychopaths.'

'Someone has to pay for medical research.'

I wasn't sure why I was playing devil's advocate. I just didn't feel like humouring her.

'Well, I don't trust those people, they're dangerous.'

She turned up the volume in conclusion, the sound of 'Dead Coast' filling the air.

•

I googled Margate as we drove through the countryside. One of the first results was a review on a travel site. 'The South East coast of England is dominated by the city of Brighton,' it said, 'the supposed jewel in the crown and the model for all other resorts. The idea goes something like this: open a cultural centre, lure in broke young artists and hope to stir up the housing market to the point that the town re-emerges as a hot new destination for London to haemorrhage its downwardly mobile middle classes. Margate was the first to attempt this scheme, to the dubious credit of Thanet Council.'

Lara pulled up outside Dreamland, its wobbly rides gyrating in their cages. Overshadowing the funfair was a colossal, Brutalist monolith – Arlington House.

We walked around the edge of the estate, passing a Tesco Metro with a smashed window on which the phrase *Every Little Helps* had been abstracted into a meaningless pattern of white marks. I saw a woman with a thin, pale face pushing a pram across the broken glass, swerving a drunk man in dirty sweatpants, a pile of wet cardboard underneath him. Above his head was a poster that said *In the future, nature and technology will work as one.*

Lara picked her way through the debris.

'This is not what you think, by the way,' Niall whispered, dropping back so she couldn't hear what he was saying. 'I just needed someone to talk to.'

'I don't need to know.'

'We get each other.'

'Do you?'

'Me and her,' he said, glancing at her dress – she was wearing a short black skirt – 'we're not cut out for normal life.'

We followed her into the Fort Road Hotel where we were greeted at the door by a woman with a clipboard. It was the launch party for an exhibition. The room was full of people from London, you could tell by their expensive but bashed-up streetwear. Lara seemed to know everyone there. The artist was a woman I'd never heard of. Niall and I sat morosely on the sidelines, watching her work the room while we drank our wine.

'What's this all about, anyway?' Niall said, looking at the

photos on the wall. They were all self-portraits taken with a selfie stick. 'Narcissus', the first one was called. We walked over to a video installation of the artist walking through a field. It looked like some sort of video game, the shape of her body morphing from a curvy fur-covered fox to a voluptuous bunny, to a sexy robot.

'It's about world-building,' Lara said as she sidled back to us. 'It's about the fluidity of digital identity.'

'Is that why she looks so hot all the time?'

She gave Niall a dirty look.

'You can do better than that,' she said.

'That's not very feminist of you, Niall,' I said.

'I am a feminist,' he said, perplexed. I could see the panic rising in his eyes. 'I'm very strongly in favour of women exploring their sexuality.'

He hovered around the installation, nursing his beer, trying to look interested.

'Jesus,' I said, once she'd abandoned us again.

'Do you think I've fucked it?'

'Fucked what?'

'Whatever the fuck this is?'

'I don't know what you're talking about.'

'What does she think of me?'

'How should I know?'

'Can you find out?'

'No.'

'What do I do?'

'I don't know, Niall. It's a shame Andrea Dworkin's dead, maybe you could have asked her.'

He looked balefully at the video which was now showing a sexy cat. He was quite good-looking in his own way, which was charmingly dishevelled. There was something about him that reminded me of Lara. I tried to kill the thought that she was actually into him, although she'd always had a thing for older men with egos as bulletproof as her own.

It was late by the time we left, the ocean a greyish, darkening mass. On the way to the car, we passed a church that looked as if it had been there forever.

'You know, I wanted to be a priest when I was younger.' Niall stopped outside to read the plaque: *Original? Are You Sure? Use your phone to click this barcode and learn about the true history of St. Austin's.* www.visitthanet.co.uk/gxwgf578

Lara caught my eye and stifled a laugh.

'What?' he said, smiling at her. 'It was a phase. It's not that unusual.'

He tried the door and it swung open, unexpectedly. Then he vanished inside, leaving us to follow him. The interior was lit with a dim electric light.

'Sometimes I think this will all come back,' he said, brushing his fingers through the dust. 'I mean, the world's a mess, isn't it? Have we really improved it since the days when people followed all of this?'

'Yes,' Lara said.

He wandered towards the pulpit, stopping abruptly in front of a chipped statue of the Virgin Mary.

'We could all do with being more like her.'

Lara caught my eye as if it to say: *What is happening?*

'Are you feeling guilty, Niall?' I said, only half joking.

He didn't answer, he seemed transfixed.

'So, you think the future should be feminine?' I asked him.

'Why not? The world's a mess. She stood for selflessness, you know? *Do nothing from selfish ambition or conceit, but in humility count others more significant than yourselves.*'

'Is he quoting the fucking bible?' Lara whispered.

I thought about the analysts at work. It was true that the industry was moving towards ever greater permeability. And for the most part, we acquiesced. It wasn't the kind of selflessness that Niall was talking about, but it was a selflessness of another kind, each individual embedded in the emergent patterns of the collective, which was another word for information. It left each one of us more subject to influence. And increasingly, to predictability. That was the business model, anyway. Maybe he was right, maybe it was for the best.

Lara gave him a strange look as if she'd never seen this side of him before.

'We can't go on like this,' he said earnestly.

'Hello?' she said. 'Can we leave?'

•

In the cold, liquid darkness of the night the sea was hard to distinguish from the land. Somewhere over Jury's Gap the rain began to pelt against the windscreen. A row of high-voltage pylons tracked our route towards the beach. The masts led to a cluster of low-rise buildings around an old power station.

'This is it.' Lara pulled up. We were outside what looked like a concrete bunker.

'Dungeness! Welcome to the desert.' She got out and started unloading the boot. Niall and I stared at the dull expanse, trying to decipher it through the rain.

'My mother hates this place so we've got it to ourselves, at least for now.'

I wondered what she meant by that.

'I thought you said it was a beach house,' Niall said, his shoes sinking into the sand.

'It is,' Lara said as she opened the safety box and retrieved the keys. She lurched heavily against the steel door, using all her weight to shove it open. She disabled the alarm and switched the lights on.

'John Betjeman wrote about this place,' she said. '*Where the roads wind like streams and the sky is always three quarters of the landscape.*'

Niall looked a little taken aback. In fact, every time she said something, he seemed surprised. Although it hadn't dampened his interest. It was obvious he couldn't believe his luck.

The rain was battering the windows, you could hear it even through the thick steel frames. There was a pile of firewood around the stove. On the table was a stack of magazines: *House & Garden*, *World of Interiors*.

'I need a drink.' Lara sank into the sofa.

'Does anyone live around here?' I asked her.

'On the beach? No one, really. That's what I like about it. It's the edge of the world.'

'It feels like it.'

'I love deserts.'

'It's hardly the Mojave,' Niall said drily.

'It's still a desert, it's the only one in Britain.'

Lara slipped her shoes off and stretched her legs across the heavy linen cushions.

'What's going on between you two?' I decided to ask outright.

'Nothing,' she said impassively. 'We're friends.'

•

Niall barely spoke to me all night. He was too busy watching Lara. I caught him staring at her blouse, it was just fine enough to make out the outline of her nipples. The more she entertained this, the more it annoyed me. Why was she humouring him? I looked down at his pale pink cords. They were starting to offend me in themselves.

Periodically, she stopped to check her phone. Meanwhile, we half carried on a conversation.

'It was sexist,' she said, filling Niall's glass. We were on the subject of the royal family. 'The whole idea of royalty is absurd.'

'I suppose it is,' Niall agreed. 'Although, for what it's worth, the aristocracy offer an alternative, don't they? I mean, whatever you think of them, at least it's a counterpoint to the bilge pouring out of the USA. That new wife – the American one – she's from LA, isn't she? She probably thinks that place is the height of civilization.'

'They're parasites,' Lara answered. 'They're Machiavellian as fuck. It's not like they aren't profiteering too. That's what they're there for, to preserve their fortune.'

'Of course, but they're decent enough to cover it up. At least there's some pretence of duty there, sacrifice – all those old-fashioned virtues. They're capable of committing to something greater than themselves, even if it's only to their own bloodline.'

For a second, I thought he was going to take her phone away.

'Is this too much effort for you?' he said instead.

'I'm committed to something more important than myself.'

'What's that?'

'Fairness. Decency. Equal access to the good things in life, for everyone, whoever they are.'

He looked at me as if to say, *Is she for real?*

'How could I forget? You're a Socialist.'

'I just don't believe in unearned privilege.'

'I suppose that's all that's left these days. You can dedicate yourself to social justice or you can dedicate yourself to science. They're the only two religions still standing. It's a shame the two are on a collision course.'

'What do you mean?'

'Well, take that thing for example,' he said, looking at her phone. 'With that kind of data, there are quants out there who've got your number. It doesn't matter what you think, statistically they know how you're going to behave. Not perfectly – not yet – but they're getting closer every day. They know who you are when no one's looking, or when you *think* no

one's looking. ~~They know you better than you know yourself.~~
And it doesn't fit your ideology. We're not all equal.'

Do they, though? I almost said, but there was no point, they
weren't listening to me.

'There's no such thing as objective truth,' Lara corrected
him. 'And anyway, it doesn't matter what they know because,
ultimately, the world is run on influence.'

'And that device of yours, that's run on influence, is it?
What about the power that heats this house? The materials
that hold it up? Reality exists. Facts exist, including facts about
human beings. Honestly, at the risk of sounding my age here,
sometimes I think people are right about your generation and
these little gadgets. No wonder you're all so obsessed with
humanitarianism – it's a comfort blanket, isn't it? The more
enthralled you are by this crap, the more blind you are to your
own dysfunction. Who do you think it is that controls these
things? You of all people should know. You're not going to fix
the world on that piece of plastic. All you're doing is allowing
yourselves to become fodder. You're nothing more than food
at this point, you're chaff for the gaping mouth of the information age.'

He sipped his wine and paused solemnly, relieved to have
won back her attention.

'I don't think that's true.'

'Of course you don't, you're just grasping for what feels
good. It's denial. It's a kind of comfort eating. Comfort politics, it should be called.'

I caught her touching his knee.

'Chill out, grandad,' she said. 'You do realize that you and
I would never have met if it wasn't for this thing?'

•

I must have fallen asleep in front of the fire because the next
thing I remember, the room was dark. The logs had almost

burnt away and I could hear a banging coming from the kitchen. I stood up, the floor lurching beneath me, and made my way towards the noise. My mouth was dry. I needed water. The back door had been left open and was banging loudly in the wind. Outside, it was raining harder than ever and the beach was pitch black apart from the faint light of a clouded moon hanging high over the ocean. As I made my way towards the shoreline, I heard the sound of something over the gale. It was a while before I realized it was Lara. She was in the sea, her body pale against its ink black surface.

I stood for a while, watching her with Niall. She was lying on her back, her breasts exposed in the moonlight. Suddenly, she pitched upright and looked straight in my direction. She didn't say a word at first. I had a strange feeling she was performing, as if she wanted me to watch her. I played along for a while, then as I turned back to the house, I heard her call my name. She was beckoning me towards the water.

It was freezing. Sharp, like ice. It took a long time before I reached her. Her skin felt warm and familiar. She smelt raw, like an animal. Lightning cracked the sky above us as rain hammered over our heads. I could feel Niall's arm around her waist. He didn't let her go as she clung onto me. I watched him kiss her but she pulled me closer. For a second, I was caught between them, the three of us wrapped around each other. Then suddenly, she let me go, swimming back towards the shore. I knew what she was doing. She was daring Niall to catch her. She disappeared beneath the surface as he lunged clumsily towards her. By the time she had re-emerged, she was out of reach. She swam back to the beach, leaving the two of us in the water. I watched stupidly as she got out and walked away, vanishing into the downpour.

•

It was almost light when she woke me up.

'What do you think of him?' she said.

'I think he's married.'

'I like him.'

'Can't we discuss this in the morning?' I closed my eyes.

'Are you going back to sleep?'

'I'm trying to.'

'Talk to me.'

'You should go back to him, or he'll notice.'

'He'll notice what?'

I wasn't going to say it. I could feel my blood stirring for her, but I didn't move. She reached for my hand.

'No one has to know,' she said quietly.

When I turned to face her, she didn't flinch. It was a split second, then it was gone. I understood exactly what she'd meant but it was too late, she'd seen my hesitation. I think she'd seen Tom on my face and it had shocked her. After that, she wouldn't look me in the eye. There was nothing else to say, she just got up and left without a word.

29

I didn't see Lara at work that week. I couldn't tell if her absence was for my benefit, but if it was, it was working. I couldn't think about anything else. I kept going over what had happened at the weekend. I drank too much coffee. I couldn't work.

In an effort to distract myself, I forced myself to think about Niall and Grace. I went over and over the situation. How had Niall met Lara in the first place? As far as I knew, I was their only connection. I was fairly certain of this because I'd looked through all of my accounts: LinkedIn, Instagram, X – it was all the same, they had no other friends in common. On the other hand, I got the impression that Niall had been hanging around the industry for a while. Piecing things together from what Grace had told me, I began to form a picture of what had happened.

It wasn't clear what Niall did for a living. He'd dabbled in miscellaneous activities from photography to acting to journalism. In his current incarnation, he was trying to be a 'thought leader' specializing in tech. He wrote articles, appeared on podcasts and, increasingly, did anything else that paid. Things hadn't been going well for a while. He did OK but it was a harsh gig, which was why he'd started plugging himself so aggressively on the internet. His image had become a part of the process. It wasn't even about the money any more. He'd come to see the work he did as more important than its cash value – probably because the alternative was giving up on yet another career. And anyway, he was surrounded by other people like him: writers, creatives, academics, many of them also the children, wives or husbands of well-paid executives like Grace. It allowed them to work not so much for the money as for the more ephemeral value of a profile. Over time, he'd succeeded in building a following. In the meantime, Grace got up each day, fed their daughter and went to work, her job, at least, offering some respite from the strange atmosphere at home.

It was only recently that she'd started to question the situation. They'd agreed that Niall would stay 'at home' with Evie so that Grace could focus on her job, and he did in fact spend most of his time there, although he wasn't keeping house so much as he was quietly nurturing his brand. He spent hours alone in his office in various online forums. He functioned quite well in this mode. It was an anesthetizing but not disagreeable existence. He felt more himself amongst the people he met online than he did when he was with his wife and child.

Grace, for her part, did what she could to keep them going. She'd known for a while that something was wrong but she loved Niall and felt that things would improve. They'd built a life together and she hadn't drifted as far from it as he had. On the other hand, she didn't like having to support him. It wasn't that she couldn't afford it exactly, she just didn't like not having a choice. Nothing in her background had prepared her for it. She imagined there were still men in the world who took pride in supporting a woman, but the opposite wasn't really true; in fact, the whole thing made her feel ashamed. There was an element of fantasy in what she wanted from him. It had something to do with being looked after, or at least in feeling that he could look after her if it came down to it. She'd started mentioning that he look for real work, something with an actual salary. She thought a normal job might dignify him, or at least get him out of the house.

Balking at the thought of regular employment, Niall had instead started messaging people. His friends from school were mostly in finance and he began to socialize with these people. He showed up at their events, he joined their Discords, he turned up at the pub when they were there. He even invested in a set of kettle bells and started working out in the park like they did. He managed to insinuate himself into a world that, now that he was almost forty, suddenly didn't seem so boring. Most of these people had been laid off by this point – the banks had been shedding jobs for years – so they had some sympathy with his predicament. Most were in the process of moving into tech. 'You have a profile,' they said. 'You could leverage that into consultancy, you'd be adding value with your network.'

Niall had come across Openr by accident not long after he and Grace had returned from Ibiza. He'd been trawling start-ups on ZDNet, trying to hawk his services to new companies. The app had fed him Lara's profile almost immediately, because it knew they had a mutual friend. After that, their circles had begun to merge, slowly at first but then more noticeably. He'd see her name cropping up more frequently. He'd catch her tagged in other people's posts. She dropped into his LinkedIn feed. They were exposed to one another systematically, their circuits slowly overlapping. The first time they actually spoke, it was as if they'd already met.

30

That Friday, Grace and Tom drove to Granta Park, an industrial estate about fifteen minutes outside Cambridge. The lab was in a sprawling hub of buildings surrounded by neat, landscaped lawns. The blocks were clad in greyish plastics, their panels slightly faded in the light. They had names like Illumina Array and Steinmenz, or occasionally more historic titles: Watson, Portway, McClintok. There was something out-of-time about the place. It reminded Grace of a golf course.

'So, you're here full-time now?' Tom asked Sunny as he came down to reception to greet them.

'Back in the hole,' he said, ushering them upstairs.

Room C4 was humming with computers.

'This is where the magic happens.' He waved around. 'I used to love this kind of work, original research and all that. These days we mostly process data. I won't lie to you, it's pretty boring.'

He motioned Grace towards a row of microscopes, urging her to take a look.

'What is it?' she asked, staring at the clumps of small, uneven blobs.

'It's Eudaxa,' Sunny said. 'Or at least, this is the source material. Cloned Piper marginatum. It's a source of MDP-1P. It's one of the few still found in nature.'

'It's a beta-keto analogue of MDA,' Tom recited, surprised he still remembered.

'Exactly. It's a psychedelic with strong empathogenic

qualities. And it isn't very stable, or at least not in its purest form, which is probably why it's never taken off as a street drug.'

'So you clone the plant source to stabilize the compound?'

'Exactly. We lab-produce the plant cells here.'

Grace moved out of the way so that Tom could take a look for himself.

'Have you tried it?' he asked Sunny.

'Me personally?'

'He's not serious,' Grace intervened, wondering why Tom would ask such a thing.

They spent a long time in Sunny's office going over the results of the clinical trials. Grace had always been thorough when it came to research, she liked to understand the product inside out. She wanted a sense of its background, of its story. It was all material as far she was concerned. Sunny, for his part, didn't seem especially engaged. In fact, he looked as if he couldn't wait for them to leave.

Later in the car park, they all shook hands.

'I hope the trip was worth your while,' Sunny said.

As he turned to leave, Grace stopped him.

'Hey Sunny, would you consider coming down to London?' she said. 'We could use someone who understands the science. Just an afternoon or two should be enough.'

He looked surprised.

'Of course,' he said, as if he couldn't imagine anything worse.

'Great,' Grace said brightly. 'Tom will be in touch.'

31

I went alone to Bruton Street that Saturday and walked around the luxury boutiques. I wandered around Berkeley Square, up Bond Street and along South Molton Street, ending up in a cafe called Zen Arabica. It was almost Christmas and the cafe was busy. I still hadn't seen Lara since Dungeness and I still couldn't stop replaying what she'd done. I now lived in an alternate reality in which something had happened between us. I'd wanted it to, although I was furious that she had dared to put me in this position. I composed a text while I waited in the queue.

How long do you think you can keep this up?

I didn't send it. I was on the verge of tears and went to the bathroom to wash my face. When I emerged, I felt light-headed. I hadn't eaten much that day and predictably, I hadn't slept much either. I looked around the cafe, I must have been hallucinating because I saw something floating in the air. It was a field of illuminated numbers, each one roaming haphazardly as if tethered to one of the other customers. The digits refreshed constantly as if modelling something about these people. It took me a while to realise, with horror, what the metric was – their desirability rating. I looked away, trying to focus on the floor which was covered with shopping bags from the fashion and beauty stores in the neighbouring streets. Most of them were filled with cosmetics, decorative clothing, jewellery. The libidinal economy was real, I thought. It was inescapable and now it could be measured.

I bought a coffee and allowed myself to imagine what a life with Lara would look like. I tried to picture what would make her happy beyond the transience of the moment. I didn't have the answer and in fact, I'm not sure she knew herself. She was too much of a visionary to ever stop searching for something loftier. On the other hand, she did pull things off that most people couldn't have imagined, which made me wonder what that meant in relationship terms. I tried to think about my coffee and 'be in the present' as Floyd would have said. The cafe was decorated like something between a Buddhist temple and a spaceship. I glanced at the man beside me, who seemed absorbed by the blurb on the menu. It was an exposition of the founder's philosophy:

Who am I?

What kind of life do I want to live?

As the great Jean-Paul Sartre said, 'Man is fully responsible for his nature and his choices.'

After finishing college, I moved to California where I settled by the ocean and immersed myself in the unique fusion of beach hippie culture.

It was there that I found time to reflect on myself until eventually, I settled on three thoughts.

• I want to follow my heart

• I want to see the world

• I want to be free from financial struggle

And it was then that the answer came to me: it was coffee.

Before I left, I decided for the hundredth time that day that I was going to message Lara. Then I restrained myself, walked to Liberty and bought her a cashmere scarf. I wandered around the shop for a while. I spent a stupid amount on wrapping paper. I had no idea what I was doing, I just wanted to do something for her.

•

On the 23rd, Tom invited me to meet his family. On the way to Brown's for lunch he told me he'd been speaking to his old friend Sunny and was thinking of paying him a visit. He hadn't been back to Luton since he'd left and he felt that a visit to see his friend was overdue. He also told me about his excursion to the lab and said he'd had a strange feeling about it.

We arrived at the restaurant to find the four of them already there – his dad, his stepmother and their children, two half-siblings, a boy and a girl. Tom had warned me that he didn't see his family very often, primarily because his stepmother couldn't stand him. It would have been a cliché if it hadn't been for his teenage misdemeanours, which somewhat complicated the situation. As we sat there, I realized he'd underplayed how bad it was.

Later, he told me that he didn't blame his stepmother for the situation. She shouldn't have had to deal with his faults and in her defence, she had visited him in rehab along with his father. The problem was, neither she nor his father had had much in common with the other families, all of whom had been encouraged to attend support groups for carers. Most of the other addicts had come from more precarious upbringings than him. They'd described real poverty. Either that or they'd been bona fide rich kids. There seemed to be a tendency in both directions, whereas Tom's stepmother, in particular, was middle-of-the-road in almost every imaginable way, from her 'Be Kind' keyring to the Sainsbury's magazines she kept piled on the counter in her chalk-white kitchen. She viewed drug addiction as an illness but only in the abstract sense that she thought of herself as a thoughtful and non-judgemental person. Faced with an actual teenage addict, she'd done everything in her power to shut him out of their lives. Even now, she kept him as far away as possible from her own offspring. I'd seen her in action. None of it was overt. What she did was make light of things. She'd say: 'My kids are everything to me . . . not *you*, Tombo!' – with a fun laugh. On the surface, it was a playful way to address the elephant in the room but it was relentless and did its job, which was to keep him in his place. I realized he suffered through this every year. It must have affected him, although he didn't show it. I took his hand in the car on the way home as we watched the Christmas lights go by.

•

Christmas Day at my mother's house was the same as always. She'd made up my old bedroom which had hardly changed since I'd left home. It still had its floral wallpaper and its thin, unlined curtains. There was an ancient Laura Ashley armchair piled with old stuffed toys. As usual, it was just the two of us this year. We didn't see the rest of the family and although I knew she had some friends, they never seemed to make an appearance over Christmas. I think she preferred it that way. She always said she wanted me to herself.

There were photos of my christening on the living room wall, my first communion, my graduation. She wasn't religious but she'd clung to the old traditions. She even had an old wooden crucifix that had once belonged to my grandmother. It had a plaque underneath that said: *Love the Lord with all thy heart, all thy soul and all thy mind. This is the first and greatest commandment. And the second is like unto it, Thou shalt love thy neighbour as thyself.* Tom's mother had probably owned something similar. I liked to think so, anyway. I took pleasure in cataloguing these small connections, as if they gave some architecture to our lives. They staved off the feeling that nothing was holding us together but ourselves, because I never knew if that would be enough.

Mum always asked the same questions: How's life? How's work? It was basic stuff but I always found it difficult to answer. I wanted to tell her the truth but I knew she wouldn't understand it. It was too far from her own experience. I felt obliged to come up with a version that might be meaningful to her. She did her best to keep things going between us but it wasn't easy. The gap was too wide. She was so deeply rooted in the past, sometime late in the twentieth century, that she might as well have been on another planet. She liked TV soaps and romance novels. She wore chunky costume jewellery and bought newspapers from a newsagent, occasionally cutting out articles which she kept for future reference in a drawer. Her social life revolved around shopping centres and coffee shops. She still kept in touch with some of the other parents she'd met while I was at school; a handful of them had stayed in the area even though their children were long gone. Of course, I pretended everything was fine, although I knew the score and I think she probably did too. I was there for her benefit, really. I felt duty-bound because she'd hung her life on me.

There was something about Christmas that broke my heart in a way I couldn't quite define. I often felt there was something wrong in the world but I felt it most sharply around that time. I wondered how long it had been like this. There must have been a time in the past when things hadn't been so difficult. It probably wasn't even that long ago. I envisioned an era in which life had moved more slowly, when it had still been possible for a parent to be a role model for a child. Not so long ago, it had gone without saying that age conferred wisdom – an assumption that had been the case for millennia – but I wasn't sure if it still held. Age had become synonymous with obsolescence.

The other thing I felt most vividly at Christmas was that you had to live anyway, you had to find a way. You had to believe there was one. I gave Mum the jumper I'd bought her and we had a glass of whisky together. She told me how much she loved me and a little drunk, I gave her a hug.

Later, I sent Tom a picture of the hand-knitted snowman she had hung on the tree. He sent me a Christmas tree emoji and a photo of his stepmother's Sainsbury's vinaigrette.

32

The journey to Luton was slow, very slow. There had been some sort of track failure. It was a freezing January morning and a layer of ice had settled on the line, coating the fields around us in a veneer of frost. It had an austere beauty that held my attention while Tom worked on his laptop. We were on our way to visit Sunny but the conversation kept circling back to Openr. Tom had pulled the website up on his screen. He was on the 'Our Team' page.

'This is her bio,' I said, pointing to the section about Georgia.

He'd been hung up on her ever since I'd shown him what I thought was her fairly bullshit-heavy presentation.

He scrolled slowly through the text.

Georgia Marchant is a branding expert, futurist and thought leader working across the digital, retail and service spaces. Pursuing the concept of 'holistic insight', Marchant takes a progressive humanist approach, balancing the needs of business with the needs of society. She zeroes in on key issues with a view to creating positive change.

'She's a bit new-agey, isn't she?' he said.
'She's not cheap, either.'
He thought about it. 'She takes private clients, though?'
'I'm sure she'd see you.'

'I think it might be worth a meeting.'

By the time we'd made it into the town centre, the sky had turned the colour of a bruise. Sunny was alone at the bar when we arrived. He hugged Tom warmly, like a close friend. The three of us sat around a table and he ordered drinks.

'So what's going on?' Tom asked him casually.

'What do you mean?'

'I know something's up.'

'No, you don't,' Sunny snorted. 'You've just forgotten what it's like. I'm in the lab all day. I don't communicate with civilians.'

He downed his lager and sat back comfortably in his seat, looking expectantly at Tom and then me.

'Is that it?' he said. 'You're here to shake me down? And here was I thinking you were paying me a visit.'

'We are,' Tom said. He seemed a little exasperated.

'Well, drink up,' Sunny insisted. 'It's your round.'

Later, he took us back to his place.

'I can't believe you're still here,' Tom said, surveying the scene as we walked through Farley Hill, past the blocks at Whipperley Ring and along the rows of mismatched semis that led to Sunny's flat in Caddington. Some of the houses were clad in pebbledash, some had greying paint from the exhaust fumes and some had giant composite stones that made them look like tiny castles. Tom recognized the flat immediately: it was the same one he'd shared with Sunny when they were younger. He remembered their neighbours being noisy. There had been a family of screamers upstairs – the kids would scream, their mother would scream for them to shut up, they'd scream back and then her boyfriend would get involved, which would produce five minutes of silence before the cycle began again. The double-glazing had barely dulled the noise and the paint in his bedroom had peeled off from the heat of the weed farm next door. He'd told me about the people in that street

being angry in a way that had infected him too. There was
something about the place that had disturbed him and whatever it was, it was no respecter of income. In fact, he'd almost
moved to Farley Hill, an area that was arguably worse off but
that had at least, maybe for that reason, retained some vestige
of community. No, there was something else about Caddington, something that he'd never been able to put his finger on.
Seeing the place again after all these years, he seemed lost in
thought. He'd told me once that he'd got the feeling it had
something to do with status. A stable life was hard to get, or at
least harder than it had been in generations, but it was also no
longer enough. Nowadays you had to reach the top – because
that's what the world had become more focused on. It was a
change that had only intensified since the media had exploded
into people's pockets. You had to win, by any means necessary. And increasingly, that meant winning some argument
that seemed to change arbitrarily and yet that people stood by
religiously, to the point of violence. Whatever was at stake, and
there were many things, the important part was not to lose.

Sunny's flat didn't smell good. It was a mixture of burnt
pizza and deodorant. There were clothes piled on the sofa
and the carpet looked as if it had never been hoovered. In the
corner was a pile of Mortal Kombat sleeves. In the bathroom,
a shelf along one wall had been stacked with various grooming products, multi-coloured gels and pastes, most of which
were oozing out of their containers. I noticed a framed photo
of his parents. It was a picture of them standing in a garden,
his father in an embroidered shalwar kameez and his mother
in an elegant red gown.

Sunny opened his laptop. He pulled up a folder of pictures
of him and Tom. The two of them looked different when
they were young, baby-faced in jeans and T-shirts. Sunny in
particular was almost unrecognizable. He'd put on a lot of
weight.

By the time it was dark, he had gone quiet, but I got the feeling he didn't want us to leave. When it was time to go, I had to admit, I was relieved.

'Is he OK?' I asked Tom after we'd left.

'I'm not sure. What do you think?'

'I think he's lonely.'

'I mean, obviously.'

'He needs help.'

'He's been like that for years.'

'You should say something.'

'What, though? I don't want to embarrass him.'

'Just let him know you're there for him.'

He looked dubious. 'I'm not sure.'

I got the feeling he knew better than I did. There was an unspoken understanding between them and words might have made things worse. I didn't really understand it so I let it go.

•

We'd missed the last train home and were in the town centre looking for a hotel. Luton was busy that night. A sticker on a lamp read: *EDUCATE AGAINST HATE*. Pools of vomit sat outside the Edge Club. I recognized the star of a reality TV show and a bunch of teens by the fire exit. Passers-by stopped to stare. Some of them even asked for a selfie. He was attracting a lot of attention. I wondered how many of these clubs existed, and how much it cost to book an appearance like this. Probably more than the average band or DJ. This was what had replaced the music scene. The man chatted for a while, then he checked the time and disappeared inside. Some of the crowd trailed behind him while others dispersed across the street.

Towns like Luton, I thought, were English in a way that wasn't really true of London any more. Despite the number of commuters to the capital and the well-documented racial tensions, Luton was a quintessentially English town. I realized this when I overheard a conversation at the station the next morning.

'The British have lost interest in their heritage,' the woman was saying. 'Look at us compared to somewhere like France or Spain, they've retained a sense of pride in their culture. What have we done?' she asked the man sitting across from her in the waiting room. She seemed furious. 'The French have banned the hijab. What have we banned?' She paused for effect. '*Fox-hunting.*' It was fair to assume from her accent that this woman had never joined a fox hunt. She probably didn't even want to. On every level, she was cognizant of the fact that her chances of entering that sport were, in this lifetime, nil. All the same, it meant something to her. She was keen to align herself with the idea.

'She's so angry,' I said to Tom.

'People take comfort in tradition.'

'But it isn't her tradition, is it?'

'Maybe not,' he said, glancing around the grey plastic chairs in the waiting room, 'but what else is there?'

I'd left Tom waiting for our train on the platform and was in the queue at Starbucks when I heard the crash. The shop window shattered, cracks spattering noisily across the glass. Before I had a chance to shield my face, a second missile hit, shards bursting through the air, raining haphazardly on my head. Outside, a man stood behind the smashed glass, his breath condensed around his mask. Behind him was a rolling crowd of bodies, protesters marching down the street. Someone held up a banner that said: *WHY DID THE POLICE TURN A BLIND EYE TO LARGELY PAKI-STANI SEX GROOMING GANGS?* Behind them there was a long white sheet emblazoned with the tag *#BELIEVE-BRITISHWOMEN.* The letters were dripping and uneven, sprayed in luminous red paint. The crowd advanced in loose lockstep, a woman at the front distributing leaflets saying *IT'S NOT JUST ROTHERHAM – GROOMING EPIDEMIC IN THE UK – 1400 GIRLS IN ROTHERHAM* ALONE. The man in the mask didn't move away. Instead he reached for a third missile. I slid down to the floor as he lobbed it hard, this time smashing the glass completely, shards raining over my head as I covered my face. Flecks of beer hit my skin. The sharp smell of urine filled the air and I realized that someone had thrown a can of piss. I felt someone's body lying on my legs. It was a long time before the police arrived. They approached seemingly out of nowhere, herding the crowd outside into narrow channels. A pair of helicopters circled above. The noise drowned out the chanting on the ground: 'NO SURRENDER – JUSTICE FOR OUR GIRLS.' When the arrests began, the marchers fought back. Some of them kicked and screamed at the authorities, while others stood and recorded them for evidence. They tracked everything on their phones, people being handcuffed and led away. I touched my face, there was blood on my hand. When I finally tried to stand up, I realized my leg wouldn't hold. I made an effort to pull myself up but I couldn't balance. My leg was swollen, fragments of glass lodged in the skin. I scanned the station, looking for Tom. I couldn't see him at first: he was cordoned off, on the far side of the concourse. His face looked grazed but otherwise he didn't seem hurt. There were leaflets all over floor: *WHY ARE WE PROTECTING MUSLIM RAPISTS?* My heart was pumping. I couldn't feel my foot. For some reason, I felt transcendentally alive.

•

At the hospital, I watched the protest on the news while I fielded messages from work. Even Lara made an appearance via email after the Dungeness debacle. This was what it had taken to break her silence. I still had her stupid scarf in my bag, wrapped up in crushed Christmas paper. I hadn't had a chance to give it to her.

I switched my phone to silent and read the news. *The Telegraph* was leading with 'White Nationalist Rioters Block Luton Streets'. *The Guardian* had gone with 'Far Right Spreads Toxic Propaganda'. The story revolved around a police investigation into the grooming of teenagers in Luton. The authorities had allegedly underplayed the crimes for fear of inflaming racial tensions. Each paper had released a version of the story. Each had a video of the chanting crowd. There was also a photo of a young girl, her mouth taped shut, her placard scrawled with: *We want Britain FREE from medieval ATTITUDES towards women.*

The people in the videos looked energized, their eyes shining with fervour. Above all, these people were impassioned. They'd been fuelled by something powerful. It wasn't only outrage, it went deeper than that. It was more like righteous conviction.

The A&E waiting room was packed. There were kids in brightly coloured fleeces with their parents, who were mostly dressed similarly. I wondered how many of these people believed in something. I'd read somewhere that human beings were genetically predisposed to faith, in the sense that – in theory, at least – it offered certain fitness advantages. The scientific revolution might have killed God – and in exchange, conferred predictive powers – but it hadn't provided a way of life, let alone a step up in the evolutionary playing field. I could feel myself spiralling as I scanned the room. Who were these people and what were their lives like? They weren't like the people at the protest. A lot of them looked listless. Their joggers were loose, their trainers scuffed. They sustained themselves on bags of crisps and fizzy drinks from the vending machine. I could feel my thoughts swirling faster. It had taken two hundred years for Western institutions to internalize the implications of the Darwinian revolution. Even now, we were in a strange position, caught between upholding Christian values – kindness, equality, personal responsibility – and abandoning all of it in the name of cash. The resulting politics were pretty minimal. They could be reduced to a single idea: follow your heart. How long would it take, I wondered, for these institutions to absorb the science of our own era? The question of free will, for example, seemed to be leaning towards the 'no' camp, at least by any classical definition. This wasn't a minor alteration. Personal choice underpinned everything around us. Without the self-determined individual, what was left for Western culture? I started sweating. Tom looked at me, concerned.

'Do you want another coffee?' he said.

While he went to fetch it, my queue number came up. I double-checked my ticket – it was 378. I tried to stand but I couldn't support my weight, so I waved at the woman at reception. According to the clock behind her desk, it was almost 2.05 a.m. I sat there for a second, trying to catch her eye as the screen flicked to 379.

33

I was stuck in traffic with Tom and Sunny, my leg was throbbing. It had only been a fortnight since I'd injured it but I'd had to drag myself out of the flat because the three of us were on our way to the world's most excruciating meeting. I couldn't understand Tom's enthusiasm for Georgia's racket but unfortunately, it hadn't diminished and she'd agreed to see us all at 11. Tom handed me his phone to check his emails.

'It starts as sadness,' I read from the message Grace had sent him. It was a quote from one of the patients at Mind. org.uk – a charity whose website opened with an old photo of the royal family, the princes William and Harry half smiling at the camera, turquoise sweatbands around their heads. The bands were emblazoned with the phrase *Heads Together*. It must have been at least five years old. 'Then I feel myself shutting down,' the quote continued, 'becoming less able to face reality. I want to be enveloped by the darkness that existed before I was born.'

'Is it true, what you told me?' I asked Tom, 'that there's no real evidence for depression? As an illness, I mean.'

'Well, the UN are saying no. They're disputing the biomedical model completely.'

'I thought it was partly genetic, anyway. Like you're born with the predisposition. Doesn't that suggest there's a chemical component?'

'To some extent,' Tom agreed, distracted. 'Major depressive disorder is hereditary in some people – up to around 35 per cent of it. That's the current understanding, anyway. Doesn't mean it's all just a chemical imbalance.'

'What do you mean?'

'Well, there's epigenetics.' He flipped off the radio. 'Painful life experiences, that kind of thing. They can affect suscepti-bility to stress. And not just in the individual but across whole generations. Stress affects DNA methylation, plus there are other factors involved – microRNAs, histone modifications – they're all affected by the endocrine system and they've all been shown to play a role in psychiatric disorders, which is why they can run in families. They don't even require a specific gene sequence. Hereditary trauma is nothing new, though. The idea has been around for centuries. It predates science by a long way. What's new is the prevalence of these diseases.'

'You think they're getting worse?'

'According to the research.'

'Isn't it just that more people are being diagnosed?'

'Well, there's that. Plus we have to rely on self-reporting for these numbers.'

'But why would people exaggerate their symptoms? What's the point?'

'A cry for help? Anything's possible. Although that scenario begs the question why. If some of this is just about attention – a desire to be noticed or "seen" – why do so many feel "unseen"? Has the world become more self-absorbed? More competitive? More narcissistic? There are theories around that too – that modernity incentivizes self-interest, that it weakens trust on some level. There's an idea that more people lack stability because they lack strong relationships. Without role models, family, friends – even social norms like belief systems – it's more difficult to regulate mood. And I'll tell you what's even more difficult – formulating a vision of the future. That's something that's fundamental to depression. Depressives are people who have nothing to look forward to.'

'So you think life is just getting worse?'

'It's possible. In certain ways. And the data suggests that unhappiness accrues.'

'Generationally, you mean?'

'Yes, but not just through genetics. Culturally, politically, economically. Mood effects are extremely complex. The brain grows 100 billion neurons in the womb – and it never stops evolving. It's not possible to quantify the number of random events that take place. The level of uncertainty is vast, even if you try to control for other factors. Regardless of the evidence we actually have, the truth is, we just don't know very much. We can't separate out the causes. Which makes it virtually impossible to identify targets for drug intervention.'

'So you think these medications are all a scam?'

'Look, we've spent the last hundred years trying to distinguish between nature and nurture. All we know about depression is this: genetic factors notwithstanding, it's caused – on some level – by stress. Why is there so much interest in these drugs? Because the market is exploding. Because what these patients are suffering from, arguably, is exposure to the twenty-first century. Depression is already the number-one disease burden for women in the world. By 2030, that figure will include men. Life expectancy is dipping in the West, mostly due to deaths of despair – alcoholism, addiction, obesity and suicide. The numbers are colossal and they're escalating, which means anything in pill form is a licence to print money. Do these drugs alleviate suffering? Long term? I haven't got a clue. No one does. It's all just speculation. No one really knows how anyone else is feeling.'

He stopped abruptly behind a truck with the message *Axis Transport – Value To Be Together*. The front of our car grazed its tailgate, prompting the driver to stick his head out.

'Cunt,' he yelled, flipping Tom the finger. Then he revved his engine, flooding us with fumes.

•

Georgia was late so we started without her. Lara was curled up in a pouffey chair. She'd kicked her shoes off and had ordered Aliya to bring us green tea, which arrived in a tall glass pot with a slice of lemon floating on top. In her hand was a report from the focus group that Georgia had commissioned the previous week. It was an overview of their attempt to collect early consumer insights on Eudaxa. Tom, Sunny and I sat quietly while she flipped through the document. She refused to meet my eye or Tom's. It was the first time I'd seen her in weeks.

'So, the results were mixed,' she said. 'Based on first impressions' – she barely looked at Tom – 'your product scored highly in the "concept" category: 86 per cent "extremely like". However, people felt it lacked something – "neither like nor dislike" – when it came to packaging.'

Georgia burst through the door. She was in a pair of red vinyl trousers. She pulled out a tablet and a small folder from her bag.

'Sorry I'm late,' she said, plumping herself down on the chair next to Lara's.

'So, one of the groups,' Lara continued, 'and I think this point is crucial, said the product felt "too clinical".'

'Too clinical?' Sunny looked perplexed.

Tom made a note on the corner of his pad.

'They found it dry,' Georgia added. 'It's too distant.'

She peered at Sunny with curiosity. For some reason, he was wearing a shirt and tie. I thought he looked good in them, although I wished I'd thought to tell him that he shouldn't.

'They're saying the product looks too *clinical*?' Sunny repeated.

He stared at the pile of boxes on the table.

'They *are* a bit dated. Is that Helvetica?' Georgia said.

'They always look like that,' he said.

'Well, our testers thought the packaging was blah.'

'And it's not just the packaging,' Lara continued. 'It's about your whole approach. The way you're handling this is simply not reflective of the society we live in.'

'But they *are* clinical,' Sunny said, still processing the earlier point.

'Basically,' Georgia ignored him, 'the socio-historical background here, the lens through which you're viewing mental health – it's all too male, pale and stale.'

Sunny looked at me then back at Georgia. There was a weird tension between them. She seemed morbidly fascinated by him, as if she'd discovered a whole new genre of man, a curiously novel specimen that she'd never encountered in the wild before. I don't think she was used to meeting people so diametrically different to herself.

'Our testers found it boring,' Lara said. 'They found it cold. They wanted something punchier. And something politically switched on, if you know what I mean?'

'Why, though?' Sunny said.

I could hear Tom sighing under his breath.

'Because, in case you haven't noticed' – Georgia plopped her notepad on the table – 'we are living in the twenty-first century.'

She gave me a look that said: *Who have you brought me?*

I glanced at Tom. He looked exhausted.

'Look, we're willing to work with what you've got, but you're going to have to be more open-minded.'

'So,' Tom said, 'your point is that we haven't been proactive enough when it comes to inclusivity?'

'Exactly,' Lara replied. 'And as a result, you're not connecting with your market.'

'It just doesn't feel like it's for *everyone*,' Georgia said, gazing at the little white boxes. 'You're going to have to try a little harder. Reach out to people. Make it *friendlier*.'

•

'What was that about?' Sunny said, as the three of us braved the Old Street roundabout on foot, trying to find our way back to the car.

'They don't usually work with medicine,' I said. 'And they're not necessarily wrong.'

'They scared the shit out of me.'

'You'll get over it.'

'So, you work with these people?'

Tom let him back into the car. I could tell it was going to be a long journey.

'Yes,' I said reluctantly.

'And what exactly is it that that you do?'

•

That weekend, Tom had arranged for Sunny to stay at his flat. He needed to be in London first thing on Monday for a meeting with Grace and there didn't seem much point in him going home. I woke up on Saturday to discover that he'd set up camp on the sofa. He'd demarcated his area with a cushion and accessorized it with a laptop, an A5 tablet, the TV remote, a miscellaneous array of power cables and a tub of Protein World's 'The Slender Blend'. He didn't seem interested in going out. I went to the hospital to get my leg checked and when I came back, he was in the same position. He was watching *Spectre* on Amazon Prime.

'You like James Bond?' I said.

'You mean a man so emotionally scarred that he just fucks girls and murders foreigners?'

'While wearing a tuxedo and a bow tie.'

'If it ain't broke.' He moved his laptop to make room for me. 'I prefer Bourne though, actually. He's a better spy. More realistic.'

'Sunny's definitely a Bourne man,' Tom said, coming in from the kitchen with a bowl of popcorn. 'Low-key. Outstanding skills. Very solid in a crisis.'

'The brains of the operation,' Sunny said.

'I can't deny it,' Tom agreed.

I sat between them feeling like a spare part. I seemed to have entered some sort of bromage-à-trois.

Stretched around the generous mound of Sunny's belly was a T-shirt printed with Mai Shiranui, the sexy ninja from Fatal Fury, her mini-skirted cheongsam riding up her thigh.

'Do you like Fatal Fury?' he said, as if there was any chance I'd know what he was talking about. I only recognized the character because I remembered people playing the game when I was at school. 'There's something about the textural rendering of a thong riding up a virtual girl's backside that does something for me no real woman ever will.'

'I don't doubt it,' I said.

He reminded me of one of those beetles that had been discovered in the Australian outback, the ones that spent their time humping empty beer bottles. He'd adapted perfectly to his environment – just not in the way that nature had intended. There was a small pile of banana powder gathered in the crease of his jeans.

'There's banana powder on your jeans,' I said.

'I'm saving it for later.'

He was doing a very good impression of someone who didn't give a shit. I got the feeling with Sunny that this was a hard-won quality. Other people's judgements couldn't touch him. God knows what kind of life he'd led but I had a certain level of respect for it.

•

Tom and Grace were due to pitch brand Eudaxa to Floyd the following week and they still weren't sure where they were going with it. I was with Tom, crossing London Bridge. It was raining. We'd agreed not to talk about work but he couldn't seem to let it go.

'Your friends, they really went for us, didn't they?'

'I warned you.'

'I'm not taking any of it personally.'

'Are you sure about that?'

'I'm not so sure about Sunny . . .' He pulled a 'yikes' face.

'He'll recover.'

We walked in silence for a while.

'Seriously though,' he said, 'I've been thinking about it. Imagine we run with this whole "inclusivity" thing. I'm thinking our tagline would be something like: *Better Together With Eudaxa*. It's about bringing people together, healing conflict, building bridges. Is that "friendly" enough for them, do you think?'

'Better Together With Eudaxa?'

'Do you think it's bland?'

'No, I think it works.'

'So, this is the message we're trying to get across. We're not just focused on the patient. It's about strengthening their network. We're creating a safe space where patients and their peers can connect with one another.'

'It's quite out there.'

'Not really. Therapy has always been about relationships.'

'But not about doping the victims.'

'Arguable.'

'OK, what about this. You could go even further and say you're rethinking mental health completely. You're taking on its patriarchal history. You're challenging the victim-blaming. Where do you draw the line between a sick person and the society they live in?'

'You're starting to sound like Floyd.'

He stopped and leaned against the railings. It was getting dark and the street lights had come on, their reflections shining across the water.

'Sometimes I think this job is making me crazy.'

'Ironic.'

It was a joke but he wasn't in the mood. 'Do you want to know what I really think?' I said.

He looked at me as if to say, *Please help me.*

'Sometimes, when I'm looking at the data-sets at work, there's so much information in those archives and yet the same patterns keep recurring: the more time people spend alone – physically alone, I mean – the more negatively it affects their mood. People pass the time with entertainment, with ideas, but it's all transient stuff. They'll get attached to some of it – to certain fandoms, tribes, movements – but underneath all of that, they're not fulfilled. They're fundamentally frustrated. And it just drives them further online. It's like they're searching for something that never comes. It's a vicious circle. It's difficult to break. There isn't an obvious way out. What I'm saying is, maybe this is a way out.'

He stayed quiet for a while.

'Because it turns people back towards each other? Instead of keeping them fixated on . . . the machine?'

I wasn't sure if that's what I'd meant, but he seemed taken with the idea.

'You've out-Floyded Floyd,' he said.

'Is that a good thing?'

He pulled out his phone. 'Better Together With Eudaxa,' he wrote. 'Machine. Freedom. Movement.'

At the pub, we made a point of sitting by the fire. I ordered the fillet of Dorset sea bream.

'I could get used to this,' I said.

Although the truth was, I already had. I couldn't hide my disappointment they were out of truffle sauce.

Tom had the green hispi salad and turbot with Maltaise dressing. By the time the food arrived, he was back on it.

'Is it too soft? They're paying us to make some noise.'

'Not this time.'

'Why?'

'Because this whole project is about rising above that stuff, isn't it? It's about lifting people out of the noise.'

'I like that,' he said.

I smiled, satisfied.

'You're good at this.'

'It's interesting.'

'I should get you on my team.'

'Not you as well.'

'I think I'd like that,' he smiled.

I kicked him softly under the table.

'I think you'd like it too much.'

34

Tom waited behind the glass wall of Floyd's office. He recognized Ian Dunstan coming out – the man who'd introduced Floyd on stage that day. He wondered who was funding all of this and how much of it was coming from people like Dunstan, who seemed just as interested in their own publicity as they did the medical side of things. Floyd looked smaller than he remembered. On stage, he'd somehow seemed more commanding. He'd requested that Grace speak to him on her own, he'd said he didn't like the formality of pitches – an unexpected change that had put her on edge. He could just about hear what they were saying.

'Psilocybin?' Grace said, surprised.

'Just a touch, it helps keep me lucid.'

Floyd offered her a drop of the yellowish fluid but she declined.

Better Together With Eudaxa it said on the title page of Grace's deck. She built her case up point by point. Her style was detailed and precise. Floyd stroked his head, staring at the marble egg on the corner of his desk. He picked it up and twirled it in his hand, tossing it up in the air as she spoke. Grace painted a meticulous vision of what she called 'a revolution in mental health', one that took the responsibility off the patient, one that focused more holistically on groups, on unlocking the potential of social networks to lift everyone up together.

'Imagine you're troubled by your relationship with your

wife,' she said. 'Family breakdown is a major indicator of depression. The patterns we inherit from our parents are the ones that damage us the most. If something's wrong, it can affect generations. In a traditional therapeutic context, that sort of problem might take months, even years to treat – and there's no guarantee that it would work. But bring Eudaxa into the mix and we see those success rates begin to rise. The evidence is clear – it's a gamechanger at this level. It offers an immediate route to empathy, to trust.'

She was still apprehensive as she wrapped things up.

'But our licence permits us to prescribe this outside of psychotherapy,' Floyd said.

'I know, but the therapeutic framework is important,' Grace replied. 'At least in the introductory phases.'

She had rehearsed this part. She leaned forward for emphasis.

'It separates us from the Prozacs of the world. That's the first hurdle we need to overcome – we need to make it clear that Eudaxa is *different* to other medications. It's about creating long-term change. It's not about papering over the cracks.'

There was a pause while Floyd appeared to consider what she was saying.

'And also,' she added, 'we don't think the industry is ready for anything more. If we place this drug in the context of psychotherapy, we're at least opening up that door. After that, we can think about other applications, but it's always better to approach these things conservatively.'

'You know,' Floyd said, 'I've long thought that in business, the biggest opportunities are the ones that no one else has managed to define. Sometimes, the problem is so pervasive that it simply goes unnoticed. It's one thing to develop a solution but it's quite another to frame a product in a way that ordinary people can digest. You're right in that there's always resistance to change. And that's true of psychiatry in particular. I think what you've brought to me today is – well, it's very faithful to our research. And yet you've drawn it on a human scale. You've made it all sound rather touching.'

He gave Grace an appreciative look.

'I think it's interesting,' he said. 'I'll have to present it to the board but yes, it's good.'

PART 3
Launch

The process of bringing a product to market, including learning from early customer behaviour and altering protocols as necessary

Why not a technology of joy, of happiness?

ABRAHAM MASLOW, *THE FARTHER REACHES*
OF HUMAN NATURE

35

We were a quarter of the way into the twenty-first century and despite escalating redundancies, the digital economy was still growing. An ambient malaise hung in the air, a vague sense that something wasn't right. It was no secret that the world was getting stranger in ways that went beyond the economy. The widespread charge to follow your bliss was not resulting in much bliss. What it seemed to produce, more than anything, was marketing. Each passing moment was drenched in it. There was an endless stream of marketed content that seeped into every moment. Under the circumstances, it was hard to concentrate, especially on other people.

Grace's birthday was no exception. There weren't many people at her house because she didn't have many friends. She'd invited Bay and Mireille, some old colleagues, a girl from school, and her sister, who'd driven up from Taunton with her husband Pete, a plasterer. Pete was built like a rock and barely said a word all night. Even Niall didn't seem himself. He hardly touched his prawn linguine. I noticed his hands were shaking; he was already on his second bottle of Merlot.

'I suppose you know what's going on?' he said, cornering me in the garden later.

'No.'

'She knows.'

'You've told her, then?'

'Fuck no.'

'What's happened?'

'She found my second phone.'

'What did she say?'

'She wants a divorce.'

He shoved his hands through his hair which had formed a ginger haze around his head.

'Isn't that what you wanted?'

'No. We've been together since we were kids.'

'You still love her?'

'Of course I do.' He looked genuinely upset. 'It's just – things change, don't they?'

'So you're staying together?'

He let out a dry laugh.

'It's not the end of the world,' I said. 'People break up all the time.'

'Everyone keeps telling me that.'

'You'll be fine.'

'Will I, though?'

He glanced through the kitchen window. Grace and Evie were sitting at the table. Their faces were illuminated in the candlelight as if they were characters in an old painting. I wondered who he would become without them.

'It's hard to say,' I acknowledged. 'I don't know.'

36

Where are you?

Lara wasn't happy.

I updated her with a photo of my leg. It was broken in three different places and had now become infected. It hurt every time I shifted my weight. The doctor had ordered me to stay at home.

I wanted to talk to you about that

I was thinking you could write something about what happened

I want the Openr take

Which is?

Your story, in your own words

Just tell me what to say

I had a feeling she was going to anyway.

If you want to know how I would do it, I'd say it's about the policing of women's bodies. These white supremacists think they own us. And they're trying to make it all about race, as if it's only brown men who commit these crimes. Grooming is pervasive. It's not a race thing

I hesitated.

Do I talk about the victims?

It's more that this kind of crime has no ethnicity

I had no idea if this was true.

Aren't there cultural differences with these things?
And anyway, what about 'Consent is our mantra'?

I watched the three dots hovering for a while. They were definitely radiating hostility.

The race-baiting is more important

Why?

Because that's where it all starts. It's all connected isn't it? The more you oppress a man, the more he'll take it out on the nearest woman

Did you just make that up?

You can have it

Why don't you write this stuff yourself?

Because I wasn't there, it wouldn't be authentic

She said it without a hint of irony. I didn't want to have to write 'my story' but I also didn't have the energy to argue.

When for?

Asap

Ok

I waited for her approval but she didn't bother.

37

Through the bathroom window at Tom's apartment I could see a woman getting dressed. I'd developed a habit of taking morning baths, my plastered ankle propped up on the edge. It was almost March but the sky was grey, a light fog muting what little light filtered through the buildings.

I was still officially working from home, which meant hours alone in Tom's flat. I'd started watching TV when he was out. The simulation of company kept me going. It was only tuned into certain channels, which I found comforting, probably because it reminded me of my childhood when I'd watched a lot of television, the whole family gathered around the box like a campfire. That morning, I settled on *Inside The Factory* while I worked through my stretches – the hospital had given me a set of exercises to try and rehabilitate my leg. Gregg Wallace from MasterChef had gone to Ireland. He was walking around a liqueur factory that processed over a million bottles of Irish cream a day. He followed the journey of a bottle as it worked its way through the production process. During the final stretch, Cherry Healey discovered where the empty bottles were recycled. This was followed by a scene in which a historian, dressed for some reason as a nun, chatted excitedly at the camera as it tracked her progress around a monastery. 'I'm in pursuit,' she said frenetically, 'of the spiritual origins of liqueur.'

At around nine, I picked up my laptop. I clicked reflexively towards the news. The headline said 'Model Bella Hadid Attends Pro-Palestinian Rally'.

Although the article had only just gone live, there were nine thousand comments underneath, some with hundreds of likes.

The Hadid girls would be stoned by Hamas and other Muslim extremists for the way the flaunt their bodies.

The fact that so many people support these people, who are not just the archenemies of the Jews but also the enemies of all non-Muslims, is a testament to how pervasive the utterly ludicrous religion of Islam is, a so-called Religion of Peace pushed onto us by open-borders lunatics, infesting the minds and psyches of the public at large. It is very sad indeed.

Can anyone tell me how marauding mobs and violence against the police on the streets of London & Manchester helps the situation in the Middle East?

I'M A PALESTINIAN, I'M A WOMAN AND I'M ALSO A FEMINIST. PALESTINIAN WOMEN LIKE ME CAN BE ANGRY ABOUT MORE THAN ONE THING

Only 5% of the UK population is Muslim, yet Muslims comprise 12% of sex offenders.

Probably because juries are more likely to convict them.

Sarah Champion, the Labour MP for Rotherham thinks there are likely at least a million child victims of Muslim rape gangs in this country. As we know from multiple enquiries, councils don't want to talk about these cases.

WTF HAS THIS GOT TO DO WITH PALESTINE? THIS COUNTRY HAS GONE INSANE

In the background, the nun explained that liqueurs were invented a world away from the 'funky downtown bars' of

Dublin and that the monks who had developed them had, in fact, been searching for the elixir of life.

I checked my phone. There was a message from Tom. No words, just a picture of the airport.

Much later, he sent me something else. It was a link to pictures of an exhibition. It was the Openr Gallery, I recognized it immediately. There were people milling around the space, drinking beer, colourfully dressed – and mounted on the walls around them, a series of huge photos on the walls. I didn't recognize myself at first. I was naked in every single shot, my body blown up across the canvases, my face and body bathed in flashlight, exposed against the black night sky. My waist and legs were obscured by what looked like a flat expanse of water. There was an orange blur in the corner, as if the photographer had left a finger over the lens. In the background, I could just about see Niall, his face flushed with alcohol, his eyes pin pricks in the distance, his hair slicked against his head as he floated, also naked, in the ocean.

What is this?

It took him seconds to reply:

I was hoping you might tell me that

I called immediately but he didn't answer.

There were ten photos on display, each one fashionably blurred. They'd been uploaded to Openr.com/blog and then spread over the company's social media. They had an eerie, almost ghostly look against the stark white walls of the gallery. Above the images was a caption: *NOCTURNAL ANIMALS – A NIGHT OF WILD SWIMMING AT DUNGENESS.*

I scrolled quickly to the bottom of the page. I was naked

in almost every shot. I messaged Lara but she didn't answer. I tried to calculate the damage as I rang her. I couldn't remember any of the photos being taken. I had no recollection of a camera that night. I hadn't seen a flash. It had been raining so hard. I had no memory of it at all.

Call me, I wrote but she didn't reply.

I tried Tom again – still nothing. I could see he was online. I sent another text. When I called him later, it went to voicemail.

•

I spent the next two days on my own. I didn't see another human being. I had no way of knowing where Tom was – all I knew was that he still hadn't come home and that he wasn't answering his phone. I still couldn't leave the flat even to buy groceries, so I immersed myself in work. I prioritized tasks and crossed them off. I wrote my articles. I monitored my stats. When information became available, I checked it, logged it and marked it on the system. I didn't hear a living voice, not even my own.

It was on the third day that I began to crack. Time had started bending into strange shapes. I picked up the piece I'd been writing about the riot. I tried to describe exactly what had happened to me that day. I tried to make it vivid for the reader but somehow, whatever I did, it didn't feel right. Unsatisfied, I sent my efforts over to Lara, who replied almost immediately: You're holding back. Make it more real

I tried to call her but again but she didn't answer. She had me pinned down like an insect on a board. I did her bidding, I amped up the 'realness', although I wasn't sure what she meant by that. It was definitely more lurid by the time I'd finished with it.

Better, she responded.

Then nothing.

I knew I was going to have to present this thing on video.

Do you want this filed or not? I said.

She didn't take long to think about it.

Yes

•

On the fourth morning of my confinement, unease began to harden into anger. I got dressed and dragged myself outside. I was determined to confront her in person.

It was around noon by the time I made it to the foyer of 180 Strand. It was London Fashion Week. I'd arrived late but the show still hadn't started. I knew she was there because she'd posted a photo of herself backstage that morning. It said *Openr* in the corner of the cards that been laid out on the seats. They always partnered with young designers, it was one way of keeping the company in the news. I looked around, trying to pick her out in the crowd. I couldn't believe she'd somehow managed to reduce me to stalking her again.

A single row of chairs snaked around the runway, which took a long and winding route around the hall. The tiles beneath my feet were gloss black. The people in the row opposite were silhouetted against a grid of glowing screens. In the darkness, I could just make out the features of the tech investor Josh Kushner and his model wife Karlie Kloss. Beside them was the German performance artist Anne Imhof and the Russian Instagram celebrity Miroslava Duma. These figures were circumscribed by a flotilla of photographers and demi-celebrities, a few of whom I recognized vaguely, although I couldn't have told you who they were. I scanned the hall but I couldn't see any sign of Lara. I tried calling her again, unsuccessfully. A tall woman in a plastic mac slouched down beside me without a word. I could feel my painkillers wearing off. I was still on antibiotics and I was starting to feel sick.

The show began with no trace of Lara. The music started

off quietly, a low hum of crackling static. The walls turned green, like a special effects screen. A single piano note built up to a muted, soft-edged symphony. 'Constant transformation,' the voiceover said. 'Continual Evolution. Fluid change.' As the models strode along the runway, light projections meandered from one image to the next: now a melting hall of mirrors, now an oozing volcanic surface. Kloss shifted in her seat, her eyes hidden by the changing lights. Immersed in a literal sea of content, she lifted her phone up to her face. At first, I thought she was snapping the clothes but then I realized that she was filming herself. 'My work,' the designer was quoted in the show notes, 'explores new bodies, new environments and how our world, our perceptions, our relationships are in a state of constant flux.' The models continued to stride past me, their footsteps fast and blunt. One was wearing a tailored skirt, another a pair of blue jeans that looked, as far as I could tell, exactly like a pair of 501s. In contrast to the models themselves, who had all been cast for their odd features, the clothes seemed to reach for normativity: a trench, a black dress, a sweatshirt. 'The journey,' the show notes explained, 'takes us through an enchanting virtual world, dreamlike architectural experiments merging into techno-futurist nightmares. The outside world collapses into inner consciousness as the show fixates us.'

Kushner stood as the lights went up and headed straight for the door. 'Constant transformation,' the voice whispered after him. 'Fluid change.' A field of cameras descended as the audience began to stir.

Still no sign of Lara. I headed backstage in search of her. The show's designer was being interviewed, the hood of his tracksuit crumpled around his neck. He'd been chosen by Openr not just for his aesthetic but also because he was a refugee. 'I use my work to express all of the difficulties I've experienced,' he'd written in his application for the money.

'Our world is full of instability and violence and that's what I try to show.' Following a partnership with Adidas, he had started expressing his pain through sportswear. A T-shirt from his range – now imbued with his politically charged trauma – was on sale in Harrods for over a thousand pounds. The people assembled in the room congratulated him in reverent tones. They liked his authenticity, his vulnerability. He was, they commented, an *artist*.

I finally recognized someone I knew: Aliya.

'Lara's not here,' she said. 'She left after the show.'

•

It took me over an hour to track her down. She was in the bar of the Delaunay. By this point my leg was burning and I knew I wouldn't be able to stand for much longer.

'What are you doing here?' she asked me.

'I could ask you the same question.'

The waiter turned up with two whiskies. It was only then that I realized she was with her father.

'This is a surprise,' he said. 'I rarely get the pleasure of meeting Lara's friends these days. I'm an embarrassment, apparently.'

She warned me wordlessly to leave but I ignored her.

'What's your poison?' he said, motioning to the waiter.

She glowered at me as I sat down.

'Vodka tonic,' I answered, ignoring her.

'So tell me, what do you make of our current overlord?' her father asked me, leaning back in his green upholstered chair. 'Sunak's an interesting character, isn't he? Funny how the browning of the UK hasn't turned out at all like Labour intended.'

'Dad!' Lara said.

'I've committed another thought crime, have I?'

This was new coming from him. Had he fallen out of love

with Tony Blair? There was a bitterness in his voice that I'd never noticed before. It sounded personal. I got the feeling he wasn't dealing well with the divorce. I wondered what had happened with Lara's mother. He changed the subject as if to placate his daughter.

'So, I hear you're working with Lara. How's that going? Do enlighten me, she never tells me anything about her life.'

'Well,' I said, unsure where to start.

'Obviously, it's all Dutch to me,' he talked over me, nursing his whisky. 'You're going to have to break it down in simple terms for an old duffer like me.'

'Leave it, Dad,' Lara said. 'Ignore him, he knows exactly what I do.'

I got the impression she wasn't just protecting me, she really didn't want the conversation to continue.

'Well, that's the thing, darling,' he replied. 'You're so mysterious about it all.'

He leaned towards me conspiratorially.

'I'm thinking of making an investment in this young lady.'

'You're not investing in anything,' she said.

She caught my eye, reddening.

'He doesn't mean it,' she said.

'Of course I do.'

He drained his glass and waved at the waiter again.

'It seems the only crime worse than a father wanting his daughter to succeed is, God forbid, one that actually invests in her.'

'You're *not* investing in me.'

She looked mortified.

It dawned on me that she was more than embarrassed by this invasion into her territory. She looked genuinely unhappy, as if something was seriously wrong. I got the sense he wasn't offering, exactly. Maybe he was trying, not very discreetly, to put his money in her name. Maybe it was something to do with the divorce. Or maybe he'd finally pushed his luck too far and taken on one too many loans. He looked both drunk and miserable. I could feel his desperation in my stomach. It was a state I'd never seen in him before, he was usually such an amiable borderline alcoholic. She glanced at me, ashamed but also hurt. From her face, he might as well have taken a shit on the carpet in front of us.

I didn't feel as if I could just leave. I looked around, as if I hadn't noticed what was happening. The room was full of after-work drinkers, sprigs of herbs poking out of their cocktails. In front of me was a tiny candle in an art deco-style holder.

Lara went to the bar and I followed her.

'What the fuck?' I said.

'Just leave, you shouldn't be here.'

'Why aren't you answering your phone?'

'It's not the time for this.'

Despite myself – and I knew she didn't care, she looked haunted by her father – I decided to force her attention.

'What was that weekend all about?'

'What are you talking about?'

'Those photos.'

'Give me a break.'

'Why?'

'They're *art* photos.'

'Nudes? Of *me*? Apart from anything else, it's unprofessional.'

She laughed. 'You're giving me advice on what's professional? I've built a fucking company from scratch. What have you done? You couldn't keep a job holding your own hand without me to do it for you.'

'You asked me to help you.'

'Well, I'm waiting. You're so checked out, I'm surprised you saw those photos.'

'It's against the law.'

'I'll take my chances.'

'Tom could lose his job.'

'Do you think I care about him?'

'I think you knew he'd see them.'

She rolled her eyes. 'Look, if you're really that offended, just blame it on me. You usually do.'

'And what if it's too late?'

'Then you can thank me for doing you a favour.'

'What is your problem?'

'You're the problem, get over yourself.'

She turned to pay the bill.

'Don't photograph me naked.'

'No one gives a fuck.'

'Post your own nudes.'

'I will.'

I wasn't finished. I opened my mouth to reply but her father rolled up beside us.

'Darling,' he said, a cloud of stale Balvenie ascending from his leather jacket. 'Our table's ready, shall we go?'

He barely acknowledged me in his determination to get to her.

38

I spent another week alone in the flat wondering whether Tom was coming back. I felt like a fraud, surrounded by his things. During that week, it became increasingly apparent that he was expecting me to leave. I realized it wasn't socially acceptable to just squat there like a creep; the right thing to do was disappear and hold on to at least some semblance of dignity. The problem was, I just couldn't bring myself to go. I couldn't stand the thought of simply fading from his life. Occasionally I opened his wardrobe just to remind myself he'd left his clothes. I even resorted to looking through his drawers for some evidence of where he'd gone. There wasn't much to find. He didn't own much. He seemed to have made it through to this stage of his life with only three or four boxes of possessions, a couple of which he hadn't even unpacked yet. It wasn't unusual in a place like London, but for some reason, that week, with nothing to do but stare at his stuff, it made me feel inexplicably despairing. I felt a paralysing hopelessness that went far beyond my own grief. Looking at the city out of the window, I sometimes felt as if the whole of London was just a holding area for workers, an airport lounge filled with transient personnel. There were still people who stayed, even people who built a life here, but it was becoming more and more difficult to pretend that the London of my childhood still existed.

·

I finally forced myself to pack my bags on the Friday. I was about to leave when I heard his key in the lock.

'You're still here,' he said noncommittally.

'Nothing happened,' I told him.

I felt like an idiot. I stood there while he threw his bag on the floor and took his coat off. He went to the kitchen, put the kettle on and made a single coffee.

'How's Grace?' I said cautiously.

'Fine.'

He finally turned to look at me.

'She's not happy, obviously,' he said.

'What did she say?'

'Not much.'

'Do you think I should speak to her?'

'Fuck no.'

'What should I do?'

'I think you should leave her alone.'

'And Niall?'

'What about him?' he said wearily.

'Do you want me to leave?'

'I'm not sure why you're still here.'

I took my bag and walked towards the door. For some reason, I stopped before I got there, hovering for a moment in the hallway. It was excruciating but I wasn't sure what to do. I had a feeling he wanted to see if I would leave, as if it was some sort of test. He sat down heavily, watching me.

'Look,' he said, 'I haven't decided yet.'

'I'm sorry.'

'Are you?'

'Of course.'

'These sex parties, or whatever the fuck they are. How long has this been going on? I mean Niall playing away is one thing but you, him and your little friend. I mean, what the fuck is that?'

'It wasn't a *sex* party,' I said. 'We just went away for the weekend. I didn't even know he was going to be there.'

'Why hide it then?'

'I was embarrassed.'

'Not as embarrassed as I am, fucking hell.'

'I know.'

'Do you really expect me to believe you?'

'Nothing *happened*,' I repeated.

'Except you're just casually fucking my friend?'

'Not me, I was asleep. I didn't even want to be there.' I didn't know what else to say.

'Your boss is a piece of work, isn't she?'

'I can't control her.'

'Neither can Niall, apparently.'

'When it comes to you and me, she's a little, you know' – I searched for the word – 'territorial.'

'So, you and her? I mean, really?'

'It was a long time ago,' I said.

'It's not like it hadn't crossed my mind, but really?' He thought about it for a second. Then he pulled an intrigued face.

'Don't,' I said.

I sat beside him on the sofa.

'Just forgive me.'

'Should I?'

'Yes.'

He looked at me thoughtfully.

'I'll think about it,' he said. 'But in the meantime, you realize I'm going to have to punish you?'

•

I could feel the tension in his body that night. He didn't tell me where he'd been for the past two weeks but I got the sense he'd spent a lot of that time alone. It had been long enough for both of us to realize that the damage had been done, just as Lara had known it would be. I found myself privately furious with her again, another arduous duel with her long shadow.

There was something different in the way Tom handled me that night. He was rough, despite my swollen leg which he'd always treated so reverently in the past. I felt as if he was searching my body for signs of Lara, trying to know for sure what it was I wanted – and to understand what he could handle. It was a tough, annihilating fight for our lives. Then later, he held himself inside me and asked me what it had been like with her. He wanted to know how she had touched me, then he made me show him. He was as aroused as he was unsure what it meant. He came before me for the first time. I didn't lie to him, I told him everything. It was an experiment as much as anything else, and between us, by the morning, we had resolved something.

'Fucking hell,' he said afterwards.

'I know,' I said.

39

If it was true that desire was a contagion – that it was just an echo of what other people wanted – then the Netflix Top 10 Today was a sobering reflection of the situation. I was watching *Dubai Hustle* on the sofa. Tom had been hauled out of town again and my leg was still swollen, although now in a plastic brace. I'd expected to spend the night on my own and was in one of his old sweatshirts, eating cereal when the doorbell rang. It was Grace. I hadn't thought she'd want to see me again. I'd sent her a long email to apologize but that had been a week ago and she hadn't replied. I opened the door to find her small, anoraked figure soaked with rain. She was carrying a bag of groceries. She filled the fridge and sat on the end of the sofa, sliding a small box of beer across the table.

'I thought you might need looking after,' she said, as if by way of reconciliation. 'I know Tom's been busy these last few weeks.'

She opened two Coronas and handed one to me.

It was cruel the pretence that there was equality in marriage. I let her pick out a film. She went for *Wuthering Heights* by Andrea Arnold. We sat through the opening scenes in what turned out to be an amicable silence.

'So, you know her,' she said eventually.

'I'm sorry I didn't tell you.'

'Why didn't you?'

'I should have done. I wish I had.'

'What's wrong with men?'

'I don't know what's wrong with Niall.'

'My life is fucked.'

'You'll be happier without him.'

'If this goes to court, I'm done.'

'You'll be fine.'

'I'm worried they'll give him Evie.'

She looked miserable.

'They won't.'

'Well, even if they don't, what then? I pay some stranger to raise her while I'm away? Sometimes I wonder what the point is.'

'This is the point,' I said. 'This is what the money is for, to give you some control.'

'You'd think so.'

There were dark circles around her eyes that she'd covered up with pale concealer. She looked like someone who was running a very long and gruelling race. I wanted to hug her but I wasn't sure how she would take it. She didn't seem like someone who was used to being touched.

'I'm sorry I covered for him.'

'It doesn't matter.'

'Thanks for coming.'

'Of course,' she said.

She didn't say much else that night, she just sat beside me and watched the film.

•

It was March by the time my brace came off although my leg was still weak from disuse. After such a long time at home, the outside world felt overwhelming. Everything felt far too real. I hadn't seen Lara since that day at the hotel, which I tried not to overthink. It was my first day back at the office. I took the Tube for the first time in weeks. It was rush hour and the sickly smell of bodies hit me as soon as I reached the platform. It stank of coconut oil and sweat.

I'm sorry about your dad, I wrote to Lara.

Then I deleted it and tried again. I spent a while composing different versions, all of which sounded too half-hearted to be real apologies, not because I didn't want to smooth things over – I did, I felt bad for her – but I also couldn't bring myself to surrender. It was pathetic but the truth was I felt too aggrieved that she'd left it up to me again. She was ruthless. I knew it was irrational but I just wasn't ready to give in to her. On the other hand, I knew we'd see each other at work. In the end, running out of time, I circled back to my original version.

There was a long and calculated wait.

It's not your problem, she answered.

That was it.

Hello old friend, I thought as I stepped back into the building that morning, the familiar sinking feeling dropping through my stomach. It was going to be a long day.

•

Grace had booked a conference room at the Crowne Plaza. She was standing on her own on a small stage, a group of sales reps from Pharmacon hanging around at the back. It was launch day for the UK sales team, which meant stepping out of the relative safety of Neura Therapeutics' little set-up and firing up the full force of Pharmacon's sales operation. Along one wall was a salad buffet, along the other a Nespresso machine and a bowl of those cheap biscuits that come in see-through plastic packets. I stood uncomfortably by the door, directing people to their seats. I'd already started looking at new jobs, and with my prospects back on life support, I'd agreed to volunteer today. The Eudaxa campaign had become a guilty pleasure, a sojourn from my life that I enjoyed at the safe distance of someone who had no responsibility for it.

Floyd was late. He'd turned up on his own in jeans and a pair of complicated trainers. He seemed a bit spaced out, as if he'd just finished his mid-morning Vipassana. Once everyone had taken their seats, I dimmed the lights.

'Eudaxa,' Grace announced solemnly, 'is here. She's here to provide the glue that has long been missing from our communities . . . from our societies . . . from our families. She's here to optimize our networks. She's here to mobilize the value lying latent within them. She is empathy, togetherness, compassion. She is a revolution in the way we live.'

She paused for a moment, glancing at Floyd who seemed intoxicated by this vision.

'Because we're all,' she gazed up at the screen, '*Better Together With Eudaxa.*'

The speech went on and on. I caught one of the execs scrolling through talkSPORT. It was dark by the time we finally made it out.

'You killed it,' Tom said.

She wasn't listening.

'Floyd looked fucking ecstatic, did you see him?'

'What's wrong?' I asked her, as we got into the car.

'Nothing,' she replied tersely.

Then she nodded at the console by the handbrake. There was a small pink metallic device lying in one of the compartments.

'It's been there since this morning. Am I going mad?'

We all knew what it was. It was one of Lara's keyring chargers. *Openr: A Safe Place to Play* it said in red Helvetica.

'Doesn't she have a car of her own to fuck my husband in?' Grace said calmly.

I caught Tom's eye, he looked panicked. I could tell he wasn't used to seeing her like this.

She started the engine and drove in silence for a while – then suddenly, she stamped on the accelerator.

'I don't know who he is any more,' she said, her voice

cracking. Her knuckles were white around the wheel. 'But I'll tell you this much, I hate the cunt.'

She started crying. Tom touched her shoulder.

'I can't keep doing this,' she said.

'You can. Listen, work is going great. Niall can wait. Let's deal with him when this is over.'

For a second, I thought she was going to calm down, but instead, she swung the car over the kerb, screeched to a halt and started banging her head against the steering wheel.

'Grace,' Tom said gently.

She didn't respond. Instead, she got out of the car and dragged Niall's kettle bells out of the boot. Then she started smashing them, one by one, against the windscreen until it shattered.

40

It was a small plot of land on La Gomera, an island off the north-west coast of Africa. It was the second smallest of the Canaries, an almost perfect green circle surrounded by a vast expanse of ocean.

'This place is in the mountains,' Tom said. 'It's close to El Cercado.'

We'd both arrived home late from work that night and were on his balcony. It was raining lightly. I studied the picture on his screen. The house was modest. It was built from stone. It looked as if it had been there for a long time. There was almost nothing around it, just a low barn and a crude driveway that cut through a field of tough-looking shrubs.

'I was going to show you earlier but I wasn't sure,' he said.

'This is where you want to go?'

'If you'll come with me.'

'You want to be a hermit?'

'Just for a while, long enough to get my head together.'

'And then what?'

'I'm not sure yet, I just want to get away from all of this.' He waved his hand around the flat, taking in my laptop, all of the devices on the table, his expensive kitchen, the tower blocks outside.

It was an obvious thing to say, but I understood why he'd said it. He wasn't motivated by work in the way I'd first assumed. It wasn't money that drove him, or even status. I think it was more the need to prove that he was OK, that there wasn't anything wrong with him.

'I've spent my life trying to influence people,' he said. 'I want to have some influence over myself.'

'You think it's possible to escape all of this?'

'I think it's easier in a place like that.'

There were vines climbing over the house and a long garden inclined towards the valley. The land was high in the mountains, surrounded by woodland that stretched out towards the coast.

'It looks like something from another time.'

'It's a bit of a backwater. That's why I like it.'

'You think we can do this?'

'Why not? I've already been approved for a mortgage on this place. I could rent it out, it'll give us an income. Not much but enough to live on for a while.'

'What would we do there?'

'Nothing, we'd just exist. And, you know,' he said nonchalantly.

'What?'

'We could think about the *future*.'

He said it so meaningfully, I almost laughed. He watched me closely, trying to gauge my reaction. I must have stayed quiet for too long because he suddenly seemed panicked.

'Is it too much?'

I looked at him.

'I don't think so,' I said.

In fact, the more I thought about it, the more it felt like the most natural thing in the world.

•

Towards the end of April I missed a call from Ashley. She left a voicemail asking if she could rent my room out. I hadn't said anything about leaving but I'd barely been home in weeks. She was sprawled on the sofa when I went over there, a damp towel wrapped around her shoulders. Her hair was packed into cling film, Vaseline smeared along her hairline. She didn't look very pleased to see me.

'Where have you been?' she said.

We'd lived together for almost three years but that night, we might as well have been strangers. In some ways, I'd barely known her at all, I had only a broken picture of who she was. I knew that she was thirty-five years old, a woman living a supposedly ordinary life. She'd told me that she'd grown up with her parents somewhere in rural Cornwall, although she'd always insisted that she didn't have much in common with them. She'd found her childhood difficult, in that she'd been raised by a man who worked away a lot – her father did something in the military – and a mother with whom she could barely communicate at all. Her mother had grown up in their village but was the only one remaining of four siblings. The place had changed completely in her lifetime, it was now empty half the year as the other houses were rented out to tourists, but she seemed entrenched in her corner of the world and rarely left, even to visit Ashley. She was a woman who seemed so packed, not just with her own memories, fantasies, gossip, everyday routines, but also with those of other people, with whom she seemed to experience no inhibitions whatso- ever. She never stopped talking, spilling out the accumulated contents of a lifetime of formless exchanges, empathizing with people, comforting them, complaining, arguing, ignoring them, gossiping. She was a porous mass of never-ending chit chat – to the point that it was difficult to know how much of what she said she really meant, or how much was even true. I got the feeling she sometimes told stories about herself that had actually happened to other people, not exactly on purpose but because she couldn't remember where her own experi- ence ended and theirs began. Ashley, by contrast, resisted her mother's attempts to infiltrate her life. She always described her mother as lacking in self-awareness, I think because she viewed her own 'self' as something to be guarded, improved upon and assessed competitively. It was a property. You had to work on it. The goal was to raise its value. 'It's about boundaries,' she told me.

'Let's stay in touch,' I said, once I'd finished packing my things.

She barely wrenched her eyes from her laptop. I knew we probably wouldn't see each other again.

•

As early as the first week of May there were signs that the campaign was going well.

'You were right,' Tom said as he sat with Grace in the corner of the Gatwick Aspire Lounge. They were on their way to the Glasgow Congress of Clinical Pharmacology. The early sales figures had come through. Press releases had gone out. Consultants from all over the world were gathering for talks about Eudaxa. All of the major conferences had been booked. The campaign was in its second month.

Grace was busy on the phone to her daughter. She seemed outwardly OK. She'd had her hair cut differently and she was wearing brand new sunglasses. She'd gone for a hard black Prada style that she'd picked up in duty free.

'These numbers are ahead of target,' Tom said.

'Well, let's not relax just yet.'

She swivelled her screen around to show Evie the airport.

Tom went to the bar anyway and returned with a celebratory glass of champagne and non-alcoholic beer for himself.

'To making it out of this project alive,' he said, raising his bottle.

Grace raised an eyebrow.

'Better Together,' she said drily.

A small boy at the table next to them was playing some kind of shooting game, his tablet propped up on his lap while he sucked on the straw of a large milkshake. He swerved hard into Tom's shoulder as he eviscerated a medieval village. Tom drank his beer and watched him.

'By the way, your phone was ringing while you were at the bar,' Grace said.

He checked his calls.

'It's just a friend, I'll call her later.'

He didn't read Lara's message until that night. The boy veered violently out of his seat, knocking the milkshake over with his elbow. The liquid splashed all over the carpet as his tablet vibrated in a fanfare of explosions.

41

Lara had arranged for both of us to meet her at a bar that Thursday. The place was almost empty when we arrived.

'Where is she?' Tom said impatiently.

Another twenty minutes passed before she finally appeared. She sat down wordlessly and slid her phone across the table to Tom.

'I thought you should probably hear it from me,' she said.

She sat in silence as he watched the video.

'So what?' Tom said. 'It's a party.'

She glanced in my direction, a little aggrieved.

'So we throw these parties,' she said patiently. 'You've been to one of them yourself.'

'And?'

'This was the last one.' She looked at him meaningfully, then back at me.

'It looks like your usual thing,' he said dismissively.

'They're on drugs.'

'So what?'

'They're high,' she repeated slowly.

'What exactly are you saying?'

'What do you think I'm saying?'

'That's not possible.'

'I'm telling you, it is.'

'At a sex party? It's prescription only.'

'Well, they're getting hold of it somehow.'

'It's not a party drug.'

'It is now.'

He looked doubtful. 'You're going to have to give me more than this.'

'Come and see for yourself, if you like. We've got another event coming up in Spain.'

'How long have these rumours been going around?'

'They're not rumours. I'm doing you a favour.'

'Why?'

'Peace offering,' she said.

He looked even more unconvinced.

'Like I said, come and see it for yourself.'

'Thanks,' I cut in diplomatically.

'You're welcome.'

'I know you didn't have to.'

'No, I didn't.'

'I owe you one.'

Under the circumstances, I thought I was being generous. She knew exactly what she'd done, but she didn't seem to share my view. She looked at me with that steely look of hers.

'Another one,' she said coolly.

•

Neither of us said much on the journey. By the time we'd arrived at Granta Park, it was almost midnight and the place was dark. Inside, the building looked sinister. Headlights flashed across one wall, the last of the technicians leaving the car park. Sunny sat a few metres from the entrance. He didn't bother hiding his annoyance.

'You're early,' he said. 'You could have been seen.'

There had been a long negotiation on the phone and he'd agreed, eventually, to meet in person, mainly because he didn't want to be overheard.

'So now you know,' he said, leading us upstairs.

'Just show me what you've got,' Tom answered. He looked rattled. He wasn't in the mood to waste time.

Sunny switched on a pair of monitors. One screen lit up with a set of charts. The other was cued to play a video. The footage showed a group of patients in a room. It was a drab, low-lit lounge that was furnished with a short row of beds, divided by thin curtains. Lying on one of the beds was an old man. He was wearing striped pyjama trousers, his bare paunch splayed out across the mattress. He was lying on his side, next to a girl who had stripped down to her bra and knickers. The girl must have been around eighteen, her long hair draped across her breasts. She seemed content. Blissed out, even. Her eyes were closed as she relaxed in his arms, her hands toying gently with his chest hair. Beside her, a woman of around fifty was slouched on the near side of the mattress. Her loose nightdress was unbuttoned and bunched down around her waist. There were another two figures on the screen, both of them boys who looked like students. One of them was grazing on this woman's neck while the other stroked her breasts lightly, tracing her large, soft nipples, cupping her and then moving his hand down to her thighs where he rubbed gently between her legs. He lifted his face towards her and started to kiss her. Sunny paused the video.

'What the fuck?' Tom said. 'What is this?'

'They're in love. Or at least, we think they are. The neuro-imaging suggests that they're experiencing limerence.'

He restarted the footage. One of the boys started nuzzling the old man's neck.

'When was this recorded?'

'Around four years ago. It's "Trial XII90: Efficacy and Safety of Bio-fabricated Stabilized MDP1P over six hours in patients with Severe Major Depressive Disorder".'

'But how?'

'We don't know the mechanism, exactly. All we know is that

at this dosage – a few milligrams higher than recommended – the results are fairly replicable. MAO-A is an enzyme that's involved in the breakdown of serotonin and dopamine. What we're not clear on is why it's producing these behaviours. At the lower dose, it elevates oxytocin, which results in mild feelings of bonding. You could also call those feelings love – a more holistic, platonic kind of love – although this isn't a brain state natural to humans. It brings up patterns that are more common in cetacean species like orcas and dolphins. The problem is, once you raise the dose' – he turned back towards the video – 'this happens.'

'They're attracted to each other?'

'It's more than that.'

'You're saying that with this higher dose, it's an aphrodisiac?'

'In the romantic sense, as well as the sexual one.'

'Can we switch the lights on, please?'

'No.' Sunny sat down on his swivel chair. 'Obviously, we can't let this get out.'

'Who knows?'

'Only the researchers on my team.'

'No one leaked it?'

'Of course they didn't. You know how it is.'

Tom leaned on the edge of the table and thought about it.

'Anyway, point is, it works,' Sunny said. 'These people aren't depressed. They've got it pretty good in there.'

'Are there any other side effects?'

'Not as far as we can tell. I mean, the effects are cumulative to some extent. They can linger. They can build up over time. People come down after a few hours, but in many cases, they remain a little softer than before. Let's say they're a little more convivial. And then the next time, they're building from that baseline, so the effects might be a little stronger. Who knows what could happen over time? But it's not toxic, if that's what you're asking. Physically, it's far less harmful than something like alcohol.'

'But you have no idea how it works?' I said.

Sunny shrugged.

'Anaesthesia,' he said. 'You think anyone knows how that works? Paracetamol? Lithium?'

'What about Floyd?'

'That guy's a moron.'

'He doesn't know?'

'Of course he does.'

'So he kept this quiet on purpose?'

'He's a salesman.'

'Is it legal?' I asked.

'Well, it's covered. If people abuse the medication, that's entirely on them. It's beyond the jurisdiction of this company.'

Tom looked at him, a little stunned.

'Look, we're not talking life or death,' Sunny said, before either of us had a chance to speak. He shut the video down and wiped its history. 'All we need to do is keep our mouths shut.'

42

In June we flew to Ibiza. Tom took his laptop and used it to watch the football. He seemed fairly relaxed as we hovered over the Pyrenees. There was something about getting lost in the game that compartmentalized things for him, as if the screen itself offered some protection from what was happening around him. It was only an illusion but it was a persistent one, as if the glass functioned like a mirror and only one side could be real at once. I reclined in my seat and gazed out over the mountains. It almost felt as if we were going on holiday.

In arrivals, we joined the passport queue where I recognized two of the men in front of us. I knew their faces but couldn't quite place them. They were both balding, slightly overweight, both dressed in shirts and cargo shorts. They didn't look like tourists, exactly. I noticed both had travelled business class. It was only later, while we waited for a taxi, that I remembered where I'd seen them before. One was Aaron Charles from Taizong Capital, the guy who'd grabbed me at the hotel party. It put me on edge immediately, a shot of cortisol breaking through the pleasantly tranquillizing aura of the flight. I almost mentioned it to Tom but he looked so calm, I didn't want to disturb him.

Ibiza Town was almost empty as we drove through it. The high season hadn't yet started and although there were people milling around the Carrer de Saint Cristofal, most of them looked like locals. As we passed the port, the landscape changed into a mass of sand and rock. Dusty shrubs with yellow flowers clung to the old stone walls beside the ocean. The thick sound of cicadas pulsed around us. I pressed my leg against Tom and he returned the gesture without thinking. We drove past a craggy inlet, the water a vivid, sapphire blue. The warmth was pleasurable and mesmeric. For a long time, it enveloped me completely.

After a few kilometres, we turned off the motorway, then again into a long, winding driveway. From the outside, the gate was almost invisible. There was just a high white wall, almost completely shrouded in a veil of bougainvillea. It was only once we'd made it inside that a gravelled courtyard appeared before us. There were a few cars parked along one side, its contours leading towards an old stone villa.

Aliya answered the door in bare feet, her greying curls tied up in a scarf. She was wearing a white bikini underneath a short embroidered tunic. She led us down a long corridor that opened up into an expansive lounge, filled with exotic plants and a marble table lined with tall raffia chairs.

'Sorry about the mess,' Aliya said, as she picked her way through a mass of cables.

Assistants stood on ladders, installing lights and hanging decorations from the ceiling. Two security guards hovered by the door, one of whom Aliya introduced as Kader – a young Idris Elba lookalike – and another whose name I didn't catch but who I would later learn was called Yannis. He reminded me of the actor Vin Diesel. The men nodded at us without much interest.

I found Lara outside on the terrace. She was on the phone and seemed preoccupied. She waved vaguely in our direction, then asked Aliya to show us to our room.

The rest of the day passed uneventfully. We swam in the pool and lay on the wooden loungers that had been arranged at the end of the garden to overlook the Mediterranean. Pristine grass stretched out on either side of us, the watering system buzzing in the heat.

Sunny arrived a few hours later, a stuffed backpack strapped across his chest. He was wearing a pair of patterned surf shorts that exposed a surprisingly sturdy pair of calves.

'I had to tell him,' Tom said. 'He wanted to come.'

'How do you know you can trust him?'

He held his hands up as if to say, *What could I do?*

Georgia arrived not long afterwards trailing a pair of vast suitcases. She was dressed in a floaty blouse with a pair of cut-off denim shorts, her hair now golden blonde like a young Taylor Swift.

When Sunny re-emerged from his room that evening, he had changed into a different pair of shorts, this time a pair of tailored trunks, his shirt tucked neatly into the waistband. Georgia gave me a questioning look.

'Who invited the deviant?' she said.

Sunny, for his part, seemed happy enough. I got the impression he didn't go to many parties.

Georgia sat beside me at dinner.

'What has he come as?' she said. 'A seaside butler?'

'You mean Sunny?'

'This is supposed to be a curated crowd.'

'Give him a chance,' I said. 'You hardly know him.'

She glanced over him disapprovingly.

'I can smell men like that a mile away. Sometimes I think we should round them all up and leave them on an island to wank themselves to death.'

'Steady on.'

She gave me a dirty look.

Giving up on Georgia, I turned my attention to Lara, who was sitting on my other side.

'Where's Niall?' I asked her.

'He's missed his flight. He's going to try and make it tomorrow. I'm glad you came.'

She looked genuinely pleased.

'I know I'm not always easy to be around,' she said. 'I'm sorry.'

It was the first time she'd apologized to me in her life.

'It's fine.'

'It's not fine. I don't know why I'm like this.' She sounded genuinely reflective. 'I'm trying to be more zen about things.'

'I can see it's killing you.'

She half smiled. Then she took my hand under the table. It felt warm. I almost pulled away but between the wine and the sunset I was feeling more forgiving than usual. It felt good, sitting there beside her.

'Gentlemen.' Georgia stood up, beaming, as Aliya introduced the executives from the airport. 'Welcome to Ibiza. I think you've already met our friends?'

•

That night, I barely slept at all. I spent hours drifting in and out of consciousness, part-suspended, as if I was under water. I surfaced occasionally but not for long. There were other people in the deep but they flowed around me like shadows. They permeated my awareness and then they dissipated into nothing. By the time I came to, around dawn, I was disoriented and bothered by the sunlight. I turned towards Tom but he was still asleep so I lay awake for a while, listening to the sound of the waves as they crashed against the rocks beneath us.

•

It was still light when the first guests arrived. They turned up in groups of two or three, a line of cars rolling up and then vanishing back into the mountains. A few of Georgia's friends arrived together, then a handful of older faces, most of them men in polo shirts, presumably VCs. Spence appeared with the same girl I'd seen him with in London – he was the only one of Lara's friends I knew. Small cliques gathered by the pool. I recognized a handful of creators, a singer and a former model who now worked as a sex columnist, her minidress stamped with the word Dior in a pattern that looked like newspaper headlines. I stood mesmerized by her for a while, wondering if she knew that the designer, John Galliano, had once been cancelled for anti-Semitism, and whether his turn-of-the-century party looks – which were back in a big way – had now taken on a meaning of their own, cut loose from the circumstances of their creator.

Not long afterwards, a well-known actor showed up with a small entourage. There was a musician who had done an ad for Apple and a fairly high profile journalist, a lifestyle and features editor who had interviewed Lara more than once. Hostesses in bikinis wandered around with trays of Cava and spirits, the wine flutes accompanied by tiny shots of Hierbas Ibicencas.

The light began to fade around nine which cued the DJ to up the tempo, dance beats merging into something less nostalgic – the kind of music that owed more to SoundCloud than any notion of a dance floor. Guests gathered on the terrace, slowly warming up to one another. A palpable energy rippled through the place as the dwindling sunlight glazed the ocean.

It took a while for the ambience to build, the sound of small talk giving way to something stranger, more unfamiliar. A handful of guests began to dance, gathering fluidly around the speakers. I looked around but I couldn't see Tom. Afraid to drink too much, I messaged Lara.

Where are you?

She didn't reply.

A little restless, I went upstairs in search of Tom but found no sign of him in our room. On my way back down, my route was blocked by a pair of indistinct figures. They were crouched low, holding tightly to one another. It was dark and it took me a while to decipher what I was seeing. It was only as I stepped over their bodies that I recognized Aliya wrapped around someone who looked a lot like Kader, the security guard. His chiselled arms were cradling her like a child, his face buried deeply in hers. I caught a glimpse of the thick shaft of his penis. Startled, I stopped still. He looked up at me. He seemed beguiled but lucid, Aliya's bony chest nestled lovingly in his hands, which were big enough to ring the whole of her bird-like torso. For her part, her cheeks were flushed, her lips parted in delight, her eyes soft with something more than only physical pleasure.

Outside, the atmosphere was charged. It was as if a dam had burst. The louche mood of the earlier hours had escalated into something more intense.

'It's like the nineties again,' I heard one of the execs say under his breath. He'd untucked his polo and was gazing hungrily across the dance floor.

Marie, the company's Head of Accounts was perched on Aaron Charles's lap, his face buried deep between her heavy breasts. By the pool was Bob de LaPuente, the Group Head of Investment Advisory. A coterie of software engineers were massaging his back, fondling the luxuriant hair on his shoulders, while Nicole, Openr's business manager, sat primly on his lap, masturbating soulfully.

My phone buzzed.

I'm in the sala

As I made my way past the terrace towards Lara, I caught sight of Sunny. He was lying topless on a lounger whispering quietly with Georgia. They were gazing indulgently at one another, their eyes locked together like magnets. I stopped in my tracks, a little traumatized. Georgia nuzzled Sunny's ear. She traced her hands around his curves.

'I see you,' she said.

'I see you too,' Sunny whispered.

He sucked softly on her lips, then moved down towards her nipples. She jiggled them playfully for him. It was both off-putting and strangely gripping. It was only after I called his name that Sunny noticed me approaching. He stopped and waved happily in my direction, making space for me to join them. Georgia smiled benevolently. She stroked his chin as it quivered in the moonlight.

I turned around quickly and fast-walked to the villa.

'Have you seen Tom?' I asked Yannis. He shook his head, smiling gently. I backed away as he tried to take my hand. He was still carrying his clipboard while bobbing genially to the music, a distant look in his eyes that suggested raw, unadulterated arousal.

I was starting to panic. I forced my way through the dance floor. When I finally caught sight of Tom, he was prowling through the crowd towards me. He looked like he'd been in a war zone.

'Where have you been?' he said.

'In a wet nightmare?'

'Your friend's a fucking lunatic.'

Behind him, Lara was brokering a deal with a woman in a candy-coloured thong, a tiny pouch hanging delicately from one of its strings.

'Eudaxa,' she announced triumphantly, pouring a handful of capsules into Tom's palm. The expression on his face shifted slightly. He seemed almost resigned to his fate.

'It's really something, isn't it?' Lara said, throwing her arm around my shoulder. She gazed indulgently at the scene around us. 'And it's still early. The show has hardly started.'

'I think I've seen enough,' Tom said. 'Is there anywhere we can sit this out?'

'Upstairs. There's a balcony in my room.'

She went to the bar and returned with a tray stacked with an ice bucket, glasses and wine. While we waited, Spence emerged from nowhere.

'Bit much, isn't it?' he said.

He was flushed with sweat, his linen shirt glued limply to his chest. He seemed to have lost his date and was roaming haplessly on his own. For a moment, I almost felt sorry for him. He seemed out of his element for once. There was a small commotion by the pool and we all turned to see what was happening. Spence bolted as quickly as he had appeared, calling his girlfriend to heel as he sped towards her. She'd taken her clothes off and was bouncing happily beside the water. She waved at him enthusiastically, then dived in before he could reach her, a group of miscellaneous execs following, dolphin-like, behind her.

'I think it's time we got out of here,' Tom said.

Lara took my hand as I reached for his, the three of us forming a chain as we snaked our way through the garden and upstairs to her room. From her balcony, the grounds of the villa stretched out expansively beneath us.

'This is too weird for me,' Tom said. 'They're possessed.'

'They're awake,' she corrected him.

'Come on.'

'I think it's beautiful. This is what a revolution looks like.'

'You can't be serious.'

'Humour me.' She leaned over the railings beside him, surveying the scene with satisfaction. She had a wild look in her eyes that I recognized from all those years ago, from the day she'd broken that pint glass in my defence. It was as if she'd given up on the world and decided to rip the whole thing up, a kind of take-no-prisoners zeal that I now found a little unnerving.

'Think about it,' she said. 'People recreate injustice through their actions.' She opened the wine and poured me a glass. 'They do it without realizing what they're doing. It's all about where you choose to live, where you work, who you spend your time with. Let's not pretend that sex is any different. Or love, for that matter.'

'You're a philosopher now?' Tom said sarcastically.

'Put it this way,' she said, ignoring him, 'you can't control how people treat you, but now, at least, you can control how you behave. You can own what you want, what you choose. It's a different kind of power. It's a radical solution, if you think about it. And of course, it's interesting for Openr.'

'You're drugging people to help your business?'

'They're drugging themselves.'

'It's ridiculous.'

'Why?'

It was difficult to tell how much she really meant it. I'd long lost track of the line between what she actually believed and what was good for business. In fact, I was starting to realize that the two were functions of one another. You couldn't separate them, each side was necessary to advance the other.

'Look, love is rare in adults,' she said pragmatically. 'Especially unconditional love. That's why we created Openr in the first place, to help people navigate that territory. Unfortunately, what we discovered is that there's a vast no man's land between what our customers want and what others are prepared to give them. And let's face it, the pre-condition for love is attraction. Without attraction, nothing happens – there's only invisibility and disappointment. And even when there *is* attraction, it's unpredictable. It doesn't last. It's volatile, it's insecure. Complacency creeps in, comfort, convenience. It's not enough. None of it is enough.'

She looked at Tom and then back at me.

'What do you think I'm trying to do here?' she tried again, once she'd seen our faces. 'This isn't just about sex. It's about what families will look like in the future. How children will be raised. It's not superficial. And in the end, it will come down to what people value most – their fleeting, personal inclinations or the long-term well-being of *everyone*. Why not take back some control? It would solve so many problems.'

She pulled out a vape and inhaled deeply. Its label read *Elite Premium Marijuana*. She offered it to Tom but he declined. He was more interested in filming the scene below.

'It's disturbing,' he said eventually. 'They're not themselves.'

'Maybe they're *more* themselves,' Lara said.

'It's annihilated their inhibitions.'

'So what?'

'Don't they regret it in the morning?'

'Why would they? There's nothing to be ashamed of. And anyway, it protects them from those feelings. It just seems to make them' – she paused, searching for the right word – 'less judgemental.'

'They're out of control.'

'They're experimenting.'

Tom joined me indoors, on the corner of the bed. 'I don't understand why anyone would do this.'

I thought about how Grace had spoken about Floyd. Maybe he'd been right all along. He'd said that human behaviour had gone awry – that the way we lived now had become deformed by an environment so many times removed from the one in which we had evolved. He'd said that none of it was sustainable, that sooner or later there would need to be a correction. I felt a little light-headed. It was hard to get a grip under the circumstances.

'Look, there's no point worrying about it now.' Lara looked shrewdly at Tom. 'There's nothing you can do about it.'

'Let's get this over with then,' he said.

She raised an eyebrow.

'I thought you'd never ask.'

He looked expectantly at me, as if he was asking for my permission. I'd had a feeling this was going to happen.

'Do you actually want to?' I said.

'Of course he does.' Lara reached across the bed and tapped a pile of tablets out of her purse.

'It's research, I suppose,' he acknowledged.

'Absolutely.' Lara gathered our glasses and chopped the tablets into a fine, white powder. There was a definite glint of triumph in her eyes.

'The thing is,' she said, hardly glancing at Tom, 'you and I, we haven't been seeing eye to eye. I thought, you know – since you're here – this might be the best way to work things out.'

'Is she always like this?' he asked me.

'It's relentless.' I took his hand.

She filled our glasses carefully, then she divided the powder evenly into each. The wine foamed as it dissolved.

'You know Tom's teetotal, don't you?'

'Of course he is.' She shook her head.

'He's an addict.'

She contemplated this news. Then she looked at him more closely, this time with a new-found level of respect.

'So he's human? Interesting.'

She handed him a glass.

'To new beginnings,' she said, raising a toast.

I felt completely disconnected.

'Are you sure about this?' he asked me.

I looked at him for reassurance. There didn't seem much point in going back.

'To new beginnings,' I said, raising my glass.
He took a deep breath and followed suit.

•

My memories of the following hours are hazy. I know Lara moved her head against mine. Her face was soft, almost fluid as she shifted its weight against my shoulder. It came to my attention that she'd unbuttoned her dress and her breasts were the colour of sand in the lamplight. I felt myself drifting back in time, back to college, the wallpaper in her old room. I had a vivid hallucination of her bare arms around my waist. She lifted her face towards mine, her lips skimming my own. Then she knelt over me, straddling my waist. Tom came closer, his eyes faded and unguarded. He leaned over to kiss me and I fell into him completely. He kissed me again and this time a surge of pure euphoria washed over me. I was aroused almost immediately. A swell of desire drove through me like a bolt. My blood thickened as Lara took my hand and worked my fingers inside herself. She was wet already and she moaned softly as I reached to touch her breasts. She took my fingers and put them in her mouth. Then she lay down on my body as Tom moved towards her, spreading her thighs, exposing her. She groaned again, reaching for my hand, laying her head on my stomach. I pulled my underwear to one side and let her kiss me there, her tongue against my skin as Tom leaned down again to kiss me. I must have lost consciousness for a while because the next thing I knew, the three of us were naked. Tom pulled Lara towards him, he was standing at the edge of the bed now, pressing his thumb against the crack of her backside, pushing lightly, circling her until she began to open for him. He slipped his thumb in deeper, up to the knuckle. He was rock hard. I began to touch myself as I watched him push himself inside her, filling her gently. She closed her eyes and my blood moved as if it was hers. I took her hand and she squeezed it hard, letting out a slow sigh. It was luminous. I felt her pleasure as if it was my own. I kissed her eyes and mouth. I sensed her rippling through me. Tom lunged against her, holding still as his orgasm broke, the three of us hanging onto one another as she came slowly against him, taking me with her, all of us together. It was boundless. It was also strangely familiar, like an echo of something that had always been there. There was no struggle, only affinity. He pulled out slowly, reaching for me as Lara's body lay between us. Later, she fell asleep in my arms and I realized how much I loved her. It was very simple that night. I loved both of them.

43

All my life, I'd had an intuition that too much pleasure was antithetical to happiness. Maybe it was a British thing – something to do with the cold. I woke up around noon, blinded by the sun, waiting cautiously for the usual morning-after dread. I gave it a few minutes, but – nothing. Surprisingly, I felt alright. Tom and Lara were still asleep so I lay in silence for a while. It occurred to me that I hadn't always been so full of trepidation. I'd spent the first few years of my life free from that nagging sense of apprehension. Like most people, I'd once been capable of straight-up contentment. It hadn't lasted long – probably until around the age of six. I could remember the end of that stage quite well, the simple joy of raw experience slowly losing its intensity, the emergence of a more neutral texture, the feeling that everything had become tempered, because inevitably, it was now filtered through the lens of all the experiences that had come before. After that, there was just the accumulation of layers, memories upon memories, a process that only seemed to become more entrenched as I got older. After decades, it was only natural to experience a certain level of disillusionment. Like any living organism, the lights slowly dimmed. Still, that morning, I felt something like that early vitality. Whatever had happened during the night had brought it back to the surface. I felt good. Surprisingly good. It was surreal but I actually felt revived.

Outside, the terrace was deserted, loungers lined up by the pool. The cleaners were already almost finished and there were

people dismantling the lights around the trellis. I nudged Tom.
He barely stirred. He was still breathing deeply. His legs were
entwined around a sheet, the other end of which was twisted
around Lara. I got up and went to the bathroom, surveying the
place as I returned. The walls looked as if they'd been plastered
by hand. It was obvious that the villa wasn't that old, its crude-
ness was just a style, but the effect was still quite believable. It
was like being in a luxurious mud hut. Lara's suitcase lay open
on the floor, her clothes spilling out, her nylon make-up bag
left open on the table. The whole place smelt of Lara. I tried to
wake her but she didn't move. Instead, I felt Tom begin to stir.

'Hello,' I said.

He looked at me quizzically, then he pulled his pillow over
his head.

'You can come out,' I said. 'It's OK.'

He rolled over, squirming in the sunlight.

'Well, that was weird,' he said eventually.

'You didn't like it?'

It took him a while to recover enough to answer.

'You don't have to lie,' I said.

'I mean . . .' he murmured.

He rubbed his eyes again.

'That was quite a night.'

I turned my attention back to Lara, who was lying motionless beside him. 'Is she OK? She's so quiet. Is she still
breathing?'

'Jesus Christ,' he said. 'Are you trying to give me a heart
attack?'

'I've got a feeling she'll survive.'

'You think she got what she wanted?'

'She always does.'

He sat up stiffly and took my hand.

'What do we do now?' he said.

'Get out of here?'

'Good idea.'

He looked blearily around the room. I wondered what he was going to do now. I told him he should just quit, but his loyalty to Grace made this seem impossible.

'You should both get out,' I said.

'I'm not sure if she would.'

'You can't know that.'

'I do know that,' he sighed, 'because I've already spoken to her about it.'

'So, she knows?'

'She knows about the trials.'

'And she's making you stay? Why would she do that?'

'She said we have to honour our contracts – that it would be more damaging if we just dropped out. After that, she said we could consider our options. She also said I'd be throwing a lot away.'

'Like what?'

'Something about my reputation. She said if I stepped back now, it would be almost impossible to come back. That I'd miss the money but also other things – the life, the culture, the sense of humour.'

'She said that?'

She obviously didn't want him leaving. I thought about one of the developers at Healthify who'd taken a job in San Francisco. Some recruiter had hauled him out there and he was now based somewhere in the Bay Area. He always described the people there as if they had something missing from their personalities. 'It's almost as if,' he once told me, 'they don't assume that everything is shit.'

'Anyway,' Tom said, 'much as I appreciate your willingness to lie for me, even if I quit now, I won't get out until the autumn.'

'That's a long time.'

'I know.'

I heard Lara stir beside me. Just as she was waking up, the door burst open. There was a figure silhouetted in the hallway. It was a man in salmon pink shorts, a straw fedora and a waxed suitcase that he dropped loudly on the floor.

'What the fuck is this?' Niall said.

He stood motionless as he took in the scene. The blood draining from his face which was already slightly burnt.

•

Health is a state of complete physical, mental and social well-being and not merely the absence of disease or infirmity.

I kept my eyes glued to the article in *The Ibizan*. It was a piece quoting the World Health Organization, something about the growth of health tourism.

Niall and Lara were sitting opposite each other. They weren't speaking. I watched as they picked through their salads. Niall poked sullenly at a slice of sobrasada, before stuffing it violently into his mouth. After almost half an hour of this, I decided to try and break the deadlock. I knew that Niall didn't exactly have a job but he liked to talk about work, so I asked him something impartial about the economy. He poured himself a glass of straight whisky, his third of the morning, and launched into a spiel about the economic forces in the Balearics. He said the islands' populations were too dependent on tourism, a sector that had become increasingly unstable and produced too many low-waged jobs. 'There'll be tourism dependency in the short term,' he said miserably, 'but beyond that, the smart money's on renewables and old-age care.'

'It's over,' Lara interrupted him.

'Don't I get a say in this?'

'No.'

He put his glass down quietly on the table. Then he stood up without a word and sloped off, unsteadily, towards the sea.

'What took you so long?' I asked her.

'I don't know.' She looked deflated. 'I'm not sure what I was doing, to be honest. Looking back, I think I just wanted your attention.'

She touched my hand and a long, slow wave of warmth washed over me. It coasted at the edge of my perception, then built up to something more profound. I wanted the moment to last forever. I could tell that she felt the same. I understood her completely. We felt it together.

'You know what I mean,' she said.

I knew she was serious but I also realized I couldn't give her what she wanted. I thought she'd pull away then, but she didn't. She noticed my reaction but nothing changed. She looked across the terrace at the pool. There was an electric cleaner buzzing across it, drifting rhythmically from side to side. Neither of us said anything else. She understood everything and she accepted it.

•

'This is too surreal for me,' Tom said.

I'd found him standing at the bottom of the garden, leaning on the balustrade that overlooked the sea. There were guests reclining on the lawn. An almost eerie calm filled the air.

'You don't like it?'

'I mean, it *feels* good.'

'What if we just went with it?'

He laughed nervously.

I looked across at the guests around the pool. They were relaxed. They seemed comfortable in their bodies and they regarded one another with approval. Even Sunny and Georgia, who were lying peaceably on neighbouring loungers. There was no rivalry, only mutual affinity. Even admiration. I recognized it as a relic of desire – just enough to assuage the anxiety that usually surrounded questions of beauty.

'It works,' I said.

He followed where I was looking. It was obvious that he could see it too. We'd stepped into a world in which the role of aspiration had been muted. There was nothing here to aspire to. The guests viewed one another as important because, in the end, it dignified them all. Regard – even affection – for total strangers was, it turned out, its own reward. It was the feeling of a circuit closing, one that had perhaps always been there, but had until now found itself continually disrupted.

'Remember, you said these drugs were sometimes worth it? That sometimes people benefited?'

'*Some* people.'

'But what if it was everyone?'

He didn't answer. He was staring over my shoulder.

'Fuck,' he said.

It was Niall. He was floating in the ocean, already quite far out. He seemed to be drifting slowly towards the horizon, his body billowing under the surface, bobbing listlessly like a seal.

Tom shouted his name but he didn't answer.

'Jesus,' he said, 'he's not going to make it back.'

•

In the taxi back to the airport, Sunny sat beside me, his pupils fixed unswervingly on the road. Niall was slumped listlessly on my other side, his skin prune-like from the sea. It had taken three lifeguards and a helicopter to winch him back into the world. He didn't seem particularly grateful. He also smelt bad, like a wet dog. He didn't say a word throughout the journey, just sat there looking morosely out of the window.

At the airport, Sunny looked spaced out, as if he'd just survived an alien abduction – one that he had enjoyed intensely but that now seemed a little worrying. I caught him texting Tom while we waited: This is above our pay grade

Tom didn't reply. Then later, having thought about it: Stay quiet. Keep out of it. You weren't here

Niall fell asleep as the plane took off. He snored beside me for the whole two hours. I had to wake him once we'd arrived at Gatwick.

'Do you think Grace will forgive me?' he said.

'No.'

'What am I going to do?'

'You'll have to talk to her.'

He looked at me as if I'd suggested he eat the green holdall he was carrying.

'For God's sake,' I said, 'just talk to her.'

44

The first quarter sales report arrived in July. By the time Tom and Grace sat down to go over the numbers, they had already discussed what they'd do next. The plan was to wait out their contract and then make a quiet departure.

'It's unusual,' Grace said as she looked at the sales feedback.

Patients were clustered around urban centres. Certain populations were displaying greater uptake. At a glance, the picture seemed to mirror the trajectory of property price growth, or of ABC1 advertising demographics, although on closer inspection it wasn't quite so simple. What the figures suggested was that Eudaxa was spiking among early adopters, in the jargon of the technological adoption model. These were people who displayed certain traits: openness, curiosity, low fear – none of them obviously associated with depression. On the contrary, sales seemed to be rising in areas of relative wealth rather than those in which depression rates were historically highest. The numbers were modest but growth was strong.

'It's all off-label,' Tom said. 'Either that or it's people with private shrinks. I don't believe these referrals are clinician-led. I think a lot of this is driven by patients.'

'That shouldn't be possible.'

'It's what we wanted.'

'Not to this extent,' she said quietly. 'The data should have foreseen this.'

·

After work, Grace went to the gym. There was a queue around the Woodway Curves, a new breed of running machine that let you power your own movement. According to the description on the wall, the Curve was: 'more natural than other machines' and had 'the organic feel of the Earth's surface'. The woman next to her looked close to tears, her jowls bouncing erratically, her T-shirt emblazoned with the words *Nevertheless she persisted*.

Stepping onto the machine, Grace caught a glimpse of her reflection in the window. She rarely thought much about her appearance but that night, she couldn't help herself. Her skin looked more or less OK, but there were hollows under her eyes. She should probably do something about it, although the thought hardly filled her with enthusiasm. It was just another chore on the long list of things that filled her time. She'd always felt quite detached from her appearance. She viewed it objectively, as a fact of life, but that didn't mean she wasn't aware of its significance. It hadn't escaped her attention, for example, that beauty standards had escalated in her lifetime. The skinny, muss-haired women of her mother's generation wouldn't have cut it in today's environment. A kind of arms race had taken hold, where what were sold first as innovations quickly hardened into expectations. There was hair to shape, remove and dye, skin to resurface and scars to remove. Nails had become a billion-pound industry; eyebrows alone brought millions into the economy. There was a kind of camp absurdity to it all that only masked the amount of work involved. Appearances were money now in a sense that hadn't been the case when she was young. It had become normal to exploit how you looked in a way that once had been the province of professionals: you took your own portraits, you edited them, you uploaded them – another time-consuming activity that had gone from optional to conventional. And of course, beauty meant youth, just as it always had. She was pragmatic about the way she looked but she also knew the deal. It was exhausting. She was already dead tired. She couldn't wait until this job was over.

Trying to slam the brakes on her anxiety, she forced herself to think about the practicalities. She and Niall were splitting up. It was done. She couldn't afford to indulge her feelings for him, even though she felt as though he'd ripped her heart out and then, moronically, tried to shove it back inside her. It was too late to salvage anything. Although predictably, Niall had done nothing, so despite the fact that she was aching for him, she'd had to take the lead as usual. She'd already asked him to move out. What she hadn't banked on was his reluctance. He had told her it was his home as much as hers, which had led to the first real argument they'd ever had. She had realized, to her disbelief – and even Niall had seemed surprised at himself – that he was actually prepared to fight her for her earnings rather than just passively consume them. The shock still hadn't quite worn off. She blamed herself for the millionth time; she felt unbelievably stupid. Then she did what she always did: she got strategic. First things first, she'd have to play for time. She was going to need every penny of her bonus, which meant holding on until after the divorce – otherwise she'd have to split it with him. It all factored into her decision to keep her head down at work for a while. With a little luck, if she timed things right, she'd be able to exit Eudaxa by the spring. It was a little later than she'd hoped, but she had a feeling Floyd would want to keep her around.

45

Nothing much happened for several weeks. The summer faded slowly into autumn. It was a bright, cold October day when Tom and I found ourselves in Ikea. This was the sort of thing we now did. It was fun, playing at 'ordinary' life. It was a novelty for both of us and, for that reason, it became a joke. I bought him a bamboo soap dispenser and he bought me a miniature cactus. We ate lunch in the cafe and counted the days until his contract was up. He had another eight weeks at Neura and then he would be free.

That night Floyd was celebrating his birthday. He'd thrown a party at the Bloomsbury Hotel. It would be the last of these events that Tom would have to go to, which coated the whole experience with an aura of relief. It must have been around nine by the time we arrived. There was another event going on in the hotel, something connected to the Frieze art fair. I'd been a little anxious all day that Lara would be there; she usually made an appearance at these things. Although anxious wasn't the right word. I hadn't felt anxious since Ibiza. If anything, I'd felt a little lighter than usual. I had a strong feeling that everything would be OK. And if Lara was there, so be it, she was my closest friend when it came down to it.

Grace had already arrived by the time we got there. She was standing at the bar with a man I couldn't place.

'Grace?' he was saying. '*Hi!* How are *you?*'

She shook his hand.

'You don't remember me?' he said. 'It's Ian. Ian Dunstan. From Cambridge.'

I knew then that I'd seen him at Floyd's lecture. He was the guy who'd been on stage that day. He was wearing the same black shirt and jeans. He introduced himself as an altruistic investor – a patron of both the sciences and the arts. He'd helped Floyd organize the party because he wanted to connect him to the 'art crowd'.

'Floyd's an artist himself,' Dunstan said, a little buzzed on his Terra Organico Prosecco. 'I think it's fascinating what he does. He paints with chemicals, systems – with *information*. With enough data, you can paint with *life*. Subjectivity is becoming the province of the sciences. Don't you think that's a fascinating phenomenon? This is territory that used to be dominated by philosophers, artists, poets.'

Grace ordered another vodka soda. I got the feeling she was past the point where she could even be bothered to feign an interest in this stuff.

'He's a smart guy,' she said cordially.

Tom scanned the room. He looked bored.

'He's a radical,' Dunstan ploughed on. 'And I don't just mean in a symbolic sense.' He waved dismissively at the artists. 'What Floyd is doing is hacking *reality*.'

He paused to gauge Grace's reaction. She smiled benignly, then she glanced at Tom as if she was hoping he'd rescue her.

'You know, Warhol said that good business is the best art but he was wrong. Technology is the best art. That's what I tell my kids, anyway.' Dunstan looked around for his off-spring. 'You should meet my son, he's at Cambridge. And my daughter Sofia's here too. She's the real geek in the family,' he chuckled. 'These kids breathe this stuff like air.'

There was something different about Grace that night. She didn't look so haunted any more. On the other hand, she wasn't her old self. It wasn't necessarily true, I thought, that what didn't kill you made you stronger. Sometimes it just made you harder. It seemed like she'd stopped caring about anything or anyone, except Evie maybe.

'Are you OK?' I asked her later.

'Why do you ask?'

'No reason.'

She downed her vodka.

'I'm not getting paid enough for this shit.'

The two of us wandered through the lobby towards the Frieze party, which was just getting started. She sat down on a sofa and surveyed the scene.

'I don't know what I'm doing here,' she said.

'You should go home, we can cover for you.'

'I don't have a home.'

'I'm sorry, Grace,' I said, although it sounded empty, probably because I'd repeated it so many times.

'Do you want to dance?' I asked her.

'What?'

'We could dance.'

She looked at me as if I'd spoken in Japanese. They were playing 'Totally Wired' by The Fall.

'Let's dance,' I said, pulling her up.

She resisted for a while, then she started bobbing uncertainly in front of me. It was a few minutes before she began to let go. We found ourselves in the middle of the dance floor. It was loud, the lights flashing across her face. Before long she was sweating, lost in sound, as if she'd finally managed to escape the world.

After a while, something caught my attention. There was something going on upstairs. A line of people was streaming steadily towards the stairwell. They looked young, early twenties or so, some of them even younger than that. Curious, I left Grace dancing and followed the trickle upstairs. I found a small gathering in one of the suites. It was a sort of make-out

room, people draped on the deep velvet sofas. The lights had
been turned down low. Drone-like music masked the quiet
hum of voices. I made my way around the lounge, stopping by
a door that led to a bedroom. Inside, a girl was kneeling on the
sheets. She looked young, around sixteen. She was crouched
on all fours, naked, her dress scrunched around her neck. Her
buttocks were turned towards two men who were also nude.
They looked easily ten years older than her. They were both
dark-skinned, perhaps East African or Middle Eastern. The
room reeked of sex. I noticed that both of the men had been
circumcised. The girl turned slightly and I recognized her. She
was Sofia Dunstan from @*peaceoutsofia*.

She caught my eye and I realized she wasn't sober. She
seemed blissfully, rapturously high. It crossed my mind that
I should speak to her. I tried to hold her gaze but she didn't
respond, just tossed her hair and arched her back as if she was
enjoying the performance. One of the men moved towards
her, his erection solid as he grabbed her thighs. I realized the
other guy was holding something. He began to record them as
I watched. He was masturbating in the corner while I stood in
silence. She spread her thighs, the first man pulling apart her
buttocks, positioning himself against her, exposing her for the
camera. Suddenly, the second man looked up. He noticed I
was watching, stood and closed the door. He smiled sheepishly
as he shut me out. I thought of knocking, or going downstairs
to find her father, but I wasn't sure if that was right. I felt
misplaced, like an adult at a teenage party. I could tell the girl
had taken something but I wasn't so sure about the men. She'd
seemed high but not exactly wasted. And whatever was going
on, she had seemed to want it.

I hovered awkwardly outside for a while. The people passing by gave me strange looks. There was a heavy atmosphere
in the suite, as if the other guests knew something I didn't. I
wasn't drunk but I felt dislocated. I had a sudden, nightmarish

illusion that the party was pulsing around me, like an organism with a coherence of its own. I couldn't breathe. I needed to get out. I pushed through the crowd to the bathroom where I splashed cold water on my face.

I didn't say much during the rest of the night but in the taxi home, I told Tom what had happened.

'It was Sofia *Dunstan*,' I said. 'You must know her. From *@peaceoutsofia*.'

He looked blank. I brought her up on my phone. She'd been posting from the party only hours earlier.

'She's Dunstan's *daughter*.'

'And?'

'It's Eudaxa.'

'Probably.'

'So, what now?'

He looked out of the window.

'We can't control everything,' he said.

'He'll find out.'

'Maybe.'

'What then?'

'We'll deal with it,' he said wearily.

Outside, it had started to rain and the street lights gleamed sharply on the glass.

•

'Jesus,' Grace said.

She'd only just got out of bed the following morning when she got the call from Floyd. The two men, it transpired, were kitchen porters. They were both immigrants, both recently arrived in the UK. They claimed to have been approached by Dunstan's daughter in the car park; they said that she'd accosted them after their shift. It wasn't clear how they'd ended up in her room but the implication was that she'd invited them. And just to make things worse, one of them had decided to share the video.

The footage, inevitably, had made it back to Dunstan, who had immediately spoken to his lawyers. He was not only suing the hotel but also Neura Therapeutics.

'And that's not all,' Floyd had continued. 'They failed to file a privacy injunction in time.'

Not only was the footage circulating in private but it had already started to disperse.

'What do you want to do?' Tom asked Grace.

The three of us were sitting in her kitchen. It was later that day. I watched her light a cigarette.

'Nothing,' she said, exhaling out of the window.

The smoke dissipated slowly into the garden.

'The company's insured,' she said pragmatically. 'They'll deal with this. They'll probably buy in some crisis management PR.'

'So, no change from us?'

'Exactly. We ride it out. We stick with our messaging, that's all.'

Better together with Eudaxa it said on the sticker she'd attached to the lid of her laptop.

'All conflict is good conflict?' Tom said.

'I can't believe I actually said that.'

'You've trained me well.'

She smiled calmly and examined her cigarette. Once she'd finished, she took out a tissue as she always did, wrapped it neatly and threw it away. It was only later as we were leaving, that I caught her looking at him for reassurance.

•

It was less than a week before the story hit the papers.

Rape Suspects Deny Using Off-Label Substance To Rape
Teen Saying Everything They Did Was Consensual

What followed was a small flurry of attention, most of it
confined to social media:

**WHAT THE FUCK IS WRONG WITH WHITE
WOMEN?**

Her body, her choice. No one else's business

THIS DRUG IS LITERAL WHITE GENOCIDE

This medical company is affiliated with Openr.com who
CONDONE sexual assault #BelieveBritishGirls

Just another case in the long and bloody history of
white women using black men's bodies and then
abandoning them, often to their deaths

**DUMB AS A ROCK RICH WHITE BITCH MAKES
SHITTY LIFE CHOICES, GETS WHAT SHE
DESERVES**

The sexual assault implied in this case is racist, pure
and simple.

•

By December, an icy calm had fallen over the city. It was freezing even by London standards and the streets were quieter
than usual. There had been strikes on the trains and buses
and the lure of a day spent indoors, free from the encumbrance
of travel, had taken half the population off the streets.

'She was right,' Tom said as he tossed a pan of pasta
together with cheese and tomatoes for dinner that night.
As he and Grace had watched in silence, Eudaxa's online

presence had grown. The drug's mentions had accumulated fast, hitting first the thousands and then the millions. It was a mini-maelstrom that criss-crossed the world, traversing the outer reaches of Brazil, through to China, Kazakhstan and back to England. The first few surges of interest took the view that Eudaxa was immoral, just another disingenuous exercise dreamt up by the one percent, and that anyone defending it was a brainwashed, virtue-signalling moron.

A second wave coalesced in the USA, after the story was picked up on public radio. These responses clustered around the conviction that the rape charge was racist. Eudaxa, they argued, was a force for good, a potentially radical weapon in the battle against unconscious bias. #*Whynot?* trended in this space, followed by #*Herbodyherchoice*.

Before long, the word #*Eudaxa* had begun to spike. There was a definite heat around the product. And the lack of a conventional publicity campaign only seemed to fuel the intrigue. A news cycle was born, one that slid from comments to memes to traditional news outlets and back again. It was a wild spiral that over time – through the sheer weight of repetition – had begun to acquire an authority of its own. People poured energy into their positions. Dissenters were ostracized. Sales rose.

Tom seemed sanguine as he ate his penne.

'Floyd's not complaining,' he said. 'Thank God.'

Floyd, in fact, was loving the attention. Neura Therapeutics was growing so fast that his own reputation had expanded. He'd joined a public speaking agency. He'd even been approached by a TV company that wanted to make a documentary about his life. He seemed more than comfortable with all of this. I'd noticed he'd started dyeing his hair.

'So, that's it,' Tom said. 'I'm out.'

'Are you still sure about this?'

'Of course.'

His contract ended on 31 December, but he'd told me that

Grace had asked for an extension. She'd sent him the paper-work but he wasn't going to sign it. 'You've told her?'

'Not yet, but I've made my mind up.'

'How's she going to take it?'

'Probably badly but it doesn't matter any more, I've had enough.'

He sat on the sofa and I lay beside him, leaning my head against his shoulder.

'I've never felt this happy before,' I said.

'I'm glad to hear it.'

'You know, all of this might easily not have happened.'

'I know. That first time I saw you, I knew we'd probably sleep together. It sounds arrogant but that's what I was think-ing. Then, when I started to realize there was more, it threw me at first. I wasn't sure what to do.'

'I don't want to think about it,' I said.

'Then you and your friend nearly gave me a fucking heart attack.'

I smiled, although it wasn't really funny. He put his arm around me and I kissed him, holding onto him as tightly as I could.

•

I got the call early the next morning. The lawyer representing Dunstan's daughter had subpoenaed me as a witness. I had to give them something in writing. They were going for negli-gence as well as fraud.

There were journalists in the street when I arrived at the law firm. I was in there for what felt like hours. By the time I finally made it out, my name had already been leaked online. One of the posts I'd written for Lara had been resurrected from the dead, attracting more clicks than it ever had the first time around. I cringed as I watched myself in the video 'sharing' my take on the Luton ruckus. It was supposed to show my raw reaction but the whole thing was overdone. It was only now, as the footage began to spread, that I realized what the caption said. I'd become hardened to Lara's taste in headlines – and it wasn't even one of her harshest takes – but she'd really outdone herself in context:

> Isn't it time we all stopped putting Basic
> White Girls on a Pedestal?

I couldn't sleep that night, I felt as if I was being watched. I went through all the usual motions – I scrolled, I orgasmed – but I couldn't relax. The screen no longer seemed to numb me. It was as if I'd passed through the lens, no longer the watcher but the watched. I checked my mentions for the hundredth time. They'd crept up since I'd gone to bed.

46

Tom lay on the carpet of Floyd's office.

'The trick with unwanted thoughts,' Floyd said, 'is to embrace them. Just accept them, like little children. See how they clamour for your attention? Just receive them, then let them go.'

Tom exhaled at the ceiling. He wondered how long this was going to take.

'The mind is like a river,' Floyd continued. 'Get out of the water and stand on the bank. There's no need to remain submerged in the violence of the passing moment.'

'I don't think I can do this any more,' Tom said.

He kept his eyes on the ceiling. It was covered in smooth plaster with some kind of carved lampshade in the centre. Where was Grace? She was supposed to be here. He was starving, he'd arrived too late for lunch and now that he'd broached the subject of leaving, Floyd was holding him hostage on the carpet. Surreptitiously, he tried to check his phone.

'No.' Floyd kicked it across the rug. 'Stop dwelling on your feelings!' he demanded. 'Simply let them float away and free yourself from all this negativity.'

•

'If it's what you want, then you should go,' Grace said reluctantly.

She didn't look happy. It was the following day, 15 December. The three of us were sitting by the window in a slightly clinical-smelling restaurant. I'd gone stir-crazy in the flat and had taken the train up to meet them at their hotel. They'd both arrived in Luton that morning for a sales event at the Pharmacon office. It was already dark outside and the motorway lights had started blinking on. Beyond them, a last flush of daylight bathed the ancient ruins of Someries Castle, its jagged walls casting a long, dark shadow over the airport. *Hilton Garden Inn Hotel* it said on the paper napkin under my glass.

Grace reached for a packet of Nicorette and popped a gum in her mouth. Despite everything, she looked well. Her face was slightly flushed from the jacuzzi and she was obviously trying to stop smoking. She'd managed to get her divorce going and Niall was living with his parents. There was a definite air of finality to it all.

'So what are you going to do?' she asked Tom.

'I don't know.'

'You know my door's always open?'

'I know,' he said. 'I appreciate it.'

'There's no other offer on the table?'

'No.'

She looked at him, a little concerned.

'And what about you?' she asked me.

I wondered if she held me responsible.

'I'm leaving too.'

'So that's it then? The pair of you are running off into the sunset?'

'Trying to.'

'Well, I hope that works.'

I think she meant it kindly but it came out a little cold. I wondered if she thought I was being reckless, allowing myself to become dependent on a man. But what was the alternative? Another job? Each seemed as precarious as the other. I tried to brush off my irritation but it was difficult not to feel a little ruffled. What did Grace know about me? We were all just trying to make our way in the world.

'I hope we'll stay in touch,' I said.

'Of course. You won't get rid of me that easily.'

She flashed her crooked smile at me, then she pressed her Amex over the bill.

47

20 December fell on a Thursday. It was Tom's penultimate day at work. He wasn't in the London office that afternoon but still in Luton at the Eudaxa lab with Sunny.

Tom watched as an assistant pulled up outside, unpacked a bag of Heineken and carried it into the kitchen.

The lab was huge, its steel doors locking off the sealed glass chamber at its centre. Inside were rows of machinery performing high-precision movements. Capsules of Eudaxa shifted down the line, mutating into retail-ready stock. It was hypnotic if you watched for long enough, the low buzz of the equipment overlaid with the sound of plastic-covered shoes.

They stopped around five and gathered in the kitchen where Sunny had broken out the beers. He stood up to raise a toast.

'This is the second time I've been dumped by Tom,' he said, 'and I think I'm safe in speaking for all of us when I say: You lucky bastard. It's alright for some.'

There was a postcard stuck to the fridge behind him, a spaniel in goggles and a lab coat, a thought bubble over its head that said: *I have no idea what I'm doing.*

They must have stood around for about an hour, then the group began to disperse.

'Have you seen this?' Tom asked Sunny as they waited for the last of the team to leave. He showed him the email he'd just received from Grace. 'IMPORTANT,' it said. Tom scrolled down to the body of the article:

Man Wins Case Against
Pharmaceuticals Giant

A mobile phone tycoon has successfully sued the pharmaceuticals company Neura Therapeutics over their controversial new release Eudaxa. Neura Therapeutics is partnered with Pharmacon, one of the world's leading multinationals. The drug, Eudaxa, is a novel antidepressant that has been subject to rumours of misuse. In an interview, the Secretary of State for Health and Social Care has stated that he will be reviewing guidance around this substance. He added, 'It's too soon for further comment.'

'What now?' Sunny said.

He was a bit drunk.

'I don't know. I suppose it's up to Floyd.'

As they made their way downstairs, Tom noticed what looked like a journalist in the car park.

'I'm looking for Tom Walsh,' the man said. 'Are you Tom Walsh?'

•

The following morning, Tom was late for his last day at work. By the time he arrived, Floyd was already in Grace's office, he could see them through the glass divider. Grace looked impassive as ever but Floyd was visibly upset. It was almost noon by the time he emerged. He grabbed his coat and left without a word, barely registering Tom's presence. He'd probably forgotten Tom was leaving but either way, it didn't matter. Tom spent some time clearing his desk. He wrote some notes for his replacement, Padita, who turned up later that morning. She was talkative and very young. He switched off almost immediately when she started chatting about Web 3.0, whether or not it was actually dead, whether blockchain would experience a renaissance.

Grace appeared and relieved him of her after lunch, but it was only later that afternoon that the two of them had a chance to speak. They took sanctuary in her office.

'Do you really have to deal with this?' he said.

'Don't worry, it's being taken care of.'

She gave him a long hug.

'I'm going to miss seeing you every day.'

'You too.'

'Take care of yourself,' she said affectionately.

She said it as if she really meant it. She had a slightly wistful look in her eye.

The lift wasn't working so he took the stairs. On the third-floor landing, something caught his eye. He went over to the window. There was a thin group of people on the pavement, some of them spilling out into the road. From what he could tell, some of them were press. There was also a scattering of women holding brightly coloured placards emblazoned with slogans like *Time's Up* and *Why Don't You Get It?* Among the placards was a group of men who looked as if they'd arrived from a different planet. One of them was holding a loudspeaker:

'The Left believe they have a monopoly over young people,' the man said. 'It's about time they woke up.'

A wave of applause rose up around him.

'There are more and more of us who've had enough.'

'Hear! Hear!' someone yelled.

'It's time we put an end to this insanity. Women in this country are not fair game.'

One of the women began to cheer while others looked away in disgust.

As Tom leaned closer to the window, he realized there was

now quite a crowd. A small scrum had gathered around the door. One of the men looked up and saw him watching. He pulled back to hide his face. Something wet smacked against the glass.

48

Leaving drinks had been arranged at the King's Head. By the time I arrived, the pub was closed. The area had already been cordoned off. There were police parked along the street, a line of officers circling the crowd. A reporter was broadcasting live, the lighting bouncing off her rain-flecked hair. I tried to push my way towards the cordon.

'This is not consent!' a woman shouted.

Tom was a few feet away from the office trying to make his way through the crowd towards the pub. A small pack had swarmed towards him, making it difficult for him to move. He was covering his head with his jacket.

'Is it true,' someone yelled, 'that this company takes no responsibility for the sexual assault of women?'

Neura Bosses Are You Listening? read one of the placards swinging in front of me. *You Are Literally Fucking Women Over.* It lurched violently around my head as I tried to force my way towards the barrier.

I came within touching distance, then I froze.

'Tom Walsh.'

It was a man's voice, piercing through the loudspeaker.

'Where is your rape apologist girlfriend?'

Tom kept moving, his head bowed down. He was shoving harder now, more bullishly. He seemed to be making headway, then he stopped. A sudden lull fell over the crowd. A space opened up around him. I strained harder to see. There was a man standing beside him, leaning against him as if they were embracing. The man's head was on Tom's shoulder, his face turned towards his neck. Someone stepped aside to let me through and I saw the expression on Tom's face. He was looking around, confused. I called his name but it was as if he couldn't hear me. There was blood pooling in his shirt, dripping heavily, soaking his shoes. His legs moved slightly as the man released him, his eyes wide open as he fell. The silence remained as he hit the ground. It was only then that a woman screamed.

•

I must have left the hospital for a while because I remember calling Lara from the car park. The rest of the night I spent awake under the strip lights on the fourth floor. The Royal London had a glass facade that looked like any other workplace, its grey windows co-ordinated with the plastic signs in intensive care.

The doctor looked youngish, tired, a little hunched, his hair gelled roughly to his head as if he hadn't had time to wash it. He said that Tom had been sedated, that they were still trying to stabilize him. He'd lost a lot of blood. They'd almost lost him during the night.

'We think there could be bleeding on the brain,' he said quietly.

I was sitting on a plastic chair in the waiting room. There was a brightly coloured mural on the wall, a flat, cartoonish tableau of London. It reminded me of the artwork on Floyd's website. There was a name for the style, what was it? I felt myself dissociating as the doctor spoke.

'We'd like to do an MRI.'

He looked closely at my face.

'Are you OK?' he said. 'Would you like something to drink?'

He asked one of the nurses to bring me a coffee. Corporate Memphis, that was it, I thought.

•

The atmosphere in the ICU was calm. Staff moved smoothly through their shifts to the rhythmic bleeps of the heart monitors. The ambient sounds of the ventilators fed into more complex patterns: nurses oscillating between beds, hushed discussions on protocols. I barely recognized Tom. There was a tube taped around his mouth. I touched his hand but he didn't move, although his skin was warm. I watched him for what must have been hours.

At one point, an alarm went off. There was a problem with a woman in the opposite bed. Her heart wasn't responding. Her eyes had already been taped shut. Her body was slumped face down. I watched as a nurse arrived, then a doctor. They handled her efficiently, trying to revive her then moving her swiftly through the system. Patients like her, it turned out, were removed fast, presumably because the bed had to go to someone else, someone who still had a chance. There was no time for ceremony. They just took her away.

I'd never thought of myself as being scared of death but I felt uneasy watching them. It was obscene, for reasons I couldn't explain. I'd always envisioned the end as something more momentous, something that involved at least a few moments of reckoning. I felt this instinctively, although I knew most patients at this stage of their lives would have come in disoriented, if not already unconscious. If they were lucky, they might have a few moments of small talk with some anaesthetist, a friendly chat as the tube went down. That was it. They left the place as senseless mounds of organic mass. I squeezed Tom's hand, then I went downstairs. There was a Costa Coffee in the lobby. I bought a cereal bar and a cup of tea. I watched people eat their Christmas sandwiches.

Grace turned up that afternoon. She brought a basket of fruit. Once she'd left, I realized I'd barely said a word to her. I hadn't known what to say. We both knew what had happened but the truth was difficult to articulate.

At some point in the night I must have fallen asleep because it was dawn when I was awoken by a different doctor. He'd brought Tom's MRI results. 'We don't think there's any point in continuing,' he said. 'There's been diffuse damage to his brain. We can't find any activity at all.' Then that old stock phrase: 'There was nothing we could do.'

•

The next few days passed inconsequentially. There was no paperwork, no formalities. I wasn't Tom's next of kin so all of that was taken care of by his father. I was just someone he'd once known. I felt as if I'd entered a different universe, one in which everything looked the same but to which it was obvious I didn't belong.

Sunny visited at the weekend. There had been reporters at his flat. Some journalist had found his number and he'd had to change his phone. We watched the news together. He showed me the report that had been published in *The Times*.

The perpetrator has been identified as John Friedman, a 28-year-old former security guard from the Caddington area of Luton. He lived with his mother, who described him as 'a quiet soul'. She said the incident had come as 'a shock' and was 'out of character for John'.

Friedman, who had live-streamed the 13-minute attack from a body camera, described himself as 'a freedom fighter', 'a Christian foot soldier' and 'a realist'. Meta said it had removed the suspect's accounts and was working to remove any copies of the footage.

A security source leaked that the attacker had a prolific online history, much of it contrarian and contradictory. He was a long-time supporter of Luton FC although he'd posted several comments denouncing football as 'a tool of the elite'. He'd made a series of videos called 'Why Are Normal Men Being Silenced?', while operating multiple social media accounts, some of which generated a small income. Despite his mother's Jewish heritage, he believed that English society was being decimated by multicultural elites. His browsing history on the morning of the attack revealed searches for God of War, sizzurp, transgenderism, fungible human resources, Lil Wayne, Anders Breivik and Mind Pump: Raw Fitness. He targeted Walsh, a marketing manager, because he viewed him as 'one of the collaborators' and 'a traitor to his own people'. He'd followed Walsh online after seeing his name embroiled in the controversy surrounding Eudaxa, an antidepressant released earlier this year by the pharmaceuticals company Pharmacon. He'd become fixated on Walsh after recognizing him from the Caddington area of Luton where Walsh had lived briefly as a postgraduate. After attacking Walsh with a hunting knife, he died by suicide on camera, slashing his wrists in front an audience of several thousand followers.

Paul Sweet KC of the UK counter-terrorism watchdog Intercept described the incident as representative of a new and increasingly prevalent form of violence, one characterized by lone actors with 'mixed, unstable and disordered ideologies'. He described the need for a different approach when it came to evaluating these individuals. 'What's required,' he said, 'is a better understanding of mental health in these investigations.'

'Mental health,' Sonny said incredulously. 'They're talking about his fucking mental health.'

He looked at me as if the world had gone crazy. 'What the fuck are we supposed to do now?'

'Wait?'

'For what?'

I had no idea. The future seemed to have evaporated.

'Why don't you stay here tonight?' I offered.

It felt like a small gesture of solidarity. There didn't seem much point in him going home.

•

A few days later, I went to Lara's. I wanted to be with someone who understood what had happened and there weren't many other candidates. I was expecting it to be just the two of us, but there were people gathered at the entrance to her flat. I could hear music throbbing from the street. Inside, the place was packed, mostly with people I didn't recognize – or at least not from real life. It was sea of fashionable strangers. They were spilling onto the pavement, sitting on the wall that overlooked the road. I came across Spence in the kitchen.

'You look fucking awful,' he said.

'Where's Lara?'

'Debauching herself upstairs.'

I found her on the landing. I could tell immediately that she was high.

'You came!' she said, as if nothing had happened.

I wanted to leave then, but she wouldn't let me. She followed me downstairs. She grabbed my hand and tugged me outside into the garden. There were people shoving past us. I felt suffocated, as if I was drowning. The scent of strangers' bodies filled my lungs, their hair and skin too close. I pulled away roughly and she stared at me, shocked at my reaction. There were people dancing on the lawn behind her. As she backed away, their bodies parted. She caught my eye one last time before they closed around her like a mouth.

The police arrived not long afterwards. I'd just left and was still on Lara's street when the cars appeared. It was cold, it had started raining, the lights of Canary Wharf in the distance. I could hear voices streaming from their radios. Someone flashed a torch in my face. There was shouting. They stopped me to take my details, then they disappeared into her flat. I stood still, watching for a while, then I started walking home.

49

I barely left Tom's flat after that. It's a strange feeling, the sensation that your life is lurching over a cliff. I did nothing – there was nothing I could do. The days passed with unnerving speed. The prime minister made an announcement. There were think pieces all over the news. A new narrative had coalesced, this one more uniform than the last. Before long, everyone had adjusted their position. There were thousands of pages on the subject. *The Guardian*, *The New York Times*, Fox, the BBC, the *Daily Mail*, almost every outlet was on board with the view that Eudaxa should never have been released. Floyd was taken down by one of the broadsheets after a whistleblower leaked his emails. There were long exposés of the drug's history, lofty critiques of its apologists. *Teen Vogue*, in particular, was full of outrage. It ran a series of fashion spreads that featured activists in string bikinis, the models' bare ribs scrawled with the words: *My property.* Openr released a torrent of its trademark essays – courageous, personal ones that 'unpacked' the Eudaxa experience across the board. The essays functioned as an exercise in damage control which Lara packaged as a fearless, honest reassessment. No one had much to say about Tom. It was as if his death didn't matter. It only served as a cue for the proliferation of more opinions.

Aliya called one day to let me know that Openr was closing down. Perhaps inevitably, it had failed to complete its last round of funding, not because the business wasn't viable – it had, in fact, been closing in on profitability, in part because of the interest in Eudaxa. It wasn't even because its investors disapproved: half of them had separate holdings in Mindbot, which was hardly a font of respectability. It was because they feared the attention turning onto themselves, they didn't want the reputational risk. There was, it turned out, such a thing as too much heat around a start-up.

I received my dismissal the following week. 'Your role at Openr' was the subject line.

> Hi,
> We regret to inform you that your employment is terminated effective immediately. This is due to the winding down of Openr Limited. Given the nature of our distributed workforce and our desire to inform impacted individuals as quickly as possible, communication for this process is taking place via email. Our operations team will be reaching out to you with offboarding instructions.
> Please address any questions to alum@openr.com
> Thanks,
> Management Team

Not long after Openr's collapse, Neura Therapeutics began its own implosion. There were new claims made against the company, presumably as a result of the stories in the press. Accusers had been emboldened by the Dunstan case. Before long, a group lawsuit was in progress.

I didn't hear much from Lara during this time, although I'd noticed she'd removed herself from social media. She texted a few times, that was all. It wasn't personal, it was just the way things were. Before she closed down her accounts, I saw her holidaying with Nico and Natasha. She must have flown out to their parents' place to lie low while things calmed down.

Grace and Niall faded away quickly after the funeral but

Sunny and I kept in touch. He'd been managed sideways into a different lab but he would drive down occasionally to see me. Out of everyone, he made an effort to stay in contact. We were one another's only link to Tom and for that reason it seemed important. In fact, the more I thought about Tom, the more I realized our lives had barely intersected. There was hardly any trace of what had happened. Only the flat, which was already on the market.

Simeon Logistics was a young company specializing in real-time transport feedback. I needed training to use their software, which I completed easily online. The job had been advertised as 'fully remote', which was another way of saying it didn't pay enough to cover the costs of living in London. It was the first thing I was offered and I took it. And in some ways, it made things easier. It forced me to let go of my former life, which was over. Although it was perhaps more accurate to say that it had never really started. I walked around the city in a daze. It was all too normal, too busy.

In the summer, I left London and started travelling aimlessly around the cheapest towns in Europe. As the days began to shorten, I found a place in Riga. It seemed as good a place as any. It was quiet, the Wi-Fi was fast and it was full of exiles like myself, remnants carrying our jobs in backpacks, haunting the city's bars and cafes. Most of us had spilled over from the more salubrious hubs of Western Europe – London, Stockholm, Berlin, themselves slowly becoming interchangeable.

I rented a room in a flat off Miera Street. The place was next to a retirement home in which the residents spent all day in armchairs watching endless episodes of *Poirot*. I missed Tom but I'd become habituated to it. My days were slow and regular. They connected to nothing in particular. I worked until seven, ate dinner and then most nights I walked around the streets. As always, I found it difficult to sleep, which meant the hours rolled by without much definition. Or more specifically, they passed without much meaning. Sometimes, I felt as if I existed inside a sealed capsule. It wasn't that I'd never felt that way before, there had been days in London like that, the difference now was that I no longer expected much to change. I could barely understand the language and I felt no desire to learn it. The world stopped at the periphery of my experience and I didn't search for anything more.

Occasionally, I caught myself in a moment of reflection. What was I supposed to be missing anyway? I was no longer suffering, exactly. I had adequate distractions when I needed them. I had a home, of sorts. I had advice on grief – there were thousands of pages on it online. I kept virtual company with other souls, most of whom I'd never meet in person but who gave me some semblance of society. There was porn. There was endless entertainment – some of it of decent quality. And if I felt the need for more than that, I could go outside and watch people on the street. The people who passed me seemed content, or something close to it.

From time to time, I wondered if things could have been different. There were moments when I became conscious of something there, something overseeing me, quietly producing me, re-routing my desires, sculpting how my path would go. The lines along which my life unfolded were, in a sense, already traced. I would have liked to have believed in my own freedom – in an open world full of opportunity. I would have liked to have fulfilled my potential in all the ways that my childhood had suggested, but the impulse no longer drove me. I wasn't sure who I had become. I also didn't know if it mattered.

One night, I received an email from Lara.

Don't miss my exclusive chat next week. As the founder of new platform NewsVerse I'll be sharing my thoughts on how different communities access the news, how to connect readerships, and how we're moving away from

a top-down model towards becoming an agile resource
that delivers the bespoke news streams customers want
and deserve.

I was sitting outside a cafe when I saw the message, watching the container boats on the Daugava. The boats had names like Maersk and X-Press. Some of them slowed down beside the port, eventually coming to a stop to unload their cargo onto trucks. The trucks then graduated onto the concourse where they were scanned and waved along the motorway. I'd seen women selling sex on that road, looking for stray clientele, the ones that hadn't been captured by the more formal channels of the online marketplace. The system sought to service every need. It created new desires and then it created ways to endure them. Its goal wasn't satiation, or even profit in the end, it was only to invent new ways of living, to produce visions of a future that remained perpetually in flux, dissolving constantly like smoke and then re-forming again. I caught my reflection in the water, my features fractured on its surface. Maybe it was true that everything was just another technical problem. Maybe it was just a matter of time before everything became reducible to code. That seemed to be the goal but at the same time, there was no locus of control, there was only the inexorable unfolding of second, third, fourth order effects – effects that went far beyond the comprehension of any single player.

I wondered if there had been a moment when I could have prevented what had happened. If such a moment had existed, I hadn't noticed it. I tried to imagine another life. I pictured friends, children, nothing special.

There was a pile of books that had been left on the windowsill, the usual stuff that tourists left behind: a couple of thrillers, a Harry Potter, a self-help book with a compass on the cover. I took a photo of the last one to send to Lara. *Follow Your Heart*, the book was called.

Acknowledgements

I want to thank my friend Luke Brown for reading the first draft and giving me so much encouragement and guidance at the beginning. I also want to thank Nicola Chang for her excellent taste. Thank you to my editor Gillian Fitzgerald-Kelly for signing me as a complete unknown and thank you to Anne Meadows for taking me on with such enthusiasm, patience and grace. Thanks also to everyone on the team at Pan Macmillan and special thanks to Rosie, for being there all along and to Daisy, who designed the cover. Finally, thank you to Steve, my muse and inspiration.

Permissions Acknowledgements

Mariel Franklin lives and works in London. She has an MA in English from Edinburgh University and later went on to study Fine Art at Goldsmiths. After graduating, she spent several years working in data administration in the tech industry.